Rosamond Lehmann

was born in Buckinghamshire in 1901, the second of the four children of R. C. Lehmann, an M.P. and a contributor to *Punch*. Her brother, John Lehmann, was also a writer and her sister, Beatrix Lehmann, an actress. Miss Lehmann was educated privately and at Girton College, Cambridge. In her early twenties she wrote her first novel, *Dusty Answer*, published to great critical acclaim. In 1928 she married the Honorable Wogan Philipps, the artist, with whom she had one son and one daughter. Her second novel, *A Note in Music*, was published in 1930. *Invitation to the Waltz* followed in 1932 and its sequel *The Weather in the Streets* in 1936. Both were dramatised as a BBC TV film in 1983. Her other books include *The Ballad and the Source* (1944), *The Echoing Grove* (1953), *The Swan in the Evening: Fragments of an Autobiography* (1967) and *The Sea-Grape Tree* (1976).

Rosamond Lehmann was a Vice-President of International PEN, Vice-President of the College of Psychic Studies and a fellow of the Royal Society of Literature. She was made a Commander of the British Empire in 1982. She died in 1990 at the age of eighty-nine. *The Times* said of her work, 'In the perspective of twentieth-century literature she will be remembered as a novelist both of contemporary manners and the individual human heart.'

Dusty Answer
A Note in Music
Invitation to the Waltz
The Weather in the Streets
The Gipsy's Baby
The Ballad and the Source
The Swan in the Evening
A Sea-Grape Tree

MODERN CLASSIC

ROSAMOND LEHMANN

The Echoing Grove

With an introduction by Jonathan Coe

Flamingo
An Imprint of HarperCollins*Publishers*

FOR MY MOTHER AND
MY FATHER

Flamingo
An Imprint of HarperCollins*Publishers*
77–85 Fulham Palace Road,
Hammersmith, London W6 8JB

A Flamingo Modern Classic 1996
9 8 7 6 5 4 3 2 1

First published in Great Britain by
William Collins & Co. Ltd 1953

ISBN 0 00 655009 6

Set in Monophoto Ehrhardt

Printed and bound in Great Britain by
Caledonian International Book Manufacturing Ltd, Glasgow

INTRODUCTION

by Jonathan Coe

The Echoing Grove, first published in 1953, completes and closes the cycle of novels Rosamond Lehmann had begun twenty-six years earlier with *Dusty Answer*. Although a final novel, *A Sea-Grape Tree*, followed in the 1970s, it is deeply informed by the spiritualism which came to Rosamond Lehmann late in life, and stands strangely apart from the rest of her fiction: and so it is to *The Echoing Grove* that we look for something approaching a final statement, a resolution of the themes which had preoccupied her for most of her writing career.

Superficially, at least, the most prominent of those themes had been romantic love: at the heart of all her novels, including *A Note in Music* (1930), *Invitation to the Waltz* (1932), *The Weather in the Streets* (1936) and *The Ballad and the Source* (1944), are women wounded, wronged or in some way let down by the men into whose trust they have placed themselves. To stress the centrality of romantic love to Lehmann's fiction is not, however (as some critics would have it) to diminish her: the romantic relationship in all of these novels assumes its overriding importance because it is seen as the touchstone, the litmus test, of an individual's standards in all other areas. Viewed in this light, the theme of Rosamond Lehmann's fiction becomes nothing less than the moral responsibility of human beings towards one another; and comparing how this theme is treated in *The Echoing Grove* and *Dusty Answer* makes us realise the enormous emotional and technical distance she had travelled in the decades between the two books.

Dusty Answer is a coming-of-age novel, in which the heroine, Judith Earle, finds her youthful expectations betrayed by the men and women with whom she falls successively in love. It is underpinned by a sweet nostalgia for childhood, and a distant, elegiac awareness of the Great War as some tragic offstage event. In *The Echoing Grove* war is inescapably present – providing both a background to much of the narrative, and a metaphoric commentary upon it – while the subject of betrayal is treated with far greater rawness and urgency, through a rueful, bitter retrospective filter. In essence, the story is simple enough: Rickie Masters – handsome, successful, practically idolised by everyone who meets him – is married to Madeleine but has fallen obsessively in love with her sister, Dinah. He and Dinah have an intense, guilt-ridden affair; Madeleine finds out about it, and their marriage, although it never dissolves, starts to crumble beyond repair; Rickie dies, and the sisters, estranged for fifteen years, finally struggle towards a taut reconciliation, so that Dinah is able to offer her sister some comfort at the moment when she is again abandoned, this time by her latest faithless lover, Jocelyn.

In their edgy dialogue during the closing pages of the book, Dinah and Madeleine speak with the strained, waspish voice of hard-won experience: we seem to be a long way from Judith Earle's breathless naivety. Rosamond Lehmann herself, however, was in no doubt that this novel was of one continuous piece with *Dusty Answer*: 'more than any of the others,' she said at the time of publication, 'this novel had something to do with the first I ever wrote. Not the same one in a fresh guise; not even a development from it; but more as if somehow – I cannot explain why – some cycle of experience that had opened when I was a girl was now coming to a close'. This sense of continuity would have been explicit if her publishers had allowed her to retain the book's original title, *Buried Day*. Apart from making sense of the section headings – which allude to the different times of the day during which the sisters attempt their reunion – this title gestures back directly towards *Dusty Answer*, being a quotation from the same poem: number 50 in Meredith's bleak verse cycle of marital incompatibility, *Modern Love*:

> But they fed not on the advancing hours:
> Their hearts held cravings for the buried day.
> Then each applied to each that fatal knife,

Deep questioning, which probes to endless dole.
Ah, what a dusty answer gets the soul
When hot for certainties in this our life!

The book's publishers were unhappy with the proposed title because they felt it contained a punning, too-obvious reference to the relationship which had consumed Rosamond Lehmann's emotional life throughout the 1940s: her public affair with the poet Cecil Day Lewis, which had been abruptly terminated in 1950. And in some respects, I think, they were right: knowledge of this affair and the ways in which it informs the novel hinders as much as it helps our understanding of *The Echoing Grove*. Milan Kundera once said that literary biography is the most destructive of all critical practices. Writers, he argued, take the chaotic, random elements of their lives and make it their job to rearrange them into beautiful edifices; the literary biographer then comes along and painstakingly reduces them to rubble again, expecting to be congratulated into the bargain. And Rosamond Lehmann was, by this stage in her career, an exceptionally inventive and formally ingenious novelist, the very reverse of an autobiographer *manqué*: to look for exact correspondences between her own life and the lives of these characters seems especially reductive. Nonetheless, the fact that this novel grew out of her own experience of a long and painful triangular relationship can hardly be irrelevant, and a brief sketch of the background might be helpful.

She began her affair with Day Lewis in the spring of 1941, and by the end of that year they were living together in a house in Kensington. His wife Mary, sitting out the war in the country with their children (as Madeleine does in *The Echoing Grove*) remained in ignorance of their relationship for about two years: after that, it was out in the open, and she and Rosamond Lehmann even embarked upon an occasional, polite correspondence.

This was at the high water-mark of Rosamond Lehmann's career. *The Ballad and the Source* had been an outstanding success, particularly in America where it had sold over 600,000 copies; on top of which, an offer for the film rights from Hollywood producer Walter Wanger had brought in £40,000, enabling her to buy a

Georgian manor house near Abingdon in Berkshire (commemorated in Day Lewis's poem 'The House-Warming'). The affair, which had begun during a raid in the Blitz (the setting for Rickie's long, rapt sexual encounter with Georgie Worthington in the 'Midnight' section of *The Echoing Grove*), continued for nine years, taking in the winter of 1947 with its great blizzards (inspiration, perhaps, for the scene in which Dinah gives birth to Rickie's child in snowbound Cornwall), and an idyllic trip to Tuscany the same year, which Day Lewis celebrated in the seven poems making up *An Italian Visit*, but which seems, in retrospect, to have marked the beginning of the end:

> *Dare I follow her through the wood of obscurity –*
> *This ilex grove where shades are lost in shade?. . .*
>
> *I imagine you really gone for ever. Clocks stop.*
> *Clouds bleed. Flames numb. My world shrunk to an echoing*
> *Memorial skull.*

(Note the vocabulary of these lines, and how Lehmann's final choice of title seems to allude to them – besides containing references to William Blake's conception of female love as 'the Infernal Grove', and to *The Echoing Green*, a poetry anthology edited by Day Lewis in the 1930s. He also, incidentally, wrote an introduction to a new edition of Meredith's *Modern Love* at exactly this time: it was published in 1948.)

This poem, dedicated to 'RNL', was interpreted by her at first simply as 'a beautiful, romantic farewell to an idyll'; but she realised that 'with hindsight it does seem strange, as if he was already denying us a future together'. In the summer of 1949 Day Lewis started seeing the actress Jill Balcon, and it was for her that he abandoned both Rosamond Lehmann and his wife: they married on his forty-seventh birthday, in 1951. 'What was almost the worst thing to bear, for both Mary and me,' Lehmann later told her lover's son, Sean Day Lewis, 'was what appeared to be his complete change of personality towards us both after he had struck us down . . . No kindness, no courtesy, sympathy or (apparently)

conscience. I daresay this was temporary but it was very appalling.'
Her decision to end *The Echoing Grove* with Jocelyn's desertion of
Madeleine for a '*New Statesman* girl' who is a little 'on the grubby
side' seems primarily to reflect her own anger and despair at this
point; as a plot development, it seems somehow discontinuous with
the main body of the novel.

From Sean Day Lewis's lucid account of these events in his
biography of his father, the reader notices not so much any specific
overlap of detail between fiction and real life, but more a strong
correlation between the diction used by Rosamond Lehmann and
Mary Day Lewis to describe their trauma ('nightmare', 'numb-
ness', 'despair', 'sink into oblivion') and the prevailing emotional
ambience of *The Echoing Grove* itself – surely the most painful and
demanding of all Lehmann's novels. 'He was a deeply divided
personality,' she once said of her lover, and it is precisely this frac-
turing of the human personality under the pressure of irreconcilable emotional commitments that *The Echoing Grove* records so
faithfully, and to which it gives such magnificent fictional shape.
Indeed it's the shape, the structure of the book that lends its story
meaning – Lehmann's extraordinary patchwork of memories, flash-
backs, events seen from different perspectives, and events narrated
at second or third hand, so that the imagery of mazes, webs and
nets which pervades the narrative corresponds to the reader's own
sense of enmeshment. The time-scheme of the novel is so complex
that the effect is almost, paradoxically, to make us feel that normal
time has been suspended, that the level of emotional intensity
achieved and endured by these characters gives rise to a bizarre
sort of timelessness.

Dinah herself puts this point more pragmatically: 'I do get
confused about time,' she admits during one brutally adversarial
conversation with Madeleine. 'If one loses one's emotional focus
. . . that's what happens. Aeons – split seconds – they interchange.
One gets outside the usual way of counting.' In *The Echoing Grove*,
getting outside the usual way of counting is something that soon
happens to the reader as well: Rosamond Lehmann engineers, in
this book, such a thorough collapse of conventional narrative time,
such a seductive blurring of memory and actuality, that once lost

in the thick of the novel we can even begin to believe, along with T S Eliot, that

> Time present and time past
> Are both perhaps present in time future,
> And time future contained in time past.

These opening words from the *Four Quartets* are in fact highly pertinent to the book. Rosamond Lehmann was an avid reader of modern poetry, and this novel abounds with echoes of Eliot as well as Day Lewis. Both Dinah ('I saw the end from the beginning') and Rickie ('In my end is my beginning. Who said that?') nearly manage to quote the famous first words of 'East Coker', 'In my beginning is my end': words which might almost, of course, describe the opening narrative gambit of the book itself. A line from 'Burnt Norton' – 'Time and the bell have buried the day' – also show that it was not only Lehmann who kept Meredith's poetry in mind. And years later, when writing her memoir *The Swan in the Evening*, she looked again at the *Four Quartets*, 'that sublime, unhopeful, consoling cluster of poems' and 'discovered, or rather rediscovered, that everything was there – everything that I have been trying, and shall be trying, to say'.

These affinities between *The Echoing Grove*, *The Swan in the Evening* and Eliot's poems suggest one final point: that this novel, while closing off the 'cycle of experience' which lay behind Lehmann's earlier life and work, also provides a moment of continuity with what came afterwards. The philosophy to which she so passionately subscribed during her last thirty years – her belief that this life is merely the pale rehearsal for a later one, and that communication between the two worlds is possible through the intervention of mediums or 'sensitives' – has often been traced to one single, traumatic event: the abrupt death of her beloved daughter Sally from polio, at the age of only twenty-three. But I think that in its way *The Echoing Grove* is already a visionary work, which foreshadows her later spiritualism.

Some people are repulsed by the book, and can see only its faults: the undoubted *longueurs*, where the dialogue becomes unlifelike and over-explicit; the loss of momentum at the start of the 'Nightfall' section, after the story of the affair itself has essentially been brought to an end. Among its hostile readers, for instance, was the critic Walter Allen, who lamented the way 'personal relations become obsessive, indulged in . . . as an end in themselves', and saw it as 'a suffocatingly claustrophobic work in which never for a moment are we allowed the least relief from the masochistic self-torture suffered by the principal characters. They never transcend their misery.' But besides posing the question of what exactly personal relations *are*, if not 'an end in themselves', a more sympathetic reading – one which is alert to the inseparability of form and content in this novel – would see that what Walter Allen refers to as the characters' 'misery' is in fact the *instrument* of their transcendence.

This, above all, is the sense in which I would describe it as a visionary novel. Most people would feel, after finishing this book, that the event which both opens and closes it is more than an affecting reunion between two middle-aged sisters: it is a moment, rather, in which personal differences – as well as normal perceptions of time – seem to collapse under the weight of intense, remembered emotional experience, and something greater is achieved: a sort of spiritual empathy which does indeed transcend even the most violent and hurtful of past conflicts. Rosamond Lehmann was already looking forward, here, to the beliefs which would become so important to her in the last years of her life; and it's this tremulous, barely voiced undercurrent which sets *The Echoing Grove* apart from her other novels and makes of it – like the *Four Quartets* themselves – something 'sublime, unhopeful and consoling'.

Jonathan Coe
February 1996

Contents

Afternoon

DIRECTLY Madeleine came to the door, Dinah said, without looking at her:

'You've got the blue tubs.'

Holding a dog tight on the lead, she went on staring at the pair of baroque objects in peacock-blue glazed pottery set one on each side of the porch; tracing the convoluted garlands, shells, tritons, dolphins with an intent expression of amusement and surprise.

'I never heard the bus,' exclaimed Madeleine, aggrieved. 'I was listening for it too.' Her rather loud voice, impulsive yet uncertain, flurried, seemed to get pinched off at the back of her nose. Head averted, she stepped out on to the flagged doorstep beside her sister, touched the dog's head, scraped a morsel of earth off the rim of the right-hand tub and said frowning: 'Yes. Mother had simply put them in the cellar. When I asked her what she'd done with them, she was so pleased. I mean ... Well, you know how she ... Pleased I remembered them.'

'*And*,' put in Dinah almost under her breath, 'that she could produce them out of her hat and hand them over. When you would naturally be suspecting her of having disposed of them.'

'Well, you know how queer she was about everything to do with the house when it was sold. She didn't seem to want to think about it.'

'She gave away a good deal. I had ... she gave me ... some things ...'

'Oh, did she? When? I mean ... Of course -- I didn't need – though I'm sorry now. She sold a lot, I remember all the stuff out of the spare rooms going into a sale. Anyway ... When I asked what had happened to the tubs, I'd always loved them, she was thrilled. She said Papa bought them on their honeymoon in Italy, but she'd always

9

thought them so very ugly. She couldn't imagine anybody wanting them.'

'I didn't know,' murmured Dinah, 'they went to Italy for their honeymoon. I can't remember their ever mentioning it. Can you?' Her eyebrows went up. 'How odd ... I wonder why she thought them ugly. I always thought they were beautiful. And now I see they are. They had hydrangeas in them.'

'No, *palms*.'

'I could swear, pink and blue hydrangeas.'

'*Never*. You're mixing them up with Granny's conservatory. They were on the landing, in the window, surely you remember, and they had revolting spiky palms in them.'

A scolding irritable note appeared in Madeleine's voice. She crouched to caress the dog in an automatic way, while he pranced on the lead and strained at her in ecstasy, marking his sense of deferred recognition. He had a loose silken black and white coat with a flouncy ruff – a mongrel with Welsh sheepdog predominant in him. 'Anyway,' she went on, still stroking, 'she made me take them *then and there*. You can imagine how she would. We'd just bought this cottage and I was furnishing. So I lugged them up and heaved them into the back of the car and brought them straight down.'

For a split second her mother stood at the top of the cellar stairs, breathing with some difficulty, calling careful, child, you'll strain yourself, throwing down a cloth to take the worst of the dust off. Intensely lit by the naked bulb at the bottom of the steps, her face had blazed out transfigured, its puffiness and fatigue dissolved in an almost incandescent animation, to herald the resurrection of the tubs. When they were set down in the hall, she began to chuckle. Satisfaction, amusement? ... Yes. But then something else, climbing from the depths to be heard out loud in another moment. So urgent, thought Madeleine with a pang of misery, that I made my departure as brisk, as joking as possible.

'I've stuffed them with bulbs,' she said. 'They've had geraniums all the summer – those magenta ones.'

'They must have been a treat.' Dinah's eyebrows went up again. 'Are you a gardener?'

'I do garden,' said Madeleine. She straightened up and rubbed her eyes and forehead hard with the fingers of both hands – a gesture that rolled back more than twenty years for Dinah ... Early married days, mornings in Montagu Square, the hours turning towards the evening climax – another successful dinner party. All over the household a disciplined increase of tension, not a fray in the glossy texture; and then at my coming into the room – I the unmarried sister, being given an opportunity to meet some suitable young man – at something I said: should I write the place cards for the table, do the flowers, or some of them? – she would rub her forehead and eyes hard thus for a moment. Quite a new trick, revealing a hostess's tension and preoccupation ... and something more. Rubbing me out of her line of vision. And after that she would decline my offer, saying: 'I do it all,' or words to that effect, in the same voice, as if stifling a yawn.

'You find it soothing?' said Dinah.

'I find it a job of hard work,' said Madeleine, sharp and light. 'But I've quite taken to it. Had to.'

'Vegetables and all?'

'Of course. I don't potter about in embroidered hessian with a dainty trowel and a raffia basket, if that's what you mean,' said Madeleine, thinking: She hasn't changed. Still the cocked eyebrow, the guarded mouth firing off remarks designed to cause discomfort; as if to say no matter what the answer, she knew its fraudulence beforehand and would transfix it. She glanced sidelong at Dinah and was struck by her expression. Tired? Sad? ... Shaky, certainly, under the film of composure. Changed, though the same; greatly changed. As I am, I suppose. It's time we looked at one another. This was a ridiculously bad start. Altering her voice to cheerfulness, she added: 'No, it's a tie and a strain and all the things we all say nowadays, but I do like it. I've let the orchard and I've got a pensioner for the digging. That did get me down.'

'It seems to suit you,' said Dinah. 'You look fine.'

They looked at one another at last, they smiled, they dropped their eyes, unable to bear the weight and meaning of what for a moment they fully exposed to one another. Flushing, Madeleine stooped to pick up the shabby suitcase, saying:

'Come in. Bring him in. Why do you keep him on the lead? You told me you were bringing him but it went out of my head. I'm sorry you had to carry this. Was it all right in the bus – with him? What's his name? I really ought to have come to meet you, only this blasted petrol business, I've only got two gallons left for a month . . .'

'Oh *no*.' Dinah followed her over the threshold, into the long, large living-room. 'I didn't expect you. We agreed . . . In fact I preferred . . .' She fumbled with the dog's lead, let it drop as if bemused, watched him start a tentative exploration of the furniture, trailing the lead behind him. 'His name is Gwilym,' she said. 'He's Welsh, he was given to me. He's perfectly house-trained, of course.' They found themselves standing in front of the log fire, lighting cigarettes unsteadily.

'Well you must have thought it odd when I wasn't at the bus stop,' said Madeleine almost crossly. Her voice expired again.

'Why on earth? It was only a step. My bag isn't that heavy, as you will have noticed. I only brought slacks and night things, and a scrap of rations. My meat for him. He sat on my lap in the bus and was as good as gold. What a heavenly road it is, coming down into the valley. I haven't been in the country for weeks. It rather goes to my head – and his. That's why I kept him on the . . . Here!' He came obediently and she reached for the lead, snapped it off and stuffed it in her pocket. 'Directly I looked along the lane,' she said, 'I knew which was your house. I didn't need to ask.'

'Well, there aren't many to choose from.'

'It's such an eligible little affair,' said Dinah, making a sketching motion with her hand. 'Such a *character*.'

'I wouldn't call it distinguished.' There was a pause, during which Madeleine threw more logs on the fire.

'You love it?' The tone suggested less of query than assertion.

'Well, yes . . . It suits – for the present anyway. One must live somewhere.' She rubbed her eyes. 'Clarissa likes it.'

'Oh, Clarissa.' Dinah nodded rapidly. 'Does she?'

'Well, she's got her pony, and friends . . . She never seems to want to go away in the holidays.'

'Do let me see her room.' She stopped. Her eyes travelled from object to object within the four walls, as if she must now start deliberately to take them in. 'I want to see everything. You've made it lovely. Of course. This is lovely. One could work here. *And* relax. Oh, you've got a piano.'

'It's the piano – you remember it. Rickie's mother's wedding present.' Now the name was said. Perfectly simple. Now the tension would begin to drop. She went on pleasantly: 'There aren't many rooms. I'll show you after lunch. Come and eat now, you must be famished. It's a picnic, I hope you don't mind. If you're going to ask: Are you a good cook? the answer is no. I can cook, but I don't enjoy it. Clarissa does it in the holidays – she spends hours poring over cookery books and inventing variations. It's an obsession.'

'Oh, is it? Does she? I'm like that,' exclaimed Dinah, following her sister towards the kitchen.

'Oh, you are. So are most of my friends. When they start exchanging tips for sauces I could scream – their voices go into a sort of tranced hum of sensual communion. But I suppose it's just envy. Clarissa's cooking makes me feel awfully inferior. You and she had better meet.'

'Yes, I do want to. I was just thinking – I don't know any girls. None of my friends seem to have daughters. What is she like?'

'Rather peculiar. Forceful.'

'Nice looking?'

'Very. So everybody says.'

'Like you?'

'Not in the least.'

No more just now about this girl, dead Rickie's daughter. Girls generally took after their fathers, so one heard.

They sat down to a lunch of eggs *au gratin* and baked apples. Unspoken, the challenging testing exchange went on beneath the ripple of superficial commentary and question, the small bursts of laughter that exploded between them like bubbles released under pressure. They were meeting to be reconciled after fifteen years. This present mood in which they sat relaxed was nothing more than the relief of two people coming back to a bombed building once familiar, shared as a dwelling, and finding all over the smashed foundations a rose-ash haze of willow herb. No more, no less. It is a ruin; but suspense at least, at least the need for sterile resolution have evaporated with the fact of the return. Terror of nothingness contracts before the contemplation of it. It is not, after all, vacancy, but space; an area razed, roped off by time; by time refertilized, sown with a transfiguration, a ruin-haunting, ghost-spun No Man's crop of grace.

After the meal, after a rapid tour of the house, they prepared themselves to take a walk.

'Your shape is exactly as it always was,' said Madeleine.

'The same to you.' Dinah looked with appreciation at her sister, tall and trim in old but well-cut tweeds.

'No, not really. My legs ... Not that it matters tuppence. But I hate myself in slacks now. Mother couldn't bear me wearing them; she said I looked like a female impersonator. You know how she had a muddled idea that women must dress to preserve the mystery of sex. However, *you* look all right in them. Fine.'

'Thanks.' Dinah's voice was dry; she smiled. 'But the mystery of sex was never my strong suit.'

'Well ...' said Madeleine vaguely, with a sense of muffled collision. 'I don't know ...'

'Mother turned in her hand about my clothes when I was seventeen.'

'Nonsense.'

'Yes. You've forgotten. It was only yours she fussed about. After my coming-out frock, God help me, I was scratched from the arena.'

'Only because you were so obstinate.'

'You weren't exactly malleable, if I remember rightly.'

The looked at one another in the mirror above the mantelpiece, tentatively familiar, their smiles retrospective; turned away.

'Poor darling, she had such awful taste,' said Madeleine, staring out of the window. 'It was based on a principle: what the *jeune fille* should look like. Mine was equally execrable I suppose. Based on a fantasy, an ideal image from the fashion mags.'

'You might have done worse than hope to look exactly like yourself.'

'I never thought so,' said Madeleine, curt and vehement.

'How odd. I did,' said Dinah slowly, also staring out of the window, her eyes blank, her nostrils faintly dilated. 'You were a perpetual reminder of how much better one might have done oneself.' She added: 'I used to console myself reading *The Ugly Duckling* in my bedroom. Also that bit in the Bible about being able to remove mountains if you believed you could.'

'How absolutely mad!' cried Madeleine. 'Considering ...'

Once more she came to a stop, as if checked in a tunnel too long, too dark and devious to pursue. At the same moment a scene, not from childhood, shot out of nowhere and presented itself before her, complete in every detail; a scene containing Rickie and his wife Madeleine in the first year of their marriage, one evening, by the fire in the small book-lined room known as the study; used for domestic evenings *tête-à-tête*. Would he, she suddenly inquired, say Dinah was attractive? Yes, he would – remarkably attractive. What ingenuous enthusiasm behind the evening paper! The shock of it! '*Really*, Rickie? I think I am surprised. What makes you think so?' 'I don't think so. I just feel so.' Worse and worse. Like one chap talking to another at the Club, out of earshot of wives – casual, masculine, sexually conspiratorial. '*Really*, do you? ... I suppose women can never tell about other women. She's not *pretty*, would you say? Or would you?' He was going to say it was her figure and she would answer yes, not bad if only she wouldn't go about so stiff and hunched; or her skin, and she would answer ... But what he said, reflectively, was: 'She's mysterious.' 'Mysterious? What *do* you mean?' she drawled. He laughed as if to himself. 'She gives nothing away.' 'Oh, I see. No, I suppose she doesn't.' She added judicially: 'What you really mean is she's secretive. Likes to cover her tracks. That's true. She always did. Cold natures are always secretive, don't you think?' To this he made no answer. Yawning – with ostentation? – he took up the paper again, while by the fireside, opposite him, she swallowed back the burning stuff and felt it settle on her chest – sediment of prophetic acid, indissoluble. What had happened? *Nothing*. Sudden destruction of security, accomplished in a trice, as if by mutual pact ... No, not sudden but gradual, working in darkness from the beginning; and the pact was triple, long ago signed unread, sealed and shoved away ... Mysterious Dinah, slyness personified, impassive, neat, small, colourless, mysterious to Rickie; different outside and in and altogether, utterly different from herself, the flowing sister, acknowledged affectionate, responsive, popular – therefore not mysterious, or no longer so, to Rickie. What he was saying, simply, taken off his guard, was that he had married the wrong sister. Moment of fatal lucidity, fatal hallucination – which? Had she, or he, in that very hour become the self-betrayed protagonist who never need have been but always was to be? Or in that hour conspiring to draw back together, had they assigned that rôle to the absent third? Nothing in fact had altered for a long time. Their marriage continued idyllic, as all their friends remarked. Dinah came and went. At the end of the first year Anthony was born; at the end of the third year, Colin. An unexpectedly difficult and exhausting birth. Dinah stayed on for weeks, was agreeable

15

company. Then she declared her engagement to a young barrister, one of the most eligible of the possible husbands for Dinah at their dinner table; a solid chap, reliable, intelligent, well-off into the bargain. There was Dinah at last established with a sensible, a prosperous if not dazzling future, conforming to the right social pattern after all. Madeleine could congratulate herself. Did not Rickie think so? Yes, on the whole Rickie thought so. Charles was a good chap ... Perhaps a bit cold-blooded. 'But she's cold-blooded too, Rickie. She always was. And very ambitious. She'll make a good lawyer's wife.' 'I dare say she will,' said Rickie. 'All the same I don't feel certain somehow she'll go through with it.' From her sofa she watched him lean back in the armchair and close his eyes. A habit of his, to rest his eyes at odd moments by closing them. He had the kind of large blue eyes that easily got inflamed: Anthony had inherited them. A month later Rickie was proved right. Dinah declared the engagement a mistake and without further explanation broke it off; everybody was fed up with her; nobody could get her to confide or break her down; she went to live on her own in a cheap room in Pimlico; wrote a subdued, not very interesting or well-written novel, semi-fantastic, about a deaf girl and a blind man, got it published; enrolled herself as a student in some school of art; grew more and more cadaverous and uneven in her spirits; next went to live in Chelsea with a person called Corrigan – a woman as it turned out, a painter of only moderate talent and tendentious appearance, with whom she knocked around the pubs ... And then, a thorough Bohemian, with a lot of impecunious, free-thinking-and-drinking, bright-witted disreputables in tow, she started to come back into their lives. And then ... And then began the end that had been waiting in the beginning.

Glancing at her, Madeleine thought with extreme surprise: 'We are both widows.'

They went out, down the garden path. From its eight square windows the house watched them go; saw one of them – Dinah – stop at the wrought-iron gate in the low brick wall and look back hard at it. Her wide-open opaque dark eyes examined its compact brick face, the half-random, half-formal lay-out of the garden: herbaceous border on the left, lawn in the middle, on the right the apple orchard separated from the garden proper by an inconclusive hedge of yew in need of clipping. Her eyes had the look of eyes

16

accustomed to observing things in themselves with close attention. She said something to her companion, who turned from a vague survey of the landscape and looked too: she was admiring the semi-circular bow window that made such a pleasing feature between the four pairs of windows.

'Who lived here before you?' she asked.

Madeleine was not sure. She believed a retired naval officer and his maiden sister had inhabited it; but it had been empty for months when they bought it. She thought it had had a number of owners; luckily the building itself had never been touched; but everybody had done something to the garden and made a mess of it. Faintly she frowned, contemplating the area of her labours, seeing what should have been, what could be done. Her eye was for the land, for the last flowers in the border, the frost-blackened dahlias that must be lifted, the rose bed that must be pruned, the apple leaves drifted on the lawn. The other stared at the windows, thinking they looked uncommunicative. Upon what terms, she wondered, did they and Madeleine agree to contain, to release their mutual and separate lives, their ghosts and substances? It was a house for a quiet couple, or for someone in retreat. Could Madeleine really have retired in her prime, become a country woman on her own, her days plotted by the seasons, evenings alone with books and wireless, or writing letters to her children; a friend occasionally for week-ends perhaps? Strange, it was she, Dinah, who had dreamed always of living in the country, of running a small farm. Madeleine had been the Londoner, in the swim, never unaccompanied, never without new clothes, shored up with layer after layer of prosperous social life. Now though still expensively dressed and carefully made up she was no longer *soignée*. Her hair was going grey, her face had hollowed underneath the cheekbones, the tremendous vitality of her youth had faded out ... no, rather sunk down in her. In her youth it had spilled out all over the place, brilliant but not warm, and rather avid, even when playing with her babies. Now she had a glow from within, like an autumn rose. Yet the years just behind her had dealt her cruel blows: her firstborn, Anthony, killed; then Rickie's death. If she had been, as she must have been, adrift in wilderness, she had planted herself again in something ... more likely, someone? Yes, more likely than the soil or the community or intellectual interests or God.

17

They went out of the gate and took the elm-bordered lane that ran down past cottages, past the Dutch barns, past the church towards the river. The early November day was windless, blooming with a muffled lustre; weak sun drew out of the damp ground a haze within whose grained iridescence shapes and colours combined to create a visionary landscape, consuming its heart of honey colour, lavender, rose, dark amber, russet, jade and violet. From the polls of the stripped willows sprang sheaves of tapering copper wands, each one luminous from groove to tip. The river lay in its crescent loop entirely without movement, an artifice of green-black liquescent marble, inlaid between the banks' curved and scalloped edges; solider far than the de-materializing forms of earth around, above it. Flat fields unearthly green, dotted with grazing cattle, stretched into the distance on the side they walked on; the other side was broken, hillocky, and patched with unkempt plantations of smouldering beech and hazel. With intermittent yelps of hysteria, Dinah's dog tore along full pelt, plunging into the pitted banks, blowing rough snorts down holes and cavities, launching himself madly into treacherous rushbeds.

'What do you do with him in London?' asked Madeleine, watching a startled moor-hen skitter out across the river.

'Take him to work with me,' said Dinah. 'I insinuated him gradually and now he's more or less in control. There's quite a lot of competition to exercise him in the lunch hour. One girls brings him her meat ration. Another's Mum queues Thursdays for offal for him. Everything is gratefully accepted. His food is rather a problem. He looks fit though, doesn't he?' She stopped to gaze with indulgent pride at his tranced and quivering stern now sticking up out of a tangle of alder roots beneath them; adding: 'I'm looking after him for someone. His master had to give up his job and go and live in the country – he got ill. He was given this puppy by a farmer in the Welsh hills. But now he's too ill – he's in a sanatorium. He asked me if I could look after him till he came out, so I went down last Spring and collected him. But I don't think he will ever come out ... He's worse. So there we are.'

'You'll have to keep the dog?'

'Of course. I should miss him dreadfully anyway. He's very intelligent and affectionate. Very pleasant company.'

Suddenly she called to him in a sharp tone: 'Gwilym! Come out of it, there's nothing there. Come out, you ass!' At once, all simple optimism and goodwill, the dog emerged and bounded off in another direction. She followed his course with a dreamy look, remarking that he was very obedient.

'How long have you been living where you are now?' asked Madeleine. The address was in the Holborn district; it sounded shabby, dismal.

'Oh ... years,' said Dinah lightly. 'It's a big room and fairly cheap. Only one bathroom in the building but the other tenants refrain from baths till Saturdays, so it's not too bad. Still, the stairs are endless and there's not a square inch of garden to let him out in. I might move now.'

By the terms of their mother's will, apart from particular legacies to her two sons – prospering one in Canada, one in South Africa – the jewellery and furniture had been divided between her daughters; her own capital – her handsome annuity ceasing on her death – she had left to Dinah. The income to be expected, from safe investments, was about two hundred and fifty pounds a year. It was to this that Dinah referred by implication.

'You live alone?' said Madeleine, rather awkwardly.

'I live alone.'

'And your job?'

'What about my job?'

'Well ... what is it exactly?'

'Oh, I see. I work in a bookshop.'

'Do you really? Just selling books?'

'Selling them and wrapping them up and making out the bills for them.'

'Do you enjoy it?'

'Very much.'

Turning over in her mind rumours that had reached her through the years of Dinah's advanced political views, Madeleine paused before asking in a delicate way:

'Is it that place that got started in the thirties – I used to see it – called The Socialist Bookshop or something like that?'

'No. It's called Bryce and Perkins.' Dinah looked amused. 'It's simply a jolly good bookshop. Not a big one.'

'Highbrow?'

'Middle to high. It does cater for what's called the cultivated reading public – and for specialists.'

'Specialists in what?'

'Oh, various branches of literature. Art historians. Foreign research students. It's got quite a flourishing foreign section even now; and a second-hand one. Mr Bryce deals with the bibliophiles – he's one himself. He's an authority on early printing and types and title pages. I find all that a bore: I don't have anything to do with it of course. He's nice; a hard taskmaster but I like that. He won't employ anybody who trips up on his standards – of culture, I mean, and education. Every employee is made to take authority in some department. It's assumed you have an area of special knowledge.'

Her voice awoke in Madeleine echoes of a series of ancient exasperations: Dinah authoritative about something or other always – the drama it might be, the dance, psychiatry, wine, Negro sculpture, dirt-track racing, Egyptology, Buddhism, jazz composition, boxing ... Dinah airing her latest piece of serious research ... Not that she showed off exactly: she was always unaggressive, courteous in argument, not exactly dogmatic, never smug. That made it worse. She had simply made up her mind from the beginning.

'What is your area?' asked Madeleine.

'Oh, political history, economics – Marxist chiefly.'

'I see.' They stopped and looked out across the river at one fisherman anchored midstream in a stumpy green punt: motionless abstraction, double image, half air-borne, half reversed in water, pinpointed through the lens of a coloured dream. Watching him, Madeleine continued in a vague and level manner: 'I didn't realize that would be your area. It absolutely isn't mine. But then I haven't got any area ...'

'Well, you've never wanted one, have you?' said Dinah as if passing judgement, not unsympathetically, on a self-evident case of human nature.

'How do you know?' Her voice sharpened.

'Your brain is as good an instrument as mine. Better, probably.'

'You mean, I haven't used it.'

'I didn't say so,' said Dinah, mild. They turned and walked on slowly. 'No ... I mean it's just another way of life. For one thing, you haven't been obliged to earn your living ...'

'God knows what I'd have done if I had,' burst out Madeleine, the prey of violent and obscure emotions: suspicion, indignation – a complex wish to lay the blame on someone and at the same time defy the critics of unearned income as a way of life. 'The ridiculous education I was given.'

'Mine was the same,' said Dinah, inexorably mild.

'I could have got a job in the war. I was offered a decent one, in the B.B.C. – translating French – Rickie wouldn't let me. He said I must stay with the children.'

'He was perfectly right.'

'God knows I worked as hard as any working-class housewife.' She flushed darkly, to her forehead. 'I *slaved*.'

'I bet.' Dinah was sympathetic.

'What did you do?'

'Oh ... various things. Nothing spectacular. Worked in rest centres mostly. Taught some children drawing for a bit; some of the evacuated ones who came back. I had a huge class in the end – in a cellar in Stepney. I enjoyed that. They were brilliant, some of them.'

Suppressing another burst of querulous resistance to the idea of this huge drawing class, Madeleine merely said:

'You were in London all the time?'

'Yes, right slap through.'

'I suppose you were called up.'

'Would have been.' Dinah stopped and lit a cigarette. She smokes, thought Madeleine, like a chimney. 'Being a widow with no home ties. Actually, I volunteered.'

There was a silence; then the other said nicely:

'You must tell me where your bookshop is. I'd like to come in, next time I'm in London.'

'Yes, do,' said Dinah, cordial. 'You look so stunning, you'd raise my prestige.'

'It doesn't sound – from what you said – as if it needed raising.'

'Then I must have given you a false impression.' She stopped again on a small bridge with white wood railings to watch a pair of swans glide from the main stream into a meandering reedy willow-bordered backwater. 'My capacity is a very humble one. I've no particular qualifications, worse luck. What I do know I've taught myself. At least, Jo started my education ...' The swans slid out of sight, making for some known evening haunt in the creek's upper reaches. 'If only,' she said with sudden eagerness, 'I could be a whole-time student for a year or two! Go to Oxford or Cambridge. Get a degree. How I'd work! How I'd love it! ... I *might*, you know, now. I might be able to afford it.' Her lifted profile, regular, delicate, looked rapt.

They strolled on again.

'What do they pay you in this job?' said Madeleine.

'Five pounds a week.'

'That's not all you – what you've been living on?'

'No. It comes to a bit more than that. I get a small bonus at Christmas – and a guinea or so for an occasional article here and there. And then of course I've still got that hundred a year – at least it's less now but it does make all the difference: what we both had from Papa when we were twenty-one.'

Doing sums in her head, Madeleine thought ruefully of the hundred a year. She had forgotten all about it, was uncertain whether it still came in, whether Rickie had long ago reinvested it, or long ago helped her to spend the capital it represented. He had had a regardless way with money in the first years: a lordly way, a generous way, as Dinah might remember ... Hush, stop, for shame, she told herself. Here was the truth: Dinah a frugal wage-earner, managing on a few hundreds: she herself comfortably provided for. She had feared a possible clause in Rickie's will: something left away from his family, for Dinah, something to mark his sense ... to say sorry, to say remember, to say love. But no: absolutely nothing.

The dog bounded back with a stick, and Dinah took it from his jaws and threw it for him, far, like a boy, from the shoulder. She said:

'Seeing that Jo was killed in the Spanish Civil War and not the Second World War, I don't, of course, get a pension.'

She seemed to throw the words after the stick, letting them go with simplicity and ease.

'I suppose not,' murmured Madeleine, thinking this was not the time ... All she knew was that in the end Dinah had married a man, a Jew, called Hermann, killed fighting in the International Brigade. 'My sister, Mrs Jo Hermann.' Strange.

Observing what they took to be a bull in the next field, they turned for home. Talking of relatives – kept up with by Madeleine, by Dinah lost sight of – they recrossed the old toll bridge with its rosy picture postcard cottage and garden brightly patched with the last Michaelmas daisies, the first chrysanthemums; and walked up a slope towards the rambling village. On their right lay the rectory, a glum neo–Gothic building girt with laurel, ilex and other dark nondeciduous shrubbery. Beyond it the church raised a fine untouched fifteenth-century tower above the remainder of its injudiciously remodelled structure. A group of poplars, still topped with lemon-coloured turbans, stood beside the gate: and crammed with nettles, long grass and lurching head-stones, the neglected graveyard ran down in rough terraces almost to the river's bank.

'Anything exciting inside?' asked Dinah, stopping.

'There's an effigy: the Lord of the Manor prone beside his wife, and twelve midgets kneeling under them. Jacobean. Rather fascinating. Come in and look at it. There's just enough light.'

'Sit,' said Dinah to the dog in the porch. He sat. 'He'll stay put till I come out,' she said.

They examined the effigy, the memorial brasses, ancient and modern, in the walls, the Tudor font, the Edwardian altar cloth, the brass-bound Bible on the lectern, the parish notices pinned up inside the door. It was chilly in the church. They came out again. The dog was no longer sitting in the porch.

Whistling and calling, Dinah went this way and that, between the graves and then behind the church. She was astonished, and said so. She said several times that he had never done such a thing before.

'Yes,' agreed Madeleine. 'You told me how obedient he was.'

'He must have seen something,' said Dinah with decision.

'Perhaps a ghost?'

On the heels of this suggestion a shape of silence, planing stealthily from nowhere, crossed the churchyard: a huge cream-coloured owl. Ravished, startled, they watched the apparition wave up and down, up and down, with rapid wing beats, low above the terraces; then, leaving a long wake of deeper silence, swoop away out over the river.

'He's always here,' murmured Madeleine, 'about this time of day.'

'Listen!'

A medley of disagreeable noises broke upon their ears: whimperings, maniacal moans, hoarse growls and chuckles: then *staccato crescendo* a volley of imperious barks. Darting forth, chin out, in the direction of the back of the tower, Dinah said madly: 'He must have seen a badger.'

But it was a rat. Down in the ditch beneath the churchyard wall; half curled on its side, as if reclining in dreadful ease, and facing its opponent: flea-bitten, sodden, its belly blown; and all of it watchful, still, grey as damnation.

'*Now* what do we do?' said Dinah, unsteady.

'We go away,' said Madeleine. 'We simply go away. He'll deal with it, won't he? It's cornered, isn't it? He's a sporting dog, isn't he?'

The dog continued to tread the ditch, forward and back as if setting to partners in The Lancers, sobbing, trembling from head to stern.

'It's his first rat,' said Dinah. She lit a cigarette, puffed, let it fall to the ground.

'Is he *frightened* of it?' asked Madeleine. 'He seems frightened of it. No wonder.' Again she said: 'We'd better go away.'

But horror-struck, they continued to stand watching.

'It's too big,' said Dinah. She swallowed; then making her voice resolute, she croaked out: 'Good boy, Gwilym. Good boy. At it. Good boy. Go on. Attaboy.'

Thus encouraged the dog pounced, caught the rat by the nape, shook it, dropped it, caught it, dropped it again.

'There,' breathed Dinah, pale as the marble angel adorning a Victorian tomb beside her. 'That's got it. He knows how ...'

But the rat began to run along the bottom of the ditch, blood on its back, its tail gliding sinuous, obscene, over the matted ivy and dead leaves. The dog went after it; and after the dog went the frantic voice of Dinah, repeating on a full chest note:

'Kill it! Kill it! Kill it!'

'This is devilish,' said Madeleine.

She hurried to the gate, looked up and down the road. Help, help! ... But help there was none. Dusk, opalescent, was beginning to enfold the empty pastoral scene. Behind her, hysteria now clamoured from a different direction. Loath to look back, she looked, and saw Dinah staring through some spiked iron rails enclosing a large square block of monumental masonry, wiping her face with her handkerchief. The dog was charging these rails with fatuous bravado, plunging his nose between the bars, and barking without intermission.

'What's happening now?' called Madeleine with a hint of threat.

'It's got inside this damned ...' Emotional, indignant, Dinah's voice broke off.

Madeleine walked slowly back and joined her; with an effort forced her eyes to focus once more upon the object. It was huddled just inside the railings, watching the dog with absolute concentration. Dinah said in a weak voice:

'It's been *fighting* him. He's done his best. He can't finish it off. Look at its eyes, just look.'

'We must leave it,' repeated Madeleine.

'We can't. It's all mauled – don't you see? We *cannot*. It's got to be killed.'

Suddenly the creature reared up on its hind legs behind the bars, teeth bared, jaws wide, and started to screech. Beneath its cursing throat, its midget hands hung pink, useless, as if in supplication: a shock for all. Again the dog plunged. It made a snake's dart; and he sprang backwards with a yelp, nipped in the lip.

'It isn't fair!' cried Dinah, grabbing him by the collar.

All at once the rat abandoned its point of vantage, turned its back on them. They watched it creep along the side of the tomb; stop; then, obscurely driven, yet as if with the terrible deliberation, the final fatal calculation of a duellist, emerge from between the bars on the farther side, and slither off on a slow track through the soaked grass. It was badly hurt.

'God!' muttered Madeleine. 'I can't stand much more of this. Of all the bloody – beastly – bungling ...' She looked with raging disgust at the incompetent animal, quiet now in Dinah's grasp. Blood and foam flecked his muzzle: he whimpered and wagged his tail in a bewildered way.

'He's not a terrier, he's a sheepdog,' explained Dinah, deadly gentle. 'They *fought* down in that ditch – you didn't see. It went for him again and again – *screeching*. He's hurt. Rat bites can be very poisonous.'

'You're telling me,' said Madeleine. 'Does that rat look to you diseased? It does to me. We'd better hurry back and ring up the vet – though I doubt if we'd get him on a Saturday evening. At least we'd better make for the Jeyes Fluid as soon as possible. Immerse him totally, and then ourselves.'

'I doubt,' said Dinah, 'If you've incurred any risk worth mentioning.

But if you're anxious, the best thing would be for me to take him straight back to London. What are the trains?'

Incurring risk to the full, she pulled up a handful of long grass and carefully wiped his muzzle. The branches of the ancient yew under which they stood enlaced them with serpentine malevolence. Turning a nasty colour, the peaceful landscape withdrew itself and left them on an island where any movement might mean electrocution. From this wired stronghold they looked out and beheld the blot, the poison-container, lying dark on the grass, like a broken flask, between two mounds. Then it moved a bit, not much ... And still no rescuer came by, no whistling rustic youth or shrewd old labourer expert in, indifferent to slaughter. They were weak women in extremis, abandoned by their natural protectors.

'Isn't there a *man* about?' cried Dinah, suddenly breaking to voice all this. 'Are there *no* men in this village? Can't you fetch your *gardener?*'

'He's seventy-three,' said Madeleine. 'Besides, he's gone to the football match. I think everybody has.'

In silence they walked together to the gate and looked once more up, down, far and near. Not a soul in sight. A sigh came out of the poplars and a few bright discs spun down and settled round their feet.

'Or the Vicar?' muttered Dinah, scarcely attempting to disguise appeal.

'No use. He's got lumbago. And even if he hadn't, he wouldn't.'

'There seems to be a boy down there by the bridge. Should we run for him? He's a country boy. He'd probably enjoy it.'

They strained their eyes in the direction of the old toll house, in whose square of garden a small figure could be seen, moving among white fowls.

'Stanley Higgs,' said Madeleine reflectively. 'I scarcely think so. He's only six; and not allowed to play with rough children.'

There was a pause.

'Ah well ...' said Dinah. 'It may be dead by now.'

'I should think it must be.'

But they did not expect it ever to be dead.

'I'm going to see,' said Dinah with sudden resolution. 'Hold him.'

She handed the lead to Madeleine and strode towards the church. The dog sat down on his haunches and trembled piteously; and after a moment Madeleine said: 'There, there,' and stroked his dishonoured head. She saw Dinah questing with caution within the rat belt; after a while she stopped dead close to the church door and stood with her head poked forward.

'Found it?' called Madeleine.

'Yes.'

'Dead?'

There was no reply. Madeleine walked forward and stood at a little distance, near enough to see the shape at Dinah's foot.

'Nearly dead,' said Dinah slowly. 'I think it's back's broken. Give me your stick.'

Madeleine handed her a crook-handled Alpenstock carved with edelweiss, saying: 'You'll never do it with that.'

'Keep Gwilym away. Don't look. On your life, don't look.'

Madeleine shut her eyes, gripped Gwilym, turned her back; and after a few moments heard a sick thread of voice remark: 'I cannot do it. I can't take life.'

Come here and hold your dog,' said Madeleine, still with her back turned. 'I'll do it.'

At once Dinah obeyed, saying shakily: 'It looked at me.'

'Oh *Christ* . . . !'

'Madeleine, you can't. Or can you? You know you can't.'

'I can. I can and I *will*.' She examined the stick and let it drop. 'This is the wrong shape. And much too light. Wait, I must hunt.'

She walked away, disappearing behind the tower, and presently returned with a large garden spade. 'The sexton's, I suppose,' she said. 'Propped against the vestry door. Careless. I think his grandson uses it to dig up worms with at week-ends.'

'*Worms?*'

'For bait.'

'In the cemetery?'

'A lot happens in this cemetery. Now keep back, for God's sake.'

She forced herself to get close enough to the rat to examine its potentialities. Stained, chewed, defeated – a piece of monstrous garbage thrown away. Not moving any more, but visibly breathing. Then suddenly it moved. On the uttermost fighting verge of life it turned its head sideways and looked at her, measured her, with brilliant fixity . . . *No, no, no, no, no, no* . . . Strike on the back of its head, don't waver. 'This is gross, this is *gross*,' she said aloud. Now. Death and *death* to it. She lifted the spade, aimed, brought the flat of it crashing down. The rat reared up full stretch in a supreme convulsion, as if about to spring. But it was done for. It rolled over, twitching. Immediately its open eyes began to film.

Dragging her gaze away, she turned to see Dinah by the gate, her back averted, busy securing the dog's lead to the post.

'It's dead,' she called; and at once, with automatic briskness, Dinah turned and advanced to stand beside her.

'I suppose the twitching is just reflex action.' Dinah's tone was clinical. Then, appreciatively: 'Good for you. I never thought you'd be able to.'

'I do a lot of things now I couldn't have done once.'

'My God, it was brave,' said Dinah, extending the scope of decent tribute.

'It certainly had reserves,' said Madeleine. 'The worst came last. It didn't turn to best.'

She fished for her handkerchief and wiped her mouth and forehead; and after a glance at her, Dinah seized the spade, saying:

'Here, give me that.'

Looking away, Madeleine said sharply:

'What are you going to do?'

'Bury it.'

'*Not here.*'

'No.' Her gaze travelled round, irresolute.

'Best thing,' said Madeleine, still looking into the distance, 'would be to take it down to the river and throw it in.'

'Far the best. Perhaps if you feel up to it, you wouldn't mind waiting here and holding Gwilym. Or rather, start walking on home – I should.'

'Well, I'll go on and make tea. We need it.'

Leading the dejected animal, Madeleine went slowly down the path, through the gate, and started up the road. Presently she stopped, looked back. The hampered figure of Dinah could be seen emerging from the gate and veering in the opposite direction. She held the spade straight out in front of her: an effort. From it the tail hung down, swinging. Like one moving in a barbaric rite of dedication towards some altar she stepped onward, onward, and disappeared

28

below the brow of the slope. Tractable, but grief-stricken, the dog began to cry.

'All right,' said Madeleine kindly. She strolled back on her tracks and stood leaning against the churchyard wall. She turned and let her eyes travel over the mounds and memorials; to the spot; then upwards along the tower's spare grey pure-shafted column, to its light-washed crown; to its arched upper window deep-set beneath crenellations, its one round turret, its weather-cock and flag-pole all supernaturally designed in the last sun's last symbol-making glow. Keep watching it, she told herself. Be empty. Rest in peace.

Dusk had perceptibly deepened before Dinah was seen to be marching briskly up the slope again, the bier across her shoulder. From some distance she waved and nodded, calling greeting and encouragement to Gwilym.

'It's after you!' called Madeleine.

She checked a glance behind her, brandished the spade.

'I won't ask for details,' said Madeleine when she reached her side.

'No.' She shuddered.

'Well, that's that.'

'We shan't recover all at once.' Dinah lit a cigarette in the manner of one taking calm stock of past catastrophe.

'There's nothing like a dog for ruining a pleasant walk,' said Madeleine, bending to remove the lead. 'Don't let him lick your hand for God's sake.'

'I suppose you've got disinfectants.' Dinah patted his ribs, adding: 'He did his best. Brave boy, you did your best. Your very, very best.'

'We all did,' said Madeleine. 'Our very, very best.'

They looked behind them at the now tenebrous graveyard spreading yet one more fold of everlasting night upon its shadow people. Dinah took a breath, as if to speak; said nothing; and Madeleine continued:

'The great thing was to get it out of here. I couldn't have done that. I admire you.'

'The great thing was to kill it. I couldn't. I'm sorry.'

We're sorry. We did our best. Stopped it going on dying, shovelled it into limbo. There's nothing more to be done, we'll go away. Darkness, close up this fissure; dust under roots and stones, consume our virulent contagion; silence, annul a mortal consternation. We must all recover.

But still the stones seemed rocked, the unsterile mounds, reim-pregnated, exhaled dust's fever; a breath, impure, of earthbound anguish.

Morning

SLEEPLESS in the small hours, Dinah switched on her lamp and looked through the pile of books upon the bedside table. A brand-new novel – Book Society Choice; an anthology of modern poetry; two thrillers; a recent collection of delicious Continental recipes; Keats's Letters; *Green Mansions*; a worn copy of *The Phoenix and the Carpet* with her name, Dinah Dorothea Burkett, pencilled inside in her own sprawling nine-year-old hand; last, a small volume in a honeycombed Victorian binding, dark blue stamped with gold; *Tuppy the Donkey*. She opened this, and an aroma of sour paper and dead nurseries came out of it. She read on the title page: John Vandeleur Burkett, on his sixth birthday, from his affectionate Mother, May 14th 1878; a time-browned script, swimming and delicate as a dragonfly. Somebody, years and years ago – John Vandeleur perhaps, her father – had crudely chalked in the illustrations. The ghost of a qualm twisted in her bowels – residue of some obscure long overlaid association with childish fear and sickness; some intimation of mortality breathed out from the engravings – boys with improbably celestial faces, sailor-hats haloing cherubic curls, short jackets and long trousers – old-fashioned boys at play, an old-fashioned donkey. Push them out of sight, bury them deep at the back of the shelf: they won't come back alive, and Tuppy's a nasty name to give a donkey.

Everything for the spare room had been remembered, just as in former days. *Cloisonné* jar filled with ginger biscuits, box filled with cigarettes, ash tray beside it. She took a biscuit and started to break and eat it with stealthy movements and glances towards the armchair where, upon an old rug of Madeleine's, Gwilym lay curled. But even this, his favourite noise, the breaking of a biscuit, failed to penetrate his total anaesthesia. Tilting the lampshade, she craned forward to peer at him. Normal respiration, no sign of swelling in the lip: thank God, he seemed all right. Surely, she told herself, lying back on the pillows, I can begin to relax. Forget the omen. I can't face anything more ... Omens are nonsense anyway. If he's O.K. tomorrow – and he will be – it will be a good omen. The rat will be gone for good to the bottom of the river, the swans will float together in light and peace. This enterprise we're on, whatever it is, whoever accompanies us – myself, herself, Rickie, our parents – who besides? – or awaits us still unknown along the road – this enterprise will bring us somehow to an extension of freedom; not end, as it still seems it might (is she thinking like thoughts, is she asleep next door?) in a place of distorting mirrors and trap doors.

The room she lay in must have been Rickie's dressing-room. She looked round it in a cautious way, but nothing made a leap out of neutrality: not the pastel portrait of him as a pretty child – fair waving hair, rose cheeks, periwinkle eyes, white blouse – above the fine mahogany chest of drawers; not the set of good sporting prints on the walls, nor the cream and green floral chintz curtains that Madeleine had drawn after tea, saying you remember these old spare room ones from home, Mother produced them about a year ago, she'd packed them away, the linings have had it, as you see, but still, these days ... Frowning, dissatisfied, twitching the folds.

Madeleine's household goods had always been expensive and well chosen, suggesting an advised taste, the aesthetic tact of the interior decorator, rather than any personal preference. These charming rooms, decorated out of what was suitable and small enough from Montagu Square (after Rickie's death she'd sold so much, thought now she'd been a fool) revealed no alteration in her formulae. Only that long room in the attic, Clarissa's room, struck with determination a note of discord. A junk shop, said Madeleine, looking round on what had been superimposed upon a basic conception of girlish simplicity, pink-painted. Did you ever see? ... but she would have it so. Shelves crammed with animals in glass and china, with snapshots in composite frames – Nannie and former cooks and housemaids, girl friends, dogs, kittens, ponies; one table reserved for studio portraits: her father and her brothers all three in uniform; also her mother. The window seat carried her radio, her gramophone, two record cases, several albums, a pile of old sporting and country magazines, a pot of Stickphast and a pair of cutting-out scissors. 'A year *at least* they've been there,' said Madeleine. 'I'm not to throw them away. She'll deal with them *in her own good time* – I ask you! She's making scrapbooks for Colin, so she says. Look at her desk ...' She flung open one drawer, then another; stuffed with old letters, theatre programmes, regimental badges, note-books, balls of knitting wool, old purses, broken wrist-watches. 'Every letter she's ever had. And things the boys had ...' She picked up an old diary, glanced inside it, put it down again, rummaged uncertainly, closed the drawer. '*Nothing* is to be touched, I've had to swear. It's always the same answer – she'll go through everything in her own good time. Where does she get this magpie streak from? Can she be maladjusted? ... But Mother hoarded, didn't she? She's like Mother in some ways. The same obstinacy too ...'

In one corner stood a cabinet containing Rickie's boyhood collection of birds' eggs; in another Anthony's old fretsaw; behind it, propped against the wall, a pair of skis once his. Colin had made the rather good models of sailing ships on top of the bookcase. The library bore witness to a decade of voracious hugger-mugger reading, ranging from Shakespeare, the Brontës and Jane Austen, E. Nesbit and Beatrix Potter, to madcap-of-the-school fiction and equestrian books, technical and romantic, by the dozen. On the wall hung a guitar adorned with many-coloured streamers; a straw boater bound with maroon gold-lettered ribbon and a wreath of faded pink roses: Rickie's, a trophy from his Eton boating days; also a couple of Van Gogh colour prints and several unframed water-colours on rough paper, casually attached by insufficient drawing pins: her own work these. Yes, conceded Madeleine, she had talent; she seemed to be able to do everything rather well. They were bold, naïve, formal – scenes of drama and violence; a shipwreck, a resurrection of the dead from tombs in a moonlit cemetery, a street of houses on fire, ladders, black figures jumping, flinging up arms of lamentation, running through lurid flames.

Opening one of the albums, they found it to be Anthony's, its stiff cardboard leaves pasted with athletic groups, the names printed neatly out below. Raking the lines of schoolboy puppets with folded arms and bare knees spread, they detected, without comment, the lost one's face, bright, blank, pre-adolescent. Another, similar, album belonged to Colin's past.

The person inhabiting this space reflected her own ego, fluid and tenacious, in all its dispositions; scaled down an immeasurable bereavement in this pious setting up of emblems: a fervent matter-of-fact heart had been at work here, intent on consolidating all its history; a girl who missed her father and her brothers. 'Not a permanent inhabitant,' Madeleine had said, describing with half-sympathetic irony the spiritual awakening which Clarissa was now undergoing as the result of recent confirmation at her school. On the one hand beckoned the dedicated life; on the other the life of selfish pleasure. But dedicated to what? Clarissa asked herself; impossible to discover; whereas pleasure presented no such problems: she wished to study tap-dancing, and to broaden the mind by riding alone through Europe on her pony. To make matters worse her two best friends had already discovered their vocations. 'They all three deplore my lack of faith. Fidelia is sorry for me and writes me helpful letters.' And turning to leave the room, Madeleine repeated: 'No, I can't tell myself I must make a home for her all that much longer ...' Yet this area staked out beneath the family roof seemed the almost clamorous assertion of an attached child. I was the same, thought Dinah, at her age; my room like hers, stuffed with nursery relics and the boys' discarded things. Yet I knew I was half-packed already.

She saw Clarissa in the attic, a big fair-skinned Nordic type of a girl, brushing out a mane of hair with vigorous perfunctory strokes, looking not into the mirror but out of the window while she shook it back. The time is coming, she thought, when we shall meet. I can advise – no, make only the most cautious suggestions, to help her keep her relics and discard them. She might give me devotion – I the black sheep, unmentioned member of the family, natural object of romantic interest to the young. Presumably she knows of my existence. What can she have been told? – or what conjecture? ... The situation is tricky, almost anything I say might cause her to admire me more than would be acceptable to Madeleine. The young take sides, she'd take mine, it couldn't be prevented ... In no time, we should be conspirators. Feeling her heart begin to thump, she lit a cigarette and lay back, drawing deep breaths, seeing again that photograph staring at her from Clarissa's table: the face of a tired man, good-looking, his hair a little thin, grey round the temples; Clarissa's father, sacred relic not to be breathed upon. It was only in corrupt literary fantasies, in the world of steel-true waifs and blade-straight wantons that daughters made pacts in their wise grave childish way with the Woman in Daddy's Life.

Let it alone, it's dead and everybody's dead except Madeleine and myself. It's a patch of scorched earth, black, scattered with incinerated bones. Whatever she's digging for will not turn up: there's nothing buried alive. What does she fear? ... He fathered her breathing children in lawful wedlock; and in the lawless dark another: mine; spilt seed, self-disinherited prodigal; non-proven proof, stopped breath, rejecting our and the whole world's complicity. What of it now?

'*Oh!* ... *It's not breathing*.' Puzzled, matter-of-fact. Not a tactful thing to remark in that tone of voice to a woman just through labour. Before that, with my eyes fast shut, I'd seen her, Corrigan, pick it up out of the tumbled bed. 'It's a boy.' Just what I'd expected to have: three normal words. I felt my huge smile flood through me, burst out of my spent body like the huge irradiated backwash of the final wave of birth. A boy. Under my shut eyes I listened, peacefully waiting for what was only to be expected – the sound of newborn crying. I wasn't worried by the silence: in all those hours I hadn't had a moment's fear; and, bound to me in our unreality, nor had she. I was travelling first class and taking her along for the privileged hell of it: wild country but *de luxe* conditions. Poor old Corrigan, she'd never done anything in style, she thought we were initiating her. We bamboozled her. She was an old clown doing her damnedest, born to the game, condemned to it, assiduously tumbling in the ring; we were the glamorous *artistes* doing the new sensational trapeze act high up among the lights with a roll of drums. Breath-taking acts, drama and suspense. Danger? Not for such star performers.

Her movements creaked, breathed round me while a timeless age went by. 'It's dead I think.' Flat statement. My lids lifted, she was holding him up, I saw his blood-stained human head. She'd cut the cord and tied it; she was clever with her hands. One couldn't say she'd lost her head ... It was just bad luck. Or it had gone on too long, we'd thrown our hands in without telling one another we knew the game was up. Thinking back afterwards, I realized there was a moment about half-way through when the imtimation reached me that ... something biding its time from the beginning had stepped

35

from ambush and taken charge. The enterprise was moving to its predestined outcome. But one is never prepared for what one has prepared to bring about. Her bulky figure blocked the low-ceilinged room, solid between lamplight dying on the table and pewter snowlight through the pane. Dawn. Some time in the small hours the blizzard had drawn ahead of me and emptied itself out. There was a cry then, animal, and it was mine. It trailed its length out of the window and died in the nine-days-hanging shroud of the dead world.

Presently, as the morning whitened, the men from the farm began to clear the lane, digging us out for the third time in ten days, hailing our dumb door as they dug towards it. They were full of rum and very jolly. She ran down and called to them, I was beginning to die by then. Distinctly I heard her say: 'I think she's dying.' That was the last thing I heard for a long time ... All the wires were down, the milk van crawled five miles on chains to the doctor. What a freak of climate in Cornwall at the end of February: only once before in living memory, fifty-eight years ago. What a grotesque disaster, all of a piece with the rest. *All of a piece* to stay in an isolated cottage at the bottom of a Cornish lane in winter when you're eight months pregnant. They told me later at the hospital that it was just one of those things, unaccountable, the heart fails suddenly in transit, nobody could have saved him; but I never have believed it. If I hadn't fatuously lain there thinking myself triumphant and past effort, if I'd sat up and given her some simple sensible instructions ...

No ...

Next thing, I was being lifted into the ambulance. Seeing her face mottled, in pieces, I said aloud: 'Your face is a smashed plate.' I saw her hand a sort of parcel wrapped in white towelling to a public Statue of Justice in a dark blue veil who placed it somewhere, with tact, out of my sight. I said: 'What a balls-up,' but nobody answered, so I thought they were shocked at my language, I'd better keep quiet. I felt hot-water bottles being pushed in all round me, her icy fingers on my pulse as we set off. I thought I'd try a medical approach and said, with calm: 'How can this haemorrhaging be dealt with?' – but there was still no answer, so perhaps I only thought I said it. Then I went on dying until I began to live again in a different place in the middle of the next night. 'Your husband has come, dear ...' Kind voice, later less kind, suspicious. I opened my eyes and there was

Rickie, who had driven for fifteen hours through thaw and snow to reach me when he got her telegram. What a blue blaze of love and grief his eyes poured over me to draw me back. What tenderness, what self-reproach and consolation ... Which suffered most then, of the three of us? Not I, perhaps ... I played the lead, and it was big stuff; supporting rôles are less rewarding. I was prostrate, absolved, pure tragic principle in the cathartic state. What they got stuck with was the guilt and conflict, clogging their vitals, not to be expelled. That's what in other words she told me later; but again I was unprepared ... While she raved and wrung her hands, while she accused and cursed me, I began to dream of shaking it all off, the love and the hate, the treachery and the fidelity, the humiliation and the reconciliation, the fear, the reassurance ... the whole claustrophobic world of the emotions where truth and falsehood exchange their masks for ever and for ever. I began to conceive of loss as liberation. But only as a moment's wild surmise, or a sudden failure of instinct in the chase. Meanwhile I heard her say she could find it in her to be sorry for Rickie, under my influence he had lost all sense of right or wrong; and sorry, damned sorry for Madeleine and she had to say so; far be it from her to judge or be censorious, but she simply had to. And revolted as I was by her dishonesty, I felt compunction; she'd gone the whole way to find that the taste of me was ashes. I'd fed her raffish power addiction, her snobbery, her temperament of a good sort cum *procureuse*. The responsibility was mine. I wasn't in the category she'd so far catered for, poor devil: I hadn't borrowed her money and drunk her gin and come to her for the abortionist's address and relied on her to see me through the botched dark deed. I was bound for a private room in the District Hospital: when my time came I'd be safe there with my layette and wedding ring. It was just bad luck that my time was premature; he had less chance by far than the snowborn lambs all gathered in and tended. He was to have saved her: a cottage in the country, a love-child, not her own, to dedicate her life to. The best of her was her nurse-mother instinct, and she'd always wanted to adopt a child. We were to have committed ourselves, somehow, to the future – constructively, religiously you might say. No more anarchy and squalor.

And then we foundered – on elementary facts. For her it was the crack-up. Poor wretched old Corrigan who from the highest motives blew the gaff on the delinquents ... What of it now? I never saw her again, I heard of her death by chance. Some pair of queens or other took her to Mexico and she died there, years ago.

It was a time that couldn't be sustained. Time of enormities. Madeleine's still got it under her skin. She's partly stuck in it still, and thinks I am, or should be: Why, says her bright stare, should she – not I – feel guilt for crimes not hers but mine?

> All of a piece without,
> Thy chase had a beast in view,
> Thy wars brought nothing about,
> Thy lovers were all untrue ...

A long time ago now that burden had faded out of earshot. Once my head was a gong, beaten on day and night: all of a piece thy chase, all of a piece thy wars, thy lovers untrue, in view, untrue, gone away, gone away ... Day in day out the stamping bold refrain; then intermittent, bursting out and fading; bad days, the beast at bay; bad nights, beast running in the jungle; then slowly, by dint of unremitting labour, with sweat, blood, tears – months, years of them? – I passed out of this circle; I gave birth to myself and entered into life. My head was purged, my hearing was absolved; my eyesight ... If I looked backwards, I saw only one of those old dim scenic paintings, featuring histrionic crag and precipice, leopard-concealing forest, storm clouds, zigzag lightning, distant prospect of lit water; and in the foreground a few figures, important in relation to the whole conception yet unemergent, kept in their proper place; dark, or transparent almost; standing or sitting for ever in repose.

But before I was made free of such a landscape, before I could arrest the flux, compose it, I had had, of course, to die. Not one *coup de grâce*, but three; and all in the same day: remarkable. *One:* Rickie; *two*, Rob; *three*, the third one, the last, the finisher ... But that enormity was still unperpetrated the last time I saw Rickie.

That time when I summoned him, the very last time, I still had it in my mind to ... What did I have in mind? ... to place myself under his protection. My brother-in-law: what more suitable? If when I telephoned he refused to see me, I told myself I intended to go straight to my sister Madeleine: an unequivocal appeal this time. 'Look, for God's sake,' I would have said, 'surely you know I'm honest? Surely my having kept my distance, silence, all these months – when after all one *could* say I had rights, seeing that Rickie had chosen to leave you and come to me, seeing that I did, so to speak, deliberately relinquish him and hand him back – surely that earns me the benefit of the doubt? Listen,' I would have said, 'I'm in trouble, I'm not up to anything; I'm frightened. I'm in the hands of crooks, thieves, perverts, *murderers*. I've been living in dreadful lodgings,' I'd have said, 'in Stepney. A working-class boy that I befriended – he spun me a hard-luck story ... He's taken all my money, and my valuable cigarette case (yes, Rickie's present, but so long ago, it's of no consequence) – and vanished. Question is, what am I to do? I can't inform my landlord because he's a German Jewish refugee ... because he thinks better of me than to think I'd mind ... because he's not my landlord but Nemesis overtaking me ... because he said all along that Rob was a stillborn soul and must be left in peace, not tampered with; and I did tamper, break in on what had to be everlasting twilight ... because in the crackpot Scheme of Things he is constructing, in which each individual soul is a world or an atom to be split – thereby releasing limitless potentialities of spiritual energy, thereby progressively creating God or the Myth or the spiritual universe – factors of moral and material order such as H.M. Police Force are false, unreal ... I'm telling you these facts,' I'd have said, 'because they'll help you to realize what I'm up against; how badly I need authoritative protection. Some male person of importance, such as Rickie, must return with me to Stepney, stand guard while I collect my property – what's left of it, repel intruders with the threat of Law, pay from his well-stuffed wallet what is owing, drive me away in his expensive car.'

This speech was not made. I betrayed no one. I got Rickie at the office, curtly made my request. Shocked pause; appointment curtly granted. I had five shillings left, I went to the Grand Central Hotel, St Pancras, and had a bath; with my last shilling saw a News Reel, watching the programme round and round; at five went along to the flat, let myself in with the keys, hoping but failing to pass unnoticed by Mrs Lilley in the basement. She nosed me out, she came up carrying her mongrel bitch in her arms to give it a bit of a change. We discussed its heart attacks. I made loud bright chat with many a Cockney quip and crack thrown in. I'd been abroad, I said; was off to the country now for an indefinite stay. Come to clear up, clear out, the lease being up. Mr Masters (yes thank you quite himself again) would be along later to settle any bill outstanding and make arrangements for the furniture. When the van came would she be a duck and keep an eye on the stuff that was going into store? To keep her sweet I made her a present of my crocks and saucepans, which with marked nonchalance she accepted – thinking me barmy or else there would turn out to be a catch in it. She was sorry to see me go: she'd miss me, so would Spot: I was quite a favourite with Spot – eh, Spotty, love? Her eyes, with snakes' tongues darting out of them, appraised me. Well she knew that my status had declined; that I was no longer wealthy gentleman-friend's young lady-friend, walking illicitly, securely, demurely, on the sunny side of the street. A thrill for her; but all the same ...

She hung about, seeming to feel uncertain; presently remarked she must be popping down, her old man would start creating. In one of his wicked old moods he was, the sinner. What with the grumbling all day and the lifting all night, she sometimes felt she'd as lief be in her grave. Still he was grateful in his way. 'You pore old cow,' he'd come out with only yesterday. Ah well, one blessing, not having the use of his legs he'd never play her no more tricks: she'd got him now, where she could lay her hand on him and serve him right. He'd been a devil in his day. But there, it was a woman's lot: give 'em the best years of our lives, the more fools us. What good, she said finally, did fretting ever do? Any girl that got herself deceived should ought to say good riddance. Plenty more fish where that one got hisself hooked, the joker ... Ah well, she wished me luck. She lifted Spot, held Spot stomach upwards, manipulating one nerveless paw in my direction. '*Bye bye Auntie, all the best,*' squawked a ventriloquist's dummy's voice.

I went on packing, turning out, filling the waste-paper baskets. Punctually at 6.15 Rickie arrived. I said hullo and got straight down to business. He was co-operative. Telephone? Gas? Electricity? – all paid up. Just one account from the wine merchant. 'Give it to me,' he commanded, stretching out his hand, pocketing it without a glance.

Last the keys. 'Ah yes.' He would look in tomorrow at the estate agent's, give formal notice, hand them in. Nothing simpler. 'Anything more?' ... I didn't, I said, want any of the furniture, only my own pictures, and a few French pottery jugs and plates I'd bought myself. 'Just as you please, of course. It's yours to keep or dispose of.' 'I don't want to sell it, simply be rid of it.' In that case he would, of course, arrange to have it removed and stored; or put in a sale. 'It isn't much anyway.' 'No, not much.' He glanced round at it. He had a patient expression; business adviser at the end of a tiring day, prepared to listen and advise but wishing to be gone. 'Oh, and your links,' I said. 'I found them in that drawer when I was turning out.' He took them from me, jingled them in his palm, closed his hand on them; then slowly his hand fell open. When presently he moved it to smooth, in an automatic way, his hair, I saw the cuff-links lying on the arm of our big chair. I watched all this; I saw when he shut his eyes. Had seen him do this a dozen, dozen times by the family hearth – never before with me. Had decided to my own satisfaction what it meant, in psychological terms; not tension, not active boredom – simply negativity. I'd often wondered how it struck her, if at all.

'Tired?' I said at last. He opened his eyes and sent a rapid blinking smile in my direction, a sort of grimace, apologetic, and said yes, no not really, he'd had rather a long day of it and then this damned pain, indigestion or whatever, had started up again. Since my telephone call, I thought, perhaps. He ought, he said, to be getting along now, he was preposterously late already: one of his words, preposterous. I noticed he was a bad colour, and drawn round the mouth. I saw how he might look in middle age. Heaving himself out of his chair, he walked to the window, stood there looking down into the street. How heavy his broad shoulders ... I sat on, and, from where he'd let them fall, the links stared glazed, thick, like eyes dropped out from broken dolls' heads. Already they looked incriminating – clues dropped, forgotten, in the room that saw the murder, objects the sleuth picks up, examines, pondering in his hand their weight of evidence. On an impulse I leaned forward, snatched them up, stuffed them in my pocket. He turned slowly from the window and looked round the room, laying a look of lead on every object. I knew that look – it meant he had resigned. It was a look I'd seen very recently on another man's face, in another room. The only difference was that Rob had laid it on *me* – marking me UNTOUCHABLE; Rickie laid it on every cherished property of the small space we had enclosed for our domestic love. *Home no more home to me* ... But he, of course, he was not homeless; he was expected back. I wasn't. Not anywhere. Whichever way I turned, my possessions were a few fag ends of human occupation: one or two suitcases, some hairpins in a drawer, a pound of tea, an empty milk bottle. Such things can spell despair, deadliest of the seven deadly sins. I kept telling myself this was after all what I had come for, after all: the final pay-off, the practical one that always has to be gone through when there has been a death. That's how I'd put it to him on the telephone, to persuade him after all these months of silence it was safe to meet me. But I knew I'd doubled back in panic terror to pick up, if I could, an old familiar trail. And didn't he know it too? I did not find out.

Once, on one of the former occasions when we had made an end, saying good-bye he said: 'I give you my life. If ever you need it, come and take it.' Wild words, meaningless, I told him; but I kept them locked in me, and after all the time had come to remind him, to bring him to the proof. But I didn't remind him. He was totally beyond my range at last: my body and mind, all known, loved once and offered back to him, anachronistic weapons. 'Rickie, help me ...' He knew I was saying that and he wouldn't hear. The coward ... But even from the last ditch, from my contempt for him, he cut me off. He was a coward, but not a coward then. His shut eyes seemed to hold authority. He had decided to resign without consulting me, *he was not ashamed of it*. He stopped me dead in my tracks.

Did he? Did he? Was it something deliberate – a choice a person capable of love might make? A person of integrity, one become wholly responsible, within his limits, in the realm of moral action? A person who had begun to face, before I had truly begun to in spite of all my fine words and gestures, the lifelong consequences of a choice that, once made, is made to be adhered to with no soft option, not even a dying grace-note to echo on in the ensuing void? Or was it merely that he had become indifferent?

No, not indifferent I know, because – I know. To resign, to be indifferent, are not synonymous. On the other hand, not to resign, to remain predatory, are also not synonymous ... And why accord such honour or what is, after all, a self-defensive impoverishment of self? I hadn't resigned, that's all; obviously not, because I felt, suddenly, an escape of pure pity for his shoulders, for his stance by the window, for his looking so dully down, then all around the vacancy:

look, stance of the disinherited. So I knew I was connected still; a *posthumous nerve*, but irreducible, intact survival. So then I was able to say: 'It's all right, Rickie.' I think that's what I said; meaning ... oh, many things. He let his eyes come to rest on me at last; they didn't brighten, but he smiled faintly. Eyes of that blue are the most vulnerable: in anger, pain, grief, sickness, the pigment drains away. His had become wall eyes ... not quite that ... transparent. A ghost gaze rested on me. So then we left the room. He went ahead of me. He had a way of running downstairs that always gave me pleasure because it made me see him as a schoolboy, practising to bring it to a fine art: an unbroken skidding run from top to bottom of the staircase, back straight, knees and ankles loose. He had charming hangovers of this sort from boyhood: accomplishments, tricks he had never quite put away. It's an upper-class thing: ways they invented in youth of playing with their ease of mind and body, decorating bored leisure with a flourish. He did it now, and it struck me with a pang that what I witnessed was a man dividing: a schoolboy giving me the slip went hurrying down ahead, improving his technique; abandoning upstairs a stock-still man with heavy shoulders. In the void of this split husk he left me cancelled ... I wonder if he went on practising in Montagu Square ... here in this house ... at the Admiralty in 1944, with death running downstairs after him, as Madeleine had described tonight. Picked up unconscious at the bottom, rushed to hospital, a burst duodenal ulcer, too late, a few hours later he was dead.

On the pavement we hesitated, pausing for a final check-up, making sure that nothing had been left undone. It was a tepid washed-out June evening, grey, steamy after a day of thunder showers; the air was penetrated with the smell of exhausted strawberries and pinks and stocks from a barrow on the corner. The person who strummed every evening upon a twanging piano in a house across the road was playing scales. A group of children burst out of the alley-way behind us, dragging an orange box screwed to a pair of rusty iron wheels. In it sat two tiny Negro children, twins, boy and girl, in magenta flannel jackets. Their faces, black, tender, designed in harmony with the skull's perfect globe, had an extraordinary abstract dignity. They tore past us brushing our legs, on up the street. Behind the opaque glass windows of the pub on the opposite corner shadows passed and re-passed. Everything looked expectant, supercharged, dramatic: opening shots in a French film, camera turning on doors, pavements, lamp-posts, street-vistas, housefronts, on selected figures; sound track picking up the thin invisible piano, the screech of a rusty wheel, shouts, motor horns and running footsteps, all intermittent between loaded silences, all to build up the atmosphere for what would happen. Anything might happen. Who would slouch shady from that narrow passage, on the heels of that penny-for-the-guy prelude, that flurry of infant mummers? Whom would the swing-swinging pub doors reveal at last, solid against the phantoms? When will they move, that pair of lovers? What are they muttering, their lips stiff, looking hard at each other, then away? She wears her hair shoulder-length, rolled under, she wears a mackintosh and carries a shabby suitcase: clearly she is the heroine. He has a virile sensuous distinction, a prosperous suit of clothes. Upper-class philanderer caught in a fatal net with waif? ... Why does that taxi crawl along the street, slow down beside them? Watch now, the plot is about to thicken.

'God, I'm late,' he exclaimed, consulting his wrist-watch. 'I don't want to cut this short but ...' He hailed the taxi. 'I've got to dine out and there'll be ructions. Can I drop you somewhere?'

'No thanks. Where I'm going would be quite off your beat.'

'Well he can take you on – wherever you're going.'

'No thanks. I don't fancy dropping you at your front door.' Off-hand voice contemptuously underlining my detachment, his lack of curiosity.

All of a sudden he changed, he was black and blazing.

'Get in. If you think I'm going to leave you on the pavement with that bloody bag ... *Go on, get in.*' Savage voice. He wrenched the bag from me, pushed me before him into the cab, jumped in, slammed the door, leaned forward to slide the glass partition back and give his address, then flopped back into his corner. I in mine.

'You can make up your mind as you go along where this machine is to deposit you. It's at your service. I shall get out before we reach my front door.' Savagely he pushed at the bag with the toe of his shoe. He hadn't noticed when I picked it up in the flat and carried it into the street. I sat up rigid in my corner, feeling his anger explode, impotent, against me. Presently he put his warm, dry hand over mine and said without expression: 'Dinah.' We bowled along hand in hand

44

as so many times before; only, the nerves in our meeting palms were dumb.

So then I said: 'Don't leave me, Rickie. You, you only, know the worst of me. Don't let me go. Where I've got to go back to if you do is much too terrible. No light, suffocation, scorching emptiness, like Hell. I told you I am expected; but in fact there is no one. The person who was there has gone.' So he took me in his arms for ever and we drove on, on, on ...

We said not another word. He stopped the cab on the far edge of the square, jumped out in a hurry, gave the driver a ten-bob note, told him to take me wherever I said, didn't look at me, went running towards his house. Never once looked back. Hurried to Madeleine waiting for him behind that door, already dressed for the party, frowning and fidgeting, preparing ructions.

I told the driver Paddington, I had to tell him somewhere. He was very genial after Rickie's generosity. He gave me a tip for the Derby when I got out; for which with a beaming smile I thanked him. I was still a pretty girl accustomed to consider myself precious. Where could I go? I could go home: catch the 7.48, be there by nine. What a joyful surprise for them. On the platform I started to have hallucinations: smelled the lime blossom in the garden, heard Bruno bark as I came up the drive. I got confused. The train was sinister, full of people sitting like ordinary people sure of where they were going, all silent, all watching me, waiting to rise and push me out if I attempted to join their ranks. I was paralysed with terror. Then I clearly saw Rob lying on the bed in the other room, the red one, waiting for me. So I made for the escalator and took the Tube and went back to him as fast as possible. He was not there.

Around midnight there was a tap on the door and in came – that final one. The last one, at last; having known his time would come, and bided it. Selbig was his scarcely ever spoken name, Ernst Selbig, Jewish doctor with a cut-off European past he never mentioned, with eyes like pits and hairy hands ... Saint, corrupt saint. Thank God he's dead too: suicide, just before war was declared ... He came to make me cry and make me drunk, and he did both. Oh, how drunk I got and cried, how I soaked his coat! The things I told him ... He wished to make me free of his rotting humourless world of wisdom and understanding, of pity for incurable humanity. Ach! Sometimes

45

I think cynics do less harm. He came to tell me Rob would never come back; he came to initiate me into the human condition, into freedom. Oh, I couldn't understand his mystic bunk ... But the more I drank the more it seemed like truth, salvation. Oh, I was drunk. Drunk, drunk ... Macerated with the tears of all humanity! As good a way to make an end as any other. Whirling, dissolving with the floor and the ceiling and the mad red roses of Rob's wallpaper and that dark breathing bulk coming down silent on me with a reek of brandy to invade my free, my free-for-all body ... Going, let go, pass out, well over the plunging edge now, all of us bubbles flying, floating all of us, all gone, all drowned together – I, my lost lovers, Selbig ... someone moaning.

Not once looking back, Rickie reached his house, ran up the steps, let himself in, slammed the door, called out:

'Darling!'

There was a pause; then, from the first floor, Madeleine's voice came down on precisely the anticipated note. '*There* you are.' Tense, querulously inquisitive. 'Where *have* you been?'

'Sorry, I was kept.'

'Do you realize we've got to start in ten minutes?'

'I do.' I do, you bet I do.

He went on into the dining-room and opened the cupboard of the sideboard. He heard her come swishing downstairs, her voice: 'Where are you?' Her head came round the door in a familiar gesture – peering on the threshold, goose-like, stretching her long neck as if to search out the lie of the land before advancing. Exasperating habit. 'Oh, that's where you are.'

'This is where I am.'

She watched him swallow half a tumblerful of whisky, opened her lips, drew in a sharp breath, said nothing. Out of the corner of an eye he took in her appearance, thinking she looked a bit garish: petunia pink evening frock, a colour he disliked, white fur wrap, diamond clips and earrings, make-up overdone, blue-shadowed eyelids between frowning forehead and hard anxious stare. She was beginning to plaster it on, he thought, like all the rest of them. All but one. One pale one. White moth among Painted Ladies, quite out of place in this our life. Brush her off, let her fly or fall ... Too late. Can't be

46

done. Impaled, look, wing-stretched, stiff, a long sharp pin through her . . . through me, impaling me.

'Very pretty, very nice. Not *quite* sure about the colour. Nice, I *think*. Yes. New?' Tumbler in hand, he slightly jerked his head towards her.

'*This* thing! Heavens no. Really, Rickie! You've seen it half a dozen times.'

Glancing again, he saw her deliberately start to alter her expression, replace it with a patient mildness.

'What kept you?' she pleasantly inquired. 'I couldn't make it out when you *knew* – I finally rang the office. I couldn't get any answer.'

'Couldn't you make that out? There's nobody on the switchboard after five-thirty, have I never told you?'

'No, never. At least I don't remember – perhaps you have. Did you go to your club?'

'No, the old man's. He collared me just as I was leaving. Kept me jawing for an hour and a half, blast him.'

'What a nuisance. He is inconsiderate. Didn't you – couldn't you get a taxi? Or did you? I didn't hear one stop. Darling, for goodness sake do hurry. We shall be hideously late.' He nodded, swallowed down the last of the whisky at a gulp. 'Tired?' She searched his face, the tumbler, all of him with controlled intensity, frantic, he could feel it.

'I had a twinge or two this afternoon. Nothing much. Had to bolt my lunch, that's why.'

'Oh *dear*!' She bit her finger, barely able to muster even a false show of sympathy. 'I wish to *God* you'd see Drysdale again. You *are* a fool, Rickie, to drink spirits – that amount too, neat. You know what he said.'

'I know what he said and to hell with it. If you want me to get through this f— evening, leave me alone, for Christ's sake.'

He saw her close her lips in long-suffering wifeliness. She turned away and said in a thistledown voice:

'I'll give Clara a ring then, tell her we've got to be late. You know what she is.'

'I know what she is.'

At the door she hesitated, then said nervously: 'If you *could* just say how long you'll be I'll have a taxi waiting.'

47

He said with compunction:

'Fifteen minutes, darling, to the second. Must have a shower. I've been in a muck sweat all day, this weather's horrible.'

She sighed and nodded.

'Shout to the boys, they're just gettting into bed. Anthony's been asking for you, he's stuck with his Meccano, but don't let him hold you up. I've put your clothes out – soft shirt, but I didn't know what links. Where are your jade ones? I couldn't find them.'

Almost, not quite imperceptibly to her, he gave a start; his hand moved towards his pocket, checked.

'They must be around, I had them – oh, the other day. Never mind, I'll find them. Thank you darling. Kind girl. I'll be with you. If Clara squawks, tell her to boil her head.'

He bolted for the door, catching as he passed her a whiff – too strong – of her expensive French scent, swerving blind through the dumb query which held her gripped, watching him; ran for the stairs, heard her voice pursuing, then cut off:

'I hope they didn't get left in a shirt and sent to the laundry, because if so . . .'

On the half landing he stopped, searched rapidly through all his pockets. Not there. Not there. Left where? – *where?* He felt her cold hand dropping them into his. Without warning the trap sprang, bit his heart; anguish, physical, bursting his chest, kept him pinned by the long landing window.

Look out: down: at an angle across the square to the opposite corner where the cab stopped. Look, it's still waiting. Run to it. Run for your life.

For five seconds he looked out, bewildered, into the vaulting branchy, green-swell of a surge of plane trees; let his gaze travel in hope and terror over the hallucinated square. The corner swam, appearing and disappearing through a screen of privet mixed with lilac; but by dint of focusing with a vast last momentary effort he thought he saw what he expected: nothing.

When he came down she was standing in the hall.

'On the dot,' she said, and turned to open the door. 'Taxi's waiting.'

Her smile now – surely her smile was triumphant, mocking, sly?

48

Or was he going mad? Smiling she led the way towards the black box on wheels, towards the impassive driver, seen in profile. Thick neck, eye and nose bulbous, grizzled walrus moustache – *the very same*. He smelt a rat. Dinah was inside, in ambush, hugging herself with laughter, preparing with Madeleine's connivance to disclose herself. In another moment he would be stripped, raked by their deadly crossfire. Strident voices would pierce him, claws seize him, drag him to and fro. The driver turned his head, was youngish, dark, clean-shaven. Rickie gave the address, opened the door of the cab, Madeleine stooped in, he followed her.

'Such luck,' she said with satisfaction. 'I just happened to see it cruising past. I'd rung three ranks.'

'Trust you!' He sank back, reprieved, staring ahead of him, pulling himself for God's sake now together. 'When have you not so happened? If in the whole of London there was but one sole solitary taxi, you'd be bound to collar it.'

But luckily there were at least two taxis in London: such luck. He suddenly laughed.

'I don't *collar*,' she protested with light petulance, encouraged to foster this auspicious banter. 'It's all a question of the correct psychological approach. I place myself in a state of total passive expectancy. Then the object of my desire materializes.'

'Does it indeed? It never does for me.'

'You don't concentrate enough.'

He suddenly laughed again, so loud that she glanced puzzled at him. His forehead was beaded with sweat. She took his silk handkerchief from his breast pocket, and with gentleness wiped away the starting dew. At this a little sound, part groan part protest, broke out of him; he gently took the handerkerchief away from her and held it crumpled in his hand. She put her own hand tentatively out and laid it over his. He did not respond, he let it lie there, thinking: 'Hand of a woman in my dead one, twice in the space of an hour ...' and turning a screw down tight on the appalling thought. In close sad separation they went bowling towards Chester Square.

'You know ...' She stopped.

'What do I know?'

'This is the first time we've dined with Tim and Clara – sort of in style – since we got going again.'

'Is it?' he said in a courteous acknowledgement. 'Yes, I suppose it is.'

'Of course,' she went on, nervous, 'I've seen Clara on my own sometimes. She does know – a bit, I did tell her a bit, not much. She can be trusted, she's very discreet.'

He nodded. 'I'm sure she is. And can be trusted to advertise her discretion widely, I should guess.'

'Oh, *no* – she's not a bit like that. You're always unfair to her. She's *really* trustworthy, and she never judges anyone, and you know they both adore you, specially Tim.'

'Oh, I know. And they're both jolly sorry for poor Madeleine. So they should be.'

'Of course they're not. They – I didn't ...' She stopped. 'Anyway, nothing has been mentioned for ages now. It's just assumed it's – all in the past never more to be referred to again.'

Once more he nodded. 'Quite right. What does it all matter – who's been discreet, who hasn't and all that? Who adores me, who thinks I'm a cad and a brute? Clara's all right I know, if you talked to her that's your business, I'm glad if it helped. Tim and I know where we are with one another, I think. He wouldn't judge me, or only mercifully, but I dare say I caused him considerable despondency. We don't let our hair down when we meet. Let's leave it at that.'

'What I really meant was – I think this party is in a way for us ... Not underlining it, of course, but a sort of little celebration.'

'I see. Oh, God!'

She was silent. Feeling her hurt, he gave her hand a light quick squeeze and put it away from him, saying:

'Afraid I won't come up to scratch? Don't worry.'

She gave a heavy sigh. 'It's only that I wish you didn't seem so – I don't know ... Low.'

'I don't feel awfully festive, but it's nothing. I'll improve as the evening goes on. I only hope they intend to celebrate in style.'

Provocatively meant, she told herself. He should not get a rise out of her. After a pause she said in an offhand voice:

'Where did you lunch?'

'Oh, a dive in the City. The usual one.'

'With anybody?'

'No one in particular. I saw one or two familiar figures along the bar.'

Something had happened, she was certain of it. He was lying or prevaricating. *Her* touch was on him once again. He'd had a letter? Seen her? ... Don't question, don't examine. Behave as if it was only what, after all, it might be: a passing mood of depression, a breath coming up again out of the buried day, as it was bound to still from time to time. These things took time; and less than a year had passed. Poor Rickie. Must be kind, patient, wifely. Most unfortunate, infuriating, that it should happen tonight, when things had gone so smoothly now for weeks and weeks. Clara would spot trouble in a trice. Why could men never put a good face on? If they were tired they yawned in your face, if they were depressed they glowered: women were expected to lump it.

It was a party of eight: besides their host and hostess and themselves there were the Wainwrights – three couples paired off in matrimony at about the same time, still living in wedlock, their offspring roughly parallel in age and number. The fourth pair, Jack Worthington and one Mrs Enthoven, were both recently divorced and about to marry one another. Jack and Rickie, each in his different way, wore the insignia of adulterous romance; in the case of Rickie a highly extravagant embarrassing affair, not easy to swallow or explain away. But it was over, all hushed up. Madeleine seemed to have played her cards with dignity and skill – one had to hand it to her. As for old Jack, his marriage had come unstuck by unspectacular orthodox degrees, to nobody's surprise or great distress. The point of interest was that he had picked on an outsider, an unknown quantity, for his second venture. This divorced woman was American. He had met her, fallen head over heels in love, in New York last year. She was a quietly dressed brown-haired woman in the middle thirties, with a subdued voice that now and then seemed to curl round and echo in her throat, with eyes and jaw both slightly protuberant: large wide-set brilliantly grey eyes, lips full and just not closing over strong regular teeth. She drank one cocktail and no more, sat trimly in her place listening with unaffected interest and composure while, amiably neglecting her, the stranger, in the English way, the rest of them gossiped together and exchanged the customary group badinage. When she did interpose remarks they were formal and courteous, also trenchant; they and her rare questions seemed to have a faint twist to them, as if with a little

51

spur – or a little curb – she might go further, verbally, than social basic. All this the English wives were to tell each other afterwards; agreeing also that at first they had thought her plain and a bore, but they weren't so sure after all, there was something about her – personality . . . or sex appeal perhaps? Clara said Tim had not thought her plain; neither, said Mary Wainwright, had Sandy: not that he ever noticed people much. Had Rickie given an opinion? Well, Rickie hadn't altogether taken to her, but he'd agreed with Madeleine that she had *something*.

It struck Madeleine almost at once what it was that this woman had: while eating salmon *mousse* to be exact, and looking across the table at Rickie and Mrs Enthoven sitting side by side. It struck her that the quiet creature was looking steadily at him with luminous myopic orbs and parted lips; and that she was formidable; and that Rickie was half turned in his chair towards her, with that look . . . abstracted and yet concentrated, drowning a blind stare in hers. Here it was again, the same thing over again: this one could do what the other one did, had done under one's eyes in other rooms, at other dinner tables; shamelessly, unexceptionably; drawing a charmed circle round one other and herself, pulling in whomsoever she chose to pick on – beside her or across the table or across the room – by the force of the current she switched on and caused to flow between them, while she searched, probed, provoked him with her curiosity . . . with an idea, always a cold idea, a subject – politics, books, art, sex, religion, science, business, law, psychology: whatever she had to find out, whatever would engross him while she calculated and drove the hot naked under-cover bargain.

Rickie's face was stripped and at the same time utterly obscured. He was lost once more in a face, *the* face, searching this one's image for another, *the* other, *the mysterious one*. They were saying it, the essential nameless thing, exchanging recognition, slipping the pass-word. If one were to say casually to him later: 'You seemed to be having an absorbing conversation at dinner with Jack's girl friend. What was it about?' he would say: 'Absorbing? Was it? I can't remember – you know I never can. It can't have been anything in particular.'

'What have you lost?' The low voice of this Mrs Enthoven penetrated his ear with such curious force that it seemed to start a reverberation in his head. He continued to stare at her, struck dumb. Then he said:

'Nothing in particular.' And after a moment: 'Why did you say that?'

She replied without hesitation: 'You've got a kind of a look on your face as if you were wondering where you could possibly have left something or other. Where was it you last had it?'

'Oh ... Like a dog with a buried bone, you mean. I know exactly.' He uttered a laugh. 'What a perspicacious woman you are. There may be something about me that forcefully suggests a canine simile. It's happened before.'

'It was your simile, not mine. Myself I wouldn't have selected it.'

Again he searched her face: composed, not looking amused. He said rather aggressively:

'Don't you ever laugh? I know someone else who doesn't laugh – at least, not at my jokes, not latterly. This person *makes* jokes though, very witty ones, at other people's expense sometimes – not always. Do you? I suspect you do. Though over here we tend to think Americans a bit solemn, much as we love them. On the serious side. What would you say to that? – as a generalization ...'

Turning to Jack Worthington on her right, Madeleine broke into effusive chatter. Revelling in his new and now drink-heightened happiness, he answered rather absent-mindedly, with bantering affection, while his eye wandered across the table, approving with a fatuous beam the spectacle of his love and his best friend getting on so famously together. For he's a jolly good fellow and she's a jolly good fellow, God bless us one and all ... It would be shocking indeed, thought Madeleine, when it began to occur to him ... when his genial coarse-veined face would stiffen, his eyes go thick.

'But *don't* you remember?' she persisted.

'Mm?' He looked at her, indulgent.

'That time at Oxford, when you and Rickie fought?'

'*Fought?* Me and Rickie? My dear girl, you dreamt it. Or you're pulling my leg – eh?'

'No, no. I don't know *why* you fought and Rickie swears he can't remember, but it's true and we've often laughed about it. Why, it was one of your landlady's classic sagas. She told it to me. Rickie took

53

me to Oxford when we were engaged and we went to call on her and she came out with the whole thing.'

'Good lord! It does ring a bell. Good lord, yes! We were as tight as ticks . . .'

'And she came in with a tray of crocks and found you locked in a wrestling bout without so much as a stitch of underwear between you. And it gave her such a turn her inside started to work like ginger beer, not that she hadn't seen plenty of young fellows up to their larks and it would take more than seeing them at it in the birthday suits to upset her at her time of life, but you were so deathly quiet the both of you and heaving to and fro like a blessed football scrum and never so much as noticed the door open, it didn't seem natural; and she was just a-wondering what to do for the best when she heard Mr Masters mutter: "*I'll get you this time, Worthington, if I have to swing for it.*" So she says to herself: "Then it's murder, is it?" and she lets out a screech to wake the dead, and bless her if you didn't drop your hands off one another like as if it was the Sunday joint you'd been caught stealing, and so she says: "Oh Mr Worthington, Mr Masters, sirs! Think of your dear mothers! Turn the other cheek! Let bygones be bygones be your motter! Don't let the sun go down on it, I beg." And Mr Masters he says: "Oh, Mrs Upex," he says, as cool as a cucumber, "is that you? I never heard you. I do sincerely trust," he says, "you'll accept our humble apologies and overlook the shock to your feelings." Oh, you were a precious pair of rascals the both of you, but mind you, always the perfect gentlemen . . .'

'I guess I was impertinent,' said Mrs Enthoven from the middle of her throat, fixing Rickie with a steady gaze.

'Dearest Mrs Discobolos!' He waved a hand across her eyes. 'Relax, relax! It is I who should feel remorse. Truth to tell, this pain makes me feel a trifle snappish.'

'What kind of a pain?'

'A pain I have sometimes. We all have one sometimes, somewhere, don't we? Where do you get yours?'

'I guess you shouldn't be here.'

'Not here? But I must be here. This is a big evening, all sorts of celebrations. Hymen in the ascendant. We're gathered together here to drink to you and Jack. A blood-curdling rumour reached me I was

54

to be the hero. False, thank God! Sh! Forget I mentioned it. Jack's my best friend. He's an extraordinarily nice chap. Nobody knows how nice, except you and me, it's not on the outside, bless his heart. I hope you're going to be very happy.' He smiled, an extremely winning smile.

'Thanks, Rickie. I hope you are too,' said Mrs Enthoven, not smiling.

'Ah, you've been tipped the wink.' Brusquely he turned a shoulder on her.

Driving on through Jack's hilarious explosions, observing the moment when Rickie turned suddenly, with a sharp jerk of his head, away from his unsmiling neighbour, Madeleine wound up:

'Kind Mrs Upex, I think she wanted to warn me, as one woman to another, that I was taking on a dangerous character.'

'A dangerous – old Rickie ...' Jack mopped his eyes. 'Ah well, perhaps she was right. Perhaps he is.' Hey, mind your step, he told himself – thin ice. 'Ah well! Boys will be boys, you know,' he added feebly, hastily. 'Not that I wouldn't take my dying oath old Rickie and I never fell out for a single moment from the day we met.'

'You can both swear on your grandmothers' graves, I'll never believe you've forgotten the incident. It was terribly disgraceful, wasn't it? – and you're too ashamed to tell me.'

'Rickie!' called Jack across the table; and immediately Rickie leaned forward with an expression of intense willingness to join in the fun. 'Help here! Your wife – I've done my best, but women, you know – tenacious animals. We're ruined. It's out at last.'

'It is, is it?' His grin stretched wary, false, too broad.

'There, you see!' cried Madeleine. 'He does know. He doesn't even ask *what's* out at last.'

'Matter of principle,' countered Rickie. 'Always plead guilty. Th' charge is immaterial. Takes th' wind out o' their sails.' He was rather drunk. Dilated, his eyes thrust at Madeleine, then from face to face, then back at her. He looked – not a tenacious animal but a tricky, nimble-witted one; and caged up; and dangerous perhaps. 'United we fall, Jack,' he said; then turning to Mrs Enthoven, added politely: 'Old English custom.'

'Stout fellow! Right, Madeleine, you've asked for it! What was it now? Remind me. What were my exact incriminating words?'

In a hush of suspended laughter everybody turned waiting upon Madeleine to elucidate the joke. She paused, sank her voice theatrically, put the words across in all their ludicrous ferocity: '*I'll get you this time, Worthington, if I have to swing for it.*'

How they laughed, what a sparking and crackle developed across that dinner table on that evening – Rickie the generator, the centripetal force. After his death, separated as they all were then by time and war, and too much preoccupied to miss and mourn him as long, as deeply as they would have wished, they did, each one of them, recall his mood that evening: never more lively and preposterous, just like his old self at school, at Oxford, or in his days of a young bachelor about town. Come to think of it, none of them could remember ever seeing him like that again. As the years passed he had seemed to draw more and more into his shell, to lose his gaiety and resilience. He must have taken a bad knock, worse than he ever let on to anybody, over that rotten business. As Tim said to another chap, walking from the House of Commons across the park towards their club one raid-free evening, when it came to women old Rickie, bless his heart, had always lacked any instinct of self-preservation. The other chap remarked that Tim surprised him. To a mere acquaintance like himself, a charmer such as Rickie had appeared eminently fitted, in the matter of women, to get away with anything. He could think of three women, straight off, who'd been in love with him, or said so. Yes, agreed Tim, they said so freely: he was that sort of chap – the sort women didn't mind people knowing they'd adored. Had a lot of loves? Tim supposed not, on the whole. He was kindness itself; he had a conscience; in spite of ... And then ... Tim fell silent, pondering; could not and did not want to express what else he had in mind. For instance, that evening ... only the pitch and tempo, rapid, pulsating, stuck in his memory; together with the feeling beyond all qualification or rational analysis that then and always Rickie had been – how to put it? – not exactly reckless but – but any moment about to do himself no good; clearly though indefinably less able than most chaps to – to take calculations and precautions, less concerned than most to provide adequate safeguards against pain to himself. Women would love him for that, but on the other hand ...

And roughly at the same moment, in a Tuscan hill town, it came

56

over Jack grieving for his oldest and best-loved, his irreplaceable friend, how it had struck him that evening that the dear old fellow was sailing a bit near the wind; that it didn't seem altogether up his street to indulge in such uproarious fooling: almost defiant once or twice, almost – if not quite unkind – antagonistic. Then suddenly, to his surprise, with a gush of nostalgic tenderness Jack remembered the thrilling peace and joy that had invaded him when, in the midst of it all, Georgie had met his eye and offered him a smile, such a smile, the one he'd waited for, he knew then, all his life; sealing an absolutely secure forever understanding and devotion. Also it came sharply back to him that later, after they got home, Georgie had remarked to him: 'That man is a tragic figure – or pretty nearly.' 'Rickie tragic? What rubbish, silly girl.' But she was always one to get her teeth into a notion and hang on. She had persisted in her cross-questioning and analysis, listening with extreme attention to his rather lame account of Rickie's recent troubles. He could see her now, lying on the sofa, drinking iced water, himself holding and stroking her small feet in his lap. He could hear her slow voice say: 'Well, I guess you're wrong. It's not all over. I'd say there was considerable trouble going on in the Masters' home right now.' Nonsense again: Rickie had told him months ago that it was finished; and that from Rickie meant it *was* finished. This girl now, she said, this sister-in-law, was she truly that much of a bitch? Absolutely: one of those real deep ones, out to play a lone game and play the innocent and stop at nothing. Hard as nails. He could see Georgie considering this judgement carefully. Did he think, she'd asked suddenly, Rickie might end up an alcoholic? No, he did *not*. Because, she went on unruffled, if he were one of her own countrymen that would with all due modesty be her prognosis; but it was on the cards that she did not yet grasp the psychology of Englishmen. She'd heard tell that over here some of these immature romantics rode it out. At that he shook her and kissed her and told her to stop being a little Yankee smart-puss. There was quite a lot about Englishmen she hadn't grasped yet, and she'd talked quite enough for one night.

Clever as she was, she'd got it wrong, he'd got it right about that marriage, as she herself admitted a long time later. She said that her prognosis had been faulty, shallow: she knew more Englishmen now and more psychology. Her conversation never failed to tickle him;

not that he personally had ever made much headway with the unconscious and the neurosis and the behaviour pattern and the rest of the mumbo jumbo. As to Madeleine and Rickie, he had been content to observe with respect and satisfaction that his two old friends had made a damned good job of their mended marriage. Hats off to both of them. A thousand pities, Georgie and Madeleine never quite hitting it off. Long after she, Georgie, had given up brooding over Rickie – 'I guess you're right, he's a love, that's all there is to it,' was her final summing-up – she went on turning Madeleine over on her tongue. 'Oh, she's a good egg really,' she'd drawl, laconic; or else: 'She's a spoilt brat'; or: 'She's disappointed too, I guess. One should give her more credit for trying. Her eyes are sad. She's kind of half hatched, it must be pretty uncomfortable. She could have been bust right open, she wouldn't have resisted it; after a while she'd have integrated into something pretty fine. Rickie is a honey, but he was the wrong guy for her to settle for. She needed what she could take – well, what woman doesn't? She could take plenty too – wouldn't you say so? But she's scared stiff. She's just a married virgin ... no, not that; she's a disappointed bride with three fine kids still wondering if this is all there is to sex. I guess it's nobody's fault but it's too bad.'

Too bad, a thousand pities ... Not in *her* sense of course, ridiculous precious Georgie ... Nobody's fault but again too bad that she hadn't had a child. Many a time he had envied Rickie those splendid children. One of them gone now missing presumed killed in North Africa in that botched counter-attack, that failure to relieve Tobruk. Blackest hour of the war. Fine boy. Devilish luck. With misery Jack recalled Rickie's brief answer to his letter of condolence: *Good of you to write. We can't get much information, probably never shall now. He was seen to fall, shot through the head – whether killed outright or finished off later we don't know – He was searched for later, but he wasn't found. Thank your lucky stars you have no sons.* No pathos, no attitude of pride or pity; not a word about the boy's mother. Flogging himself stoically along a bit further to the lonely finish. Was it morbid to feel now that that was how it had been; and that Georgie in the course of her theoretic excavations had perhaps struck her spade on something solid, something that gave back a hard hollow ring? ... Too late to mend, any of it. Georgie had written that she'd seen him for a brief evening in London. He had aged, lost weight, gone grey, a tired man obviously but otherwise seemed normal. He had shown her a cute picture of Clarissa and they had talked of old times and old friends and had a few jokes as well. She hadn't tried to approach him and he had referred only indirectly to the tragedy by asking her to spare the time to go down and visit Madeleine in the country. He was too tied, he said, to be able to be much good to her.

So, on a subsequent short leave from her Ministry, Georgie had gone down to their cottage in the country and spent a day and a night; found Madeleine friendly, calm but haggard, rushing from vegetable garden to hens to cooking stove; drugging herself with a housewife's physical tasks. 'But after all,' Georgie had written to him, 'they're real in their way, they do make ground under your feet, you've got to go on doing them. She doesn't talk about gardening in a green-fingered way, but practical, tough, like a labourer almost. The same if you watch her prepare a meal: there's a kind of *coarseness* comes out in her that's encouraging. She's bent, I think, on growing a different kind of sensory equipment. Maybe she will, and it will save her. I see that if you can't break down into humanity (she's far from that) the next best thing would be to break down into a piece of country and primitive forms of contact like fetching the milk and planting lettuces and rearing pullets: better for convalescence than taking to gin or parties or lovers. That really might end in atrophy, but this, what she's doing, seems more like a sort of *earthing up*. It needs courage and she's got it. She treated me like a body to be fed, aired (a five-mile tramp) and bedded; it was refreshing, I'm pretty tired and over-conscious. I could tell you more about her if I'd seen her with the children, but Colin is at Sandhurst and Clarissa visiting a grandparent. She talked about Anthony's death quite unemotionally, asked me if I had any kind of religion, she had none; said she supposed that was a pity, but since the worst thing that could happen had happened and God still seemed irrelevant she must be a case of complete tone-deafness to God. The one personal thing she said was *rude*, and that also was rather encouraging: "I always thought you were the sort who pulled fast ones on other women. You reminded me of someone I once knew who did." (Query her sister?) "But I think now I was wrong. Perhaps I was wrong about the other one too. I've got a jealous nature." She said she wasn't lonely, the only trouble sleeping rather badly and worrying about Rickie. She felt she ought to go to London and look after him. "But he doesn't want me to. I agree with him my job is to keep a country base going for the children; still I wish – I wish there was *someone* some good to him."' And Georgie had concluded: 'She kissed me when I left, said she was glad I'd come, said: "Do see Rickie when you can." Oh, Jack! All they can give each other is remorseful pity – gift of the one sad friend. Such cold comfort.'

At the time he had thought her language fanciful. But a knock like this, your best friend's death, gave a jar to your routine outlook: all kinds of buried relics, making up a now futile but essential sum, pushed up and showed their faces, insisting now that it was too late on being looked at and preserved; on being dedicated without fear or favour to Rickie's memory. So now in Libya he admitted at last the qualm that had crossed him – just come and gone – that jolly evening. He heard the tone of voice in which Madeleine, laughing with the rest of them at Rickie's broadsides, had suddenly inserted a sharp comment ... his 'new transatlantic technique' or words to that effect, which Rickie picked up with a pounce, rapping out with an odd look and smile, What, darling, precisely did she mean? And she: 'Well ... Groucho Marx. With a *touch* of Peter Arno?' – and laughed again, a loud laugh cut off, nervous. Yes, a qualm *had* crossed him; for a moment he had felt a chill, a claw; had envisaged – why? – the possibility of wandering lost again in the deserts of disunion.

Then Georgie had looked at him, smiling their secret, across the dinner table.

'You get the idea,' remarked Rickie to his neighbour in a rapid undertone. 'Bringing the sex war out into the open.'

'Sure. Much healthier.'

'Does it make you feel at home?'

'Was that your intention?'

'That was my intention.'

'You are so courteous and considerate. But I guess you shouldn't put out such an effort. I *am* at home. Wherever Jack is I feel fine.'

'Ah!' cried Rickie. 'Aha! Is that so?'

'It is so. Thanks all the same.'

'Well, there's no place like home. These great social reformers your country produces – they all stress that, I take it?'

'Well . . . For instance?'

'Well, my wife's mentioned one or two. But she's wrong about me. I'm not a Marx boy or an Arno-ite – I haven't the necessary impetuosity. I'm on the parlour mantelpiece with Thurber's undislodgeables. All good lads and true.'

Madeleine caught the word mantelpiece, which puzzled her; saw Rickie brusquely turn away again, draining his glass; a moment later found herself being steadily scrutinized by Mrs Enthoven. Staring at one another, they broke into faint smiles. Then the eyes and smile opposite her passed on, came to rest on Jack, calmly expanded.

Later in the evening, they went on to a night club, arriving in time for the midnight cabaret. A troupe of young ladies danced a *can-can* with good humour and a touch of condescension; a red-haired English woman did some clever imitations of theatrical celebrities. There was also a quite brilliant Hungarian conjurer with a new line in patter. Then a foreign woman with a guitar came trailing among the tables. Ravaged, her huge eyes burning out of a thick surround of mascara and cobalt eye shadow, she stopped in front of Rickie and sang straight at him out of the depths of the man-eating cavern of her mouth:

> *La belle si tu voulais*
> *Nous dormirions ensemble*
> *Dans un grand lit carré*
> *Orné de taille blanche . . .*

Regrettable. It was one of Dinah's songs, in the days when she sang to a guitar in a tiny pure and plaintive soprano, sitting intent and abstracted on the hearth rug before the drawing-room fire, singing to entertain Anthony; this, and *Frankie and Johnnie* and a song about a bull frog she had sung over and over again for Anthony tranced on Rickie's knee, his face flushed, blank with total receptivity, at rest on Rickie's shoulder.

> *Dans le miton du lit*
> *La rivière est profonde . . .*

Rickie had been listening with an inexpressive face, his head bent down, but now, just as she was about to move on, he looked up at her and began half to sing half to speak the words with her, a murmuring bass accompaniment to the rocking, rocking harmony.

As if in urgent taut mutually acknowledged communion, he with his perfectly expressionless face lifted to her, she with a semblance of deferring to him then picking up words, tune, beat, and leading him, her eyes observant on him but unprovocative, as if intent on compelling him to acquit himself well in the duet, they sang to the last stanza's dying close.

> *Et là nous dormirions*
> *Jusqu'à la fin du monde.*

He got up and made her a bow, stiff yet unselfconscious, while amid clapping and laughter she dipped down before him in a deep curtsey, pulled a red rose from the bosom of her low-cut black bodice, offered it to him with formal grace, and on six-inch heels went swimming away.

That was that. The lights went up again, the band burst out. The party complimented Rickie rather loudly, stressing amused surprise, concealing faint but definite embarrassment.

'Congratulations, Rickie. Bravo!'

'Almost in tune too.' Madeleine felt her smile like a grimace.

'You clicked that time, old boy, with a vengeance.'

'Predatory type, what? Not quite my cup of tea. My word she knows her stuff though. That last thing fairly hits you in the midriff. What is it, Rickie?'

'How come you know it, Rickie? What a sly brute you are – hiding your light under a bushel all these years.'

'It's an old French song. I learnt it in my cradle,' said Rickie calmly. 'I had a French nurse.' He stuck the rose in his buttonhole.

'Honestly, did you?' cried Clara. 'I think it's *divine*.'

'Very haunting,' agreed Rickie.

'What are the words? Can you say them? Could you write them down for me?'

'It's the most Freudian song in the world,' said Madeleine. 'I can't *think* what the psycho-analysts would say to it. They'd *burst*.'

'*Freudian?* How do you mean? I thought it was an old French folk song.'

'It is,' said Rickie. 'All about being born and dying, so my nurse told me. All about sleeping in a deep, deep river, Clara, and floating in a deep, deep bed and being drowned till the end of the world. That's the idea.'

'Oh ... How extraordinary.'

'Isn't it? And all the King's horses – they mustn't be forgotten.'

'Oh ... What did they do?'

'Nothing. They couldn't. Surely you know about *them*? In point of fact, this song says they could have. But they didn't.'

'Well, it sounds to me quite mad.'

At this moment, to his extreme horror, something happened to him – a kind of snap or twang, like a snapped harp string, deep inside his skull. His head was invaded by a clangour, then by a noise like the soft anaesthetizing roar of a distant fall of water. Dinah's face appeared, afloat on rushing darkness, bloodless, whirling away drowned, mouth open wide in the rigor of dumb anguish, like the mouth on a mask: the silent square-lipped howl on the mask of classic tragedy.

What next! ... This is It, watch out, beat it off, in a moment I'll be mad! *I'm going mad.*

He sprang up, throttled, and making a blind grab at what lay closest to his hand, caught Mary Wainwright by the elbow and pulled her to her feet, saying with a grin: 'Let's dance.' He had ignored her most of the evening and in consequence she felt a twinge of gratified surprise. Romantically devoted to his image this many a year, she had disciplined herself never to hope to fascinate him. Sympathy was her strong suit; she felt, as she had felt in other cases while watching the tide of passion flow past and away from her towards this or that sister, cousin, bosom friend, that she understood the needs of his nature and could, would be if only called upon, his faithful confidante. She was always to remember dancing with him that night. They danced and danced, in silence, and she felt in his hand against her back, in the hand that held hers, a continuously vibrating tremor, and in sacrificial ecstasy received its indecipherable message, knowing it not for her. Close in his arms she observed beneath lowered lids the other couples of the party: Jack dancing happily with his bride-to-be, her husband volubly with Clara, Tim and Madeleine wearing the look of contented boredom suitable to old friends. Where then, what then ... ? Tim jostled them on a corner of the crowded dance floor, and Madeleine threw them a word in jest, making, thought Mary, an attempt – unsuccessful – to catch Rickie's eye. Then as Tim guided her on and away, her glance slid to Mary, they exchanged smiles. Sly, dreamy, Mary's sweet smile broadened upon her old friend Madeleine, hushing the tacit query, blunting the quest's sharp nose – hers, Madeleine's, everybody's ... Trusting her, as indeed he could and knew it, Rickie had picked her out to share his unknown secret. There, there, Rickie, no need for words ... Any other woman – certainly that American woman – would have imagined that he was in the grip of well-nigh uncontrollable sexual excitement, and made officious movements of response or of withdrawal.

When the band stopped playing, he waited with her on the floor, then when it started again put out an arm as if mechanically, encircled her and set himself once more in motion. He stopped trembling; but presently he seemed both to wake from a trance and to collapse. It was disappointing. His feet dragged, missing the beat, and suddenly he came to a standstill. With a sense, not unfamiliar, of bracing up for readjustment, she looked up at him and saw that he was yawning.

'Sorry, Mary.' He put a hand over his mouth in an exaggerated gesture of mock etiquette. 'It's this atmosphere. Miasmic, isn't it? I must be getting old. I can't stand asphyxiation the way I used to as a stripling.' His voice was as flat as a voice on the edge of sleep, and his eyes looked extinct.

'You're tired, aren't you? Poor Rickie,' she said, brightly, feeling in her chest the sag of rejected self-abnegation.

'Well, I don't know. Do you think that's it? One can't be tired at a party, can one? It's so anti-social.'

'Silly billy. It's getting late. I expect it's time we all went home.' She simulated a yawn to outmatch his.

'Oh, no. Surely not,' he said vaguely, following her back to their table. 'Surely, surely not. Thank you, my dear Mary. That was very pleasant.'

'Sandy gets done in too at the end of the week,' she said, all gentle pity for men. 'He misses the exercise. I do think office life is bad for you all.'

Jack and Mrs Enthoven were still dancing. Tim had just taken the floor with Clara, only Madeleine and Sandy were sitting at the table, chatting with an earnest air. Once more the two women exchanged smiles, to seal the handing-over – no harm done or dreamed of – of each husband to his lawful mate.

'Well, well, well, Mrs W.!' roared Sandy. 'What about giving your old man a turn?'

Facetious only with his wife, and that only in company, because she caused him to fear that he was not amusing, Sandy was a sterling fellow, entirely innocent of the aggressiveness which his bristling moustache and crest of ginger hair, his bawling voice appeared to indicate.

Dismissing them with effusive nods, Madeleine and Rickie remained sitting side by side.

'Light,' said Madeleine after a long silence.

'Mm?'

'Could I trouble you for a light, please?'

'Sorry.' He whipped out the matches and lit her cigarette with care, his hand, he noticed, steady. They smoked, staring at the dancing couples, at the band, the waiters, at everything moving smooth and meaningless, two-dimensional like figures on a film screen, on the other side of the glass prison in which they sat together.

'Fancy *choosing* nut-brown lace!' said Madeleine loudly.

'Mm?'

'Mary. Brown lace, of all things, for a dance frock.'

'Oh ...' He studied Mary for a moment as she passed. 'It isn't the height of glamour, I suppose. Still it suits her all right – it's rather neat. She's not a showy dresser, ever.'

'*Showy?* ... I wasn't objecting on that score ... However, I suppose she thinks she looks like a little brown bird – a dear little Jenny Wren. Have I ever had a *penchant* for showy clothes?'

'Have you? I do hope not.'

'You know I haven't. Quite the reverse.'

'Then we are at one.' He looked stonily ahead of him.

After another long silence, Madeleine said:

'It might look better if we danced together *once*.'

'Oh, would you like to? Right. Let's dance.'

To the strains of a curdling Blues they took the floor.

'What do you make of her?' asked Madeleine, more pleasantly.

'Who?'

'Jack's woman.'

'Ah!' He looked across the floor to where the bridal pair were dancing cheek to cheek. 'Rather nice, I think, don't you? Agreeable woman.'

'Is she? I wouldn't know. We've hardly exchanged a word. I don't think she finds women as interesting as men.'

'Oh, really?'

'Something about her . . . I think she'll lead old Jack a dance.'

'I hope not. But probably. However, he seems happy enough for the moment.'

'Terribly happy. I *can* see she's attractive in a way. Can't you?'

'Mm. Yes. Not unattractive.'

'Amusing too, I expect. What did you find to talk about at dinner?'

'I can't remember. You know I never can. Nothing in particular.'

'Well, at least you weren't bored. I was so relieved, knowing you were feeling low. You looked absolutely engrossed, whatever it was. How are you feeling now?'

'I feel all right now.'

'Pain gone?'

'Pain gone.'

It was true. No pain. No vertigo. Nothing in his head now but vacancy, which, when he tested it, as he had done once or twice with acute apprehension, seemed to give out merely a hollow continuous ringing whisper like the sound of a sea shell held against one's ear.

They danced on in silence for a couple of minutes. She saw their reflections in the wall of mirrors at one end of the room – an ungratifying spectacle: a not-so-young woman dressed rather showily, like a rather respectable tart, her hair set unbecomingly, trying to adapt herself to the slack grasp and shuffle of a bored and exhausted-looking man.

She said in a thin nasal voice:

'At least you might *look* as if you could just bear to dance with me – even if you can't.'

He gave a start. Holding her at arm's length away from him, he gaped at her, his jaw dropping with theatrical imbecility, as if he couldn't believe his ears.

'Didn't you hear?' she said, smiling. 'I know it's frightful for you to have to dance with me, but need you look *quite* so abject with self-pity? Could you possibly, for the sake of social decency, try to put a better face on it?'

On the edge of the dance floor, close to the band, he came to a dead stop; his arms dropped down nerveless, a thick dusky surge of blood suffused his neck, face, forehead. Then very deliberately he swung on his heel and walked away, treading a steady path between the tables. For a split second his back, portentous, was printed in empty space; then she obliterated him. She remained where he had left her, exposed to the grin, the insinuating eyes of the coloured drummer; then with a distant gracious smile and nod of acknowledgement towards the demonic convulsions of wrists, knees, ankles, instruments, strolled in the direction of Rickie's vanished figure. Pausing by the exit, she looked back, cautiously scanning the whole room, half expecting to see him materialize treading a gay measure with a member of the party – or perhaps with a total stranger picked up to pay her out – or drinking and joking at their table. But topped by two bottles in an ice bucket, the table was deserted; she marked them all down one after the other on the floor, dancing to her favourite rumba. She sauntered through into the corridor, passing on her right the claustrophobic little lounge with its modernist bar and furniture and discreet strip lighting: empty. The *avant garde* clock on the wall said 2 a.m. A solitary attendant in uniform stood by the revolving entrance door. Should she stroll up and sweetly inquire if a tall fair gentleman had just gone out? No, she would not .. He might be in the Gents, might emerge in a minute. Perhaps taken ill there ... The man was watching her curiously, waiting for the question he could answer. The answer would be yes ... She turned purposefully and entered the door marked Ladies, lingered a few moments pouring cold water on her wrists, combing her hair, repainting her stiff lips, gave the attendant a dreamy smile, hurried back to the noise and lights. Through the bonfire effect produced by smoke and rose illumination she saw them all sitting round their table. No Rickie.

Well, he'd done it, he'd simply gone – walked out on her. Public humiliation. Where was he? It might have been a vanishing trick by Maskelyne. Let him wait, let him just wait till ... I've put up with a lot, God knows I have and so do all our friends, but make no mistake I won't stand for this sort of thing. What do you suppose

67

they thought of you? I told them, I told them exactly what had happened, well, what else could I do? They all agreed, too monstrous, your bloody-mindedness, insufferable rudeness to me, to everybody, how you're going to apologize to Clara and Tim I cannot think, their party ruined, all so sorry for me, pleasant for me, wasn't it? ... Supported by this inner monologue, she approached them with a smile, sat down, opened her bag, took out her compact and powdered her nose.

'Madeleine, my dear child, allow me to pour you out a little glass ...'

'No more, thank you, Tim darling. Really, I must go home soon.'

'Just a *soupçon*. We're all going home soon. Getting on towards bed-time, I begin to think.' He glanced at her, arrested by a certain tenseness. 'What's wrong, eh? Where's that husband of yours?'

She leaned towards him and murmured, rueful, close to his ear:

'My dear, he's slipped off home. Ssh! He didn't feel awfully well. You know since this wretched gastric trouble he collapses rather if he has late nights. He just hasn't got any reserve energy, though he won't admit it. And of course he really ought *not* to drink, though it seems such a shame on a festive occasion, I can't bear to be governessy about it.'

'Oh, the poor old chap!' exclaimed Tim, all compunction and concern. 'I *am* sorry. Was he feeling like hell?'

'Ssh! – no, nothing much. Just a bit giddy and sick. He's put down a good deal tonight, you know. We went outside to get some air, then he thought – we both thought – he'd better not come back. Don't make a thing about it, will you? He told me to make his excuses – he was so afraid of breaking up the party.'

'Bless his heart. But what a shame. I wish I'd known. It did strike me he looked all in a little while ago – never gave it another thought. Rotten. Take a turn with me, my dear. Or are you worried?'

'No, I'm not worried. I know so well it's only sleep he needs. I'd love to take a turn with you.'

They took a long turn together. Tim's style of dancing was a restful affair of shuffle, sway and turn, coupled with a potent grip of his outspread palm and thumb on her shoulder blades. They discussed the improvement in Rickie's health, schools for their respective sons, the possibility of sharing a villa near Dinard for September, and other

68

soothing topics. Presently she ceased to cast surreptitious glances towards the entrance, to brace herself for Rickie's reappearance, the blood of murderous hate still mantling his black face. While Tim's ripe, husky, rather coaxing and deprecatory voice meandered on, she felt almost herself again. The boiling sense of outrage, the icy sense of panic – both had sunk down. She felt purged, confident, also coolly charitable, almost amused: almost as if all of it had happened in a dream. Owing this to Tim and wishing to show affectionate gratitude, she listened and responded to his conversation with particular sympathy. Goodwill flowed between them; a cosiness with a nostalgic undercurrent. He permitted his memory to dwell upon a romantic passage in a Sussex garden the deuce of a long time ago. He'd been a callow cub then, experimenting with girls and demi-girls and other sorts, considerably more business-like than idealistic; but he'd never quite forgotten how sweet she'd been at eighteen years old, the prettiest girl in the room, and the most oncoming you'd think – and then like as not wincing away like a filly or turning the ice on between one minute and the next. Ready to meet you half-way and a good bit more, solemn, teasing, anxious, laughing – you never knew where you were with her ... one kiss in the dark, gauche, inexpert, with no sequel; he'd found out what he wanted to know. She was hot stuff all right – would be when she got into her stride. Might have flown off the handle ... never had? Surprising under the circumstances ... They must get on well in bed together. That often kept a woman faithful when the chap had other women. Might still? ... Nothing would be easier, tonight, more tempting to suggest; nothing, thank God, more absolutely out of the question. Ah well, they were all settling down now, there were compensations ...

Prey to the fervour of devoted gratitude aroused in him, not for the first time, by the lineaments of ungratified desire, he gathered her to his chest and pressed her tenderly. She relaxed against him, kind masculine friend to whom one could confide so much but never would. So she was still attractive to him: a comfort; had often wondered if he remembered that never since mentioned episode in the Vances' garden the night of Sylvia's coming-out dance. Almost her first house party and her frock split at the waist. Fairy lights in the trees, a bush of syringa they'd buried their faces in, his anticipated but in the event unbargained-for embrace which, shaken in her self-respect, she had discussed next morning in her bedroom with a girl friend. 'I'm afraid he's *very* physical.' 'How far did he *go*?' 'Well ... I can only say I *hope* I'll never be kissed like that again.' 'Perhaps you ought to have slapped his face?' 'Perhaps I ought.' 'You don't think you *encouraged* him?' 'Certainly *not*.' 'And you didn't sort of *enjoy* it?' 'No, not at *all*.' Hysterical gales of giggling, comparing notes and agreeing that men must have desires completely unknown to women, and thoroughly distasteful. Next year when after a few weeks only of part-tearful, part-ecstatic sensations of inevitability, she had got engaged, he had written her a letter saying: *Darling Madeleine: congratulations. Rickie is a very lucky man. Ah me!* – which she had taken as a pleasing delicate hint that he hadn't forgotten, or dismissed that incident in a cynical way; and ever since she had felt with him a secret emotional security; almost as if in some half dream, unanalysed, on the threshold of experience, he had taken, without violence, her virginity.

And he's never been able to stand Dinah – thought Rickie must be out of his senses: Clara had said as much at the time of the worst trouble – another consolation ... Oh, she could tell him anything. She would tell him now, he would give her sound advice. She looked up suddenly with her great blue-black dilated eyes, her forehead puckered.

'What's the big worry, my sweet?' He gave her another hug.

'I *am* worried. Oh, Tim, it's Rickie. What am I to do?'

He looked blank, bending his ear down towards her lips. 'Couldn't catch.'

'You're too tall. You never do hear what I say.'

'I always hear what you say. But the band makes such an infernal row. Try again.'

'I said I was wondering what to do.'

'What to do about what, my love?'

'Wondering where he is. Rickie.'

'Wondering where he is?' He looked at her in simple astonishment. 'Why, just about tucked up in bed by now, I should hope.'

'Do you think so? I don't. I can't somehow picture it. But perhaps you're right. Perhaps that's where he is – tucked up and sleeping peacefully.'

But no, it was implausible. Something cataclysmic had occurred, too terrible to explain. Before her eyes he had performed an act of total rejection, stepped over the dance floor into limbo. She had no bearings now.

'Even supposing he walked home,' said Tim, 'it couldn't have taken him more than fifteen minutes. But he'd take a cab surely if he was feeling a bit queasy?'

'I don't know what he did.' Direction, goal, motive all equally unpredictable. And after all she could not tell Tim anything. She had cried out to him: 'I don't know what to do' – a cry from the heart, and he had not even heard her. A grotesque flop – ironic. 'But sweetie,' she went on, 'I think I'll disappear. You do understand, don't you? I know it's fussy but I've slightly lost my nerve since he had that haemorrhage. I'm glad we had this' – she lightly caressed his shoulder – 'but now I'd like to go. Explain to Clara. I'll give her a ring in the morning.'

This sort of appeal, to his sentimental protectiveness, was what he most enjoyed. Deprecating her wifely anxiety yet responsive to it, he escorted her out with his arm through hers, summoned her taxi and, as she leaned out from it for one more grateful farewell, dipped his sleek head in and kissed her cheek.

'You're a ravishing woman,' he said. 'Always were and always will be. God bless.'

'Good night, dear Tim. Don't forget me.'

Silly thing to say. He wouldn't question it; one more sweet titillating nothing, appropriate to the silly time and place.

Not a valediction.

He had not come back. Hall, study, dining-room, drawing-room: she opened doors and saw the face of each in turn, sunk in lugubrious hostility, emanating greyness and decay, like animals behind bars, or manic-depressives in a private bin. Already midsummer dawn fainted pre-natally in the high uncurtained windows. He was upstairs ... But already she knew along the vibrations of her nerves that there was nobody on the next floor. The house of a widow. Above the married floor, the floor of the children sunk in the routine of normal nursery sleep seemed cut off as if by a zone of concrete.

She climbed slowly to her bedroom; and it was not till she had rapidly undressed and washed that she looked almost perfunctorily into his dressing-room and saw his empty bed, pyjamas laid out upon it, sheet turned down. She shut the door, drew the blue silk curtains close, got into her big bed and switched the lamp off.

He was everywhere outside in the whole of London, he was nowhere. Gone to his club. Walking the streets. Gone to a hotel. Picked up a tart and gone home with her. Gone — but it wasn't possible? — to Dinah. Yes, it was possible. Certain in fact. She'd known it all the evening. Almost at once she fell into bemused half-consciousness, then slept a whirling sleep for half an hour, started broad awake again, the inside of her head stretched dry and taut, and ringing like a shaken tambourine. Someone was moving in the house. Above, in the night nursery? No. Below her, far down, and not a noise at all, but ponderable silence, as if someone heavy with intention were standing still: as a burglar might stand, or a murderer. She lay in a super-sensory trance, conjuring footsteps, breathing, creaking, a hand brushing her forehead, from invaded space. He was in the house. He was weight, silence. He was still no one, nothing.

The door of his dressing-room flew open soundlessly. He turned from the wash-basin and saw her standing in the doorway in her nightdress, her hair rumpled, her eyes like hot coals boring into him. He finished drinking a tumblerful of water in long gulps without a break.

'Thirsty,' he said. He put down the glass and mopped his forehead with a towel. 'Whew! Ain't it stuffy? The air's like a damp dishcloth in this house.'

His voice was level, matter-of-fact: he might just have come in from the office on an ordinary day. He twisted himself to examine his dinner jacket: one sleeve and shoulder were streaked with whitish dust. He picked up a clothes brush and started removing this in a collected way. His face in the half light looked perfectly calm, unnaturally pale.

She vanished, closing the door noiselessly.

He took off his clothes and lay down on the bed naked, his feet crossed, his hands behind his head — a reflective pose. After a while he swung himself into a sitting position on the bed's edge, propped his elbows on his knees, sank his forehead in his hands and remained thus, absent-mindedly running his fingers through his hair till it stood on end, and groaning once or twice vaguely under his breath like a person disturbed in sleep. Presently he got up, opened the door into her bedroom, stood a moment considering the dark blot of her head against heaped pillows, the mound of her body curled sideways under the blanket, then stalked across the room and sat down on the bed, near the foot of it.

After a few minutes she turned on her back and scrutinized him under lowered eyelids. What an extraordinary sight – planted there in an attitude that seemed one of contemplation, without a stitch on, his hands clasped loose between his thighs, his powerful shoulders easy. A long time since she had seen him stripped. A fine specimen, with muscle and youthful spareness still intact. What happens next?

'What time is it?' she said at last in an exhausted voice.

'I don't know,' was his amiable reply. 'Between four and five, I should think.' He yawned. 'Sorry if I woke you up.'

'You didn't wake me up. I haven't been asleep.' Disregarding the bitter meaning in this statement, he said with a sort of sprightliness: 'I'm jolly hungry.'

She stretched an arm out to the painted biscuit box on the table beside her, handed it to him.

'Ah, thank you,' he said, opening it. 'Digestive. Excellent. Have one?'

'No, thank you.'

Offering her the biscuit tin, his mouth full, his hair standing up in a mad crest, he looked, in his nudity, extremely comic. She wanted to laugh, and turned her head away upon the pillow. This was not the scene, not any sort of scene that could have been imagined. He was in a very queer frame of mind: not guilty or repentant or aggressive or on the defensive. Simply null and void, as if he had been washed up somewhere by a broken dam – stranded irrevocably in the flood's wake and resting now in a state of harmless emotional regression; as indifferent to the moral challenge, or to the rudiments of etiquette, as a babe new-born. Above all, out of reach – stubbornly so: as if his will had operated a deliberate assumption of irresponsibility; an absolutely ruthless withdrawal into self-preservation. There he sat naked, munching biscuits, yawning, complaining of thirst, of the weather . . .

'No pyjamas?'

He cocked a *distrait* eye at his abdomen and said as if mildly surprised:

'No. More comfortable without – cooler. Do you object?'

'Not in the least. I merely thought perhaps they hadn't been laid out and you didn't know where to look.'

'I'm quite capable of finding my own pyjamas.'

'Well ...' Her tone was lightly sceptical, exposing the whole area of his acknowledged incompetence: ransacking of shirts known to be at the laundry, failure to recognize anything in the airing cupboard for what it was, mislaying of studs, loss of cuff links ...

'By the way, did you find those links?'

'No.'

'I'll have a hunt tomorrow.'

'You won't find them.'

'You know I always find things.'

'I assure you you won't.'

He leaned forward, shifted a book on the bed table, tilted it to read the title, let it drop again. His eyes travelled vacantly here and there in the twilit room, resting on objects, never once on her. Every reduced remark and gesture seemed intended to convey: 'See, if you care to, how bare I am. Scooped out to the marrow. Helpless.'

'Where on earth have you been?' A heavy sigh from him incensed her and she added: 'Your abrupt departure took a little explaining away, to say the least of it.'

'I suppose it did.'

'I don't enjoy being humiliated.'

'Who does?'

'It would never occur to you, of course, to apologize.'

'I don't object at all to apologizing. Who expects me to? Everybody?'

She was silent; and after a moment he said with faint curiosity:

'Was there a public scandal?'

After a pause she muttered: 'No.'

'Did you say no?' – again with curiosity. She remained silent, bursting with indignation, and he added in a detached way: 'You're good at that sort of thing. Face saving. Women usually are. I should have been stumped.'

'You might at least apologize to me. Never never never in all my ...' she choked.

'I do apologize. It was disgustingly bad manners. I'm sorry.'

'I suppose you thought you were paying me out.'

He brooded; then said: 'I see it must have seemed so. Perhaps that was it – I don't know. I was surprised myself afterwards. At the time I just wanted to get away.'

It was like listening to a child's self-analysis: like Anthony at three years old, reproved for howling without warning at the Infants' dancing class, reflecting, then replying in a reasonable way: 'Well you see, I didn't know which I was – a tiny baby or a big boy.' Watching the mindless preoccupations of his shifting hands and eyes, she felt apologies, indignation and the rest of it irrelevant. The fact was, they were plunged in the thick of an experience without precedent in all their years of marriage. A strange man was sitting naked on her bed: situation fraught with alarming fascination.

'What did you do?' she said with interest.

'Walked about. I must have covered miles.'

'How did your clothes get in such a mess? Your coat looked as if you'd squeezed through a trap-door in a loft.'

'Not exactly.' He looked amused. 'I suppose it'll clean off ... No; that was from insinuating my person through an extremely narrow and filthy window.'

'Where? Here? Hadn't you got a latch key?'

'No, not here.' He fetched a sigh or yawn from the pit of his stomach. 'I went back to look for my cuff links.'

An explosion rocked her whole nervous system. Pushing herself down in the bed, she stretched her legs straight out, pressed them together.

'Where?'

'In Dinah's flat. I must have left them there months ago. I'd no idea. I hadn't missed them. It was a queer coincidence, wasn't it, you should mention them this evening?'

'I don't quite follow.'

'Well, I'm telling you. They were in her flat.'

'So you said.'

'They *were* ...' He shrugged his shoulders. 'Perhaps that woman's pinched them. Well, that's that.'

'What woman?'

'Caretaker woman – in the basement – where I got in.'

She fancied that he was smiling to himself. Hearing her heart beat in loud rapid thumps through her thin voice, she said: 'I didn't realize you were still seeing Dinah. As a matter of fact, I thought she'd gone abroad – for a long time. Not that I'd know her movements. Perhaps she didn't go abroad. Or if she did, I presume she's back. Safe and sound and everything as usual, I suppose. Since when, if it isn't too personal a question?'

He looked puzzled; then, with an effort, patient.

'I've no idea since when. I haven't been seeing her. At least, not till today. I did see her today – or rather yesterday, I suppose.'

'I knew it! I knew the moment you came in. All your lies – why bother? I shall always know. Oh well ... What are your plans now?'

He frowned, a frown of faintly irritated query.

'I haven't any plans. None in particular. How do you mean?'

'*Her* plans, I should have said. Her plans for you. Your joint scheme for the future. That's what I mean. I'm sorry to seem nagging, but I'd rather know.'

He hunched himself, as if her voice grated intolerably on his ears, and remained silent. So she went on:

'The moment she's back she rings you up. The moment she rings you up you gallop round for a glorious reunion. So overwhelmingly glorious that you can't be civil to your old friends for one evening – let alone to me – you can't wait to see her again. You pick a quarrel with me to give you an excuse to gallop off again and visit her in the small hours. She's waiting – oh yes! – you'd told her you'd get to her by hook or by crook. Pretending I've insulted you – you told her – oh, how indignant she'd be! – and comfort you ...' Her arms flung over her face, she thrashed about. 'Utter humiliation – utter – utter – utter ...' she went on gasping through paroxysms of dry sobs.

The room she had seen once only, suppressed for ever, glared at her again in all its details: deep settee, brown with lemon-coloured cushions, brilliant red curtains, Khelim rugs, a dresser covered with painted bowls, plates, jugs – foreign-looking, cheap but attractive, one huge round glass lamp on a low table strewn with portfolios, art books, magazines: material, doubtless, for intimate cultural evenings, Dinah teaching him all about Picasso, Matisse, Renoir, Greek and Persian art, before they went to bed. Place of treachery and passion, broken in upon, exposed, sealed up, vacated ... Reassembled again;

Dinah sitting there once more with a closed smile of mockery and triumph, knowing that she would never open her door again to admit Madeleine to see – what once she had shown her.

Not a word came out of Rickie, till finally he said in the tone of one upon whom a great light dawns:

'Oh, that's what you think – I see. Do be quiet, Madeleine. You've got it all wrong, I promise you. Stop.' He put his hands on the mound her knees made and shook it, repeating peremptorily: 'Stop!' At once she did stop; a stiff hysterical silence followed. He did not remove his hand; and presently began to pat her knee – the first personal gesture he had made. Uncovering her face, she saw that he was looking at her. For the first time. Something about him suggested an increase of animation, if not of sensibility; as if her outburst had penetrated to some nerve centre in him and administered shock treatment.

'Are you listening?' he asked in a stern voice.

'Yes.' She shut her eyes.

'She rang me up this morning at the office. I nearly jumped out of my skin. I hadn't seen her since – or heard a whisper of her since last – whenever it was. You can imagine I was startled. She said she was going to the flat to pack up for good and clear out, and would I come along for half an hour or so, just to settle up a few things – business things. It was in my name, you know – the flat.'

'I didn't know.'

'The rent was paid till September, but she'd decided to get out.'

'You paid it.'

'I paid it.'

'I didn't realize she was so completely your kept woman.'

'She wasn't,' he said unprotestingly. 'I simply paid the rent of this flat. She didn't want that even, but I insisted.' He paused: added bitterly: 'To soothe my conscience.'

'She was on your conscience?'

'Oh, everybody was on my conscience. *You* were – are ...' He uttered a brief snort of laughter. 'Naturally I felt responsible for her.'

So put that in your pipe, she told herself, and smoke it. But the sense of outrage burned in her like a corrosive chemical.

'You know,' he continued, 'how independent she is.' Tone of one discussing an acquaintance about whose character they had long been in agreement.

'Oh yes! It's not a quality one necessarily admires. It's easy to flaunt one's independence at other people's expense. In other words to be a ruthless egotist.'

'Well, it can mean that,' he conceded, judicial. 'I didn't say I necessarily admired it. Though as a matter of fact in her I do.'

So put *that* in your pipe ... 'And your precious sense of responsibility!' she cried, half choking. 'It's just your hopeless weakness. She can twist you round her little finger.'

'So can you then,' he said with a smile. 'I never did give myself marks for it. But there it is: it must be put up with.'

She felt suddenly ashamed; and then despairing.

'Are we *never* to get rid of her then? Is that what you're telling me? Will you never get over it – get free of her? Is she going to turn up again for ever, to make my life hell, to whistle you back whenever she feels inclined, to ruin our future? Because if so ...'

'Hush!' he said sharply. He took his hand away, and fixing her with a look of mingled anger and desperation, added: 'If you're going to start a scene again, I must go. I shall go to my room.'

He rose as if to carry out this threat, but as she remained dumb, sank down again. He sat rather bowed with his hands spread out on his knees, and said at last in a quiet voice:

'I shan't see her again. There wasn't any question of it. I don't know where she's been, I don't know where she went. Where she is now. She left when I did and handed me the keys and went I don't know where.'

After a silence she said timidly:

'Then you haven't been with her just now?'

'No, I have not. The flat is empty.' He stared at the waxing light in the blue curtains.

'I wish,' she said with a sigh, 'you hadn't gone there when she asked you to. It was bound to – be a mistake. Still, I suppose you felt you must.'

He did not answer this. Throwing away the words, she said:

'How is she?'

'Well. At least ... No. Ill, I think. She looked it. I don't know. An awful colour.'

'She's always been an awful colour. It doesn't mean anything. At least,' she added, seeing the protest in his face, 'she's always been pale.'

78

'Mm. Oh, pale, yes – she's always been pale ... She's as thin as a wraith. All eyes. I don't mind betting she hasn't had a square meal for weeks. Sort of transparent.'

'I expect she's having a non-eating period. She's done it before. People said how ethereal she'd grown to look, how spiritual. Or perhaps she's starving simply for the experience.' Masquerading as reassurance, hostility made her voice tense and thin. Destroy, destroy this too potent image of pathos and misfortune, she told herself. At all costs let him not pity, not wish to protect. But the face – all eyes – stared from its ambush, sickening his heart with pity, hatred, shame and yearning.

'You may be right.' He blew out a shuddering sort of sigh.

'So you went round, to settle things up.'

'Yes. For about an hour – oh, less. It was all quite formal.' His nostrils dilated. 'Extremely formal. Ceremonial handing over of the keys.'

'What is she doing now? I mean, where is she living? Has she ...' Seeing him set his lips, she checked herself and added quietly: 'All right. Don't tell me anything. I don't want to know.'

Dinah's muted voice was in his ears, saying in answer to some question of his: 'Oh no, I haven't been here for a long time – until today'; and then his own voice saying:

'You've been abroad haven't you?'

'What made you think that?'

'Someone told me so. Mentioned it. I think it must have been your mother. But perhaps I got it wrong.'

'Oh, I see.' She paused; something – amusement? – contracted her face for a moment, throwing cheek-bones and temples into even sharper relief. 'You must have got it wrong. I haven't been abroad. Have you seen Mother lately?'

'Not very lately. She's pretty tired, as you know. She can't leave your father – or won't.'

She lowered her eyes, and was silent. Presently he said:

'You've been – where then?'

She looked at him, raising her eyebrows as if in surprise, and said:

'In London.' Silence. 'Quite in another quarter though.'

'Alone?'

'No. With someone.'

'I see. I hope you're happy.'

'Yes, thank you, perfectly happy.'

'May I know with whom?'

'No, I don't think so,' she said without hesitation, still in that muted voice.

The snub made him wince, but he said politely: 'Just as you choose. I'm sorry if I appeared impertinent. I'm very glad to hear you're happy, and I hope this chap will prove more satisfactory than I did. Not that *that* would be difficult. He's expecting you back?'

Did she hesitate then? Was it only inside himself that a screw tightened as she replied: 'I'm going straight back.' Was that, in fact, what she did say? Certainly he could still hear the very telling lines he was given next.

'Well, ask him from me to take you out for a change and give you a steak and a bottle of good claret.'

Her eyes seemed to narrow, then fixed him in wide open blankness. *Touché!* Just as he'd guessed: some down and out, some cad or cripple.

'You're not looking very well,' she said. 'Have you quite recovered?'

'Yes, thank you. Entirely recovered.'

'And you're happy?'

'Oh yes. I wouldn't go so far as to say *perfectly* happy, like yourself. But I get along.'

'Children well?'

'Splendid.'

'I found these cuff links in a drawer.' She passed them to him, adding in a preoccupied way: 'I don't think there was anything else of yours.'

'Oh, thank you. Very careless of me. Funny I hadn't missed them.'

'Oh well, you have others . . .'

From first to last no kindness, and no truth.

Madeleine said nervously:

'You went back for your cuff links . . . I don't quite . . .'

'Oh yes. She'd found them when she was clearing out. She gave them to me – that I'm sure of. But what I did with them, God knows. I never thought about them again till I came in and you said – that. Later on, when I left in that abrupt and offensive manner, it occurred to me – after a bit – to go along and see if they were still there. I don't like loose ends, they trip you up.'

'Did you ring?'

'Yes, I rang.' His lip curled faintly. 'I didn't really expect anybody to come to the door, and nobody did. So I decided to break in.'

'How did you manage?'

'Easy, once I put my mind to it. There's a bit of low spiked area railing on the right. I vaulted that – just missed crashing down the area steps – and landed up between the wall of the house and a sort of partition wall on the corner. There was a thread of path to get round to the back by. I found a window, a small one, unlatched, about the level of my head. I guessed it was a lavatory and it was – a most unsavoury one. I clawed on the window and pushed it down as far as it would go, and got a grip on the top of the frame and swung up. I just managed to wriggle through and went in head first groping for the lavatory seat and pretty well turned a somersault. It was damned uncomfortable.' He stopped and glanced at her, as if suddenly aware that his voice was expressing nothing more nor less than simple pride and satisfaction in his exploit. 'I knew,' he went on, 'that Mrs Thingummy slept somewhere around, not to speak of an antediluvian yapping terrier bitch, but on the deaf side both of them, thank God. Anyway there wasn't a sound from any one of us. Then I took my shoes off and went up several flights of stairs. As I told you, there was nobody. Nothing.'

She made an effort, drew a hand from under the bedclothes, took his, and said with sympathy:

'It must have been horrible.'

'It was rather.'

'You'd been hoping she might have come back. Might still be there.'

Letting his hand lie in hers, he studied the carpet.

'I don't know,' he said, after a brooding silence. 'What good would it have been? – no good at all. It was the unreality ... earlier on. I got it into my head, if I checked up I'd – recover my sense of direction. However, there was nothing there. No links – not of any kind! Not a clue.' His mouth twisting ironically, he gave her hand a sudden quick pressure.

'You've no idea what she's doing?'

'Living with someone. That's all I know. She said that.'

Ah! ... Her heart struck like a clock.

'Who?'

'God knows.'

I bet I know.

'Did she tell you?'

'She said just that. Someone.'

A complex of emotions made her say quickly:

'Well, *that* won't last long, take it from me.'

He sent her an inquiring glance, opened his lips to speak, but only shrugged his shoulders. She murmured:

'Do you mind so dreadfully?'

'Oh well ... It's never altogether pleasant, you know. A blow to vanity.'

'I do know.' Still her predominant wish was to console him.

He nodded. 'However much one might reasonably expect it. Or even wish it.'

'You did ...' she said hurriedly; added: 'Wish it.'

'Oh certainly. I've been hoping – well, hope's the wrong word ... but if I knew she was being looked after, it would be a load off. I might not exactly relish it but – it would be a load off.'

'I don't suppose one would be likely to thank – one's ex-lover – for being so magnanimous,' she said after a silence.

'I'm not magnanimous. It's easy putting on a magnanimous act if you're indifferent. But in fact,' he said, curt, 'I'm not.'

She bit on this in silence, in almost physical pain.

'No,' he went on, 'it's my streak of realism. It generally operates too late. And neither of you ever appreciated it.' He lightly pressed her hand again. 'Not that I expect thanks – from either of you.' His nostrils stretched, in self-contemptuous amusement.

'I cannot bear it,' she cried, 'that you feel responsible for her. I cannot bear it.' He was silent and, struggling for composure, she went on: 'I know her better than you do. Twenty-eight years I've known her. She's well able to take care of herself.'

'I wish I could believe you,' he said soberly.

'She's quite unscrupulous. She only cares about what she wants.'

'What does she want?'

'You, I suppose. Me out of the way – destroyed – and you at her disposal. Utterly ... Don't you see this is just another move in the same old game? She wanted to find out if you'd still come when she whistled. And you did. Oh, round you trotted. And now you're on a string again. And off she goes, *mysteriously*, knowing you won't rest now till you've found her. Which is exactly what she wanted.'

He bent his head and meditated, as if debating the strength of this case against Dinah.

'She didn't behave as if' – he stopped – 'as if that was exactly what she wanted.'

'How did she behave?'

'As if she was' – he stopped again – 'in a bad way.'

'I thought you said it was all very formal.'

'Yes. She's not usually formal. Why should she be like that? She's so direct as a rule: not exactly *in*formal, ever, but absolutely direct.'

'You amaze me,' she replied, with subdued but passionate sarcasm. 'If that's your considered judgement you amaze me. I think one of us must be confusing terms. To me, direct means honest, it doesn't mean self-assured. I grant you she's *that*. However ...'

'Mm. Yes. Honest,' he repeated in a tone of preoccupied corroboration. 'That's what I do mean. That's how I think of her.' A spasm of distress crossed his face; as if what had passed between him and Dinah was at last beginning to take form, substance, colour, at last becoming evidence he recognized. He added: 'She wasn't self-assured. Quite the opposite.'

'Feeling her way perhaps. A bit embarrassed. I can't remember ever seeing her embarrassed but she may be capable of it.' He looked at her with vague inquiry. 'I mean, she was telling you, wasn't she, she'd already – found someone else ...'

'Oh, that wouldn't embarrass her,' he said decisively. A look sardonic, indulgent, appeared on his lips: distasteful to observe, seeming to uncover secret vistas of experience sexually shared, imparted without guilt. 'She never made any bones about that sort of thing.'

'I suppose she played you up with – descriptions. I believe some women do.'

The look altered sharply to a wary reticence, and then to blankness. 'Oddly enough,' he said with detachment, 'I never minded what she might be up to. Yet I'm as jealous as the next man. Horribly jealous, in fact.' He frowned in a surprised way. 'I suppose she gave me confidence ... It didn't matter ... I knew, or rather ...' He checked himself, then concluded: 'Oh no, she's freer than some in her – private life, but she's not a bitch. She'd never get me round to cock a snook at me.'

The tide was beginning to crawl in again: unpredictable tide that rose now and then from somewhere beyond the farthest point of ebb and swung them off the treacherous flats they stood on. She felt it start to lift her, stinging and cleansing the raw abscess in her breast. Hold on, she told herself, soon we shall be afloat, we shall have drawn one another in.

'I *have* seen her unsure of herself,' she presently allowed. 'It's when somebody whose opinion she values gives her a – real telling off. You didn't, I suppose?'

'Tell her off? Not in the least.' He smiled a wintry smile. 'No, the boot's always been on the other foot. I've never been in much of a position to criticize.'

'Nor has she, my God!' she said indignantly, but without venom. 'But I suppose that hasn't prevented her. I suppose she's been highly critical of you – and even more of me.'

'No,' he said after consideration. 'She's not a very critical person. At least, not censorious.'

Admitting to herself, for what it was worth, the truth of this, she said: 'You never criticize either. Sometimes I wish you did.'

He threw his head back suddenly, and a sound that was laughter as dry and hard as sobbing came out of his throat.

'Oh, I shall start now! I'm a reformed rake, you know. There's nothing more censorious.'

'Hush, Rickie, stop!'

She sat up in bed, speaking low and keeping his hand in hers; but he jerked it away and flung up both arms, a gesture so uncharacteristic in its dramatic last-ditch surrender that she was shocked.

'There's nothing,' he said. 'I'm nothing. That's what's happened. There's *nothing*; do you hear? I can't feel a thing. I'm done for. That's how it all ends – loving – and the rest of it.'

'It will come back,' she whispered. 'Nobody can stop feeling. Not for long.'

'Can't they? *Can't* they? I seem to see them all round me, wherever I go, wherever I dare look. Dead people. Dead pans. Petrified.'

She came to sit curled against his side and put her arms round him. He felt cold, cold.

84

'Darling, I love you,' she said. 'I do love you.'

Her cheek against his, her side pressing his, she listened with her whole body; but nothing stirred in him. She said:

'You still love her?'

He gave a sort of shudder, impossible to interpret.

'You want to go to her?'

'I told you. It's finished. She's gone.'

'We can find her.' She clasped him closer. 'I'll find her. She can't have simply vanished into limbo.'

'Oh, but she has.' He sighed wearily. 'I know now what hell is like. Not burning and howling. It's seeing people you've cared about, hearing them ask for help, and not being able to give *that* ...' He snapped his fingers. 'Not even giving a refusal. Just a mechanical needle scratching a graph. Record of human agony. It shoots up and down. You separate yourself from it and examine it. But it remains a black jagged crazy line on a chart. No meaning attached.'

'Then she did ask for help ...'

'Yes,' he said like lead. 'I'm sure she did. Not in so many words. She was too far gone. And I was simply observing her – so she didn't get a crumb of a chance. In the end we were both observing the needles scratching – each other's – our own – I don't know which ...'

They were both silent, breathing against one another, no more. Presently a light early morning commotion arose from above, the nursery quarters: voices, the sound of a curtain drawn back. They heard a thump, then one of the children ran rapidly across the floor. Day had begun.

Rickie said in a slow matter-of-fact voice:

'Somebody has given her a bad knock.'

'Oh *no*, Rickie! ... Are you sure?'

'Certain. Looking back on it. Well, I knew it at the time, and that's what stopped me ticking. It was written all over her.' In the same level voice he added: 'I know her.'

'What can we do?' Her clasp tightened round him.

'Nothing.'

He fell against her, she drew him down on the pillows, and soon they lay with their arms round one another, cold and still. Almost at once he fell fast asleep; his heavy respiration fanned her shoulder in regular beats. *Lost–won, lost–won* said his breath in her ear. *Won.*

85

Won. Alas ... The purest triumph, pain, loss of her life. *Gone – where? – gone* ...

She began to relax; a current of animal warmth started at last to flow between her drowsy and his unconscious body. Suddenly he roused up and without a word or a sign or a caress took her into an embrace, brief, violent, anonymous; then fell over on his side away from her and plunged into a yet deeper, more solitary annihilation.

That morning Clarissa was conceived, and might, they were both separately inclined to fear during the months of pregnancy, have turned out any incalculable kind of a failed fruit – little mad thing, gross misconception, star-crossed waif, accusing ghost; but instead was born without a hitch, punctual to the day, the flower of the flock, a spanking ten-pounder with fists doubled and lungs open full stretch; so firmly planted in the earth, so squared for the attack that she seemed from her first hour a laughing matter, a child of fortune.

It was during those months that he began to feel that if he was not careful to avoid unnecessary strain his health would become completely undermined: his family would have a crock on their hands, or – possibly? – possibly not? – worse – be left without a father. He began to be anxious about himself, and consulted the doctor of his own accord and followed his advice about diet, rest and medicine. When the pain nagged he thought about the relation between worry and his acid juices, and did his level best to stop worrying. He made a point of getting back from the City in time to play with the little boys before their bed-time, and this he quite looked forward to, though they sometimes made him feel irritable. After a *tête-à-tête* dinner with Madeleine, he was inclined to lie back in his armchair with his eyes shut. From the sofa where she lay reading her book, Madeleine could look at him occasionally and wonder if he had rather prematurely reached the age when men dropped off after dinner. His hair was thinner in front, he was fatter in the face: he had to drink a lot of milk. Did he miss Dinah? Think about her? Was he still unhappy? Could he possibly be seeing her? Unlikely: he was regular and domesticated, never went out without her in the evenings.

Lapped in a quiescence part aqueous part vegetable she felt the memories of jealousy and anguish, of vows to cherish and console him push at her coldly, languidly, like the forms of fishes flicking the

86

dark weeds, pushing the nebulous glass of an aquarium. Then he would open his eyes, smile faintly, suggest a game of piquet or a little reading aloud, or early bed for both of them.

When about midnight one night that eminent gynaecologist looked into the book-room and said a girl, both splendid, he was pierced suddenly with such an unexpected pang of emotion that he could only grin and stammer and look away like a schoolboy to hide his brimming eyes. A little later he went up to the dressing-room and saw in a Moses basket on a stand his daughter. The nurse returned to Madeleine and reported that he was as pleased as a dog with two tails; and a little later still when he went into the still ether-laden room to see his wife, he kissed her and sat beside her bed with her hand in his; and they were both a little tearful and both delighted.

Undressing in the spare room, warily testing his heart for the first time for months, he decided that he still felt different. *Better*. Hope had come back, or life; perhaps they were the same thing. He had heard said that nobody could go on living without any hope at all: he had wondered for a long time whether it was true. He told himself that now again he had a bit of something to live for, and promised his daughter love, and felt a stirring of tenderness and gratitude towards the mother.

He got into bed and lay on his back, his arms crossed behind his head, thinking of his luck – the fine healthy offspring he had fathered. For the first time for months, Dinah's real face appeared, looking calmly up at him; one of her real faces. When she wore it, she had been lying under blankets in a high narrow bed with an iron headrail and looking most curiously complete yet incomplete. Something had left her body yet was still informing it. With a sense of shock he told himself that his last child had been stillborn: his by Dinah.

Bad business; fantastic; criminal, paid for with only agony. The tune began again: *To make the punishment fit the crime, the punishment fit the crime* ... That refrain had pranced in his head, a mouthing Prance of the Madmen, for weeks, weeks, weeks, when all was over; yet once he had felt – or thought he had felt – no guilt or fear; only a kind of exultation in the thought of the child to be born, a passion of protectiveness towards his love; and nothing else, no room for anything else, except an occasional visitation or jet of positive irresponsibility, a compulsion to defy, to proclaim, to destroy, to be off at a gallop, headlong, anywhere, anywhere, away, away … *Sad mad and bad*. Who said that? How did it go on? *But oh, how passing sweet*. No, not quite right. *And dangerous to know … How mad bad sad and sweet … and dangerous to know my Dinah dear …* That also could be fitted to a tune: he hummed it over in his head, jazzed it up, trying out various syncopated stresses. Pot-pourri rag-time. Ha! Ha! Memory's cracked bowlful of time-rotted debris.

Failure of, loss of memory. *Can't* remember must mean don't want to, won't: that much he suspected without psychiatrical assistance. And so he must have fixed it – and God! at what a cost to him – he must have consigned it to perdition: the true story of his love. Only true love of my life.

Beginning of loss of memory had been – when? – yes, *as if at a signal prearranged*. It had started with that cryptic telegram, extravagantly discreet, not even signed – prearranged with Corrigan, the signal which was to be taken to announce that Dinah's time had come, she had gone to hospital. Why, when it reached him at the office had he forthwith interpreted it favourably, in a slap-happy blur of emotional relief? All over, all well, thank the Lord, I'm coming, I'm with her, this is it – an uprush of hysteria on those lines; a last race, breathless, witless, blindfold, to get away with it, to outstrip Nemesis.

Late afternoon, moon-coloured street-and-roofscape, lucent, pied with the snow's last vestige of shroud, the shovelled stuff heaped greyish in the gutters, a spectral sky, green-tinged, an air he drank as he ran – ice water laced with fire; afternoon of a Friday, Madeleine gone to the country with the children (whooping cough convalescence) and not expecting him: God on his side as usual. He ran, he had packed a bag, was in the car and out of London before dusk, before he had even begun to use his loaf. But once an inky night had fallen, once well out on the first long lap to the south-west, and unable to make speed on the tricky though sanded roads – then he had time to reflect. The farther he went south, the harder to mitigate stark meteorological facts. Snow flurries swarmed, white bees, against the windscreen, whirled iridescent in the tunnel of his headlamps; and beyond this travelling gold shaft of energy and light, mile after mile the stiffening world unrolled its winding sheets.

Where had he put that telegram? While with one hand he ransacked every pocket, the car made a dizzy glide across the road: a skid, a nasty one. This drive was going to be tough – insane perhaps. What had the infernal weather report been last night, this morning? Severe blizzard in the south-west, such and such areas cut off, warnings to motorists ... *No!* ... Ever since the accursed snow had started to take charge ten days ago he had turned an eye made blind on earth and sky, blocked fast his ears each time – dozens of times – that the weather hit the headlines. Seeing the last of London's blizzard shovelled up yesterday, he had told himself that the wind had veered, thaw must be general. Where was the bloody telegram? What had that blasted woman put?

Slight delay now safe at destination come

That was it surely. Think now. What exactly did it mean? What sort of delay? And why? *Come* was the last word, certainly. Now why bother to put that, as if he needed telling, when it had been understood between them all he needed was the signal, by hook or by crook he'd be on his way. He strove to remember what formula he had agreed on the last time he had managed to get down to see her. That was on New Year's Eve, he had got there by breaking and keeping promises all round. Weather like April, soft and sunny. Dinah looking suddenly anonymous, like any pregnant woman, in a loose coat and maternity jacket, touchingly disfigured, moving with a kind of undulation and extended rhythm like a small ship putting out of harbour under sail – in all physical ways the contrary of her normal discreetly defined and moderated self. They had joked, actually joked, inventing messages for every comical eventuality. Corrigan mercifully absent, they had spent two days and nights of tranquil domesticity, walking, cooking, sitting by the fire, discussing plans for the year to come. Once or twice something seemed to threaten ... the drag of a claw, thrust of a beak in a dream: once or twice he looked at her in amazement, seeing them both in such straits as beggared all description, and she didn't see it. It was not for him, who had brought her to this pass, to air his qualms. 'I can't help wishing, darling, you hadn't so completely stuck your toes in about getting rid of this ...' A nice thing that would have been to come out with. Supposing she were to die in childbirth ... What a scandal! How to break it to her parents, to whom he was devoted, let alone to Madeleine? But she wouldn't die. As soon as she was out of hospital she was going to

France with the baby and Corrigan. Somewhere in Provence they were to compose a unit dedicated to freedom, creative freedom and responsibility; Corrigan painting, Dinah writing, the child to be nourished on sun, milk, wine and happiness; Rickie to send funds – only the minimum – and come like a god at intervals, to shower down love and drink it back ... Morally, socially, financially, it was all sewed up, there wasn't a loose stitch anywhere. Of course it would be known, sooner or later, that she had had a child. What of it? She had always told her friends that she intended one day to pick a lover deliberately and have a child by him; no bourgeois bonds; no divorce court or registry office; life the pure gift out of desire from man to woman, freely offered, freely accepted; an act of entirely uncorrupted passion involving moral choice. People would say, of course ... well, let them say; she was retiring, lips sealed, wasn't she? – she was embarrassing nobody. As for her mother, she felt sure that when the moment of revelation came, Mother would surprise them all by giving the enterprise her sanction; reluctant, dismayed perhaps at first, not overt; but in the end whole-hearted. Mother was an old donkey in some ways, but she had a strong streak of unconventionality: she had declared more than once in the bosom of the family that every woman had the right to have a child. One thing was certain: even if in her secret heart she half suspected whose child this was, she would not only not inquire, but firmly resist enlightenment. As for Madeleine – oh, Madeleine would never suspect. She took such a disgusted view of Dinah anyway, said Dinah, that she would assume the child to be the result of some piece of casual promiscuity. She would be curious, no doubt, and ... oh, sexually agitated; but chiefly she would decide to shrug her shoulders and sterilize the scandal by keeping it at one contemptuous remove ... 'And if you think,' Dinah had said, teasing him, 'That he'll look like you, you're wrong. I *know*. I can see him. He looks exactly like himself ...'

Didn't one have to register births? Yes, of course one did. They had overlooked that little awkwardness. But time enough. Apart from that, all the arrangements were scrupulously unscrupulous. Her letters written in her childish hand and addressed to the office had continued to breathe reassurance: always brief, terse, always with their odd naïve and caustic undertone, their tiny piercing sting of intimacy. The last, three days ago, had been like all the others. A blizzard over the week-end, she wrote, had blocked them in, all the telephone wires down, Corrigan in a fuss, but that was nonsense. She had another three weeks at least to go, and by that time spring would have come. She was doing her exercises and leading the most wholesome and regular of lives. A lot of lambs had been born, they had had a bad time at the farm but they hadn't lost any ... something about twin lambs she was helping to bottle feed.

Why, when he had torn open the orange envelope, had his eyes, or mind, immediately – done something to the message dancing on the flimsy paper – censored it somehow, rejected it? Delay, delay ...

Severe delay: sudden delay: slight delay: serious delay ... now safe, not safe, now saved ... which, which? Oh, *destination*, ominous word! *Come* ... to the place she had reached, where it was appointed that he should come to meet her. *I knew it all along*, he told himself. I sent her to death, her destination; persuading her, himself, that the impossible was child's play; that the plot, so monstrous, so plausible, devised with such cunning ingenuity, could outsmart the God of Wrath. *Punishment. Crime* ... His hands on the wheel went limp, began to shake. *Hate* ... He fixed on her, on Corrigan, for its incarnation and its object. Her large white powdered cheeks – obscene; her fine hard prominent brown eyes, her rubbery amplitudes of bust and hip bursting from grubby slacks and jumpers; her over-emphatic slang, her dirty stories, her roars of heartily yea-saying laughter, her romantic devotion to his cause and Dinah's, everything that revealed in her the *fausse bonne femme*, masked an aggressive Lesbianism. He might have known – he'd always known – she was a common fraud; that she would loom on him at the last in full obstetrical regalia, reciting evidence, pronouncing sentence, self-exculpation, and – most hideous of all – stout words of consolation and stiff upper lip that time she stooped and with dramatic flourish lifted the sheet from what lay under: frozen irrevocable image of reality; stark dead, authentic Dinah ... Morbid rubbish, he addressed himself – snap out of it, keep cool, keep going. At the next open garage and road-house he stopped, swallowed coffee and a sandwich, had the chains put on; they told him that farther west the roads were shocking, to proceed would be inadvisable to say the least. Slowly, steadily he drove on, pausing occasionally to take a nip of brandy from his flask, to light a cigarette, to rub his aching eyes. About six o'clock in the morning he came to the final county and found himself suddenly, between one market town and the next village, in Polar wastes, his landmarks all obliterated; swerved incautiously to read a signpost and ditched the car feet deep in drifted snow.

He tumbled out, sank up to his thighs, scooped, shovelled with his hands, flung himself flat, shoulder beneath the running board, heaved, grunted, heaved in a madman's effort to lift the car; gave up at last, stood sweating, panting, snow in his hair, ears, collar, pockets, shoes, alone in lunar vacancies crossed with black poles or gibbets, scrawled with skeleton tree shapes, and smudged in the middle distance by a long dragonish mass of crouching darkness, snow-mantled, ante-diluvian – an area of afforestation. Pipped on the post. Another twenty miles at most to go.

He took his bag from the car, locked it, removed the key, left it sunk at an angle of forty-five degrees and started steadily walking forward, following the direction of the signpost towards a village he remembered. He was wearing fleece-lined suède overshoes – he had actually taken that precaution – and at each successive hole he crunched out under him appeared a patch like a stain of brownish blood. *Blood was in the very sod* he chanted to himself. After three hours he reached the village. Nine o'clock in the morning, a cataleptic day, livid with frost-fog. At the inn, the astounded garrulous pessimistically jovial proprietress served him fried eggs and bacon, a strong brew of tea; he felt an access of superhuman energy and power. He tramped off to the station, and at eleven-ten took his seat in the branch train which, groaning, hissing, crawling, and stopping at random, brought him long after midday to the destined place.

He was by her bedside, he had her in his arms; through the bare succour of his finger-tips beneath her shoulder blades he was lifting her dying body into resurrection, he was all incandescent, ablaze with the pure total life of the world of death which to reach and save her he had traversed.

And that was the crack-up. He saved her through the power of love, and that was the end of the power of love. There was no way out for it, it had so overreached itself; it burst against negativity and was extinct. He went on for a bit, holding her hand but clueless, turned back, forward again along the same blind alley among the same suffocating shadows lit fitfully at times by luring beams, to end once more and yet once more against the same claustrophobic wall; holding her and losing her, hearing her voice, succumbing to it, denying it – her voice of truth, of falsehood, of gratitude, reproach; of pride, surrender, of love, of whips and scorpions; answering it tenderly, roughly, firmly, weakly; not answering; beating about for help, and terrified lest, searching in the dark, he should see suddenly from what unknown quarter help was coming.

And help did come. Oh yes, it came; as it was bound to.

It came in a letter handed to him one morning by Madeleine when he looked in on her to say good morning on his way to the office. She was sitting up in the big bed – from which he had these many months removed himself, having developed a most tiresome twitch in one leg which kept them both awake – in a blue bed wrap, on her knees her breakfast tray. When he said: 'Just off, darling. I'll be a bit late back – not much' (for he had promised to go round for an hour or so to Dinah just back with faithful accomplice from the South of France) – Madeleine, looking rather stupidly at a point above his head, said nothing. What then struck in him like a muffled gong, made him say lightly:

'Any interesting letters?'

After a pause she said: 'One *curiously* interesting.' She lowered her eyes to stare at him, then put her hand down slowly and picked from the morning's mail strewn round her a broad thick sheet of paper of a dismal beige. 'It might be as well if you spared a moment to read it.'

His first thought was that he had never seen a more revolting handwriting. The whole thing looked like a conglomeration of beetles on a dung heap. Next, the signature outraged his susceptibilities: Elaine M. Corrigan, with a theatrical flourish – nauseating. *Elaine* indeed! – what a name for a bloody old cow. The letter said that after deep suffering and many a night of anxious questioning she had been guided, now saw her moral duty, wished to make atonement, to save three lives from an Evil to which in her blindness and mistaken loyalty she had hitherto contributed. She had always, if she dared say so, greatly admired Madeleine; would Madeleine see her? She thought, in all humility, it was in her power to help – help everybody still. Sincerely, Elaine M. Corrigan.

He took it all in in a couple of seconds, tossed it back on to the bed, stood waiting, with a sensation of extreme, of almost blissful calm. He watched Madeleine lift the coffee pot; her hand shook, he noticed, and the coffee spurted over the sheet.

'What's it all about?' she said, stirring her cup briskly.

'How do you mean?'

'I mean, is she a lunatic? Or what? She's that creature Dinah goes about with, isn't she? So far as I remember I've only set eyes on her once – at one of those ghastly bottle parties you were so keen on a year or two ago. I don't quite seem to take it in.'

Daring one splinter of a glance at him, she saw that his eyes had gone pale, oddly sleepy looking. He said:

'She's a lunatic. But it's all down there.'

'I still don't follow ... Why should she admire me?'

'I suppose she thinks you've behaved with great dignity and self-control. She's offering you her tribute.' Seeing her stretch a hand out to pick up the letter again, he said quickly, savagely: 'Oh leave the filthy thing alone. Burn it.'

'Yes,' she said musingly after a minute or two. 'I will. It's horrible.' Again she said, not looking at him: 'What's it all about?'

'Well, you've read it ... It's about me – you ...' With a frightful effort he added: 'Dinah.'

'She seems to imply that you and Dinah ... that you've been having an affair – for a long time.'

'Yes.'

'Which couldn't make sense – or could it?'

'If you mean is it true, it is.'

'And it's still going on,' she said in the same musing way.

After a pause he said: 'I haven't seen her for a long time.'

'Where is she?'

'She's been abroad.'

'So I understood. Coming back when?'

'Soon ... I believe.' His mind raced like a weasel in a cage, intent on one problem only: how much, by keeping cool, he could still manage not to say.

'You *believe* ...' She rubbed her eyes. 'And then you carry on again, as usual. Is that the idea?'

'I can't answer that,' he said huffily. How cheaply she expressed herself, how squalid the whole thing was being made to look.

'One's own sister ... It does seem a bit – out of the ordinary. This

94

letter seems to imply her intention is – or your joint intention is – to break up our marriage. It's rather frowned on, isn't it? – in that list of relations, I mean, in the Prayer Book.'

'Oh yes,' he agreed politely. 'That's putting it mildly.'

'Not even *deceased* wife's sister.' She burst out laughing, checked herself. 'What a liar you are, Rickie, aren't you? Stunning. All these sudden important business journeys. Kept at the office. Business dinners. Extraordinary, *extraordinary!* Packing me off to the country, so concerned about my insomnia. Insomnia, yes! I *see* now why I lay awake tossing and ... I *knew* ... all the time.'

'Then why didn't you do something to stop it?' He spat this out.

She gave a gasp, pushed all her hair up in a familiar gesture, lay back with flaming cheeks on the prosperous pillows.

'I suppose I trusted you,' she said in a quiet incredulous voice that got him on the raw.

'Well, I suppose I must get along to the office,' he said finally. He made a movement of departure, then stopped and waited. Up flew her eyelids.

'Is that all you have to say?'

'What can I say?'

'No.' A grimace twisted her mouth. 'There's nothing you can say. Let me see ... What could one say? ... Sorry – didn't mean it? Couldn't help it? Surely there's nothing to make *much* fuss about – after all it's just a little family affair?' She started to laugh again.

He said fatally: 'I am sorry,' and at this she made a violent spring in the bed, as if to leap at him, overturning the tray and scattering its contents in hideous mess and clatter.

'Don't say it!' she blazed at him. 'Don't dare! *She*'ll talk you round! *She*'ll tell you nothing matters – trust, marriage, children, nothing. Not even *decency*. Experience is the great thing! Taste life to the full! Devil, *devil* – she's done it – ruined my life, she always meant to.' Then as he dissolved before her eyes, rooted there, escaping from her, she began under her breath, neck craned, to stone him. 'Get out of here. Get out. Get out. Get out.'

He turned and walked away, shutting the door on it all with careful quietness, thought of running up to see the boys, but instead made straight for the front door and went by Underground as usual, reading *The Times*, to his office in the City.

He was late, and his secretary was waiting in his room; after a cheery good morning she told him at once that his sister-in-law had telephoned half an hour ago. Oh really? Any message? Just would he ring her back as soon as possible. Thanks. It struck him how often he'd heard said that any secretary worth her salt knew, and kept, all her boss's secrets, and was convinced that Miss Matthews knew and always had known everything. His uncle sent for him and he spent a fairly busy morning; then Miss Matthews, poker-faced, retired, and he telephoned to Dinah. Yes, she too had heard from Corrigan. She sounded calmly contemptuous and amused. Would he come as soon as he could leave the office? Yes, he would come. She said, which was rare for her: 'I love you,' and rang off.

He went out in the lunch hour, trudged to the Tube, took train towards home, got out at an intermediate station, came back, pursued by Madeleine's eyes, cheeks, hair, by her voice – 'I trusted you.' Her voice – 'Get out! Get out!' He was frightened, he wished to go to her, to be reassured and to comfort her. He could not: she was wronged, she knew it, he was found out. Torn with pity, remorse, self-loathing, he had to stop at the bottom of the Exit staircase and lean against the wall. That was the first time the Thing caught him in the midriff, a twisting screw, then suffocation. *Caught* ... He took a taxi to his club, drank several whiskies, found old Sam Lipiatt there with another chap, drank more, and made them laugh. Never in better form.

He came back optimistic to the office at three-thirty, read two reports laid on his desk during his absence, couldn't make head or tail of them, threw up his window, saw, separated from him by a hair's breadth yet worlds, worlds out of reach, blue sky, a plump white cloud of May, sun in the streets and people walking at peace, enjoying it; saw also – no more, no less horrible – a sign he had never noticed before in red glass lettering on the fourth storey of the building opposite: Uhlmann Trusses Abdominal Belts. He sat down again at his desk and put his head in his hands.

Think things out now. Pretty drunk. He thought hard: truth came to him. Corrigan was the evil one, the killer: Corrigan, not he. Break her door in, fall on her, kick her till she bellows, drag her by the scruff, show her the filthy mess she's made and rub her nose in it. That was the stuff. Face her with his wife distraught, his children weeping, the roof tree crashed in ruins. Pah! – but he couldn't look at her, couldn't touch her, it would be touching dung. Better hang around a bit longer, then go straight to Dinah. Have some more drink with her. She'd keep her head and *think of a way out*. He *must* go to her: obviously somebody must go. It was the obvious sensible thing to do, the right thing, the – manly thing; the thing he'd craved for, at intervals, for weeks and months: intoxication, anaesthetic. My love. Hollow words. He could not focus her: she seemed to be covered with cobwebs. He didn't want to go to her, he feared her like the plague. He wanted to see someone outside all this, take someone out to a good dinner, say to someone later in the evening when with the help of wine he had got himself together: 'Look here, I'm in rather a jam . . .' He cast about in his mind for the right person, grasped at this and that one: bachelor friends, friends of his married world; not friends of Dinah's. Nobody seemed quite right.

It was five o'clock. He must keep his word to Dinah. Be resolute. He put the reports in a drawer, locked it and left the room. As he shut the door after him the telephone rang. He hesitated, went straight on, hearing it shrill, shrill, shrill, demented, as he shut himself into the lift, pressed the button and shot down.

When she opened the door to him his first impression was an odd one: he was looking not at but through her: she had become transparent. Then she materialized and he followed her upstairs. She was sun-tanned but thinner than ever; extremely off hand and therefore, he knew, nervous. He said:

'Darling. How are you?' He stood looking at her, unable to approach or kiss her, and keeping her distance, she mixed a strong cocktail, handed him his, and sat down with hers in her usual chair – a small low Victorian affair with a high scalloped back, upholstered in a wool and beadwork tapestry of lilies and red roses: a piece that said, like all her domestic objects: Dinah's choice.

'How are *you*?' She fixed him with enormous eyes. 'You look . . .'

'How do I look?' He feebly smiled.

'In a panic.'

'I'm not in a panic,' he said, stung. 'Naturally, I feel rather – upset.'

'How exactly?' Business-like, she lit a cigarette.

'Well ... you won't be altogether surprised to hear it was not very pleasant at home this morning. In fact, it was hell.'

'It must have been,' she agreed after reflection. 'I'm sorry. I ought to have foreseen this. Should have realized, I mean, what way this bestial madwoman would be bound to jump. I see it now, of course. It's psychopathic logic.'

'Oh, is it? That's something gained then. We understand psychopathic logic.'

She dropped her eyelids, scrutinized him for a moment from under them, looked away.

'Is she – Madeleine – in a frightful state?' She spoke with sudden timidity. He had begun to walk up and down, up and down the room, as he always did under pressure; and there was silence between them until he burst out in a painful mutter:

'She seemed to go mad. I've – she'll never ...' He stopped, on the verge of announcing to Dinah that Madeleine would never trust him again, that he had let her down and failed her utterly.

'She won't go mad,' said Dinah. 'You can dismiss that worry at least, I assure you. She's got very strong feelings' – she paused – 'about her personal life, and I can imagine she'd be extremely hysterical. But she won't go mad.'

On the point of declaring: 'Well then, *I* shall,' he checked himself again; mixed himself another stiff drink and set it down untouched, in sudden revulsion to the spectacle of himself drinking his way out. He thought what a hard streak Dinah had – sarcastic too. Both these sisters were very sarcastic.

'How did it end?' she said at last.

'She told me to get out.'

Her heart gave a leap; her heart dropped leaden in a vacuum. She said: 'She didn't mean it. If that's what's worrying you.'

'God knows what anybody means. Or anything.'

He came and sat down in his usual chair, opposite her, tried to look at her and smile, and sighed 'Oh, darling ...'

This was the moment, she told herself, to lower and deflect the tension. She began to speak of her time at Cap Ferrat, of the first signs – which like a fool she said she had not foreseen – of the brewing-up of Corrigan's psychological collapse: *her* loss, not Dinah's, of the baby, *her* agony, her sacrifice; the brute ingratitude of the wicked pair whom she alone had stood by. The cumulative determination to rid herself of her guilt by blowing the gaff, going over, while the going was good, to the side of the angels.

'I suppose she explained in her letter how high-minded her motives were?'

'Words to that effect. Atonement was the keynote.' He shuddered.

'I never thought she'd go to such lengths. I thought I could deal with her.' She brooded. 'I suppose she came clean in a big way? I mean – made the situation clear beyond a shadow of a doubt.'

'I don't remember anything explicit. But it seemed clear enough to Madeleine.'

'And it was a complete shock and surprise...'

'It seemed to be. Though she did say she'd really known it all along.'

'I dare say that's true in a sense,' said Dinah in the tone which sometimes irritated him, and did so now – it seemed to sum up the case with such judicial certainty and leave so little room for any individual case of understanding. Yet he knew that this was only half of the heart of the matter: that the tone was the one she seized on, in pride and fear, when her self-esteem or confidence had received a sudden shock. 'Presumably,' she went on, 'any wife not utterly indifferent to her husband would be bound to feel he'd changed towards her.'

'I don't know that I did change towards her,' he said rather querulously, biting his thumb – another trick of his. He saw her slow rare unbecoming flush and felt that he had touched yet another new low. 'I suppose I did. Of course I did,' he added lamely; then with a change of voice: 'But I'm a bloody good liar, you know. And a bloody good actor. And she's singularly unsuspicious ... Sorry! Old-fashioned way of putting things. I mean, she's an escapist, of course ... And I'm on the schizophrenic side. That looks after everything, I think – except you, my love. Elaine M. Corrigan we've dealt with, haven't we? She's a psychopath. with paranoiac delusions based on guilt ...' Slowly Dinah raised her drooping head and slowly let it fall back against the back of her little chair. He watched this movement closely, with detachment and curiosity. Her face at this new angle had a look of pathos and stricken dignity, and he noted that the colour had drained out of it: also that under her lowered lids she was looking into space. He said conversationally: 'Go on about your time in France.'

99

She waited a moment or two, then went on, her voice at first almost inaudible, then gradually assuming a more normal resonance. Last week, she said, a scene to end all scenes had brewed up in the small hours. Corrigan had rushed drunk, hysterical, to the station and entrained for England, leaving most of her clothes and a stack of canvases behind and snatching a wad of notes from Dinah's handbag. Dinah had enjoyed a few quiet days in the hotel, bathing, walking, reading; then at the appointed time – yesterday – returned. Late last night she found the note in the letter-box:

One day you will forgive me for what I have done: realize that I was the best friend you ever had or ever will have: and now as always am acting in your true interests. Nothing explicitly set down. 'But I guessed, of course, what she'd been up to.' She had been telephoning at intervals all day. Each time, hearing her voice, Dinah had simply replaced the receiver.

Her story finished, she glanced across at him. He was still nibbling the skin round his thumb nail and he seemed to her to have shrunk in weight and height; also there was something darting, flickering about his eyes, like an animal at bay ... a predatory, hunted animal. He said in a tone of reflection:

'It's all extraordinarily squalid. Gutter press tit-bit. I suppose it always was.'

At Oxford he had had an intense if short-lived relationship with a gifted undergraduate who read modern poetry aloud to him in a punt on the Cherwell. A fragment he could not place had been recurring to him for the last hour or so: *For so the game is ended That should not have begun* ... Apt but not helpful. How many, many traitors, tricked at last, must have reached the same conclusion! Stockbrokers, politicians, priests, gangsters, poets, lovers, murderers ... Taking a rapid mental survey, he could not, off hand, think of a single chap of his acquaintance who had not behaved badly to some woman or other; or to some other chap on account of a woman. 'His best friend's wife' – a banal phrase, joke almost. He'd heard of a chap who'd gone off with his own daughter-in-law; of a woman who lived contentedly in sin with her husband's father. Then there was incest, very natural in a way – as Byron had discovered – and not by a long chalk only Byron ... He tried to think if he'd ever come across anybody known to have resisted a really strong temptation. Such people must obviously exist, but he couldn't call any to mind: wouldn't care for them anyway, wouldn't feel easy ... If a friend came to him and confessed to having fallen in love with his sister-in-law he'd think it not monstrous but the most natural thing in the world. As indeed it was ... On the other hand he would certainly recommend flight. 'Chuck it,' he'd say, 'before it's too late. It isn't worth it.'

Dinah had risen and disappeared into the kitchen. When she came back carrying a dish of curry – his favourite supper – he watched her set it down and then, catching her eye, smiled. Poor girl. The pathos of going through all the customary domestic routine ... They ate in silence, sitting side by side as usual; as usual he praised and thanked her. He took her hand, which was cold and limp.

'Say something,' she said faintly.

'What can I say?' His reply rang a jarring bell in him.

'You're not thinking about me at all.'

He answered coldly: 'I'm trying to think about everybody.'

After a long pause she said: 'Yes, Rickie, I know – I know you are.' Her voice was gentle, pitying; the first kind words he'd heard that day. They melted his frozen heart. He put his head down on her shoulder and whispered:

'I do love you. You know I do.'

'And I love you.'

They got up and drifted to the sofa and sank down on it with their arms tight round one another.

'Forgive me,' he said.

'There's nothing to forgive you,' she said in the deep voice he loved; not her everyday voice, but the one he listened for, that was for him alone – he was sure of it – that seemed when it returned – how rarely lately! – to transport them to another, a visionary world, bare of superfluities, purged of calculations and confusions. 'Or if so, I must say it equally: forgive me. But we knew – we decided all this at the very beginning. Don't you remember? We said we forgave one another everything beforehand. And that there would never be anything to forgive.'

'Could you still say so?' he murmured. 'No, you couldn't.'

'Of course, I can, of course. Can you?'

'Need you ask? But I feel so poor,' he said, feeling it no longer. 'So useless to you.' He sat up and mopped his eyes.

'Useless to me?' Her large eyes opened and dilated as if in ecstatic surprise. 'Why, love, you gave me back my life. To do anything – everything with. I never forget it for a single instant, I never shall. Snow. Blood. I was dying. Remember.' He remembered these essentials. He took her in his arms again. 'You saved me. You do know that, don't you?' He sighed. If she said so, then it was so. 'We knew then that we knew something very few people in the world have even an inkling of. We can't unlearn that, can we? – whatever happens to us.'

'People do sometimes forget what they've learnt.' He pressed her to him, to show that this was said in confident disbelief, almost *pour rire*.

'We're not people. And if I ever could come to feel I *had* got anything to forgive you ...'

'Yes?'

She said with a pale smile: 'It would be your saying it was all extraordinarily squalid.'

'I'm sorry.'

'It might well be but it isn't. And it won't be. Nobody outside has the right to judge us. We're responsible to one another, aren't we?'

'I hope so,' he said soberly. He had been accusing himself all day of criminal irresponsibility.

'This is the test of us.' She sounded elated. 'Of her too,' she added. 'Madeleine.'

'I can't see that she comes into this except as the – victim of it. She wasn't responsible.'

'Oh, Rickie, "victim" – "fault"! I never did believe in victims, unless they choose the rôle.' With what cold certainty she burned; with what contempt for weakness. 'She told you, didn't she, she'd known it all along? Why didn't she face it?'

'Perhaps that was her way of facing it.'

She drew a little away from him, as if total communication had been partly severed; but after a pause, said in the same quiet confident tone: 'No. That *is* one way. It would have been Mother's, for instance' – she faintly smiled – 'she's clear, she's real in her own peculiar way, she takes up a stand. But not Madeleine. She's not real, not about you or the children or anything – never has been. She plays everybody up, she gets by. Don't think I'm censorious. She doesn't mean to.

In some ways she's so wonderful; it's right to love her – when I say right I mean – inevitable. She'll always be loved, I know I won't be. In fact I shall always love her, she'll always hate me. She hated me when you and she were engaged; after you were married, when she was always asking me to stay, she hated me even more.'

'No. More likely feared you,' he interposed.

'Hate – fear, they're the same. She knew I knew.'

'Knew what?'

'Oh, I've told you all this before. That she was running away – cheating. That she didn't love you.'

'Oh, I think she did,' he protested mildly. 'We were very much in love, weren't we? In a beglamoured bemused sort of youthful way?'

'She shouldn't have married you,' said Dinah with finality. 'And she knew it. And she always wanted me to prove to her that she shouldn't have – or should have. Well, I did. I hope she won't cheat her way out of this now.'

'Ah well,' he said, getting up and stretching. 'It hardly becomes me, I feel, to tell her I'm offering her the chance of her finest hour.'

She got up too and stood in the middle of the room with her arms folded, her eyes fixed, ruminating. Finally she said:

'Shall I go and see her? Shall I come with you now?'

'No!' he said quickly, in horror. 'At least – no. I don't think it would be at all a good idea.'

'I think I should. However, if you feel so strongly ... Do you think she'll see Corrigan?'

'No,' he said, again in horror. 'She wouldn't dream of it, I'm sure.' He added grimly: 'I'll see there's no question of *that*, anyway.'

'I agree with you, she wouldn't want to.' She took a breath and said, her voice shaken for the first time: 'There's one thing I would hate her to know about. Last February. The baby.'

'Never,' he said passionately. 'Never, never. I promise.'

She turned slowly on her heel and stared out of the window saying as if to herself: 'Or has she really known it all the time?'

'I must go,' he said. He came and took her in his arms.

'Yes, I suppose you must.' She sighed. 'I hope all will be well.'

'I hope so.'

'When will you come back?'

'I don't know. I can't tell.'

'Will you telephone?'

'Yes, I'll telephone.'

'When?'

'Tomorrow. Some time tomorrow. I can't say when. It depends.'

They looked into each other's eyes; but what, if anything, they saw they could-not read. They managed to smile at one another.

'Ah!' he said. 'You're terrible. I love you. Whatever happens, you'll always be the only person I could ever tell the truth with.'

He kissed her with all of the truth, whatever truth was, upon his lips. He was gone.

She looked at the clock and saw that it was only ten o'clock. Hours and hours of night to be got through. She watched herself take off the telephone receiver, undress, get into bed, reach for a book, open it, light a cigarette, start composedly to read. After a time she put the book down and heard herself say clearly: 'This is the end.' Make it so, once and for all. Pull up the anchor, set forth once more, transparent yet solid, to the ocean. It was best so. Put away those wretched years: nothing but wear and tear, concealment, lies, suspicion; only half a person. Now I can be true only to myself again. Leave them to clean up the mess – or not: I wash my hands of it.

She felt calm. 'Calm as the blessed saints above,' she said aloud: a nursery phrase, one of old Nannie's, incorporated long ago among the family tags.

Where was he now? What was now being unfolded, brought to light, only a mile or so out of earshot? What betrayals was he preparing? – sanctioning? When would he telephone? Would he?

The usual clocks struck the night hours. One after another the hours stalked by.

He stood in front of his house and scanned the windows. No light on the ground floor, but a glow in her bedroom curtains. He went in, went up, opened her door. She was lying in bed, flushed, haggard, and when she saw him she held out her arms, saying brokenly:

'I thought you might never come back.'

Murmuring: 'I had to come,' he went and flung himself down on his knees by her side. Nothing could have touched him more than such a greeting. In a moment he was all at sea again; the raft – not his construction – he had got his balance on as he came from the other one crumbled beneath, around him in jagged spars and broken ropes. He was all at sea but he was flung a lifeline. He held it, let it go in revolt and in despair when she sobbed for her outraged heart and flayed him for his crimes and Dinah's; clutched it again, somehow, in despair, when she forgave him, asked forgiveness, appealed in the name of home and children, for help in a fresh start. It did not draw him in: it held him floating, swinging, helpless; it held him – saved? or done for?

In the end, completely exhausted, they agreed that they must try and get some sleep. He dropped a kiss on her hand and went away to his dressing-room; she turned over on her pillows and sank into unconsciousness. Undressing, he told himself dimly that this generosity she'd shown, this humility ... as impossible to counterfeit as to reject. He was not a stick or a stone. It was *real*, whatever Dinah ... He was grateful, touched; grateful – oh God! – to both of them, but just at this moment touched, heartwrung, by one alone. The other was strong, clear, stoical, disinterested, an alarming elevating influence; this one petty, proud, yielding, generous, sensible, silly, open, dishonest, kindly, cruel ... everything. Shamelessly human, natural. Yes, she was pretty awful taking it by and large, but somehow it seemed more *natural*. '*I'm* bloody awful,' he muttered, drunk with fatigue. It struck him that they had not mentioned the word love. Was that natural? Yes, it was. Not a word to use ... 'in such rumbustical circumstances,' he said, half aloud again, falling into bed. His senses, numbed, released him till on the very edge of sleep one sound returned to pierce him for a moment: a telephone bell shrilling, shrilling in the room he'd fled from. That had been Madeleine terrified, she told him, imploring him to come at once. The sound sank with him, deeper than his consciousness: symbol of defeat, capitulation; of a man in flight, of a man caught.

Next day, feeling wretched, he took a holiday from the office and motored with Madeleine into the country. They took the children too, and a picnic lunch, hired a punt at Cookham and spent a peaceful afternoon on the river, under Clivedon woods. It was – how long? – years since they had gone out all together as a family unit, for a treat, a Happy Day. He was a jolly paterfamilias, teaching Anthony to wield a paddle, lifting Colin on his shoulder in the lock to watch the keeper close the sluice gates. He and their mother rested in a place they had almost ignored for ages, or forgotten about – the place where they could exchange looks, winks, smiles parental, co-operative, above the children's heads. The little fellows had never seemed to him more attractive; pathetic too, so innocent and vulnerable. He could be proud, and he was, of their sturdy, handsome looks. He was charmed, too, by Madeleine's youthful yet maternal bearing. What a girl she was still! He was conscious again today of the primitive thing in her which had moved him the first time he ever saw her: the something wild, threatened, at once warm and cold, laughter-loving, melancholy, helpless and protective; not a mysterious nature exactly, but one for ever disturbed, in flux. Past, present and future were all poignant to him as he watched her lying in the bottom of the punt with her eyes closed and a smile playing on her tired but peaceful face, patiently answering the children and letting them clamber over her. All this was what had been so long, so blindly, wantonly jeopardized ... Was still in jeopardy? ... No doubt.

At intervals the thought of Dinah rose black and churning, choking him like a wave of nausea. Once or twice an image of her of his own projection burst upon his sight: she was lying flat on her bed, her hands crossed on her breast above the sheet, her face, severe, impassive, turned towards the wall ... More disgusted looking than severe, more beaten than impassive. He was sick of seeing women lying in despair upon their beds. He had not telephoned to her.

What was she likely to be doing? Could that repudiating profile be a prophetic vision? Had she decided to hand him once and for all his ticket? If so, was he relieved or – frightened? He must ring her up this evening somehow, because he'd promised to. How could he, without starting another row with Madeleine? He had promised her not to leave her today. Man of his word to both of them – it was farcical. What the hell did they expect? The whole business made him feel so utterly dead beat that he could only yearn to go off alone somewhere for ever and ever ... Well, anyway, for a bit.

This was in fact what he did. Lucky as usual, he scarcely had to work for his reprieve: within a few days it was handed to him. Perhaps Madeleine had been more active than appeared; he never asked, she never told him; only, when he announced the news, received it with unselfish enthusiasm. The uncles ordered him to Italy and Rumania for a month, on business for the firm.

He did not ring up Dinah as he had promised – neither that day nor any subsequent day. On the following Saturday his conscience goading him to do what most he dreaded and avoided, namely to visit his mother, he went down by himself to Norfolk. Home; the soil and landscape and architecture of his ancestors. None of it remaining in the family now, except for the small Jacobean dower house which he had withdrawn from the market, furnished and given to his mother when he had sold his heritage. Here, along with two ageing retainers from the former staff, she continued piously, rheumatically to fade, fret, potter. From his bedroom window he could see the Park, and, through known tree-tops, the clock tower above the stable courtyard; could hear and name the cries of waterfowl haunting the unforgotten sedges, shallows, deeps of his lost lake. And his mother, once oiled and barbed with ostentatious unreproach, had become merely garrulous, pathetic, grateful for his company. The whole thing was painful to the point of trauma. From thence he wrote to Dinah a brief note saying he felt it best not to see her till he was less utterly befogged and shattered; that he thought about her practically the whole time and would write again as soon as he could. No more time now before post. On the Tuesday after this week-end as he was hurrying round the corner from the office in the lunch hour, she suddenly appeared from nowhere on the pavement beside him. This gave him a terrible turn. She said she was hungry and wanted a good lunch, and fitting her step to his swung along with him, shoulder to shoulder. She was even paler, but more animated, than usual; also she looked in her subdued way more chic, more delicately wrought than ever, in the kind of plain black figure-moulding frock that exactly suited his taste in women's clothes. He congratulated her on it and asked if it was new. She said yes, off the peg in Kensington High Street, defurbished and remodelled by herself. They discussed where they should eat and settled on a small French restaurant in Soho; they hailed a taxi and drove to it. It was a long but not an awkward drive; they might have parted only yesterday upon the usual terms. She kept the conversation going on a light level, half impersonal, half intimate. He prayed not to see anyone he knew in the restaurant, and his prayer was granted. He asked her what she had been doing and she answered, oh, going out a good deal with various friends, going dancing in the coloured night club, thoroughly enjoying herself. Her energy, she said, had all come back at last. 'You look remarkably well,' he said rather stiffly, considering with distaste the night club and the kind of types likely to take her dancing there. He thought of saying he'd telephoned several times and got no answer, but decided better not risk the lie. He told her he had got fixed up yesterday to go abroad and had been about to write and let her know.

She was silent then. Her whole face became suffused with that dusky flush it had shocked him to observe the other night. Madeleine blushed easily, brilliantly; Dinah like this, and almost never.

'When?' she said.

'In a few days' time ... actually.'

She sat staring at the tablecloth, breaking up toast with a hand that trembled. Part of him fled; part of him remarked with satisfaction that he had called her bluff. The silence prolonged itself while they swallowed chicken *à la King* and gulped *vin rosé*.

'Whose turn was it to speak?' she said at last, looking at him in what seemed to him a slightly dotty way, with a squint.

He said he thought he had better be getting back to the office.

'You were going abroad,' she said, 'without letting me know. Or perhaps a little scrawl was going to reach me the morning after your departure.'

He denied this curtly, coldly.

'Don't lie to me,' she said, blowing out a long trail of cigarette smoke.

He got up violently; then hesitated.

'I'm afraid,' she said bright and brisk, 'I haven't enough money on me to pay the bill'; and he sat down again, observed with curiosity by Madame at the desk.

'I told you,' he muttered, 'it would be a mistake to meet. At present.'

'It isn't a mistake.' She lit another cigarette from the stub in her hand. 'Come and see me tonight. We can't talk here. Please.'

He was silent; and presently she said: 'If you don't come to me I shall come to you. To your house.'

'No.'

'You wouldn't admit me?'

'Oh ... I couldn't prevent your being admitted. But I wouldn't be there.' He signed to the waiter to bring the bill.

She said in a quiet distinct voice: 'Then if neither the one nor the other, I shall end my life.'

He rounded on her fiercely, dumb.

'Blackmail?' she said, raising her eyebrows. 'I see how it must strike you. I apologize, but I can't help it. I do mean it – I thought I ought to tell you frankly. You see I'm quite calm, don't you? I'm not an *hystérique*. This is a thought-out thing.'

'That makes it sensible, I suppose,' he said with cold contempt. 'And helpful. And splendid and courageous. *You've* thought it out, so of course it must be. Right! It will solve everything.'

After a long pause she said softly, as if with relief:

'When you talk like that I know you're still you. It's this stone wall ... Why are you afraid of me? I didn't dream you would leave me like this in outer darkness. I'm in this too, aren't I? – up to the neck. You can't just – go to earth as if I didn't exist. Or present me, some time or other, at your own discretion, with a *fait accompli*. What's to happen must be *my* choice, *my* responsibility as well as yours. And Madeleine's,' she added.

He said obstinately, sweeping breadcrumbs off the table into this hand and pouring them on to a plate: 'I don't see it like that.'

'If you deny me my share of responsibility you deny me the basis of my life.'

'I don't follow,' he said. 'However ... I'll come.' It ... knew, said graciously.

'What time?'

'As soon as I can get away. Six at the latest. I'm afraid I shan't be able to stay long.'

Her face contracted; she said quickly: 'I haven't asked you to.' But a moment after she looked at him with her broad melancholy humorous smile and said: 'Darling, don't look so sulky and distraught. It's quite all right. I promise you it will be painless.'

'Ah ... That's as may be,' he said, and had to smile himself.

'Now, please, if you've time, may I have a brandy?'

He ordered two *fines*, and while they sipped them she exercised her wit to entertain him. She even made him laugh; he had not laughed, no, nor come anywhere near laughter for a week. Once she caught his gaze fixed on her in sheer bewilderment and stopped short in mid sentence, her eyebrows up. He shook his head and looked away. He couldn't tell her ... Here they were sitting together in one of their old haunts, their hands touching, their voices caressing one another, everything solid, customary, following out its continuity; and at the same time all this *had ceased to have a real existence*. They were shadows, ghosts. It was all in the past, all over. He had stared at her bewildered, wondering why she, so sharp of sight, so hard to hoodwink, should be sitting blindfold opposite to him. She was his clear eyes, yet she did not see what he saw. Which of them was mad?

He put a call through to Madeleine in the afternoon and told her he would be a bit late home: he had just discovered that his passport had expired and he had to get it along urgently to a chap he knew in the Foreign Office who had promised to expedite its renewal. Truth and falsehood. This, he told himself as he put down the receiver, was the last f— lie he'd ever tell her or anyone. From now on, open book if not clean sheet. Dinah could argue her head off: he had made up his mind to be resolute and say good-bye to her for ever. Lingering on in the office till the clock struck six, he read the evening paper from cover to cover. He was going to cut this interview as fine as possible: no point whatsoever in prolonging the agony.

When he arrived he found her in a curious frame of mind, feverish and inattentive, garrulous, side-stepping the straight approach he had rehearsed. He wondered if she had been drinking, and when he saw her put back a double gin neat, and then another, he was sure of it. He loathed hard-drinking women and well she knew it. For the last two years and more, since their relationship had become, in its hidden, exposed, its ever-threatened way a total thing, a rock – no, no, a *stake*, oh, a stake driven into their hearts – she had led a regular domesticated life, away from her disreputable pub-crawling companions ... apart of course from Corrigan. But to give her her due, the old bag wasn't a drunk. He had been tempted to wonder once or twice whether, in the end, he would find himself according that sordid double-crosser a bitter gratitude.

He drank the martini she mixed for him, but when she took up the gin again he sharply refused. Her face set stubbornly; she tilted the bottle towards her own glass and filled it; he snatched it from her hand, strode to the kitchen and poured it down the sink; strode back and came to stand over her, breathing hard.

'Now give me another,' she said.

'You've had enough.'

She laughed. He looked at her. Something in her expression – something insolent, malevolent – snapped his last thread of self-control. He took a grip on her arm, above the elbow, and shook and shook and shook her. When he let go she stared at him, a heavy unblinking stare – reptilian, he thought – then suddenly slapped his face. The blow was a well-aimed stinger, and the pain of it shocked him into a sort of calm. She saw that his eyes rested on her with an electric glint ... His mouth, not made for grimness, remained grim. She felt a stupefied, fatuous admiration for them both. *Crack*, like a pistol shot, plumb on the jaw, the brute, it must have stung, he hadn't winced ... Hollywood trailer – Throbbing, Searing, Sensational, Dynamic! At one foggy remove from the dramatic action, she saw her head sink before the dangerous expression in his eyes. She started slowly to roll her sleeve back and exposed her wounds. When he saw the five marks of his fingers standing out dark already on her thin white arm he took a sharp breath.

'You hurt me,' she said; and after a pause: 'I'm sorry.' She buried her face in her hands.

He turned away and began to pace up and down again.

'Sorry?' he burst out. 'Sorry? Sorry? What have *you* got to be sorry about? *You*'ve nothing to reproach yourself with.'

'I got drunk. I thought you weren't going to come. I'm sorry.'

'I hate you drinking, I hate it. You know I hate it.' He approached her with remorse yet with reluctance and put an arm round her. 'Don't do it, darling. Don't. Don't.'

She flung her arms round his neck and kissed him passionately. Her lips were salty, gin-tainted, burning, and the tears pouring out of her closed eyes scalded his cheek. He drew away in uncontrollable distaste, wiped his face and handed her his big silk handkerchief.

'I must go,' he said. He was sick to death of the sound of these three crass monosyllables which he seemed always to be reiterating.

She sat down, holding the handkerchief, and said feebly: 'I wanted you to stay.' Then: 'I've got a headache.'

'Do you want some aspirin? Shall I get you some? Where is it?'

She shook her head, whimpering faintly.

He had never seen her like this. It reminded him of his mother, of Madeleine, of every female association from which he had hitherto dissociated her. At one fell stroke she seemed to have lost her essential difference from all others ...

'You'd better go to bed,' he said coldly, sharply.

'I won't go to bed. Unless you stay with me.'

'I can't stay, Dinah. I told you so.'

'I want to talk to you. I've got some things I must say to you.'

'I think you'd better not say them now. Another time.'

She lifted her head, opened huge vacant eyes and stared at him.

'When are you going?'

'I'm not sure,' he said lying. 'I shan't know for certain till tomorrow. But in a day or so. There's a hell of a lot to see to before I go.'

'How long?'

'I'm not sure. Not long. About three weeks – a month, perhaps.'

He waited a moment and nothing more was said. Well then, this was good-bye – not according to plan. He couldn't say it. He said: 'I'll write to you.'

He stooped to take his handkerchief gently away from her; and to kiss her cheek.

'Please take care of yourself,' he said. 'Promise me ... Will you? Promise me not to ...'

Still nothing more was said. He went away.

That evening after a quiet domestic dinner spent in discussing plans for the summer holidays, he told Madeleine that he had seen Dinah. He said it quite calmly, sitting in his armchair, throwing aside the evening paper; and she, looking up from the *petit point* stool cover she was embroidering, received the news with perfect calm. He said, with truth, that he had not sought out Dinah, that she had waylaid him outside the office and insisted on an interview. He passed over in silence the matter of the lunch.

'So I went,' he said. 'I didn't go to see a chap about my passport. I went round to see her.'

'How was she?' asked Madeleine, sorting strands of wool.

'Oh, not exactly ...' He shrugged his shoulders, not attempting to disguise his wretchedness. 'As you can imagine.'

'No, I can't imagine,' said Madeleine in a thoughtful drawl. 'I've decided not to go in for that any more – I mean, imagining probable aspects of this situation. One doesn't want to go off one's head. If you were in my place you might see the point.'

'Oh, very possibly,' he said with courteous restraint. 'If I were in your place I could dispense with imagining *one* aspect of the situation, couldn't I? I'd know. I don't say I would succeed, like you, in eliminating every probable aspect. Yet one doesn't, as you say, want to go off one's head.'

She threaded a needle in silence; then said in a practical voice: 'I rather wish you hadn't – felt you must agree to go and see her. But perhaps – probably – you wanted to. How should I know? That's your own affair, I suppose. What did she want to see you about?'

'I don't know.'

She raised her head from the work and sent him a look he did not meet but was aware of. He said:

'I didn't discover. She was in no fit state – it wasn't any use. So I came away – as you were able to see for yourself.'

'What do you mean, in no fit state?' He did not reply, and she added: 'Upset? Drunk?'

Overcoming an inner spasm, after a moment he nodded.

'I see. She's difficult when she's drunk. Argumentative – truculent rather.' He slightly shook his head. 'Or at another stage,' she continued, maintaining the practical level, 'low in her spirits. Tearful.'

'I expect you're right,' he said, polite. 'I haven't had much opportunity myself of observing these various stages. I happen not to have seen Dinah the worse for drink – that is, not what you'd call absolutely inebriated.'

'You *know* she drinks like a fish.'

Raw, coarse, the words escaped, and hung between them offensive, ponderous as a hanged body. He got up in a leisurely way, stretched, his gaze travelling round with the look of one vaguely noting and dismissing objects before leaving a room – perhaps for ever.

'Rickie!' She found herself on her feet, confronting his inert figure and dead eyes. 'Are you ill? Do you feel it?' She reached for his hand and felt it cold and clammy. He drew it away.

'No.'

'Sit down.'

He did not mean to obey her, but found himself dropping heavily back, without volition, into his armchair. He was taking a stiff whisky from her and thanking her and hearing her say gently: 'There, drink that, darling. Lie back. You're tired, that's all.'

'I'm all right – except I'm in a muck sweat. I'll have a shower.'

'Presently.'

She was kind, she was quiet, she was in charge. He focused his eyes on her and saw her at first through an effect of blurred vision, then distinctly, sitting in her usual place opposite to him, her elbows propped on her knees and her chin on her palms, leaning forward to scrutinize him with an expression of authoritative solicitude; a beautiful, kind woman, at once familiar and a stranger. They smiled at one another. She said:

'You looked such an awful colour, I thought you were going to pass out.'

He shook his head; but he felt thoroughly weakened, helpless, he wanted only sympathy and guidance. He wanted to say: 'For God's sake, take over, I don't know what to do'; and so finally collapse in a last expenditure of shame and frustration.

Next moment he said it, almost under his breath: 'I don't know what to do.' He felt his face working and heard convulsive sighs emanating from his own aching throat; also a voice from nowhere, from the pit, icily shrill, rejoicing: '*I say, you chaps! – here's Masters blubbing again.*'

He was grateful to her because she did not come maternally to draw his head down on her breast, but went on sitting, half turned away, in a familiar attitude again, her immature, imperfect, charming profile unconscious of itself in deep reflection, drawn down into a schoolgirl's double chin.

'Listen, Rickie,' she said presently. 'Wash out the bitchy things I said. I'm sorry.'

'*You*'ve nothing to be sorry for,' he said: to this one too.

'Yes, I have. And I am. You're terribly worried about her?'

'Yes. Oh yes. But there's nothing I can do about her.' He sat up and blew his nose.

'She's really in a bad way?'

'I think so.'

'You're afraid she'll take to the bottle again?'

The statement, clinical, made without an edge of diffidence or even of query, caused him another surge of suffocation, this time quickly suppressed. It seemed to him in everybody's interest to surrender Dinah's pride.

'I don't know that I'd exactly pin it down to that,' he said, uncomfortably. 'She *had* been drinking this evening and judging by . . . the state of the kitchen . . .'

'What was the state of the kitchen?' Her head came round, she looked across at him with lively curiosity.

'Well . . . quite a number of empty bottles . . . I should be inclined to think – yesterday and the day before and the day before as well . . . and probably tomorrow and the day after . . . How should I know? It's not my business anyway – it's nobody's business how she . . . But of course it was painful. To have my nose rubbed in it. What I am responsible for. On top of everything else, I mean.'

She took up her work again and said after a moment or two, in a considered way: 'You shouldn't feel too responsible. Some people always do drink their way through trouble. I couldn't myself, nor could you, but as she's done it before, I suppose she's that sort of person: she'll do it again. She stopped before. She'll very very probably stop again. But it is upsetting.' She laid down her work, brooding. 'Horrid altogether. And awful for you, I do see.'

'Christ!' He burst into a laugh and checked it, telling himself that to counter with bitterness and sarcasm would be to start the vicious duel again. 'That's not the point, is it – my lacerated feelings? Hers seem to me a lot more important. I can't subscribe, you know, to this simplified view. Apart from which, I call it taking on a pretty big responsibility to label anybody a drunk.'

'I don't,' she protested quickly, as if a little hurt and shocked. 'On the contrary, I said I thought – this was only temporary. She's very resilient.'

He was moved to remark aloud upon the similarity of the comments these girls made about one another; he refrained. He said rather shortly:

'I misunderstood you, then. I'm glad we've cleared that up.'

He wondered if perhaps there was now nothing more to say. He put his arms out along the arms of the chair, leaned his head back, closed his eyes and said:

'She's drinking because she's alone and because she's in despair. If she did it before, you know, and I know, that was why she did it. You know why she stopped: because I stopped her. Not forcibly, of course. Because she stopped being alone. And because I was able to make her happy. We don't need to go into how – everlastingly regrettable that was on my part. Not again. What's bothering me is that I can't stop her this time ... As for you, I don't know what's going on in your head. I can't imagine. You're behaving very well, I must say.'

The more he talked, the more the drone of his own voice seemed to anaesthetize him. He might, he thought, have gone on much longer, but on the other hand it was a bit less trouble not to go on any longer. He continued to lie somnolent, every muscle slack, his mouth fallen slightly open. It crossed his mind that if he could remain thus, he was in a very strong position – yes, scoring proper bull's-eyes, like a person coming round from chloroform. No use for the nurse to bridle, flounce, scold, weep, coax, cross-examine: he was entirely excused; she simply had to take it.

'Shall I go and see her?' said her voice, at last, from afar; and he replied, at last, from an equal distance:

'Would that be a good idea?'

'Goodness knows.' He heard her get up and rustle about, brushing, smothing, tucking in chair covers, emptying an ash-tray with brusque-sounding movements. 'But you wouldn't object?'

'It's not for me to object.'

'Oh, do shut up saying it's not for you to this and that. I'm fed up with it, it's so feeble and priggish. I merely wanted to make sure I don't get bawled out by either of you afterwards for my utterly crass, gross, tasteless, tactless, beastly cheek – just like me – even to suggest such a thing.'

'I can't answer for her,' he said, opening one eye. He watched her snatch up a harmless cushion, beat it into shape, fling it back into its correct position. 'She might not trust you – beforehand ... as I do.'

He saw her pause in her brisk automatic tasks, standing still with her head lifted as if listening attentively for the meaning of his last words.

'Well, she ought to trust me,' she said finally, rather aggrieved. 'After all, we've known each other since ...' She shrugged her shoulders. 'But I'm glad you do,' she added with a light sigh, sardonic possibly.

'What will you do?' he murmured.

'Do?'

'Say. If – when – you meet.'

'*That* I shall never tell you.' He opened both eyes wide to see her posed before the fireplace, drawn up to more than her full height, looking extraordinarily dignified, dramatic. 'And I must ask you now to give me your solemn word never, never to question me.'

'I swear it.' Sitting as it were at her feet in his armchair, he felt at a disadvantage.

'And I must rely on you never, never, *never* to question her.'

'You can rely on me.'

'It's the first thing I shall tell her – if I see her: that you've given me your word. And she must too. That's my condition: it's to be between myself and her, and nobody else.'

He tried to imagine Dinah thus confronted. Would she feel, as he did, impressed, abashed and hypnotized?

'Why are you shaking your head?' asked Madeleine, rather sharply.

'I didn't know I was.' He sat up, yawned. 'It must have been reflex action. Something – what is it? – walking over my grave.'

'It is fantastic,' she agreed, rubbing her eyes. 'Perhaps I'm still numb. Or dotty. If I let myself think about it I'd ...' She stooped and began to gather up her work and fold it into a large quilted bag. 'Mind you, I haven't decided yet if I'll do it at all. If I can possibly face it – apart from whether it's any use.' She switched off the lamp on the table by her chair. 'But *some*body's got to take action, I suppose. We can't sit at home making wax figures and sticking pins in them and burning each other in effigy. With you scurrying between us to collect the drips.'

He did not care for his rôle. He got up and said politely:

'Well, I'm going to bed now. And I'm extremely grateful.'

He dragged his heavy limbs upstairs, telling himself that women were formidable, really relentless; not a nerve in their bodies.

He fell asleep at once and dreamed that he was bouncing two hard rubber balls on the asphalt floor of something like a school games yard, watched by his mother and somebody like Corrigan. Bounce, bounce, higher, higher! 'Look out!' 'It's quite all right,' said he, or someone, reassuringly. 'They're made of elastic. Very, very, very resilient.'

The floor began to crack and tilt.

Two days later he went abroad. During this time Madeleine remained active, serene and wifely. The children were round him while he shaved and dressed, and both evenings were devoted to pleasant social engagements in the company of friends of their mutual circle. Looking beautiful, her brilliance misted in an aërial web swathed over a small white straw hat with two white roses nestling in its brim, she accompanied him to the airport to see him off. He went first to Milan, then to Rome, then to Bucharest. He was a poor correspondent, but he wrote regularly to Madeleine – sketchy travel bulletins; her letters, long, affectionate, amusing, arrived regularly at every address he wired to her. She said she missed him; he told her in reply that he often wished her with him; but wherever he went, whatever he saw, it was Dinah that he missed. Five, six times he started the letter to Dinah, the final true terrible letter of love, the ineluctable farewell; each time he tore it up.

After three weeks, on his way back through Rome, he looked up a certain Italian count, a light-hearted chap, who had been his contemporary at Oxford, went dining and dancing, was introduced to a rather attractive woman, youngish, married but husbandless, *plantureuse*, unromantic but amorous, and to their great mutual pleasure spent the night with her in her luxurious apartment. Unfaithful at last to Dinah after all these years. Next morning, in a generally unadhering frame of mind, he got a short note off to her, told her he thought of her very often, sadly and helplessly, hoped she was getting out and seeing people, feeling better in every way; wished to God there was something he could do for her. He supposed he'd be back, he said, before very long: he couldn't help dreading London and the dismal grind. With his love always, Rickie. Then he scrawled a postscript: if there was anything he could do, anything practical, would she promise to let him know? But they could not meet, she *must* see that by now, as plainly as he did. He could never forgive himself but clung to the hope that one day, looking back on it all, she would remember only their love which was something he would never forget and be able to forgive him. His greatest wish was for her happiness.

That was that, he told himself, dropping it into the letter-box; pretty poor, but the best he could manage. Occasionally, during the forty-eight ensuing hours before he caught the home-bound plane, he reflected that he would try for the present to get abroad as often as possible. He had made excellent contacts, brought off three deals with which he had been entrusted: the uncles would certainly be pleased with him. More than once he considered ringing up his Italian bed-fellow to make another date. He did not do so. In retrospect she talked too much and he found her tuberose scent, still clinging to his suit, rather cloying and sickly. He sent her a box of red carnations. He told himself that in future, while seeking no amorous adventure, he would take whatever came along. Nothing, oh nothing on the grand scale, nothing ever any more to shame and torture. He would do his duty by Madeleine, poor girl, and by the children. He longed to be old and past the game that no one ever won. He was tempted to wish that he was fitted to become a monk.

On his return, Madeleine greeted him with the news that they were moving into her old country home near Reading for the summer. Her father had been ordered a long sea voyage to ward off a threatened physical breakdown, and, with her mother, had embarked for South Africa. He was sorry about his father-in-law, of whom he was fond, and whose reminiscences, as a retired K.C. and excellent *raconteur*, he enjoyed; but he quite saw what made a temporary move from London so opportune; and he accepted her dispositions in a spirit of passivity tinged with glum relief.

That summer was a fine one and he quite relished motoring out of town each evening, bringing a friend or two at week-ends, sitting and strolling late in the warm shrubby thrush-chiming garden. He felt it incumbent on him to resume what he understood to be known as a full married life with Madeleine, and they made panicky approaches to one another; but it was a failure. The twitch in his leg was as troublesome as ever, and he retreated with feelings of thankfulness and embarrassment to his dressing-room, out of range of the tears which Madeleine attempted both to bring to his notice and to conceal from him. This frightful awkwardness which had started really after the birth of Anthony seemed past mending. Humiliating for her, equally so for him. Bad for their nerves. Perhaps in time it would come right ... unless he were to become completely impotent. His thoughts travelled to Dinah, and two or three times she was his partner in erotic dreams.

This state of affairs continued for several weeks during which there was no letter from Dinah, no word of her on anybody's lips, no telephone call, no dreaded hoped-for shock of meeting her round any corner. Then came help from the hills, the invisible hills towards which his prisoned gaze had long been strained. A cable to Madeleine from South Africa: *Father dangerously ill*. She cabled back to say she would start at once by air. Within forty-eight hours she was on her way.

The evening before her departure she remarked: 'I was told to inform everybody. I haven't informed everybody.'

He inquired nervously if she wished him to attend to this, and she replied that she didn't give a damn one way or the other. 'I expect,' she added, 'she'll be turning up anyway, the moment my back is turned.'

'No,' he said quickly, vehemently.

She went on to say that this summer had been a complete and hideous fiasco, that he could not have shown more plainly his boredom and distaste for her, that all her efforts – her patience, her cheerful front, her willingness to forgive – had gone for nothing. Then she checked herself and declared that by this time Papa was probably lying dead and here she was worrying about their squalid personal lives instead of thinking about Papa. Here goes again, he told himself, observing the tears course down her cheeks; and offering a shoulder, did his best to comfort her.

All solicitude and practical attentions, he drove her to the airport. On the way she asked him to get out of London as early as possible each evening, so that the children should see him before bedtime. He promised. She smiled, pathetic, wan, and said:

'I don't ask you for any other promises.'

'You don't need to,' he replied in all sincerity.

'And by the way I rang up Aunt Lilian, of course, the day the cable came, and asked her to pass on the news to Dinah.'

'Oh, you did.'

'Well, naturally. After all, it's Papa – I'm not the only duaghter. I asked her to help by taking on the job of telling all the relations. Of course she was delighted.'

'Of course.'

'I said I'd cable to her as well as to you, and she'd better go on keeping *everybody* posted.'

'I see. Then I'll leave it all to her.'

'By now, if Papa's alive, he'll know I'm coming. I wonder if it could possibly make just that particle of difference – as they say it does in books ...'

'Easily darling, it might. It'll help him hold on. You know how he adores you.'

'Yes. I'm his spoilt favourite child ... Whom would you want to send for if you were dying?'

'Sh!' He took his hand off the driving wheel, caught hers and gripped it hard, in tender repudiation and reproach.

This time it was he who stood at the barrier watching her walk away from him towards the giant blunt-snouted bull with wings. When she turned back finally to wave and smile at him he felt extremely moved; and when her first cable came saying *Arrived safely Papa definitely better*, his relief was enormous. Her airmail letter gave him details. Now that anxiety was over, she was thoroughly enjoying herself, staying on her brother's farm, riding, and doing tremendous motor expeditions. She expected to sail for home with her parents in three weeks' time: this meant that late September would see her home.

Late August, the dog days, the fag end of the stale season, brought him the next help. The door to a sealed room, long airless, rank with the sour undissipated odours of fumigation – that door cracked, shook, swung ajar. He advanced, reluctant, unresisting; transparent, clotted.

It was Corrigan again, Corrigan (Elaine) to the rescue. When he got the appalling letter he told himself beware! – it was only another trap. He discerned, without words for what was evident, the pyramiding guilt, the false atonement; he saw the track, serpentining back again to him, by which the tricky jungle runner, ignored by Madeleine, had run again with hot confidential news.

She dared no longer keep him uninformed, announced that thick backward-leaning script; no doubt he thought of her harshly, cursed her in his heart perhaps: this was her cross and she must bear it. She had done all for the best, as she saw it, without thought of self, and would continue so to do. Three weeks ago Dinah had turned up at her door dead drunk. She had taken her in, nursed her, kept her from the bottle and her drinking companions. (A memory rigidly suppressed now stabbed him sharply: Madeleine, that evening before she left, hysteria climbing in her: 'As for – if you think – if you only ...' then with a gasp stopping, biting on a finger as if to bite back ... well, he'd guessed what: almost, the curtain had been stripped back; the Scene with Two Fingers, never to be revealed, revealed.) She had seemed better, the letter went on to say; but suddenly, a few nights ago, a terrible thing had happened: Dinah had discovered where she, Corrigan, hid the tablets some doctor – a personal friend, it seemed – had prescribed her for insomnia, taken them secretly from the drawer and swallowed the whole bottleful. She had been rushed in the nick of time to hospital ... she would spare him a medical account. With the utmost difficulty, the authorities had been dissuaded from informing her next-of-kin: she, Corrigan, had invented a plausible story and managed to put it across. Yesterday Dinah was discharged, was now in her house, in bed, had given her solemn promise; but had lost, her friend felt, the will to live; had said quietly this morning that if only she could see Rickie her mind would be at rest. Therefore, would he in his goodness come as soon as possible?

So he rang up Corrigan and told her, briefly, that he would be along that evening. He came along, and she opened the door to him; he saw again without one glance at her the overpowering bosom, the buttocks in dirty slacks, the caramel eyes rapacious, cringing on him, waiting to reassume control of his emotions. He heard her give one of her great windy sighs and felt her about to lay a strong comradely hand upon his shoulder. He said, looking over her head:

'How is she?' and was conscious of her pause for readjustment before she answered with imitative curtness:

'Expecting you. Be careful, won't you? She's still sedated – mildly of course.'

'On whose instructions?'

'The doctor's,' she said, haughtily; adding: 'I haven't left her day or night.'

'Well, leave us now,' he said.

She stumped ahead of him, opened a door at the end of the passage, said softly, brightly: 'Dearie, here's your visitor,' and carefully shutting the door, withdrew.

He did not know what he had most feared to be confronted with: white waif, prostrate, in effigy, after the style of the death mask of the drowned girl of the Seine which a man he'd known at Oxford had had laid out on a black velvet catafalque on top of his bookcase; or worse, a piece of rubbish thrown away, unrecognizable, abject. He did not expect what in fact he saw: a dear little soul with freshly combed hair sitting up in bed in a striped silk pyjama jacket, listening to a dance band on a portable wireless. This she switched off, then held out loving arms, smiling in joyful welcome. He went and gathered her to him, lost in another surge of tenderness, remorse and gratitude. He kissed her cheeks and lips, and begged her not to cry, and drew up a chair and wiped his own wet eyes. She said:

'I'm glad you've come. I've missed you horribly.'

'Don't you suppose I've missed *you*?'

'Don't let's talk about what's happened.'

'No, *no*.'

'I was crazy. You needn't be afraid – I'll never do it again.' Comically grimacing, pointing towards the door, she said in a stage whisper: 'Might she be listening?'

They waited, ears pricked. He shook his head, murmuring grimly:

'I think I settled her hash.'

'Were you distant?'

'Very.'

In a moment they heard the front door bang, and she leaned back, and said: 'She's gone out – she promised she would. You'll stop, won't you, till she comes back? I'm all right, but when I think I'm alone in the house I get claustrophobia.'

She held out a hand and he folded it in both of his, telling himself that it would be unwise in the extreme to say that he had promised to take Anthony fishing before supper.

'The poor old cow,' she remarked with a sigh. 'I've given her a pasting. She's been incredible – marvellous to me. I'm grateful. It's hell having to be grateful to someone you loathe.'

He said shuddering: 'I can't bring myself to look at her.'

'I know. Poor Rickie, poor darling. All my fault.'

'Nothing has been your fault,' he said for the hundredth time.

'God knows,' she said very much in her old clipped pseudo-magisterial manner, 'I've read enough about the behaviour patterns of psychotics: I ought to have applied it. If you choose to embark on a relationship with a psychotic, you must expect what's coming to you. I got it.'

It flashed across his mind that, whatever Corrigan had expected, Corrigan had got something too. Aloud he said ruefully: 'She's a psychotic, is she? Is that the same as psychopathic?'

She let this pass. Presently her face lit up. She said with sparkling eyes: 'And what do you think? She's through with painting, she's taken to lit. *She's writing a play*.'

'What about?' he exclaimed in simple horror. 'Us? I bet it's about us.'

'God knows. I should think it's more than likely.' She beamed with malice and amusement, indifferent to this unnerving aspect of Corrigan's activities. 'She taps away on her typewriter into the small hours. I can hear her. I'm not to read it till it's finished. Don't you *see* how it all fits in? She *would*. Bet you she'll deliver the goods too – she's no fool. Oh, I see it all! "At last a play that looks contemporary problems squarely in the face, burking no issue, pulling no punches, but informed withal with infinite wisdom and compassion" ... Oh, and bits of poetry and philosophy thrown in, and some Freud as well. And the cleverness of her! Shall I tell you what will happen? She'll make a bee-line for les Boys, the Big Boys – and Bob's your uncle! You'll see: they'll dine her and wine her and dress her up to kill and take her down to their cottages for cosy week-ends. They'll give madly funny imitations of her behind her back, but never mind, they'll dote on her. What's more, with that deadly instinct of theirs, they'll know what they've hooked and they'll respect it: the real rare Box-Office-busting matriarch, the real McCoy! She'll go galumphing straight to her apotheosis on the first night, she'll make such a packet! I do hope so.'

Was she perhaps a little overwrought, he wondered, a little wild and over-voluble? He took a look at her, this week-old suicide, his victim, Corrigan's, and saw her in a glow, twinkling, never in better spirits. There was no end, none, to his bewilderment about women. He would have liked to enter into the fun, but he could not help a feeling of discomfiture, due possibly to his surroundings: this cramped bedroom with its aggressive walls painted in panels and strips of brilliant colour – turquoise, acid yellow, magenta – and further covered with largish specimens of Corrigan's abstract period; its small window, its general appearance of having been tacked up roughly in cheap material over a framework of scrap iron and packing cases. This bed she lay in, under a Paisley rug ... clean, of course, but so poor, so narrow ... He wiped his forehead.

Presently her contented expression faded, and she asked abruptly, in an agitated voice, what news there was from her mother. He reassured her, and she said, taking several big breaths:

'Thank God. I haven't written once, I couldn't, what will they think of me? I did send a cable ... It was the last straw, being punished like that by – both of you ...'

'Punished?'

'Yes, locked in the schoolroom with Aunt Lilian pushing my bread and water in and croaking at me through the keyhole. *Aunt Lilian!* She was so delighted to tell me you and Madeleine had charged her to keep me taped. I couldn't be trusted, of course, to come in on decent terms at the death of my own father, I must be shown where I belonged ...'

'Oh, darling, don't! It wasn't like that, not meant to be ...'

'No. But if you'll forgive my saying so, what a show-up. I'll never forgive her ... So she flew out?'

'Yes.'

'Coming back when?'

He told her, and she relapsed into silence, holding his hand tight. Then she said: 'Look here, Rickie, I've never asked you for help, not really, have I? I've never asked anyone for help – my damned pride, but it's broken. I do need a bit of help now.'

He stared at her pretty hand that he adored, bent down and put a kiss on it. Help. Help. In a moment it would be too late, it was too late already, to take counsel with that truly sensible man he so often felt to be his second self, or his only temporarily absent twin.

'How can I help you?' he asked sadly.

'Don't you want to?'

'Of course I do.'

'I'm not asking much, I promise. Nothing with secret clauses in it. Just something to tide me over. Then I'll be all right.' She swallowed. To see her in such straits caused him mixed sensations – pity, embarrassment, protectiveness, and behind these a kind of cold triumph and curiosity: she was not free of him, she was at his mercy.

'It's this,' she went on, swallowing. 'Will you take me away for a little holiday? Ten days – a week even. I *cannot* stay here, she's driving me nuts. I know she's saved my life, but imagine what it's like lying here after everything that's happened. And I know I'm not quite ready to go back to – living alone without a little break. You're the only person, the *only* person I can bear to be with while I'm still rather shaky. If I could be by the sea, somewhere quiet, for a short time alone with you, I know I'd – be healed in no time. And after that you'll see – I'll be no trouble.'

So he agreed at once. What else could he have done? It was a cry from the heart, it must take precedence, on pain of something he was not prepared to face – his own heart's atrophy. At once she relaxed, grateful, happy as a child. His pity, fear, remorse went underground; his pity, fear, remorse, crushed out of shape, revived: put forth fresh shoots, a wild growth, rampant.

There was no trouble about his taking a little holiday. Obstacles fell away with that smooth complicity, the co-operative subservience which characterizes obstacles conspiring towards the fatal act. Two days later he stopped his car at her door, and she emerged, pale in a lime green linen suit, and took her place beside him. They drove west by easy stages, stopping in cathedral towns they had never visited, exploring them together, she enthralled, intent on history and architecture, he fired by her enthusiasm. Each night it was he who lay awake an hour or so, listening to her quiet sleep beside him.

By the afternoon of the fourth day they had reached the north coast of Wales; bare outlines harmoniously interlaced and modulated, low broken promontories of rock, broad sands; colours subdued – grey, greenish, tawny, azure, silvered, violet: an early Christian, holy coast. They had been recommended, in the last town, to try the farm opened only a few weeks previously as a guest-house. Whitewashed, with blue shutters, it squatted almost on the sand's edge, looking towards the sea, the islands and the setting sun. Miraculously, a vacant double room, fresh, pretty, comfortable. Going about their tasks, the young maids spoke in Welsh to one another: it was like being abroad, as she said, and like a dream; it was the place she had been dreaming of, she had seen it, this very bay, in a dream, she recognized it.

They walked hand in hand, bathed, picnicked, prawned; in a few days they were tanned, salty, ravenous. Before the week was ended he was hopelessly in love with her again; seeing her run barefoot over the sands, turn laughing in the sea and swim towards him made his attentive heart turn over. On the last day they walked along the coast for miles; she made a collection of wild flowers and taught him their names; when he forgot or got them muddled she rehearsed them with him over and over again. They sat in a coign of the cliff with the gulls circling and complaining over them. They saw, quite close inshore, a school of porpoises go in their procession round the headland, hurled and set wheeling from below, it seemed, like oceanic weapons in some archaic ritual game. Never was such a seaside idyll. How right, how easy to love one only, and therefore to be at peace with all creation.

That night they went for a last bathe by moonlight before going to bed. She was the stronger swimmer and went ahead of him, driving on steadily, in silence. He would never catch her up, she would never wait. Suddenly depressed, exhausted, he turned for the shore, stumbled up the beach over the cobbles, dressed again in their shallow cave under the cliff-face, sat down on a rock to wait for her.

Presently dread began to grip him. She had left him deliberately, never to come back, she would swim on, on until she could swim no more, then give up and let the waves close over her. It would be like her; like her to go without a hint to him, without a word of warning, a last word of love. Heartless, fanatical, inhuman ... What was he to do now? The pinch closed under his ribs, he had to hold both hands there, hard against the scaffolding of bones.

When next moment he thought he saw, was sure he saw, the dark sphere of her head bobbing serenely back towards him in the moon's wake, he got up quickly and stalked away. He heard her *coo-ee* once, twice, and strode straight on into the house, up the stairs, ignoring the friendly young manager hovering as usual in the deserted lounge for a good night chat and a glass of beer. Dragging his suit-case out from under the bed, he started to fling things into it; until, hearing her voice, her step downstairs, he hurried to the bathroom at the end of the passage and locked himself inside. When after several minutes he emerged and loomed in the doorway, she was standing in front of the dressing-table, drying her hair with a rough towel. She saw his reflection in the mirror and turned sharp round.

'*Rickie!* What's the matter?'

'Nothing's the matter.' He took a cigarette from the packet by the bed and lit it with deliberation.

She came up to him and laid a hand on his hard-pressed ribs, searching his shuttered face.

'Did you get cold? You're pale. You feel cold. I called to you but you didn't hear. Or did you? Why didn't you wait for me? *What is it?*'

He tried shrouding himself and binding the shroud with ropes until it seemed to himself he must be visibly encased, stiff, blacked-out, knotted, mutilated; he tried loosening a rope to lash her with the end of it. She fought him off without turning a hair, fought step by step towards him; and suddenly she touched him, and darkness and bonds all fell together. They dissolved one into the other, drawing breath and speech from one another in a world of the senses never before apprehended. They were one, they could not live apart, they knew it. In the morning, before he left, they agreed upon their future course. He would await Madeleine's return, then at once, straightforwardly, tell her that his mind was made up, he was going away with Dinah. Where? Never mind that now. Some island on the other side of the world ... Why not? Or travelling from enchanted place to place together, over the whole globe, out of reach of regret and execration. He would settle all the money on Madeleine and the children, leaving only just enough ... Meanwhile he must get back to the office. Dinah would stay on here another fortnight, eat, rest, get strong, occupy herself by starting to write the book for children she had long meditated.

All was clear, solid at last, resolved. They parted in exalted peace of mind. He drove back through a day of impending never-breaking thunderstorms to the home of these women's parents and to his sons.

His relatives returned from their long journey. He met them at Victoria from the boat-train and drove them down to the country. He did what he could to enter into the spirit of family reunion; but when he saw the children, delirious with rapture, rush out of the front door towards their mother, his spirits sank to his boots and he had to go away. Later, at dinner, Mrs Burkett remarked that he looked thin and tired; and where was his appetite? This was in passing, for her true eyes were only for one – that frail, shockingly altered man her husband. He was almost relieved to hear her throw the comment off so briskly. She was a woman with antennae: he told himself that if she had detected anything amiss she would have refrained from drawing attention to his appearance. But they were all tired, and went early to bed. He had not long composed himself between the sheets when Madeleine appeared in her dressing-gown, looked at him with stony eyes and said:

'So you've been seeing her.'

He answered yes.

'I knew the moment I saw you. Before I left I knew what would happen. There's only one thing I want to say to you tonight: will you kindly assist me to preserve a front till Monday? I must insist on this. My parents have been through enough – we've got to put a face on it.'

He said certainly, he also had thought of this aspect of the situation. She was not, he implied, the only one with consideration for others.

'And perhaps you will kindly keep Monday night free. We shall have to review our situation.'

Feeling that her language was unnecessarily formal, not to say stagey, he answered that that had all along been his intention. She left him without another word. It was a great strain getting through the next two days; but what with neighbours dropping in, and most of Sunday on the golf links, the time passed.

Monday evening saw them back in Montagu Square, among the shimmer of new chintzes and cleaned brocades, the glint of polished wood, glass, silver, in the pervasive aroma of turpentine and beeswax. They dined together – a silent meal – then betook themselves to the book-room, where, at once, they had the show-down. He told her fairly truthfully and quite without emotion the whole story, beginning with Dinah's attempted suicide right through to the end of their holiday together. He said he had intended, had tried to break with Dinah: he had failed to do so. There was nothing he could do or wished to plead by way of excuse or justification. All he could say was that if he remained any longer in an impossibly false situation, three lives would be ruined – hers, Dinah's, and for what it was worth, his own.

Madeleine appeared calm and said she took it then that he was totally indifferent to his children and their fate. He replied that on the contrary he loved his children.

'You realize,' she said, 'that you would never, never, *never* set eyes on them again: at least until they are grown up and out of my control.'

He said that this he must accept: she had the right to keep them from him if she felt this course to be in their best interests. It was difficult for him to judge, he said, how much boys suffered from being brought up without a father. He himself had been twelve years old, as she probably remembered, at the time of his own father's death in action in 1914. He had always known, and knew more clearly the older he grew, the irreparable damage to him, let alone the loss. He was haunted still by his mother's grief, by her broken voice telling him that he was all she had now, they must live for one another.

'I was twelve,' he said. 'My last year at my private. I told her I'd look after her. She told me I was her little son who was going to be a man now for Father's sake. With my head on her shoulder I told her yes, that was how it would be, for Father's sake. I went and lay on my bed face down, and told myself yes, now that Father was dead I must be a man. But the more I went on insisting on it the less I' – he paused – 'the less I seemed to know what to do about it. I *had* to be one, I'd promised, but I couldn't think what it was that I – what responsibilities went with the title. My father had been – more than just *my* great pride and admiration: it seemed from the letters and all that that he'd been everybody's: gallant, handsome, brilliant, honourable, and dead for England. I'd got to make it up to my mother by being like him, taking his place. I didn't know how to. I was afraid. I knew if I ever did anything disgraceful . . . I'd see his avenging ghost.'

For the first time that evening, she was impelled to look at him; and saw a face that she was never to forget: face, re-emerged, of the boy aged twelve, in fear, perplexity and suffering. For a second she told herself that this had been all a nightmare: she had awakened to find him as close to her as in the time of their first love, with its first mutual surrender of old secret pains and shames. But next moment she said bitterly: 'Your mother is a spoilt, greedy, sentimental woman. She's been the ruin of you. She's pretended to be so devoted to me but she's always hated me. I hate her.'

'Oh, you exaggerate, I think,' he said with a sigh. 'On every count.

Poor woman, she's had a raw deal. She wanted to marry again, you know, after the war, but the chap let her down. She didn't think I knew, but I did. I wasn't really much good to her by that time. She won't like this at all ... However, that's beside the point. Naturally I've thought a lot about the boys. But you're a very good mother. And Nanny's all right. I fancy at their present stage they won't miss me much, or for long: it would have been harder for them if they were a bit older. Of course I hope you – can find it in you not to condemn me – well, too explicitly, to them: I mean of course for their sakes. I'd sooner fade out as far as they're concerned: to have a disgraced father is worse, I should imagine, than to have a dead one. However, that's up to you. I'm not quite so megalomaniac as to attempt to lay down rules of conduct for you.'

Volcanoes of invective and abuse boiled up in her towards explosion – sank down again, leaving her inert. It was his detachment that paralysed her power of initiative, whether in attack, defence, or counter-attack. He was not challenging her: he was merely announcing to her that since he had decided to retire, the fight was off, the field was hers. But for the fixed cold shadow in his eyes – that and his pallor – he seemed his everyday collected self. She told herself that what she was observing was a mental breakdown: he had gone quietly mad and must be humoured. While she was debating, if so, how to do so, he spoke again:

'As for divorcing me, I imagine you'll want to start proceedings as soon as possible.'

'I shan't divorce you,' she said in a stunned voice.

'Oh ... Are you certain about that? I should have thought you'd want to get shut of me at once – or at least I should have advised it. I shall never come back.' He paused: 'You're not under the delusion, are you, that the law allows me to marry Dinah? No, you can't be.'

'No.'

'She and I do both perfectly realize we're in the wilderness – we're – what's it called? – social pariahs, for good and all.'

'And oh,' she said in the same flat way, 'how she will enjoy that. Root up! Destroy! Burn your boats! Throw off your chains! All for love. Or rather all for her. What a thrill. But *you* won't enjoy it for long.'

He seemed to listen, to reflect, then shook his head as if what she was saying made no sense; or as if, she told herself, stiffening in her chair, he was perfectly indifferent to the sense or to the lack of it. It was all over. *He was gone.* She was alone with a stranger, or with a madman, or with a dead man out of whom emanated looks, words, gestures of grey ashes settling thick, thicker on him, on her, and coating greyly all the room's familiar continuities: the material objects they had owned together, waiting in simplicity around them for tomorrow and tomorrow.

He returned in a business-like way to his plans. Probably the best solution for everybody would be for him to take Dinah abroad as soon as possible. She, Madeleine, had her marriage settlement; and he proposed to hand over to her a lot more capital; financially at least she would be very comfortable. And there would be other compensations he said, heaving himself out of his chair and starting to pace slowly up and down. She had plenty of friends and would not be lonely. And she would certainly be able to count on an enormous amount of sympathy.

'Sympathy!' she gasped, galvanized at last. 'I don't want sympathy.' He looked at her with his ashen eyes, as if to say: What did she want? She said: 'I want my life.' He looked at her again, with curiosity. 'I love you,' she said. He stopped in his pacing and looked round the room. It seemed to her that for the first time something in him was returning to contemplate what he had done to it. He said:

'That's the first time you've said that.'

Instinct deserted her again; she expostulated, flustered:

'What did you expect – at a time like this – considering what you've said? Did you expect me to go down on my knees to you?'

'No,' he said with the ghost of a smile. 'I didn't expect that.'

'As if you didn't know it ...'

'Know what?'

'That I love you.' It was harder to say it this time; it sounded unconvincing. It choked her.

He considered; then he said:

'I think if it was true you'd have said it sooner.'

An icy cramp descended on her. The return had been a spurious one: he was really gone. He had gone into a world where he alone proposed, disposed – the self-elected Judge and sole protagonist. She was condemned, without appeal, for reasons stated, of having convinced him that she did not love him.

'Rickie, you're saying terrible things.' She could scarcely raise her voice above a whisper. 'And you're going to do something terrible.'

He turned and looked at her once more; and if she read, as she thought, despair in his face, she knew she read nothing else: no faith, fear, pity, remorse or cry for help. He had damned himself and given himself absolution; lost himself; washed his shriven soul.

'I'd better go now,' he said.

'Is she expecting you?'

'Yes, she's expecting me.'

'You can't go ...'

It sounded feeble; and still she could not get up, even to stand before him, let alone put hands on him to stop him. He said, almost with regret:

'Oh darling, don't, it's no use.'

'Don't go.'

But he had left the room. A few minutes later she heard the front door bang.

It was midnight. He rang the bell of Dinah's flat. She put her head out of the window on the third floor, called softly: 'I'm coming'; and after a lifetime, no time, let him in.

'Dinah,' he said under his breath.

She gave him her hand, and in silence they went up together. On the second landing she suddenly let his hand go and dropped behind him. He walked up the last flight with the last breath squeezed out of his chest, seeing light stream towards him from the open door of her sitting-room. As soon as they were inside and the door was shut she looked at him, a dwelling look, and said quietly:

'Well?'

'Here I am,' he said.

She was silent a moment.

'You've talked?'

He nodded. The next thing she said was unexpected. What she said was: 'Mother rang me up this morning. She's awfully worried.'

'What about?' His heart gave a lurch.

'About you. She says she's sure there's something quite terribly wrong. She thinks you must be either in trouble or sickening for something or other of the gravest nature. She and Papa find you so changed, she said.'

After a pause he said irritably:

'Why should she say it to *you*?'

'She wondered,' she said, after a glance at him, 'if I'd seen anything of you while Madeleine was away – if I had any clue. She said it was really to ease Papa's mind that she was ringing up. He'd been worrying and worrying: he's so devoted to you, she said, and you'd been so different with him, and he gets so easily depressed.'

'Different? I wasn't different with him,' muttered Rickie. 'I could take my oath on it.' The hours he'd spent sitting with the old man ... What next? 'If she was so worried about me, why couldn't she ask *me* what was wrong?'

The silence was a long one.

'Oh, don't you see?' she burst out, though without raising her voice. 'She's guessed. I've suspected she's always guessed, though she's never even hinted at it. She must be really on the war-path – this is her way of telling me. She's coming up tomorrow – to do some shopping. She's asked me to put her up for a couple of nights. Dying to have a good long chat, she said. That's another thing she's never asked me – to give her a bed. She's always preferred to go to Aunt Lilian. Never even been in for a cup of tea – always insisted on meeting me in a bun shop. I guessed she wanted to steer clear of the aroma, the aura ... Then I'm to go back with her to see Papa. I couldn't say no. Could I?'

He threw himself speechless on to the settee.

'Has she spoken to Madeleine?' he presently inquired.

'I shouldn't think so. No, I shouldn't *think* so.' Glancing at her, he saw irony in her eyes and lips. 'Surely you've got the idea by this time? Or haven't you *ever* realized? She and Madeleine are two matrons, with identical views on marriage and all that. Things are taken for granted, *not* discussed. She would talk to Madeleine about housekeeping, about the children, their bringing-up – never about *you*. She's not going to talk to *me* either – not unless I force it. At least, that's how I see it. You know her. Anything ticklish is always under cover. But she sees her duty clearly.' A smile crossed her face. 'When she smells danger she lies doggo. When she sees it really operating, she *acts*.'

134

'You really think ...' He broke off. He was beginning to feel in a turmoil, as if the vacuum he had been suspended in had begun at last to be invaded by cross-currents, winds, tides, that might sweep him anywhere, independent of his own volition.

'How did it go – with Madeleine?' She sounded diffident, almost apologetic.

'It went ill – as it had to. It's over. There wasn't any noise. Or anger.'

She moved, and in passing him lightly touched his hair; went on into the kitchen. When after a few moments, she came back he said:

'Will you come away with me at once?'

She looked at him without hesitation; without yes or no; without a query.

He got up and began to pace, then went to the window and looked out; and she came and stood looking out beside him. It was a perfect night, starry, windless. He thought about his mother-in-law.

'You're feeling caged up,' she said. 'Shall we go for a walk?'

They left the flat, picked up a taxi and got themselves dropped by Battersea Bridge. They walked eastwards slowly, arm in arm, in a world of stone and water, of light and light's splintered exhalations; in a world of muffled and diminished evidences of the presence of humanity: One that coughed on a bench; One that whistled a tune in the distance; One that laughed with a companion; One that stopped to light a cigarette and sent the match spinning; in a world where presently the landscape they advanced through seemed not so much to thin out around them as to shrivel, then to vanish, as if touched by an enchanter's wand. They were in a desert, dry, limitless, bleached and blackened; banal as grief or death. They came as if by tacit signal to a halt, and went to lean against the parapet, looking down into the river's fire-dappled, somnolent, molten obsidian mass. She said:

'It will never change. Hundreds of years back, hundreds of years to come. But every fraction of a split second it *is* changing: it's never the same. Not for the fraction of a split second.'

He murmured assent. He had such an overwhelming impulse to jump and be gone for ever into this ever-dissolving permanence that he took her by the arm and pulled her back. She said:

'So what shall we do now?'

They hailed the next cruising taxi and went back to Bloomsbury. He was so exhausted that when he got upstairs he reeled and stumbled on his feet. Sleep kept falling upon him in irresistible waves; and she put him into bed as if he were a child. By the time she slipped in beside him he was out, unconscious, totally unresponsive to her whisper and her touch.

Next day was the day that a great deal happened.

He woke up late, his limbs like lead, his head in a fog, and found Dinah afoot, making breakfast; and found Dinah changed. She brought him coffee in bed, and when he said he couldn't manage it, sat by him and quietly urged him to try to get it down. She was automatically gentle and remote, as if she existed with elementary functions only: such as, to glide about as if on domes of silence, to bring him hot drinks and take them away again, to turn his bath on and when he was in it peep through the door from time to time and ask him if he was all right. He said yes, of course he was; and though getting out of the bath and drying and dressing needed the most careful expenditure of energy and resources, he accomplished all these labours. He had just gone back to the bedroom to dial TIM when he was seized with an appalling attack of giddiness and, dropping the receiver with a crash, collapsed face downwards on the bed. Presently he heard her voice in the distance saying:

'It's all right, Rickie.' She was holding him. 'Just wait a few minutes. Then we'll get you back to bed.'

But he assured her it was nothing, the bath had been too hot, with a bit of fresh air on the way to the office he'd be perfectly all right. Presently she ceased protesting, put a brandy flask in his pocket, gave him a last searching look and sent him off, saying:

'Come back at lunch-time. I'll have a meal for you. And if you feel in the least peculiar between now and then ring me up. Promise. I'll come at once and fetch you.'

He promised; but he pooh-poohed the idea of having another come-over. He put his arms round her and gave her a long unimpassioned kiss, and went downstairs, into the street, towards the Tube. Almost at once the pavement started to heave and whirl and, just in time, he hailed a cab and sat inside it leaning forward, taking deep breaths from the open window, cursing himself, bewildered. Could it be food-poisoning? Not drink: he had had nothing except one beer the night before. He tried, and failed, to remember what he had eaten at his last meal with Madeleine. Arsenic in the soup perhaps ... Could he be sure she was incapable of it? He heard himself laugh.

About midday, drenched in icy sweat, having dictated several letters to Miss Matthews, he got up from his desk, took a step, and pitched headlong in a dead faint. When he came to he was alone, but then she was kneeling beside him, pressing a glass of water to his lips and calling: 'Mr Masters! Mr Masters!' He pushed the glass aside, wiped the spilled liquid from his collar, and with her agitated assistance dragged himself to a chair and sank in it with his head between his knees.

'Oh, Mr Masters, just stay exactly as you are. I'll run and fetch your uncle. Just keep as you are. I'll fetch Sir Godfrey to you.'

Galvanized by this threat, he said in quite a strong voice: 'No. Don't fetch anybody. Not Sir Godfrey on your life. I'm all right. Sorry.'

He opened his eyes and saw her kneeling on the floor beside him, her face mottled, her eyes behind pebble lenses glaring consternation. They looked at one another. He made a statement: 'I'm in trouble.' This he was always to regret. She nodded slowly once, twice, thrice, with total comprehension, and put her hand on his.

'You've looked shockingly seedy for a long time,' she said. 'I've been quite worried. Oh dear. Well. Never mind.'

He sat upright and said with an approach to his usual tone with her – a compound of delicacy, sexual dismay and humorously formal deference:

'My dear ridiculous Miss Matthews, what a waste of worry. Never fitter. Only this morning ... Ate something that disagreed. Must have.'

He remembered the brandy flask, extracted it from his pocket and swallowed half the contents.

'Lucky this wasn't broken in the crash.'

'Mr Masters,' she said. 'Do you really think you ought? Till you know? You might be in for something internal, mightn't you? I'm sure I was taught in my First Aid Course that spirits can be very dangerous. Should there be bleeding, I mean, or anything.'

Reviving further, he stared at her and grinned.

'I haven't been run over,' he said. 'Unless you trampled on me while I lay stretched unconscious at your feet.'

She was not amused.

'I do earnestly beg and implore of you,' she said, permitting herself a scolding note, 'to get along home at once now and pop straight into bed. And if you take my advice you'll see a doctor. It may be nothing serious but with a nasty faint like this you never know. Shouldn't I – should I ring through to anyone and warn them?'

'No thanks,' he said, appalled. 'Don't you do any such thing now, promise me. If you do, I'll never forgive you.'

'Just as you please,' she said, with what he feared to be another significant look. 'The last thing I would wish is to seem officious.'

'Perhaps I'll take your advice though, and go home. I seem to have a splitting headache. You may well say this is a hangover, Miss Matthews – only in fact it isn't. Be all right tomorrow. See you then. You've been extraordinarily kind – can't thank you enough.'

'Are you sure now you can trust yourself not to have another turn?' More and more tartly maternal. 'I do really think it might be advisable for me just to come with you to your door – I really do.'

Once more masking his horror he protested, thanked, reassured her, got away. Her last words were:

'If I had my way, your doctor would give you a thorough overhaul at once.'

Not a bad idea, he said, as the lift gates closed between them. It seemed to him that the time was approaching, somehow, for his resignation. Then everybody else would have their way.

The very moment that yet one more cab deposited him at Dinah's, the door opened and she was standing in the entrance.

'You're late,' she said. 'I was getting worried.'

He told her of his extraordinary misfortune. This fainting was utterly ludicrous, fantastic; he was telling her so, going upstairs with her arm supporting him and laughing weakly, when the whole thing started again: giddiness, black whirling sinking clouds of it, through which she struggled to bear him on. Stretched on the bed where, after removing his shoes and loosening his collar, she immediately placed him, he kept asking himself what the devil he could be playing at? There was so much that needed his attention – he couldn't pack up like this.

But as the afternoon wore on there was nothing left but a Something of the utmost urgency, something incomprehensible, beginning to invade his whole body. He heard himself murmur:

'Perhaps it was the brandy'; and heard her ask him, close to his ear: 'What do you mean, Rickie?'

'Worst thing for bleeding. So she said. Matthews.' The memory of Miss Matthews passed over his dimming-out consciousness, and he had to laugh.

'Why do you say that?' She sounded scared, and this he regretted. She was holding his hand and he tried to press it to reassure her; but the truth was, it was he who wanted someone to give him a reassuring pressure, considering how dark the room was now. 'Rickie, why do you say that? Bleeding . . .'

He shook his head. Presently he announced:

'I've been ill for a long time.' That sounded reasonable. He wished to God he'd said that, not the other, to Miss Matthews.

'Rickie, love, what is the name of your doctor?'

He thought hard, groaned, suddenly remembered: 'Murray.' He added after another interval: 'More Madeleine's . . . children's. Don't know any other. Let it go.'

'I won't be a minute. I'm going to telephone from downstairs.'

He made a protest, it was so unkind of her to leave him, but when he opened his eyes she had left the room. He was in great discomfort, he would take the opportunity to get next door, to the bathroom. Once on his feet, he set himself with a will to cover the distance. He did it, he got there . . . or rather, he was aware that by this Something his body was conveyed. It got him there, to get him . . . get him once and for all. *Death*. Ah well . . . Death in the bathroom. He'd done all he could in the way of what was impossible, he could do no more. He cried out once, a loud long cry; gave up.

He was on the bed, flat as a flat fish, someone had taken away the pillows, someone had lit the table-lamp and covered it with a green scarf, someone was sitting beside him, some chap with a well-groomed look and an immaculate dark head brushed in two polished wings. This chap was holding him by his wrist, and his fingers felt cold like the touch of glass beads. He sighed and said: 'Hullo.'

'All right, old chap. Don't move, eh? You'll be all right. Don't worry. Just keep perfectly quiet, just as you are.'

It was Murray, nice chap, great charm of manner, great cricketer, old Blue . . . jolly good when Anthony had that near shave, mastoid.

'What's the matter with me?'

'Can't tell you yet, old chap. We're going to get you shifted soon where you'll be more comfortable.' He relinquished his wrist. 'You gave us a fright, but you're going to be all right. I'll see you again in an hour or so.'

He had a virile pleasant authoritative voice, a chap you could trust to keep his head in a crisis. Pity he'd gone away. He felt lonely again and moaned to himself. Someone came towards him with a noiseless urgency and laid a hand, another cool one, on his forehead.

'Try not to move at all, my darling. It's important.'

'Oh, Dinah.' She said hush, hush, hush, with great firmness, and put arms round him. 'I did try,' he said, and felt her nod her head rapidly above him. A drop of something scorching fell on his cheek. Hot tears. Dinah's.

'What's going to be done with me?'

'You're going to a Nursing Home, darling. It's the ambulance again – your turn this time, darling. We don't seem able to avoid it, do we?' She joked in a thin light voice.

'God,' he said, disgusted. 'What a lot's been going on. I'm sorry. I can't help it.'

'Don't worry,' she murmured. 'Everything's taken care of. Do you like this smell or hate it? Frozoclone.' She was passing something icy, solid, pungent across his forehead.

'Thank you.' A fearful anxiety began to beset him: he became aware that they were not, as he thought, alone. 'Who's here? *She*'s not here, is she?'

'Who, Rickie?'

'That . . .' He couldn't say it, the name, the befouler, the rescuer.

'Oh, Mother's here,' said Dinah quickly, cheerfully, as if stating what should be obvious. 'You remember I told you she was coming.' And immediately he heard the voice of Mrs Burkett saying:

'Lie still, dear boy. Dinah, that was the bell. I expect the ambulance has come.'

He opened his eyes and saw her standing in the doorway. Dinah got up from her knees, hurried past her, vanished.

'*You* here,' he said. 'This is a pretty kettle of fish.'

'You're going to that very nice Nursing Home Papa was in,' she said, as if announcing a great treat in store. 'You'll be so comfortable

– and such good nursing. Matron is really a most charming woman.'

He sighed, looked at her and said: 'What about Madeleine?'

'Of course,' she said at once in her strong voice. 'Don't worry about Madeleine. Don't worry about anything, dear boy.'

He gave up.

'Well . . .' he said. 'You deal with it.'

'I will.'

There was, next moment, a subdued but powerful display of energy around, beneath his person; he was being wrapped in blankets, lifted on to a stretcher and heaved down, down round turn after turn of the narrow staircase by two uncommunicative stalwarts in uniform. He turned his head once or twice to look for Dinah, but she was nowhere to be seen.

His little stay in the Nursing Home prolonged itself to four weeks. Duodenal ulcer was what he had; a haemorrhage was the Something that had taken his body by surprise that afternoon. In the small hours he had another, and was a goner, wife and mother sent for; but on the last stroke of zero a blood transfusion brought him back. He was neither thankful nor regretful, merely surprised, when they told him later what a close shave he'd had; but afterwards, thinking it over while he sipped his beastly milk, he came to the irrational conclusion that he preferred to be alive. Thanks to his excellent constitution he rallied steadily, and took a particular fancy to one of the night nurses, an Irish girl, plump, with a dark creamy voice. Madeleine came mornings and evenings for a short visit and read him light fiction; she was popular with the staff and much admired. When she took him home his household received him with so much joy that he was deeply touched. Nannie blanched, and shook like an aspen. Mrs Moon the cook burst into tears; she was from his old home in Norfolk, child of his grandfather's head keeper, and had known him from a boy. Nannie had always preferred him to the children's Mummy; many a time she had passed the remark downstairs that the Daddy's was the sweeter nature. And his dear old friends rang up, dropped in to see him. Ah, and how nearly, unknown to all of them, he had shocked, rocked this entire structure, how recklessly jeopardized their faith in him. Well, there it was, they had been mercifully spared; they would never know what he'd put in their pipes to smoke on a certain evening last month; what transparencies, what bagatelles they had seemed who now so unquestionably were settling his hash; were bearing him along with the insensibility, the jolt-reducing purpose of shock-absorbers in the domestic bodywork. There it was. So much for moral choice.

He didn't see Dinah again, he didn't hear from her. When he was well enough to read his letters and Sister archly laid the whole stack beside him, asking him if he couldn't spare some for less lucky people, his pulses well-nigh pounded him to pieces as he looked through them. Nothing. Nothing. Day after day he furtively watched the door of his room, fancying it about to open to admit her. 'Your sister-in-law to see you, Mr Masters.' What more natural? It didn't happen. Nor was he told that a young lady had called to inquire, left him this bunch of flowers but hadn't left her name, or any message. He would have got her message from the flowers she chose, from her arrangement of them; but she did not send them.

Madeleine took him to Bournemouth for a fortnight; and then he was more or less himself again and returned to his office, to confront Miss Matthews. But Miss Matthews' father had had a stroke and she had left to nurse him; she had done him this last good turn. At Bournemouth he and Madeleine had had a talk, just one, conducted on a highly civilized level of goodwill and common sense. They had agreed to let the past be past, and stay together and rebuild their married life.

He never saw Dinah again, he never heard from her or heard her name mentioned – until the day she summoned him to meet her at the flat. Up to that moment he went on moving in a trance, apathetic-ally dividing time into regulated lengths: to the next meal, to going out, to coming back, to bed-time. What was love? Guilt? Pity? Love? All equally nothing, articles without function, useless, and therefore without value. Dust and ashes. Which was it – conscience? – mere animal instinct of self-preservation? – that in the nick of time had totally invaded him, burrowing in his bowels to get at the tap to drain his life blood out ... to bleed him of his sin? Strange how repeatedly the rhythm of this business had swung to physical disasters, the failure of the body: Dinah's, her father's, Dinah's again, then this. He was fed up with the Nursing Home *motif*. Some chaps got out by drink, drugs, work, change of scene, religion, other women; an ulcer in the guts had got him out. It was laughable. Henceforth he would stay put, not move an inch to right or left. If that was what they wanted, that was what they'd get. He went on wondering, wondering about Dinah – a mental process in the nature of background music, exacerbating yet compulsively turned on again, again, to drown the silence.

He wondered; and when he saw her again that time she gave him his cuff-links and he lost them, he asked her, or tried to ask her how it had been with her. She did not answer. He felt that by inquiring he was only doing further damage: the image of a stone on a buried body rose to his mind; he was trying to prise it up and she to stamp it down and drag him from it. It was not to bare it and examine it that she had summoned him. She was looking for ... asking for ... There was nothing in him, he was no use to her, if she'd had any sense she might have known it. Yet how sad he had been to have to show her he had handed back his ticket; considered as pure sorrow it was the worst moment of his life, the very nadir. It caused in him such trouble as might have arisen from the apparition of a revenant, holding up before him all the stillborn freedom of his life.

He wished as he turned over and began to fall asleep that he could hear that her life had taken a really better turn. A turn for the better, as his own had. His house was silent, sleeping: baby, nurse and mother on the floor below him; the boys away in the country: not, regrettably, with his mother-in-law. A few hours ago when he had rung her up to give the splendid news she had told him she had been obliged to send them with Nannie to the seaside: Papa's bronchitis was now pneumonia, yes, it was serious, but he was holding his own: on no account was he to worry Madeleine over it. Was Dinah with her? He hoped so. He couldn't ask. She didn't say so. He wished that everybody's prospects were favourable, temperate, settled. He wished that things could so pan out that Dinah would come into his house looking amused and pleased again, as in the old days; and sit and gossip with Madeleine; and play with the boys, and sing her songs to this one too, to the baby daughter ...

He turned over to fall asleep at last in the spare room. Dinah's room in the old days of her visits; in the bed where she had been lying that far-off night; the night he had opened the door, closed it behind him like a thief, a murderer, a lover; and standing in the dark, called:

'Dinah.' Just above his breath.

'Yes.' She did not stir or switch the light on.

'You're not going through with this, you know.' Her engagement, so recently announced.

'I've got to.'

'You can't. You know why.'

'Yes.'

'Break it off.'

'Yes.'

In suddenly enormous time and space he waited. Poised on the giddy steeple. Over, all over. Driving headlong, embraced with a bare monosyllable. Perfectly certain, perfectly cool and steady; perfectly vacant. Not one step towards her bedside, not another word. Turning from the threshold, swift the door open, noiseless closed again. Back along the passage to his dressing-room.

And so it had all begun.

Nightfall

AND so all these years later, in another room in another house of his, vacated by him in perpetuity, lying awaiting no one in the bed, the same, in which she had once lain to be taken by him, bodilessly penetrated through the darkness and in separation at a given time by the long-awaited breaking of his silence, Dinah now turned away from him, rejecting – she could, she was still alive – his wistful thoughts of her; breaking resolutely – she must, life must go on – from the trap of his pursuing shadow.

Lament no more. These things are so.

From the heart of nowhere, an elegiac voice tolled out the line.

Water, mist, moonlight, shapes of wood and stone ... Dwell only upon these inorganic matters, assimilate them, deliver your shaken senses by composing them. Tomorrow I will start a picture of the tower. Yew tree. Headstones. Wall in the foreground at a certain angle. She placed the forms, relating each to each in her mind's eye. A good way, the only satisfactory one, to cast that virus out, drop the rat for ever to the bottom of the river.

Rickie, thank God, was buried far from here. Another silent voice arose in her, spoke in the haunted, sterile room, evaporated. *'He is humbled in the dust.'*

She began to fall asleep; and yet another sprang without warning from some forgotten niche of time, remarking in her mother's ringing authoritative Edwardian tone: *'How is it I wonder that you have never learnt humility?'*

Good joke that, coming from the person who had said it. When I went to see her after Rickie's death she was in anguish. I saw her bow in a storm of sobs and leave the room. A shock to see such torrential passion break from the fountain-head of disciplined authority.

She slept. The shadow overtook her, accompanied her all night through labyrinths of the past and done with, not meaning any harm.

'He was a good man. They are rare,' said Mrs Burkett; but emotion choked her and she got up in a hurry and turned her back on Dinah; who, lying stretched upon the sofa, had the tact not to ask her to repeat herself, or to delay her as she hurried from the room.

Once safe in her bedroom, she addressed herself sternly, bathed her eyes, blew her nose; then opened a locked drawer in her bureau and took from it the vellum-bound book with gilt clasps in which at intervals during her life from the age of eighteen onwards she had copied out passages from her favourite authors. She read:

> Then look around
> And choose thy ground
> And take thy rest.

took a pen and wrote under the quotation RLM, with the date of his death; thus dedicating it to Rickie for his epitaph.

It was not a broken life and not a failed one, she declared passionately to herself: he had chosen it with his eyes open and completed it ... Cruelty was the one thing besides humbug that she censured, and cruel he had never been. Only weak; and she could pity weakness if it was not, as so often it was nowadays, given a moral not to say mystic sanction: as if to play fast and loose with other people's lives took natural priority over duty and self-control. Dinah scorned weakness; Madeleine, confused by it – afraid of it perhaps – could not judge it with detachment. *Autres temps autres mœurs* of course; her children ridiculed her code and gave her to understand that the facts of life were still concealed from her. One simple fact had never crossed their minds, the fools: she understood men and they did not. She had not lost the instinct for the art of sex, inherited from her mother and her grandmother. If she had not been able to hand it on as she had received it, it was not for lack of fostering tradition, precept and example. But nowadays they were bent, all of them, on fulfilling themselves with the aid of text-books: every bodily and mental function explained, explored and practised with business-like

146

thoroughness and zeal. All very well, all very sensible ... but oh! deplorable. So much frankness and obtuse perversity, so much enlightenment and atrophy, so much progress and *dégringolade*.

What they little realize, either of them, she told herself with a vicious secretive spurt of triumph, is that Rickie knew that he and I ... that I understood him. No need to look facts in the face and call spades spades. We knew there was a link between us. Ah, why not acknowledge him – my spirit's son, as the twins, sons of my body, had never been? – dear fellows, but frankly dull. Looking over Clarissa's head on her third birthday: 'She's like *you*,' he said, 'I couldn't be more delighted'; and his smile caressed my heart. Again we knew what we knew. That was the day I told him that Dinah's husband had been killed in Spain. His face altered, he uttered an exclamation of distress.

'That's bad, isn't it?' he said.

'Very bad.'

'He was a good chap? She was happy?'

'Very happy.'

I took her letter from my handbag and offered it to him; he hesitated, then accepted it. I showed the child a picture book while he went over to the window and read it with his back turned. Well I remember that dreadful document, setting out firm bald reasons for marching on breast forward, never doubting – placing the enlargement of my political horizon before her private grief ... Dinah has never learnt to express herself in an adult, educated way. Very curious. She had excellent governesses, also the freedom of the library; yet give her a pen and she cannot be trusted not to express herself in clichés, like a schoolgirl with a smear of the popular slick journalist. But she is *mal entourée*, hobnobs with riff-raff, people with opinions and no breeding, always has – so odd ... As if composing a primer for the indoctrination of a housemaid she set down for me that poor little man's odyssey, her hundred per cent backing of it, his life laid down to prevent – to bring about ... Ah, and in spite of because of her strident brave trumpet-blasts I admired her, prayed for her faith and his. It gave her comfort when I said how right he was, how gallant, admirable ... So he was. But oh, the waste. She had settled down at last. An extraordinary choice but they were suited, I saw that. 'Whatever becomes of me,' she wrote, 'however hard it seems at present to live without him, I shall go on working for the Cause. I have his torch as well as mine to carry now, and I shall always be proud to think I married a true pioneer of the future, one of the heroes of the new People's Democracy that is going to be born. Fascism *will* be defeated in Spain in spite of all the bombs and tanks of the Dictators, in spite of the British Government's iniquitous non-intervention policy playing into the hands of Franco's abominable reactionary conspiracy' – and so on and so forth. 'Jo wrote in his last letter that if only I could see for myself the spirit of the Spanish people and the International Brigade I couldn't have the shadow of a doubt. He had none. He was *absolutely* happy. He loved life more than anyone I ever knew, and more fully than anyone I ever knew he was prepared to lay it down. He *chose*. He was a hero.'

Rickie pushed the letter back into its envelope. Standing above me and Clarissa on my lap, he said:

'Her letters are always so – I suppose they're like her in a way but ...'

'Disappointing. Not the best of her,' I said.

'Well, yes. These Good Cheer messages from Supreme Head-quarters. And the worse things go the more confident the pep talk.' He gave a nervous laugh. 'I suppose she's got to do it. Poor girl, poor Dinah. She never could bear to be in straits. Does she believe all this, do you suppose, or is it to make *you* feel less upset about her? She's so generous in all her impulses ...' He tapped his chin with the envelope. 'I hope to God she – I wish ... There's nothing I can do. I can't imagine what we'd say to one another now if we did meet. She must have become extremely formidable.'

'She hasn't changed,' I said.

'Well, she must be even more formidable than she ...' He handed the letter back. 'It's damnable,' he said in a voice of compassion. 'This Jo must have been such a good chap. I'm glad she found someone with the guts to go all out for what he believed in, someone – well, *whole*, to take the whole of her along with him. She was always looking for that. A hero ... I hope she may be right about the rewards. Seems to me heroism is like patriotism, not enough. But she wouldn't agree.'

Then Madeleine came in. I said: 'I have just been telling Rickie that Dinah's husband has been killed in Spain.' She shot him a look, which he did not meet, and said in a sincere voice of shock

148

and sympathy: 'I'm terribly sorry.' He quietly turned the subject.

Now Rickie too was dead. If ever a man laid down his life for his country it was he. Most unpretentious, unspectacular of casualties, how preposterous he would have considered any tribute. 'But he *was* a hero,' she whispered fiercely. Perfect self-sacrifice; no less, no more than Anthony's. No brand of ideology could make a corner in heroes any more: that was one blessing about the war, she would say bitterly to Dinah ... No, no, she would not, unthinkable, the very idea of making a remark with such poisoning possibilities; of giving Dinah an opening perhaps for argument, comparison between ... of analysis of what went to make a hero. Heroes chose their deaths, she would say; were not imposed upon. Anthony chose no death. He had been ordered, simply, to enter the vast duped ranks of youth with no prospect of a future: he had shrugged his shoulders and obeyed. Had not Rickie chosen? *Rickie?* – Good heavens, no! Not thrown his life away? Ah, but not positively! – not with a summing-up, a creed, a testament. Thrown up the sponge, bled out his life or rather let it bleed, dead beat, indifferent ... The voice of Dinah with its disquieting edge (her nerves are in a bad state, she should be *forced* to rest, give up) seemed to ring in the silence like a humming wire. *Hero*, it twanged, *hero*: fanatical reverberation.

Was there nowhere left in all the world for the dead to lie down brotherly, equally defeated? – equally innocent, triumphant?

She snapped the book shut and laid it back in its place and locked the drawer. She was trembling. It was merely that she was tired: it had been an ordeal describing to Dinah the village gathering in Norfolk for the funeral. The brunt of this, practically speaking, she had had to bear, his poor tiresome mother being dead, Madeleine bewildered, and all the men of the family too busy or abroad. Staring in the mirror she noted her thin discoloured hair, the bright single rose of age, ephemeral, flaring in her cheeks, her eyes brilliant in their sunken sockets. Posthumous youth: out of grief by memory. Nobody living cared much now what she in her own identity might want or could remember. This rose revived was out of time and season. She would be expected to think only of his widow, of his orphaned little daughter; she must not call for sympathy herself. It was not *comme il faut* in the old to expect great personal consolation: they should be accustomed to bereavement. And I do not expect it, she told herself, going downstairs again to tell Dinah to keep her feet up and have her supper on a tray; my life has passed beyond such tensions and fluctuations, death is the next experience, I must make the best of it. Above all, *and at once*, I must shed this load of sour hostility towards Dinah, this corroding wish to tell her, teach her – what?

But Dinah did say, after supper:

'*You*'ll miss him dreadfully. He was so fond of you.'

She could not at once reply and Dinah went on, as if amused: 'Of the three of us I think he liked you best. You'd have suited him best, too.'

It was easier to speak then, assuming the dry tone that was part of the game – the particular type of backhand volley they practised enjoyably together.

'Thank you. The subject never arose, I cannot think why. Perhaps because I found myself reasonably well suited by your father.'

'Always?' Dinah shifted lightly on the sofa to get a less oblique view of her, where she sat knitting and bespectacled on the other side of the hearth. 'From the very dawn of romance to the very end?'

'Certainly.'

'Well, I never! What astounding luck,' said Dinah after a musing silence.

'I would not call it entirely luck. There has never been a marriage, however thoroughly consolidated in appearance, that has not been found to be steered for the rocks – at a certain moment.'

'Yours was found to be so?'

'Mine was no exception.'

She knitted swiftly on. Dinah lay back again on the cushions and lit a cigarette.

'You have given me quite a turn,' she said presently. 'It only goes to show ... It takes two, I suppose, at the tiller when the moment comes?'

'Not always. As a rough and ready rule it takes the wife. I am not suggesting that this applied in my own particular case.'

'I bet you'd have left Papa if he'd been really unsatisfactory.'

'Oh, very possibly. But he was not really so. We made allowances for one another.'

'Is it true,' asked Dinah in a voice of girlish delicacy after another silence, 'what one hears – that men have a funny time?'

Mrs Burkett shot her a suspicious glance; but Dinah was looking meekly at the ceiling.

'Men are different in certain circumstances and respects. It is a matter of physiology. The sooner this is faced in married life the less trouble for everybody concerned.'

'Considering how different men are, it seems so curious that it is always women who have to face it. One never hears, does one, of a man facing his difference? It would almost seem that his instinct was to turn his back on it.'

The tension in Mrs Burkett's features underwent a sudden relaxation; she let her knitting fall in her lap and leaned back, feeling something flutter deep inside her, like the intimation of one more quickening of the sense of life; as if after all there could be no such thing as loss without replacement. But how irritating to see this perpetual cigarette in Dinah's lips or fingers: ugly, unwholesome common habit; she would speak her mind about it.

In the silence Dinah's nerve-ends crept, contracted, listening for the guns, the sirens. Absurd: this was the heart of Berkshire; outside this pleasant cottage which Madeleine and Rickie had found for her mother when war broke out, was a cherry orchard, beehives, nightingales in the thicket just beyond; farther, a village pub, a store, church, vicarage, manor, farm; still farther, torrents of aromatic foam of wild parsley in the banks; and all around, the architectural masses and perspectives of the Downs, sheep-cropped, thymy, spattered with juniper bushes, cut with immemorial chalk tracks. In widening rings she placed the night-folded features of the landscape. She began to hear a steady giant pulse. The old woman from the village who obliged for Mrs Burkett had told her earlier that when Victory Day came the beacons would be lit from ridge to ridge as they had been for the Armada and for Bonaparte. Yes, she had called him Bony.

Her mother took up her knitting again and critically examined it. It was an ambitious work – an entire frock for Clarissa, whose measurements and other physical characteristics her grandmother now discussed; with comparisons leading on to recollections of her own childhood and of her children's childhood.

'I suppose,' mused Dinah, 'if ever a generation knew its own strength it was yours: or rather *didn't* know it, as the saying goes, meaning it's so tremendous it hasn't got to be consciously considered, for good or ill. We inherited your Juggernaut momentum; but of course not your sphere of operations.'

'Indeed!'

'That started to be blocked. And we seized up. Rickie must have known it in his bones long before we did. We weren't conditioned like him, not deeply, by ruling class mentality. You needn't get on your snobby-horse' – for her mother had snorted – 'I couldn't be more thankful for the good sound upper-middle stock I come of. It's meant a sort of solid ground floor of family security and class confidence that's been a great stand-by. But Rickie hadn't got it. He was a romantic orphan boy, irrevocably out of the top drawer. He was never at home in his situation, was he? – I mean the contemporary one, the crack-up – not just the general human situation of wondering why you're born.'

There was no answer. Mrs Burkett polished her spectacles.

'Coming down in the world must cause as many strains and stresses as going up in it,' continued Dinah, inhaling and blowing out trails of smoke. 'I've sometimes thought, if Jo had lived and we'd had children, they might have felt it.'

'Ah, you compare the alliances,' said Mrs Burkett on a formidably unprejudiced and deferring note. 'Poor Colin and Clarissa, dear me! To think they do not appear to recognize what they might well feel.'

'I merely meant that Madeleine and I both married out of our walk in life,' said Dinah in a voice which sounded to her mother intolerably patient, condescending. 'Only a degree or so in her case – drastically in mine. I know you'll resent my saying it, but Rickie and Jo did have something in common: a sort of frailty, as if they had no compost round their roots ... Jo would have got bedded down, if he'd lived; but Rickie ... You see, Jo had the advantage of a trained political mind. He knew where we were, in history. He taught me to see ourselves historically.'

'Ah, in that case,' said Mrs Burkett pleasantly, after a pause for counting stitches, 'you are certainly more advantageously placed than most of us. What can one hope to do without training? Only one's duty according to one's *very* narrow lights.'

Suiting action to words she briskly rose, drew the black-out curtains across the window, switched on two darkly shaded lamps and returned to her chair.

'I don't mean to give the impression,' said Dinah, 'that Jo looked on our marriage as a social experiment.'

'I should hope *not*,' snapped Mrs Burkett. She pressed her lips together, then added: 'As you know I only met him once. He appeared to me to behave like any nice young man in love – the usual excess of humility, the usual over-estimation. I didn't see him in terms of the potting shed, I must admit: but then I never noticed Rickie's difficulties in the matter of manure. I simply felt he – Jo – was genuine. I liked him very much.'

Her thoughts travelled back to the day when he had turned up without warning in a battered two-seater, and announced his intention of marrying her younger daughter. Spring 1936 it must have been? A dark plump glowing little man with intelligent eyes behind horn-rimmed glasses, a bright pink shirt, a loud check jacket and easy manners. Excellent teeth. Face expressive, mouth a shade too mobile. Hands cared for, sensitive. Warmth in his voice to compensate for the Jewish-Cockney twang. His father was dead. He and his mother ran a big bakery in East London, he spoke of her with endearing pride. An affectionate boy, a good son, a taking little man. Interested in literature, in education: these they had discussed, not politics. What she remembered best were his shouts of laughter once she had got over the initial shock and put him at his ease. A laughing little man. 'Aren't you a duchess, though!' he said. His eyes teased, admired, delighted in her. 'I don't mind telling you I wasn't looking forward to this interview – though I'd made a vow I'd go through with it on my loney-own. I thought you'd be sure to come it over me, in spite of Diney saying no, not on the whole you wouldn't, not if I played my cards right.' A shout of laughter. 'But aren't you lovely? Diney did say you were a classic but I got the picture wrong: I took it from those old-style musical comedy favourites – you know those picture-postcard photos, Edwardian Beauties, the ample type as you might say, all bust and fuzzy fringe and a face like a love-sick spaniel mooning at you.' Another shout of laughter. 'I'll tell Diney she's not a patch on you for looks. Not that she isn't what I call perfect in her own way. It's a funny thing, she doesn't take after you but I'd know you were related: your skeletons 'ud be the dead spit of one another.' How tender and serious when he talked of Dinah, what admiration, also what shrewd perception; also what pity, what humour.

'God bless you,' he said at parting, wringing her hand till her fingers ached.

'What an act you put on for me, didn't you? Gorgeous. I'm common – that's why I appreciate it.' Another shout. 'I wish you could meet my mother and her you – you'd hit it off. I'll bet you've never bounced anybody in your life and nor has she. And wouldn't she revel in a place like this! – she loves nice things. Her and Dinah get on a treat.' His last words sober: 'I get your point of view, don't think I don't. It's a facer for you, in a way. But there's one thing Diney needs as things have turned out for her – two things rather: one's to stay where she is because she believes in what she's doing: the other is someone to look after her, someone that wants to, mind you, because he believes in her and she helps him to believe in himself. I'm the guy that wants to, and what's more I'm going to.'

She had told him that she too believed in him. She had never seen him again. A week or so later they were married at a Registry Office in London: by friendly consent it was not made a family affair. Jo's mother and his aunts and uncles still practised the Jewish faith; and what with this, and her own Anglicanism – still potent in her though not formally professed except at Christmas and at Easter – and the aura of dogmatic atheism or of dialectical materialism (whatever that might be) around the bridal couple, there seemed no common meeting ground for the ceremony of marriage. They were married, they were happy in two rooms in Stepney. Dinah went on with her job – clerical work it appeared to be in some local clothing factory – and wrote that they would love to come and stay for a few days in September when they had their fortnight's holiday. Presently she wrote to say that she had left the clothing factory to take on an organizing job for the Spanish Republican cause: unpaid, it meant real poverty, but that was nothing. And they did not come in September. By then Jo was in Spain with the International Brigade. He did not come back, he did not look after Dinah. Waste, tragic folly, criminal waste and folly.

'What I meant was,' said Dinah with the harping persistence of one who has felt a dig, 'it must have been more of a wrench for Rickie than we realized, selling up his estates and going into business. He'd been brought up to be landed gentry like his fathers. It was a whole way of life gone – not just his own personal one: all his racial memories, you might call them. He couldn't have helped feeling he was letting down a lot of people – tenants and retainers – shrinking his responsibilities. One shouldn't underestimate that sort of dislocation.'

'So you have remarked before,' said Mrs Burkett, thinking: what a prig she is becoming, a pedantic spinster, nothing but views, no man would stand for it – no proper man. 'Since I am not equipped for these discussions, let us stick to the particulars, let us stick to simple economic facts.'

'Yes?' said Dinah in a tone of mannerly encouragement.

'Rickie, I take it,' began Mrs Burkett rapidly, 'inherited a certain property and like most of what you term the landed gentry – indeed so do I but without feeling called upon like you to impose a particular inflection upon my vocal chords – found himself crippled by taxation, whether justly or unjustly is a matter of opinion though I am sometimes tempted to consider it more a matter of *taste* – and being a young man of foresight, intelligence and initiative, and luckily empowered to break the entail, he came to a sensible decision.' She paused for respiration, and disregarding the '*whew!*' that Dinah uttered on a long whistling note, drove on: 'And above all wishing to marry young, for love, not money . . .'

'Ah, we were forgetting that . . . He could have bettered himself, couldn't he, by a more – advantageous match.'

'Do you suggest,' said Mrs Burkett after a pregnant pause, 'that cynicism was even *possible* to Rickie?' A violence in which some threat, some accusation of betrayal thrashed like a half-glimpsed subterranean monster began to swell in her. She kept her eyes fixed on her knitting needles, thinking: 'For two pins I would get up and beat to a jelly my own flesh and blood.' And as if the suppressed image had been formulated she heard Dinah murmur in a thin exhausted voice:

'No. He was on the side of the betrayed more than the betrayers . . . It's still in the Henry James *genre* though, if one could follow out the threads.'

Re-orientated by the further check of this apparently gratuitous irrelevance Mrs Burkett was able to continue:

'Be that as it may, he came to your father for advice, on his engagement. How old would he have been? Twenty-three? Not more.' She heaved a heavy sigh. 'You would not remember that.'

'Of course I remember their engagement. I wasn't in the nursery, or mad.'

'The practical aspect, I mean, you would not have realized. He wanted to fall in with Madeleine's preference for London life ... And then money, as I said ... In fact he was looking for an opening in business. Through your uncles, your father was able to procure him the very thing. He had great faith in Rickie's judgement and common sense. So had your uncles. In the end.'

Silence fell. Presently Dinah said in a drowsy voice:

'I remember Rickie telling me once about his twenty-first birthday party. The celebrations.'

'Ah, no doubt there would have been,' agreed Mrs Burkett, with enthusiasm, taken off her guard. 'Madeleine went down to Norfolk for that party, I think? I rather fancy it was then that they first got to know one another. Or would that have been some other house party?'

'That I couldn't say. He didn't mention that aspect. But if so,' said Dinah, yawning, 'it was a closer shave for Madeleine than she realized. Touch and go, if he was to be credited. I know we're not worldly, but he *was* a catch, wasn't he? Not the catch of the season of course, but by no means to be sneezed at.'

'What are you talking about?' said Mrs Burkett sharply.

'About that coming-of-age party. He told me such a curious thing, I've never forgotten it.'

'And what may that have been?'

'Well, only that in the middle of it he had a sudden – crisis, explosion, brainstorm. When all the speech-making and health-drinking and fireworks display was over and everyone had retired to sleep it off, he suddenly had an awful come-over. And he got up in the dead of night and crept downstairs and got his gun and loaded it ...'

'Hmm, yes, what nonsense. No doubt,' cut in Mrs Burkett, knitting in rapid jerks, 'he had taken a great deal too much to drink.'

'That's what he thought must have accounted for it – the sudden attack of depression. He was convinced he wanted to blow his brains out.'

'Young people get these turns,' said Mrs Burkett after a second's silence. 'Particularly young men. It is mostly moodiness and play-acting.'

'That's what he finally concluded – at the time – it must be. Anyway,

156

after sitting in the gun-room for about twenty minutes working out the most elaborate sort of cat's cradle of string from his big toe to the trigger, he undid the whole thing and went back to bed.'

Brusquely Mrs Burkett glanced towards the window, then apparently detecting a chink between the curtains, got up and hurried towards it. Standing there twitching at the black-out material, she said with her back turned:

'Perhaps you would prefer not to discuss Rickie any more. I think I would prefer it.'

Dinah stirred on the sofa: her look of amusement faded; her hands clenched, relaxed.

'Just as you choose.'

'How is it, I wonder, that you have never learnt humility.'

It was less a query than a statement, made in the resolutely uncomplaining tone of one taking up a cross, one more, unmerited.

'If you don't mind,' said Dinah, 'we won't go into that.' Pause. 'If you think what you seem to think, you're wrong – and stupid too. I haven't forgotten Rickie. Or what we did to him.'

Returning at a brisk blind march, Mrs Burkett stooped to grasp the poker, pushed it between the logs, tossed them noisily, muttered: 'Damp wood again,' seized Dinah's ash-tray, shook out its contents with evident disgust, then said:

'Speak for yourself.' Planted stiff upon the hearthrug, she fought audibly for control of breath. '*I* did what lay in my power to prevent a terrible tragedy.'

'Oh, we all did that, you know. Having done what lay in our power to cause it. Still, let's not bring it into court, now that Rickie's dead ... I haven't forgotten him, or what *I* did to him. Is that better?'

'Parvenus ... *We!* Juggernauts ...' She struck her chest. 'An old old elephant in a circus would be more apt. You may have noticed their gait and their expression.' Her voice started to expand, daemonic, harsh. 'Oh, right and wrong are old-fashioned terms no doubt you'll tell me, but they come home to roost. *We* had our point of view, your father and I, though we were sneered at for old fogies ...'

'Oh Ma, we never!' Fearing to see her mother's face contorted, she closed her eyes.

'Oh yes! You need not sigh at me so patiently. I was perfectly aware of it. Well do I remember, though his name has mercifully escaped me, some youth, I believe he styled himself a writer, one of you girls, I dare say it would be *you*, brought down one Sunday. "You see, Mrs Burkett," he said to me – so gracious of him! – in the course of conversation, I was trying, I dare say, to discover his aims and interests – "You see, Mrs Burkett, the fact is Western civilization is in *decline* and those of us like *myself* who are *aware* of it must reflect it in our *lives* before crystallizing it in our *work*. We cannot be expected to *behave*." '

A stifled laugh sounded from the sofa; the ensuing pause was ominous; Dinah said with more lightness than she felt:

'What a ghastly ass – who can it have been? To think of you chalking that up against him all these years. I expect he only wanted to be mothered.'

The pause prolonged itself; then suddenly became the end of the expended storm. Presently Mrs Burkett said with an approach to mildness:

'I always loathed a prig. So did your father. And what with the chatter-chatter and the effeteness and nothing but bottle parties bottle parties and those cynical sexy novels ...'

'Oh, you haven't been reading them *again*, have you?'

'I have *not* been reading them again. In war-time, no indeed! Though I am at a loss to know what authors you understand to be in question. No. I have been glued to the Great Victorians and shall continue so to be. Yes. But no wonder that we asked ourselves ... However ... that is in the past. You and I must never quarrel, Dinah, it would be unthinkable. What I should have said, and no more, is ...' She hesitated, fastening upon her daughter the remote yet piercing gaze of her long-sighted aquamarine eyes, 'a terrible tragedy was prevented. Or at all events its bitterest fruits.'

But Dinah lay unresponsive, one arm flung over her eyes; and turning away, her mother addressed an invisible audience at the other end of the room.

'I did not take it upon myself to judge. I never apportioned blame. Such matters are in God's province, not mine. Naturally I – though I struggled not to ... how a girl of your bringing-up and a man with his code – responsibilities – I shall never understand. But one must not measure the temptations of others by one's own. And the greater

158

the height the greater the fall. And Madeleine, poor child, with all her splendid qualities was *not* the right wife for him. The same applies on his side. It was *not* one of those partnerships one could call truly right. As for you ...'

She turned again, to see Dinah's arm drop down and lie along her side with strange inertia; as if to imply an added weight to her passivity. Listening? Bored? Mocking? Sullen? Wounded? Or mere rejection? For the first time, and with a pang whose edge bewildered her, it struck her that she could trace a family likeness in Dinah after all: to her little sister Alice, fifth among the brood of nine – plain child (quaint was the word used then), the only sallow one; when she was six they cut her hair short because it grew in rats' tails; once tamed a hedgehog for a pet; loved newts and toads; once dug a tunnel under asparagus bed hoping to reach Australia, got into trouble; always in trouble; once after disobedience punished by governess, ran away from home, was brought back mud-and-rain-drenched after dark by postman; died in her tenth year of meningitis ... What trick of feature, facial angle or proportion, accidental pose, expression, could have summoned back that long-forgotten child?

'As for you, dear ...' This time it was clearly an appeal.

'Well?' Dinah's eyebrows went up. She appeared to smile.

'I always had such faith in you – your moral stamina – even at the worst.' She laughed briefly with a quaver. 'You had to find your own way out, I wished not to interfere, though it was sad for us when you so completely cut adrift from us, we missed you ... I have led a comparatively sheltered life, but I have always understood the need to choose the hardest way. Ah, more than understood! – felt the *temptation* of it. Yes. I remember saying to Aunt Lilian when you children were all babies – Oh, *you* were in your cradle: "if there is one blessing above all others I would wish for them," I said, "it is that they should grow up to discover a vocation. Because that means happiness," I said. Oh, not to have you all in nunneries and monasteries – vocation in the broad sense, whatever form it took – medicine, nursing, the arts – I have often thought now *botany*, what could be more delightful? – or possibly marine biology ... However it was not to be. Charles's bent for farming, Henry's for engineering, much to be thankful for, but not what I ... You were the only one, in fact, who ever showed a sign of it, though I must say at one time I was hard put to it to ... Well, never mind. I *detest* what I know of the political views you have come to hold, but I admire you greatly, Dinah. Rickie fought his fight too in another way – none knew it better than I, though it was never spoken of – he has left a fair name and a good report behind him. And when your time comes so will you. Though, dear me, that won't be, I trust, for many and many a year.'

'The same to you,' said Dinah in a strangled voice. 'Ditto ditto in fact. Because if there's one thing certain, so will you.'

At this moment an eldritch and imperious clamour arose outside the door.

'Oh, now hush! Wait! I am coming,' called Mrs Burkett, and adding joyfully: 'He will *not* be kept waiting,' thrust away her handkerchief and sped with the lightness of a girl to admit an exceptionally large masterful-looking neuter cat, smooth-coated, black with a white dickie, white paws and whiskers, and a white imperial.

'Oh, Griswold, noisy fellow,' she exclaimed with pride, crouching to stroke him in strong sweeps from nape to stern; while behind her on the sofa Dinah stealthily wiped her eyes. 'Bad boy. What have you been getting up to? That particular *pealing* or *tolling* note – did you notice it? – is apt to mean he has brought in his kill. Let us hope not. Should it have been a young rabbit he will have left it on the kitchen table for Mrs Hobbs to cook for him. He will *not* eat them raw, as for mice and rats he merely casts them at my feet – a tribute one might think, if tributes seemed more in keeping with his character. Now Griswold, you know quite well who is here. Call him, Dinah.'

Dinah emitted a high muted call from the back of her throat and immediately he underwent a functional adjustment, pared out a stream-lined track towards her and, expressing nothing but studied rejection of the goal in view, leaped upon her stomach.

'There!' cried Mrs Burkett, elated. 'I thought so! The whole thing was planned. I have never known him to fail to appear from nowhere for a member of the family. This time I was dubious, I must confess; I regret to state that his hunting season is at the peak. Besides he has not seen you for a year.' She watched him wreathe and pour himself, his eyes lambent, abstracted, yet lunatically intent, around Dinah's enfolding arms. 'Don't let him start that dreadful *kneading*. On the other hand, if you correct him he will only take offence. Better

160

nerve yourself. He will soon stop and settle down and we can all be cosy.'

'I'm afraid you're putty in his paws,' said Dinah, nerving herself without flinching to endure the ritual trampling.

'Oh, but his cleverness! The cleverest cat I have ever had.' Mrs Burkett resumed her chair with a look of contemplative happiness.

'He looks prosperous.'

'Oh yes, he is in tiptop form. I can get all the milk he can swallow. So lucky.'

Gradually, softly he collapsed and lay along Dinah's thighs, voluptuously at ease. He bowed his head and slipped his lower lids up. One ear gave a rapid shiver; then another. His purr expanded, reverberating like the rhythmic snore of a flight of bombers passing high, in the distance.

Having missed the nine o'clock news, Mrs Burkett switched on punctually for the ten o'clock, listened to the headlines, switched off again, made her comments upon the military situation, reported those of a retired naval captain and a retired Indian Army colonel, both her neighbours. She glanced frequently at the clock, according to her habit. Life had taught her much, but not to tolerate the repose of others; and the spectacle of Dinah's supine body, although the upper layer of her consciousness approved it, caused in her depths a disturbance, an increase of restlessness. So much to do, so little done. So much to say, to leave unsaid ...

Presently she left the room and was absent for about fifteen minutes.

'I was just heating up some milk,' she announced on her return. 'I know you will refuse it, but I find it such a comfort in the night. Two o'clock onwards is my wakeful time – so tiresome. I have a thermos by my bed and it soothes me off again. I have put one in your room. Do drink it. You and Griswold look quite settled for the night, but I think bed is the best place for you, so come dear.' She lifted Griswold, limp as a hank of knitting wool, from Dinah's lap and held him to her check. 'I have just been telephoning to Madeleine,' she remarked. 'Colin has had week-end leave from Sandhurst, so that was nice. She sounded fairly cheerful. Clarissa has gone back to school, of course. Somerset. There is an excellent air-raid shelter but so far, touch wood, they have not so much as heard those abominable sirens. The Vicar here is very kind with lifts. He passes near Madeleine's on his way to his county council meetings – of course he gets extra petrol. So I am hoping to pop over and spend the afternoon with her on Wednesday.'

'Perhaps you could give her my love,' said Dinah, slowly swinging her legs down and sitting up.

'Now Griswold, which is it to be? The open spaces or your basket?' She let him jump from her arms and watched him stand somnolent, collecting himself for action, on the hearthrug. 'Sometimes the one, sometimes the other,' she vaguely remarked. 'He cannot be coerced ... Yes, dearest, if I get the opportunity I will gladly give your message to Madeleine.'

'I haven't written to her.'

'No?'

'I wasn't sure – what sort of gesture that would seem to her. After all, I've quite dropped out. To offer myself back – at his death ...'

'She might perhaps feel like taking the first step,' said Mrs Burkett cautiously.

'I suppose she hasn't mentioned me.'

'Not so far. There is still a state of considerable shock, you know, and a great many problems to be settled.' Folding away her knitting, hunting for her spectacle case, she added: 'But when the impulse comes, and I think it will, she will act upon it, you know. She would be unlikely to mention it to me beforehand.'

'Curious, but true,' said Dinah, still sitting on the sofa's edge. 'I did write to her, ten days ago. The morning after the night that Rickie died.'

'Ah, you did. No, she has not mentioned it – so far. I thought you said ... However, it seems to me most natural on your part. You felt you must send her a word. I am glad.'

'Oh, I didn't send it. It was curious because I didn't know he was dead. I wrote before I got your wire. I wrote because I'd had a dream about him.'

Wheeling sharply, Mrs Burkett exposed to her an acute dismay. '*Now* what?' said her fatigued face, braced for the supernatural.

'Oh, nothing prophetic.' Dinah looked amused. 'Not a relevant dream. Rather the kind I sometimes have about Papa. More an atmosphere ... An atmosphere of being young; and him appearing,

162

generally in the garden, and everything ordinary, so that though part of me knows in the dream that he's dead I don't feel a pang or a tremor. He says the 4.45 got in three and a half minutes late, or some remark of that sort ... generally about time. This was the same kind of dream. He – Rickie – appeared, looking like himself, with no – emotion attached to him; and said – I forget what really – something perfectly trivial and polite, like: "Not just now, another time, I'm in a hurry." But I had the dream about the time he actually did die. I was on duty at the Centre; I'd dropped off to sleep in my chair, in the early hours. I woke up feeling surprised to have dreamed about him, because I hadn't – consciously – thought about him for years, I began to think about Madeleine. I wondered what kind of way she thought about *me* now – if she ever did – whether she found, like me, that the war and the bombing and all had ploughed up the past so thoroughly that nothing came back from it now but these – sort of stingless ghosts: as if things in the past were *themselves* now, with no trailing fringes left, and only a kind of mathematical pure density. I wanted to write and ask her – it seemed the obvious moment. So I did write. Then later that morning I got your wire. It was a shock, you can imagine. So the letter didn't go.'

'Very strange,' murmured Mrs Burkett; then conclusively: 'You should have sent it. It was a splendid opportunity lost.'

'I debated. I opened the envelope and scrawled at the end: "I wrote this before knowing he was dead." But it looked so fishy I tore it up. She wouldn't have believed it.' Lifting her hand, she spread the long fingers and through narrowed eyes examined their outline of lucent rose against the light of the lamp. 'And if she had believed it she wouldn't have cared for it.'

'What makes you think so?'

'Well, don't you see, the dream ...? I'd described it. My idea, of course, was to suggest that so far as I was concerned there was nothing now to prevent a reconciliation. But under the circumstances it looked as if I was suggesting the opposite.'

'I do not follow.'

'How could I tell, she might have felt it as – one last thrust I'd always bided my time for. She always thought everything I did so typical of me. How could I be sure it wasn't?' Then seeing her mother

163

still groping, frowning, she added impatiently: 'Oh, don't you see – the pay-off? My little way, *don't* you see, of letting her know that Rickie and I were – in contact, together, when he died?'

'Telepathy!' exclaimed Mrs Burkett. She looked suddenly grave: then wistful, dreamy.

'I'm not saying so,' said Dinah, getting briskly to her feet. The immaterial sounding-board between each generation and its off-spring threw back an echo neither was aware of: she had assumed her mother's voice. 'It was odd, I grant you, but probably pure coincidence. After all, one dreams often enough of people who aren't dying or just dead.'

'True. Yes, coincidence perhaps,' said Mrs Burkett. 'And perhaps not. Who knows? He was unconscious for hours. Who knows where the mind wanders at such times? Last words are often so very curious.' She picked up *The Times* and dropped it into the waste-paper basket. 'It would not seem to me beyond the bounds of probability that Rickie should have thought of you: it is open to you to decide whether or not you could have picked the thought up. A dying man might well remember the woman he had loved.' Opening the door and noting with satisfaction that Griswold was streaking up the stairs ahead of her, she added: 'You must know that nothing now could give me greater pleasure than to see you and Madeleine reconciled. Mind you, I am not asking it for *my* sake. It will come about one day. It is merely that I would be pleased if it were to happen in my lifetime.'

But what with one thing and another it did not happen in her lifetime; or rather, since in so far as it could bring her pleasure or its opposite her life was over, she was not present at the reunion of her daughters.

'*Why not? Why not?*' cried someone, tearing Madeleine out of sleep. Her heart was racing; she craned her neck to see the luminous clock on the bed-table beside her: five-thirty, a bad time of the morning to wake up; still totally dark. She lay down flat, struggling to plunge, to burrow back down again below this rocked and splintering level into which she had been hurled. What had happened? This was no way to wake to face a difficult day. Why difficult? She cast about, remembered: Dinah was in her house. For a split second it seemed so unlikely that she was tempted to get up, cross the passage, open the door opposite and discover – yes, the head of Dinah darkening the pillow with a blot of silence; not the head she might have seen, had seen so often when she slipped in to wake him in the morning; saw always with the twofold vision of a person in love: tranquil intensity of recognition doubled with astonished joy. Each time, she found him flung into a non-consciousness so total that the very bed seemed to say: *touch me not*; each time, when finally she touched him he woke up at once, looked at her in surprise, then with delight.

She strained her ears for some actual repercussion that might have roused her – the dog worse, perhaps, or asking to be let out, Dinah creeping downstairs; but nothing was astir. Uneasily her mind ranged from room to room after the manner of women whose children are away; wondering which of them? what pain or nightmare? – before remembering that their beds are empty.

She did not often greatly miss her children; indeed, since she had had a lover found herself disposed at times to be thankful for their absence; but now she felt a tugging hollow in her diaphragm, longed to be able to place them within earshot, under her eye, as they had been when she first came here ... centuries and a moment of time ago: the boys sharing the room at the end of the passage, Clarissa in the midget room next door; above, the attic, a jolly sort of place where they retired to smoke cigarettes in secret, so they imagined, to play the gramophone, read magazines or simply lie about squawking with laughter and doing nothing at all for hours on end instead of taking healthy exercise. That was family life; and now she had none. She had kept it going as long as possible; it had survived the beginning of the war – even blossomed and solidified after Rickie had vanished abroad in 1940 on a secret mission; the boys still safe at Eton, Clarissa's nursery-governess-turned-cook-general married and departed, herself learning to cook, to wash and press, to plant vegetables, raise chickens. 'More fun these holidays that I ever remember,' Anthony had written. He had praised her ironing of his shirts; Colin, rightly more critical, had preferred to do his own ironing. Cursing Clarissa for her weight, they had pedalled all over the countryside with her on the carriers of their bicycles, taking turns. They had taught her to jump her pony; and at harvest driven a tractor for a neighbouring farmer. Gone out with their guns at Christmas ... What a happy time! A halcyon interlude in spite of all. No Anthony the following summer, except for one brief leave: he was an officer cadet by that time (not as tall as he had promised to be, and though such sweet looks not splendid like his father and his grandfather); but Colin, emerging at last from round-shouldered doughy puberty and developing an original face, a taste for chamber music and a *désabusé* wit, had worked again in the harvest and brought home a young schoolmaster called Jocelyn Penrose one evening for supper: agreeable chap, not a bit like the usual run of beaks, rejected for the Army because of infantile paralysis in youth. But only when he was tired could one detect that one leg dragged a little. He was tanned, fair, shortish, muscular, ripe corn colour all over: romantic ploughboy looks, except for the nervous fineness of his hands. Angry to be teaching, not to be in the Army, he worked fiercely in the fields, on the ricks, in the apple orchards, working off his rage. He liked music, he read modern poetry. He had an attractive rather sad quiet voice. He took to Colin. He eyed Clarissa and teased her and she blushed. He dropped in often to supper. He left his lodging in the next village and came to stay for the last week of the holidays, and met Anthony. They had all hoped that Rickie might get away from the Admiralty for at least one night, but at the last moment he was prevented. All through that week, under his eyes that flicked, glided in their sockets like a pair of shining green-flecked fishes, she felt her beauty flowering, serenely flowering. A family affair. Colin and Clarissa went back to school; he had one more night before his own term started, so he stayed one more night. He came to her room and into her bed and was her lover. She was a woman in love at last, she was unfaithful to her husband.

Rickie was dead, and Anthony dead, Colin in South Africa; Clarissa with a set jaw had transferred herself lock stock and barrel to the attic. When her school friends came to stay they had the boys' room, which had been redecorated to make it less of a reminder. Jocelyn still came to stay, she was still in love with him, he still made love to her; leaving her round about dawn to sleep for a few hours alone in the room opposite; but since he never put his imprint on it, never left behind so much as a book with his name in it, the room remained what it had always been – anonymous. Yes, Rickie's dressing-room of course; but under that title it could never, even in Clarissa's eyes, have assumed a sanctified identity. Rickie had occupied it so little; after Anthony's death, she could count on the fingers of one hand the times he had come to share the house with her. Could he have guessed about Jocelyn? She never knew, he gave no indication. He had seemed – something else as well as bereaved and over-tired ... Rather *distrait?* Not so much that, not exactly indifferent; kind, friendly as ever, not in the least hostile or suspicious: simply more detached, more shadowy than seemed natural. Because of this she had not confessed as she had meant to ... As the months went on he had seemed one might say to *prefer* to stay in London. He was glad enough to see her when she went up every ten days or so to lunch with him; but the only week-ends he ever jotted down were those of Clarissa's half-term holidays. To these he never omitted to accompany her: unreal interludes in a chintzy Tudor-style hotel not far from the school grounds, country house atmosphere, period *décor*, old-world latches on the doors, Clarissa and several polite best friends for lunch and tea ... The strain, the rain, the draughts, the tepid bath water, the boredom, the dreaded yet welcome hour of departure on Sunday evening, the farewells artificially alleviated on both sides with Mars bars and jokes and home-made rock cakes in a tin, the sadness of the school hats stuck on at the last moment, of the hands waving out of the over-loaded taxi, Clarissa's loud final '*Write!*' coming out of the dark with a note of desperation, to cause unformulated remores, each time, in the night watches ... But Rickie had seemed always to relax, amused and sympathetic, playing any card or paper game suggested, watching and listening to Clarissa, his manners gratifyingly courteous to her self-possessed accomplices.

When he came across the lawn that morning she was in the garden, picking peas into a basket. She knew it when she saw him. Anthony had been killed. She said so, and he nodded, and took the basket from her and led her into the house with his arm round her shoulders. He gave her a stiff brandy and helped her pack a bag and put her into the car, and they went first to Eton to pick up Colin and then straight down to Clarissa. Then they went on, all four of them ... she was never quite sure where. Seven days in a little house on the banks of the Wye, lent to them, staff and all, by a friend of Rickie's in the Admiralty; the last time they were ever together as a family; Rickie had arranged it all. They did everything as usual: fished, walked, picnicked, made jokes; motored one day to St David's and looked at the fabulous cathedral. They cheered the landing (with Rickie's assistance) of Clarissa's first salmon. They talked about Anthony; and again and again when Clarissa broke down, when Colin's anguish ...

when Rickie and I clasped but could not comfort one another. No, it was not supportable, either then or now; only it had had to be lived through. They had had to improvise a method for doing so, and somehow it had worked: the best their kind of family could do under the circumstances, to help each other to commemorate. Their strong determination – to be brave, to be unmorbid and unselfish, to go on living as usual for Anthony's sake – had accomplished something: held them as it were out of time for those seven days, exposed yet cradled, hand in hand: a breathing space in which to begin to look for the materials that must be found to build a bridge. On the way back they stopped in Bath and Rickie took Clarissa to the cinema, and she and Colin visited the Abbey and the Roman ruins. Leaving Clarissa at school was a bad moment; and then Colin went back to Eton and Rickie to London; and she went to her mother. After that, the hours became more and more difficult to live through. She collapsed and was put to bed for three weeks in a dark room, under sedatives. When she recovered, she returned to the cottage and Jocelyn came to see her. He helped her in the garden and read aloud to her and slept with her in his arms, comforting her with tenderness, patience and compassion. Rickie came for a long week-end at the beginning of the next holidays; Colin had a fortnight before he was called up. In September, Clarissa having gone to stay with a best friend, she went with Jocelyn to a farmhouse in the middle of Dartmoor. Fathoms deep in love, she scarcely gave a thought to her family. Rickie in any case had left London on another secret mission and was incommunicado. Very rarely during the remainder of the time left to him before his death did he return to the cottage. It was as if – she thought now suddenly, her heart turning over – he had been relinquishing his stake in it; by gradual stages, with no word said, vacating it.

There was one time she could not place when she had telephoned to tell him she was going to Clara for a few days' rest. When she came back she found a friendly note from him: he had been given a weekend unexpectedly, too late to let her know, in any case wouldn't have wanted to upset her plans, hoped she'd had a good rest as he had – he'd slept pretty well the clock round, got Mrs Dobson in to cook for him, read a bit, walked a bit, got some letters written. *Darling*, he headed it, and at the end: *Love, darling*.

She had not failed him ... not fundamentally. It was not as though he had been even curious about Jocelyn, let alone suspicious: the name had come up many times in the children's conversation. When Clarissa blew faint doleful blasts on her recorder and told him it was a birthday present from Jos he had merely looked amused; and if he guessed the clue to her own revived interest in poetry he never gave a hint. She had stuck to the job for which he counted on her – the preservation in the midst of chaos of a base, a place of security from which his children could, when they must, depart; to which they might, if they could, return. His trust in her for that had been complete; she had not let him down. He would not have minded about anything else; had long forfeited any right to expect from her physical fidelity; and for the rest was generous enough to welcome any comfort or companionship she might turn towards to alleviate her loneliness and heal her grief. For all she knew he had had somebody himself in London: that might well have been the reason for what she had sensed in him – that aura of shadowy withdrawal. Secretive by nature, he preferred secretiveness in others ... Feline, taut, wary in his passions, swiftly abashed, made poor by poverty of welcome ... Yes, but also the obverse, which she knew in that second, that ghost-self of disjoined marriage who lies embraced for ever with its former partner, continuing to generate those once-conceivable forms they slew or failed to fertilize – the obverse also: swiftly responsive, rich, triumphant in delight, pride, passionate gratitude ... as Dinah knew, none better, in her flesh and blood; as once in one split second of blind pre-vision she had known, known certainly though not believed, that Dinah was going to know. Not that it mattered now. Don't think about it. *Stop.*

She tried; but all the same the ambushed image sprang.

Anthony suddenly appeared fondling the hand of Dinah, crying with ardent love: 'Your cherry hand!' He was three years old.

'Nose, cherry *nose*,' corrected Rickie, smiling, while Dinah leaning towards the little boy said in soft mockery: 'Cowslip cheeks.'

At this he had looked first gratified, then perplexed, touching his nose and cheek and then the hand he held in both his own, saying finally, with loss of assurance:

'*Not* nose. And not those red kind of cherries. That other sort – what's in the dining-room.'

He watched their faces anxiously, awaiting revelation. Then:

'Ah, *white* hearts,' said Rickie, lounging on the arm of Dinah's chair, also leaning forward, his shoulder pressing hers, to tweak his son's ear. Then as if on an idle impulse he picked up that hand of Dinah's, polished, waxy, edged with a half-transparent coral flush, turned it over, examined the pronounced, delicate structure of its bones and joints, said low:

'Cherry. Yes, *I* see. Clever little boy.' Then holding out the hand to him, in a provocative whisper: '*Bite!*'

Anthony's eyes opened in wild surmise; Dinah with uncharacteristic brusqueness pulled her hand away. All over. Innocent pretty fooling, meet for children's hour. Rickie's glance slid towards me, he came over to the sofa and stroked my forehead. I was convalescent from the birth of Colin – sharper-eyed perhaps than usual. I saw Rickie turn Dinah's hand towards me to show me what lay coiled inside its palm ... but I told myself nonsense, neurotic fancy.

All over, all painless now; images, words without power or colour, their meaning within meaning long ago exhausted ... No, not *all*, not over, never to be over. She turned on her side, awaiting what was now ineluctable: apparition of the child, bursting again without warning through yet one more crack in time, focused dead centre against toneless shadows, blazing with inextinguishable terror, pity; searing a shaft down into limitless naught; infinitely removed yet always near, clear and exact – Anthony in the very flesh and hair, the clothes, the mood and gestures of whatever hour he arbitrarily selected to present himself. The voice called pipingly: 'Your cherry hand!' Or wailed: 'I dreamed you lost me'; or asked: 'Could anybody's heart break if they weren't careful?' Or: 'Flowers can have a sick smell,' it said in a knowing way; or in a way of anguish: 'Must we be dead?' – such things as children say. The voice piped its own dirge, the words wove a little shroud of pathos to contain them, dwindled and crouched down harmless. The words stirred, bred, the shroud convulsed grew great, it groaned with swelling symbols, with proliferating echoes, the voice burst through and split the world.

She waited for this to happen; but this time she was spared. He vanished quietly in his white blouse and buttoned-on pants and scarlet slippers; leaving behind him his customary offering – a taste of poison, the old one with the new fashionable name. *Angst*; more popularly known as guilt.

Quite a common thing; as common, so one heard, to humanity as having a father and a mother. One day, perhaps, she would give up and go to an analyst to discover who it was who played this claustrophobic game with her – Grandmother's Steps or Looking Back; or the game of the Stalker Stalked. Creep up, creep up, one step and then another; pause; risk a little run; pause, big step forward; TOUCHED! She crept, she was crept up on; she stiffly ran and stopped; she heard through her crawling spine that wing-beat sound, pounced on it just in time or rather just too late; in time, too late was pounced upon ... But who was the other player? Who called: '*Back to the beginning!*' – or faceless fled away back beyond recall? What panic echoing what desire could possibly engage with her in such equivocal sport?

Death wish. Birth trauma. Narcissism, sadism, masochism: the terms of reference were all available. The games ceased, or went underground, after the young man, the young lover, Jocelyn, came forward to embrace her; returned with excruciating variations after the young man, the young son lost his life ... Oh but there were no words for the cat and mouse game that went on then. But whoever appeared and vanished in her nights, it was never Rickie. He seemed to have retired for ever from the scene, leaving no travesties of himself as legacy, no reminders behind the keyholes, in the cellars. Why should he spare her? Why should Anthony, her best-beloved, hunt her so ruthlessly? She was not guilty towards him – had never destroyed his confidence or let him down; except perhaps twice, but in such minor ways ... Once at the swimming baths when she had publicly rejected him because among other people's fearless children he was the only one to be a coward, a humiliating child; once – rather worse – when he had come upon her weeping in her bedroom and asked her why, and she had answered because Daddy had been unkind to her. Bad that, of course – a classical example. On both occasions he had received the shock in the same way: a look of chill exhaustion, a lid half-lowered, veiling an eye gone dead ... as if he had been given a hypodermic shot. She had been scared, telling herself that this, already, was his method, the way he dealt with suffering imposed upon him. Out of this, murmured a voice in her, would come the means and method, one day, of imposing it. Could anybody's heart break if they weren't careful? Yes, Anthony was going to be careful, unless one was careful, never to let his own heart break.

But who could define heart? – how was it to be measured, where did it reside? Cold poets who fed on hearts – the true, the false – and spat out the remains, they celebrated it. Practitioners in psychology had other terms for it, Jocelyn, with his turn for paradox, insisted that heart was never a commodity exchanged in that least disinterested of all human phenomena, the passionate idyll. *'What do you mean, Jocelyn, by a passionate idyll?' 'You should know.'* Radiantly he smiled. Pinning down heart, qualifying, separating kindness, disallowing generosity, he concluded at last that it could best be defined by considering its opposite, the void: it was the reverse of the void in the being's centre; nothing to do with a code of morality, by no means always recognizable in good conduct. It was a residue, an essence ... something more like grace. Not unselfishness, but the capacity for freedom from self – the void-containing self. He more than suspected himself of lacking heart. *'But why?'* Because he was capable only of passion; only of self-torture, not of suffering; only of intensity of soul, not of expansion. If she did not believe it now, she would discover it one day: a treat in store for her.

'And what about me, Jocelyn, my heart?' 'Ah, you! ...' Radiantly he smiled. People with hearts could die of them, he said; they could not petrify or shrivel. Age was the final testing time, the time of resurrection – or of none. Lying in his arms she entered a dark maze where, lightly, he and Rickie set to partners, each holding her by a hand.

'Strong passions from a child but not much heart.' Whose well-known voice of summing-up resounding in her ears? Her mother's. Pronouncing verdict on her eldest child. But when pronounced? Never in my hearing, thought Madeleine; certainly never repeated to me. What then? Mere morbid self-accusation, self-begotten ... Yet it went on sounding, with an authentic note, as if it were the record of an ultimate judgement never delivered, locked up, so the judge had fancied, to die with her; yet in her last unconsciousness she had exhaled it; and I, thought Madeleine, received it ... but never heard it until now? When I sat with Dinah by her bed in the nursing home a month ago, when I saw Dinah face to face at last, when we knew she would not rally: then was the moment when from her fading mind she yielded it up and I received it. When all was over I broke down and said: 'I wish she'd known we were here together. Do you think

she might have known? Surely she must have.' Dinah, also in tears, doubtless thinking me hysterical and childish, went on holding my hand but did not answer. We were reconciled.

But it should have been brought about on the living side of their mother's lifetime, and it had not been. *Why not? Why not?* At last she had tracked it down – the cry torn out of the pit of her with her waking. It was her fault, her failure of heart and no one else's.

A matter chiefly of procrastination; a matter not sufficiently important to warrant the effort, the emotional disturbance bound to be involved. Time enough, time enough to see which way the cat jumped. She had been rescued from despair, snatched from the core of the furnace; she was reprieved, she was safe at last, but still so vulnerable that she must be given time to relax, to consolidate herself; she must be allowed to care only for one person, the one to whom she owed her life given back to her, who needed her at last as much as she needed him. Anybody likely to interfere, to ask questions, to give an opinion on the relationship must be set at a certain distance for fear of some contagion. Anybody who might with one finger touch her security and set it rocking; might smile, secretive, with a stretch of the nostrils, a twisted eyebrow; might come again to the door, a waif, *mysterious*, in straits, on the prowl, on the make, but seeming to be the one with no demands to make because she had taken steps to corner all the answers ... Or, worst of all, if one came again to *her* door, palms icily sweating, lungs paralyzed from terror, determined as before to swallow pride and be less pardoner than suppliant, bent on offering terms of surrender so rare, so honourable that they would, they must be freely accepted and adhered to; only to find, as before, so grotesque a discrepancy between one's preconception of the drama to be unfolded and what had actually been played out; to be caught out in fact once again by the unforeseeable, seen ... seen this time by Dinah, as Dinah had once been seen by Madeleine: *double-faced*.

The door had opened to admit her; she had walked straight upstairs, intent on saving Rickie, walked straight into treachery. Found two, not one, awaiting her. *Rickie betrayed.*

That was how she would be seen by Dinah if she came holding out the olive branch; came unaccompanied yet with someone doubtless visible to Dinah behind her shoulder, turning her face and Dinah's towards the ambush where once more Rickie would be hidden and Rickie would be betrayed.

The taxi deposited her and drove off; she cast a tense and furtive glance upwards over the high dingy peeling façade of the building that on one floor or another concealed the actual form of Dinah; and mounted the steps towards the front door. A dog in the basement set up a shrill yapping. On her right a row of starveling privet bushes flanked a segment of wall truncated, crookedly slanting, seemingly sinister, like a portion of a surrealist film set. A stunted tabby cat without a tail shot out of the area, leaped the railings and vanished along the narrow pathway between this wall and the side of the building. An unfamiliar square, a drab secretive part of London. Curious to think of Rickie approaching it so many many times, hurrying up these steps, closing this dark door after him in lively anticipation – freeman of a second area of domesticity, more private, more tempting than the one on the other side of the park, where also he was expected, to which sooner or later he would return, wrapped in the cloak of a double life – rank cloak, invisible. She bent to examine the four bell buttons each with a card above it on the left of the door, then straightened up again, opened her handbag and rapidly surveyed herself in the square of mirror, taking courage from the flawless mask that gleamed back at her from behind a finely-spotted black veil. Very becoming, these veils; a disguise she had come to rely on for self-confidence. For a second she wondered whether this growing dislike, mounting to phobia almost, of exposure to full daylight, could be connected with the psychology of rejection; whether if she had a lover ...

She started to ascend, her tread echoing round the steep well of the uncarpeted stone staircase, her imagination stiffly apprehending fragments of Dinah's actual, unsubjectivized identity. She was going to confront the person who was at home here; she was going to break in on this person's independent social life: an orderly life, not the life of an adulterous dipsomaniacal waif awaiting rescue willy nilly by the sister she had wronged.

On the second floor landing, her breath caught in her throat, her pulses hammering, she stopped dead, relinquishing a project that now seemed to her insane. A door above her opened, closed again, someone came winding with a measured tread down the last short wooden flight, emerged before her: elderly stoutish man, dark, sallow, foreign-looking, dressed with a certain dandified distinction – grey suit, silk shirt, lavender bow tie; something about him – his eyes? – not ordinary or reassuring. His face, an engrossed one, closed as it took the shock of this unbargained-for encounter; the sunken eyes searched hers, were quickly lowered. With a murmured 'Good evening. Excuse me,' he passed her deferentially and continued his descent. *Who?* Who possibly? Doctor? Professor in exile? Representing what further portion of the now terrifying identity silent, hidden just above her head? *Murderer?* Dinah strangled on the bed or with her throat cut ... Dinah having a few friends in for a drink ... Anything was possible, all possibilities equally appalling. But now there was no turning back. She went on, found herself before a door painted canary yellow, touched a bell.

Almost at once the door was flung open. A young man in grey flannels and black polo-necked sweater stood staring at her, a smile that seemed at first both welcoming and teasing fading sharply as he took her in. Behind him, out of sight, a voice, Dinah's, called out in a tone – familiar, lightly mocking – to match his smile: 'Come in, come in. What have you forgotten *this* time?'

Still blocking the entrance, the young man said quickly: 'It's not him.' Dinah was well guarded. Next moment, while Madeleine with a sense of final loss of bearings began to stammer: 'I came – I wondered if ...' Dinah appeared behind his shoulder.

'Oh, it's you.' Cold nasal languid voice after a moment's pause. 'What a surprise.' She put a hand on the young man's shoulder and added: 'Come in.' She elbowed him gently aside, turned her back, and Madeleine followed her into a low rectangular room decorated, it seemed to her stupefied sense of vision, with an effect of brilliant splashes of colour against darkness; a full room, a lived-in, book-strewn yet not untidy room, original and charming.

'Sit down,' said Dinah, giving a small armchair a perfunctory push. Madeleine sat down. Everything that was happening was mechanical. Dinah stood looking down at her, her hands in the pockets of a black overall tied tightly round her fragile waist, her hair falling thick, lop-sided over one eye and loose on her shoulders, her face a spectral mask. And what can mine be? thought Madeleine, trembling.

'Well, what's happened?' said Dinah in the same voice.

In dumb query Madeleine looked up. 'Accident?' drawled the voice. 'Illness? Or what?' Then suddenly, metallic, strident: 'I *said, what's happened?*'

'Nothing's happened.'

'Oh. I thought perhaps you were a widow. With the *chic* veil. Do push it up or something. I feel at a disadvantage.' She laughed, a brief impertinent sound; then as Madeleine with one scornful gesture removed hat, veil and all, turned brusquely away, walked to the mantelpiece, took a cigarette from a packet and lit it with deliberation. 'We thought,' she continued, keeping her head averted, 'it was Selby back for something he'd left, didn't we, Rob?'

'That's right,' agreed the young man who had remained standing by the door, his blank eyes fixed on space.

'Selby's a very absent-minded man. Did you pass him on the stairs? You must have.'

'I did pass somebody.'

'How funny! He's a friend of ours, of Rob's at least – Selbig his name is really, Dr Ernst Selbig. Oh, my manners! I haven't introduced you. This is Rob Edwards. Rob, this is my sister, Mrs Masters.'

The young man now advanced to wring Madeleine's hand, saying: 'Pleased to meet you' in a stylized way. His grip drove the rings into her flesh, she was unable not to wince from pain. It seemed less a clasp of greeting than a violent muscular spasm. His appearance was extremely striking: pale yellow hair, a shock of it, straight, silky, a long face of curiously perfect cut and finish, and biscuit-coloured, as if carried out in thick glazed china, with prominent cheek-bones and sculpturally modelled lips; the eyes put in last – yellow-green glass, transparent.

'Should I fix a drink?' he inquired of Dinah in a transatlantic accent of the bonhomous-host type, strangely at odds with given circumstances and with some other half-throttled more natural mode of speech.

'Not for me,' Madeleine said hastily. 'I can't stay long. I . . .' She added: 'Thank you.'

'Oh, come on, we shan't poison you,' said Dinah briskly. 'You're not on the wagon, are you? If you're considering me or Rob it's quite all right. We *were* both on a bend up till recently and we *did* have to lay off, didn't we, Rob?'

'That's right.' A faint transparent smile crossed his expressionless face.

'But now we just drink in a mild domestic way and take turns winding up the gramophone. I *cannot* think why you've come, but I suppose you'll tell me in your own good time.'

Waiting till the youth had withdrawn, she hoped with tactful timing, through the door towards the kitchen, Madeleine burst out in angry wounded protest:

'I haven't had much chance yet, have I? This isn't any easier or pleasanter for me than it is for you. I realize it's a shock for you, my coming, but at least give me credit ... I don't propose to bounce you into seeing me. If you refuse to talk, just say so and I'll go. But stop slicking it up into cheap melodrama. I haven't come for hush-money. And I'm not from the Rescue and Preventive.' She was conscious of the dark flush rising to scorch and settle in her cheeks.

Raising her eyebrows and assuming the expression of one who remarks: 'The little spitfire!' Dinah emitted a long pseudo-appreciative whistle. The door to the kitchen opened and the youth came in with his light tread, stopped in the middle of the room and stood like a peaceable animal at home with but indifferent to man.

'None left?' inquired Dinah. Leaning against the mantelpiece she smiled at him.

He shook his head. She lifted the cover of a small white and gold porcelain bowl beside her, took a pound note from it and held it out to him.

'There you are,' she said in an oddly formal yet encouraging voice. 'Be back soon if you can, and fix us a drink.'

'O.K.,' he said, without expression, pocketing the note; then to Madeleine, amiably: 'So long'; and was noiselessly gone.

'How long will he be?' asked Madeleine nervously, glancing at her wrist-watch.

Dinah appeared to ignore the question. Her stance suggested both abstraction and intentness, as if her ears were following some other, remoter, auditory line. The front door was faintly, clearly heard to bang. She came slowly then and took a chair facing Madeleine – a low Victorian nursing chair upholstered in a rich bright tapestry of wool and beads against whose high scalloped back her presence seemed designed, disposed, with deliberate economy and grace, as if she had become a portrait of herself. Then, while Madeleine cast about through a wave of physical nausea, through the drum-taps of the silence, for the true start with the right words, she remarked as if to herself:

'He won't come back.'

'You mean – not till I've gone? I thought . . .' She stopped. It seemed unsuitable to suggest that she was expecting the refreshment so recently offered.

'He won't come back at all. That's what I mean.'

'Why not?' Alarm gripped her; she glanced at Dinah thinking that perhaps Rickie had been right: Dinah was far gone indeed. But though once more ignoring a straight question, Dinah said presently, in a normal manner:

'What did you make of him?'

'He's frightfully good-looking,' said Madeleine with caution. 'Who is he?'

'Incredible looks, aren't they? I've never seen their equal.' She sounded pleased; meditated; then continued with a characteristic sniff: 'It's a handicap he won't surmount – everybody will see to that. He's a working-class character, one of the ones Bruce Corder picked up and did no good to. You may remember Bruce: he took to cocaine and killed himself a year or two ago. I'd lost sight of Rob. Bruce used to bring him to parties, and I never remember an evening it didn't end in tears – oh, the hell of a shindy, boo-hooing and bashing and smashing.' Her reminiscent smile broadened; all of a sudden she burst out laughing as if at some irresistibly comic memory; then her face set again, rejecting its moment of relaxation. 'I thought it was a shame. Rob was all right – not awfully bright but lovable. We always got on. His jokes amused me . . . He's from Nottingham . . .' Her eyes clouded, her jaw dropped slightly; she let her head fall back lifelessly against the chair. 'I don't know why I . . . This doesn't interest you,' she muttered.

'It does,' said Madeleine timidly. 'Truly it does. Very much.'

But nothing in the image of utter fatigue and melancholy confronting her responded. After some moments, however, the lips opened to say:

'Why have you come?'

'I'm not absolutely certain – now – yet . . .' Madeleine could not suppress a quavering laugh. 'I'm sorry. I do know really, I'm not trying to ... But I can't start till it starts coming in the right way. If you don't mind my staying a bit longer ...'

'Oh, I don't mind. Now you're here.'

Her tone seemed unequivocal, indifferent. She sat forward and lit a cigarette and while she did so Madeleine ventured a chary inspection of the room – books, ornaments, rugs, curtains, pictures. Pinned on one wall among miscellaneous paintings in oil and gouache which bore every mark of being the work of Dinah's friends, was a profile sketch of a man's head, life size, executed in red chalk. Rickie. A living line, distinctly a good likeness. She averted her eyes. Yet, she felt suddenly, it would have been an easy matter to comment critically: 'That's good of Rickie.' One turn one click and all could have been re-established, it seemed to her, on the old footing; only irrelevancies dividing them from the old schoolroom, from hours that seemed beyond time and change secure, discussing their future fates or the behaviour of their callow suitors. She waited in silence, too confused to adopt a course in any one direction; or else the initiative, she told herself, had passed to Dinah.

'He hadn't a chance,' said Dinah presently. She rose sharply to her feet and started to walk up and down, her head thrust forward, her hands pushed into the pockets of her overall. With every swerve in her pacing towards, away from Madeleine, her face seemed ground to a more harsh, a finer edge; and the broken sentences she laboured to bring forth fell heavily from her mouth like lumps of stone spat out. 'They got their rotten rotting teeth in him. *They've* got the belts and ties and rings and bracelet watches. And all the words. *Avant garde* passwords. And the freedom of the hunting grounds. All the happy hunting grounds mapped out, combed over. Barracks, pubs, ports, tube stations, public lavatories. How could he possibly be missed! The classiest piece of goods on the market. Bought and paid for. A *whizzing* beauty! Really but really a knock-out. And really but really amoral and uncorrupted and out of the bottom drawer! A natural gangster, a natural innocent. A natural. An enemy of society. *Done time!* – actually done time – for housebreaking! *Actually actively* anti-bourgeois. A real moronic proletarian high-brow. And a judge of character – well, that's true. He's been brought up to know his onions, he looks romantic, but he isn't – not he! Would you believe it? – he's not interested in personal relationships! But his manners are very good, you saw that for yourself. He was prepared to do right by Bruce according to his standards, but poor old Bruce, he didn't measure up. Rob thinks he made a monkey of him, parading him around one day and whisking him into purdah the next and sobbing and creating and turning sarcastic. It gave Rob the fair sick. Rob's got his pride. Poor Bruce, he had none. To the end he believed in salvation. It was a clash really of two – irreconcilable – standards of unscrupulousness. Rob doesn't know words like that. He just thinks we're all shockers, bastards, bitches. He disapproves of our messy mushy sex lives and our filthy language. What does he like? He likes going to the pictures, and betting on the dogs, and all-in wrestling, and going dancing, and being taken for rides in supercharged open sports cars. And drinks he likes, and money: he likes to be given lots of both. And me he likes. And Selby ... I can't say *I* do. And he's very fond of children; and he's partial to a day at Brighton – and I meant to take him. We shan't go now.' She dropped into her chair, as if suddenly dead beat. Her lids sank. She said again: 'He won't come back'; then added listlessly: 'You ought to be more careful.'

'*I* ought ...? You mean it's *my* fault he's not coming back? Why? I don't know what you mean. I don't understand. It all sounds mad. I ...'

Flushing darkly, Madeleine jumped up, seizing her handbag and dropping her gloves. Shocked pride, indignation contended in her with a painful sense of rejection, of mortification that seemed allied to guilt. Her enterprise, so arduous, resolved upon with such selfless intent of generosity, had foundered. She was a bungler, a humiliated figure; once again proved unacceptable by Dinah's standards, summed up, contemptuously walked out on by one of this crew, her Betters. And suddenly as she stood pulling on her gloves, she had an explosion of memory; that hated, hating voice rasped in her ears again. 'You're a great big gorgeous girl, you Madeleine, aren't you? – and of course I want to go to bed with you, damn you, but you're not a patch on little sister, are you? Are you now? Look at her! Look at that modelling. Plain one of the family, I take it? *Aha! Ha! Ha!* My God, if I could get that head on canvas ...' and so on and so forth. What gross, red-kerchiefed, corduroyed, unshaven drunk of a so-called artist, utter stranger; what outrageous, beer-and-sex-stained party years ago? Dinah's studio period, after she'd broken off her engagement and gone to live seedily on her own among raffish intellectuals; and after lying low for months started to invite us, just for the hell of it, to meet her interesting set; and Rickie became the rage and paid for all their drinks and bought at Dinah's prompting their ghastly daubs ... Amusing that Dinah should have classy relations with money, amusing to make suckers of them ... Going up to Rickie at that party, wishing to say: 'Look after me, take me away'; but able only brightly to suggest the lateness of the hour, a headache; and someone screeched: 'Oh, my *dear*! What *can* you be getting up to? You naughty double-faced disloyal thing you – making off with Rickie. Honestly, come come now, is it cricket? He's just your dish, we all know, but we *must* learn not to be a greedy girl, now mustn't we?' And Rickie with sheepish endearments, his eyes sliding, let me go away alone. We only had one latchkey. 'My dears, stop fussing. Darling Madeleine, cross my heart, I'll buckle him into his chastity belt and tuck him up *myself*, if it's romps in the dorm you're worrying about. Now *don't* be governessy, there's a good girl, I'll brush him down, the madcap, and get him along to you fresh as a rose for breakfast.' Thus we avoided the stigma of being the kind of stuffy bourgeois couple who left a party together. Thus amid the plaudits of the conspirators Rickie compassed his objective: swirled out, bemused, in the amorous maze, turning, turning, turning, embraced with the Belle of the Ball ... The truth was under my nose like a thing under a stone. I didn't lift the stone. It was forced up at last by what was breeding under it: the Thing, worm-generating, bedded in blood, roots, clay.

'I must apologize,' said Madeleine, 'for not being more careful. What you wish me to feel is that my tactlessness has been inexcusable. I just hoped – expected – to find you alone. I'm sure I don't know why. And I see that my turning up like this without warning must seem to you simply one more typical example of my utter insensitiveness and bad taste. I won't attempt to justify it. I'll go now.'

'Oh, come off it,' said Dinah still languidly but with a touch of something that might have been compunction in her voice. 'You don't need to justify it. There's obviously something – God knows what – you felt you had to say to me; and if you'd written or telephoned beforehand I should have had the option of saying no; and you couldn't risk that, you felt. So you plumped for shock tactics.'

'They were a risk too.' Madeleine went to the window and remained with her back turned, blindly looking out. 'You're not the only one to be subjected to shocks. I'm not the only one to inflict them.'

'No – o ...' drawled Dinah in a judicial tone. 'The shocks have been pretty evenly distributed.'

'Your friend, for instance. His shock appears to have been total.'

'Don't take it personally.' There was a hint of amusement in her voice; but turning from the window, Madeleine saw her face still clarified and stamped with its cold inward naught. 'I'm sure he thought you were a smasher. If I saw him again he'd rave about you – you really embody his ideal of womanhood. But I shan't see him again ... or not for God knows how long. You see ...' She stopped, shrugged her shoulders; then said peremptorily: 'Sit down again.'

Madeleine resumed her chair. Dinah's eye ran over her, an appraising glance. She said partly to herself: 'That's a good suit. Who made it?' – then as if cutting in on her own frivolous train of thought, continued hurriedly:

'What was I saying? Yes. I'll tell you. We were trying to start up some sort of a life together – look after one another, keep ourselves ticking over – see? It wouldn't make sense to you perhaps – I can't go into it. You see, we were drinking. We drink when we're in trouble – very weak of us, very unconstructive. He was in trouble too. It started about three weeks ago. I was sitting on a bench in Regent's Park; and he came by. I hadn't seen him for a long time. He was in very bad shape, that was obvious at a glance. I called out to him and then he went stiff all over, like an animal in danger. I thought he was going to bolt. But then suddenly he recognized me, he didn't bolt, he came straight up and sat down beside me. He'd been kicked out of – someone's flat, for stealing; and then the police had got on to him and picked him up; and some wealthy nobleman or other he'd expected would rally to him and bail him out had refused to help him – denied him thrice, in fact, to the police, as one might have expected. All very sordid. He was hysterical and melodramatic. He was going to blow the gaff on the lot of them, give 'em the works – blackmail – God knows what.' She paused to light a cigarette. 'I'd been sitting there seriously considering doing myself in – bringing my life to an end. But now here was someone as lonely as myself: it seemed *meant* I should go on living. So I brought him back ... He didn't exactly jump at the idea; on the other hand he didn't say me nay. And here we've been mewed up ever since in this eccentric fashion. Not a very solid ground plan, I suppose. But it's been company. I love his stories, they make me laugh – he's got such an eye, such an ear for – well, human behaviour. We understand one another. He's fond of me, I think. Is he my lover? That's what you're wondering, aren't you? Mr and Mrs Masters didn't envisage *that* when they discussed my case. Flat on my back of course, among the empty bottles, but not another *man* sharing my enseamèd bed. I was to be put in my place – put on probation – or in a Home for Inebriates.' With every sentence her voice grew quieter, flatter, as if driven back further, further towards total concentration of energy without release. She put a hand up, forbidding interruption. 'I know, *I* know. He folded up on you, he passed the buck. I saw it all, I heard it as if I was in the room with you – that night he shook off my miasmic presence and scuttled back to you crying help, help!'

'Shut up! Don't be ridiculous. He didn't.'

'Oh yes, he did.'

'He was so worried ...'

'Oh, I know all about his worries. We both know all about them now. He betrayed me to you.'

'He did *not* betray you. He was in despair ...'

'I'd sooner he'd kicked me in the teeth. Cleaner ... He thought I'd cracked up, he was scared. Poor brute, who can blame him? Poor Rickie. He's handed over, you're to be his conscience. I never would be that! *He*'s the one who's done for, not me. You can tell him so from me.'

'You're wrong, you're mad. It's wicked of you. It's not like that.'

'Isn't it? What is it then? He sent you to see me, didn't he?'

'No, he did *not*. It was my own idea.'

'Begged you to take pity on me. Lend a helping hand. Oh, and he'd make it clear you could afford to. Because at last he's come to his senses, he's quite himself again. You can see eye to eye about me at long last. A drunken tart, pretty well past praying for.'

Covering her face with her hands Madeleine said: 'I can't stand this any more.'

It was the low thick almost guttural sound of the voice that she meant, rather than the horror of what was being said. But the sound ceased. Dinah sat still, upright, in a characteristic attitude, knees

183

crossed, one high-arched foot in a green leather mule slanting downwards at its own odd steep angle. Still with her face buried, Madeleine
brought out with heavy sighs, reluctantly: 'If you think that of Rickie,
you can't love him.'

Her hands dropped down. Her eyes and those of Dinah met; they
stared together, surrendering at last to one another the image, helpless
and threatening, of the undone man between them. Presently Dinah
said in a faint light voice:

'Where is he? When is he coming back? . . . No, don't tell me, what's
the use? How are the children?'

'Very well.'

'I hope you're all right, all of you – will be. I'm not. But there's
nothing to be done. Thank you for coming – whatever you came for.'

'Where has he gone?' Dinah raised apathetically inquiring eyes.
'Him, Rob.' She hesitated over the semi-anonymous truncated name,
feeling it stick suddenly in her throat, become a symbol for all she
feared and hated – the levelling de-individualizing new order to whose
massed ranks something in Dinah was committed.

'Oh, Rob . . . God knows. I only know I'm sure he's hopped it.
Given me the bird.' Her smile was wintry, wry.

'But *why*? Aren't you – surely you're being morbid? Why should
he? – if he and you . . . You talk as if he was an escaped prisoner.
I thought you said it worked – that you were getting on together . . .'

Passionately she wanted Dinah to have this life with Rob. If it would
do to go on with, it must be restored to her: they must all be
immunized against the dire possibility of Dinah being left with
nothing.

'I suppose,' said Dinah after a moment, 'he felt a prisoner. Well,
I know he did. We both did in a way. But I hoped to make it work;
and I suppose he had no hope. I could only deal with the material
he let me deal with. What he was suppressing I could only – accept
as being there and leave alone. There was plenty pushed down inside
me too for him to leave alone. But for me it was different: I didn't
want to make a get-away; and sometimes he did want to. I've felt
it more than once these last ten days. I hoped it was a phase that
would pass once he got more confidence in – in his ability to lead
a positive life.' She paused, with a ghost of the forceful sniff that
Madeleine had learnt in the schoolroom to associate with Dinah's

formulas for living: some plan or other laid down beforehand, expounded with this committee-woman's sniff. Her face brightened for a moment, as if a gleam of curiosity, or of satisfaction in the untying of an intellectual knot were passing through her mind. 'No, not hope,' she murmured. 'I just insisted to myself. I *wanted* it to work – and he was negative – he let me have a bash at it. He's past *wanting*. Or never got as far as wanting ...' Her voice petered out on an edge of query; her face darkened again.

'But you're talking about him,' said Madeleine, 'as if it had all happened a long time ago. He's only been out of the room about half an hour.'

She felt the protest to be, if not altogether convincing, at least sensible and bracing; and was startled to see Dinah's mouth drop open as if she had received a shock: like a person, she thought uneasily, brought brutally to see herself in unsuspected straits, cut off.

'Yes,' she said presently, now totally incurious. 'Yes, he's only been gone ... What does it mean that I'm talking about him in the past? It means that I saw the end from the beginning. But you gave me a turn when you pointed it out.' Again a wry amusement touched her lips. 'I do get confused about time. If one loses one's emotional focus' – she stopped, struggled, went on huskily – 'that's what happens. Aeons – split seconds – they interchange. One gets outside the usual way of counting: *you* know – meal times, morning, afternoon, evening, night, if one goes on sitting in this ... if one has nobody to check up with.'

'Oh, Dinah.' Madeleine leaned forward, impulsively stretched out a hand. 'Darling.' But Dinah, though her eyes followed the movement without hostility, remained sitting bolt upright, not a muscle relaxing; and there was nothing to do except withdraw the hand. 'I don't know, I can't know, what it's all about; but I'm sure he will come back.'

'*He? Which?*' The monosyllables were a pounce, the glance accompanying them a sudden glare, the smile a grin. Madeleine looked away, less with a sense of outrage than of dread. Silence fell.

'Sorry,' continued Dinah, in thin staccato tones. 'Uncalled for. I go too far and no mistake. Everybody has always told me so; or if not told me *shown* me so. What does one do about it? I must resign. Then I can hurt nobody and nobody can hurt me. What makes you sure that Rob will come back?'

185

The question was rapped out with no perceptible change of tone; yet Madeleine felt, or feared to discover, behind it an appeal for reassurance; as if even she, Dinah, might in the pass she had come to be willing to believe that her judgement might be faulty; and that someone coming fresh to Rob might have detected something she had overlooked or dared not build on.

'It seems so dotty ...' she feebly began.

'You mean, because if a visitor drops in unexpectedly and one offers them a drink and then finds one's out of gin one naturally goes out to buy another bottle and naturally comes back with it?'

'Well, roughly that. It all seemed to me quite natural – normal ...? He didn't appear in the least – upset or peculiar? You didn't seem to mind. You gave him the money ...'

It was all she could say; but still it weighed on her that their last chance had gone of saving this situation on any deeper, equalizing level. 'Might your being sure conceivably make sense?' had been the unutterable cry or question. Frankly, she had answered, she had observed nothing beyond what had been apparent: that he had quietly popped out to remedy the most trivial of social predicaments. It was all she had found to say and it was the truth: or rather it was honest. Going further than was necessary in honesty, she could have added that she had been half looking forward to the reappearance of this unusually decorative male figure; personally regretted his non-return. But the truth required of her had been of another order. If only she could have said, for instance: 'Because from the way he looked at you it was perfectly clear to me that he adores you.' Even the opposite, some barely formulated conjecture told her, would have conferred grace, or the right prelude for it, upon this botched, maimed scene; if she could have said something on the lines of: 'No, I was judging superficially. Looking back I see now that everything was abnormal – looks, words, the way he took the note and didn't say thank you and made off. You are probably right when you say he won't come back. We must face the probability.' Ah yes, if she could have seized her cue and spoken the lines that would have led with artifice to 'we', not 'I' and 'you' ... Insight, in fact, plus magnanimity were what had been required, not honesty.

'Yes, I did give him the money,' agreed Dinah with slow cold satisfaction. 'Thank God for that anyway – I didn't prevent him. If anything brings him back, that will.' She looked fully across the gulf at Madeleine. 'You see, we hadn't run out of gin. There's two-thirds of a bottle in the kitchen. We didn't hide it or pour it down the sink or lock it up. We'd got to the point of being able to look at it together.' This time her laugh held a hint of rueful avowal in it: part of the void became a human area. 'You little know what drunks get up to – their ruses and stratagems. The thing is, the moment I called him in the park and he stopped, and didn't run away – the moment he came towards me *I* was – well, saved's a word I avoid – cured say, temporarily cured. I had good and sufficient reason to do what I preferred – snap out of it. But it wasn't the same for him. I was just the offchance he saw of giving himself a breather. And then the offchance we neither of us mentioned that ... However, *that* takes more than an act of hope on one side – which is all that it amounted to. Real hope isn't like that, is it? It's a state. For instance, being pregnant is a state of hope, real hope; but knowing it's on the cards one might become so isn't. He'd simply gone to earth. Men do that more than women, perhaps you've noticed. Isn't it queer to sleep in a shroud with someone? Perhaps you never have; but *if* you have by any chance you'll know one can't be said to have a lover in one's bed. That's the answer to your inquiry.'

'I didn't inquire,' the other murmured. 'It's not my business any-way.'

'No, it isn't, but I don't mind telling you.'

But I mind hearing, thought Madeleine, shrinking from the revelation. Such sexual confidences they had never, even in the old days, attempted to exchange. She curled herself sideways in her chair, one elbow propped on the arm and her chin in her hand: look and pose of a schoolgirl, nonplussed, chagrined, with flushed cheek and thick-lashed eyes cast down. I haven't much experience, she thought, abashed, uneasy, knowing that what Dinah had so violently exposed would germinate in her, pushing up wild shoots in territories fallow now for years; never to be explored, since her sole tenant, to whom she was still bound, disturbing once the virgin surface, taking the thin sweet-and-sour-tasting crop, had left her soil unhusbanded. Null sleep she knew, the neutral double nights of unembracing, casting no light or shadow; not folded, not released ... Not in a shroud: not what they meant, not the level that they pierced, those words half

187

understood that haunted her: *youth pined away, snow-shrouded virgin; fiend; rose; sick rose; invisible worm.*

'The dark night of the senses,' said a strangled voice: out of the corner of her eye, she saw white hands clench in a black lap. Then: 'He's my brother,' said Dinah, uttering in a voice almost gone dumb what seemed a sudden cry.

'Then he hasn't gone,' answered Madeleine as if hypnotized.

'Why not? Brothers do go.' Her dry laugh cracked, broke off. 'The unexpected apparition of yourself' – she held a hand up – 'that's not meant to be sarcastic – it shook him. You see, he hasn't any roots. Anybody, anything almost, breaking in from outside could blow him in another direction. You blew in like a breath of fresh air.' Not hostile, her eyes teased Madeleine.

'I didn't feel like one.'

'Oh, you don't understand about being in a trap. Forgive me if I sound high-hat – I don't think you can possibly understand it. Directly he came back without the bottle I knew he was announcing he must be off. Naturally I had to make it easy for him. He hasn't a bean.'

'What do you think he will do?'

'Couldn't say. Oh, drift round the pubs, I dare say, pick up some cronies – get stood a slap-up dinner and a comfortable lodging ... How should I know?'

'But what about his things? He must have left some clothes here?'

'Oh, those.' Her face lit up for a moment, as if the question tickled her. 'You're always practical ... Well, yes. Yes, I did buy him a couple of shirts and a toothbrush. His wardrobe is an intermittent sort of affair – quite extensive sometimes. This is a slump period. I suppose he might need the shirts. It depends on his luck.' She meditated. 'He might send Selby for them. I should hate that. I wonder if he's gone to Selby ... No, I doubt it. But sooner or later he will; or Selby will track him down. He always does. That's why I asked him round this evening – to show him how safe and sound Rob was.'

'Why? Is he responsible for Rob? Who is he?'

'Selby now ... Selby is a middle-European character who is interested in Rob. Also in me. He's interested in types. No, that's not strictly accurate. He does really love Rob, I think: he comes pounding and tiptoeing after him like the Hound of Heaven. The nosy old bastard ... Or could he be a saint? In actual fact he's some kind of a philosophical psychiatrist, Jewish of course, who left Germany for a number of good reasons; and he lives in Stepney in a large derelict hulk of a house with a grand piano in it and a picture he claims is a Caravaggio and might well be, and some Persian rugs and not much else – except bugs, I suspect. He owns this house and people seem to stay in it rent free – it's like a kind of crazy raffish Mental Home and slum tenement combined. He looks after these people – patients – treats them, rehabilitates them, God knows what – and a rare ripe lot they seem to be from what Rob tells me. Selby merely calls them a typical cross-section of humanity. I don't know what principle he picks them on, or how he sets to work on them: it seems everything from stammerers and bed-wetters through drunks and thieves to maniacs; with a sprinkling of financial down-and-outs with nowhere else to be. They come and go ... Oh, *I* can't make out what he is or what he's up to.' She frowned, rapt in the contemplation of a problem of personality; again the schoolroom seemed to project around them its former furniture and climate. 'How he picked up Rob,' she went on, 'is a mystery I've never solved; but Rob had a room there when he first came to London, and I know he can go back there whenever he feels – cornered. He took me there once some time ago when he got a fit of the horrors in the middle of a party. Such a room! – I still can't be sure I didn't invent it.'

'What was it like?'

'Low, dark, *red*. Suffocated with vast blocks of furniture: a Victorian dining-room suite – monstrous great sideboard and table, carved black varnished oak; four chairs with the stuffing bursting out of torn leather. A sour red ink smell from the Turkey carpet, and a smell of dry rot. Red plush curtains. Wallpaper – ah, the wallpaper!'

'What was that?'

'A smother of red roses, life-size, romping up trellis work, complete with particularly brown thorny stems and luxuriant green foliage ...'

'Goodness! Had he chosen it?'

'I think not. I think it was there and he decorated up to it. He was devoted to it. He said it made him feel he was living in a bower, those roses were so real. The furniture he'd bought in one lot at an auction when he first came to London – that was the time he was thinking of marrying a pure girl of sixteen from back home, and he felt it was real class – homey yet voluptous. He has a very domestic side, has Rob.' She fell into a brooding silence. 'Then he took me downstairs to call on Selby. Selby had gone to bed but he got up and let us in and made coffee and we talked. And then Selby played the piano. He told me he'd had a fashionable practice – as a specialist in nervous diseases – once in Germany; he had a hospital; but his methods were unorthodox; and he was one of the first to fall under suspicion of nameless Jewish crimes ... He got out of Germany in the nick of time.' She stopped again, frowning. 'He seems to have money ... He seems to be *expiating* something ... What? Something Jewish, terrible for him. Perhaps he left his family in trouble. Perhaps they're all in concentration camps, or dead. Rob says he never lets anything drop, not a word.'

'Do you see him often?'

'He turns up now and then, to check up on me. He gives me the feeling that he wants to *find out something* from me ... as if he was testing, putting me to the proof; not me personally, not exploiting me emotionally for himself ... but using me all the same, working something out through me, to reach some conclusion or other ...' Throwing her head up with sudden vigour, as if she had at least discovered her own meaning, she added: 'Some *foregone* conclusion of his own.'

'I shouldn't fancy that at all.'

'No, you wouldn't. I don't think I do. Did he look at you? What did you make of him?'

'I thought he looked – well, foreign. Interesting,' said Madeleine with caution. 'Queer eyes. We nearly bumped into each other on the landing. He looked startled – as if he hadn't heard me coming – I'd heard him, of course. Startled out of being too sunk in thought to hear me.'

'Ah yes,' said Dinah with an overtone of satisfaction. 'He'd be pre-occupied. He always is. He's a metaphysician. You never know where you are with them. Yes, you must have been a shock for him. He'd take you all in: another highly significant factor for him to weigh in the situation.'

'Why highly significant?' said Madeleine with annoyance, seeing herself scrutinized by an eye at once ungentlemanly, addle-pated and omniscient, and with Dinah's smug know-all connivance. 'Why can't seeing me unexpectedly give him a bit of a jump? Why pitch it up into a *situation* – cosmic?'

'He wouldn't pitch it up. That's what I was trying to explain about him. He doesn't manipulate – he simply arranges his material in an orderly scale of values. Whatever he is – and I'm still not sure – he's not a phoney middle man. He sees life in terms of moral or spiritual drama. It's a point of view. As for *you* – don't you see he knows enough about this set-up to know that *whoever* you were coming up the stairs – friend, foe, stranger – he couldn't discard you as casual or immaterial?'

'Then all I can say ...' began Madeleine; but what she could say she was unable to; and weakly, in disgust, she added: 'I wish I'd never run into him. It was most unfortunate.'

Her own mission, she felt, had been one of sufficient difficulty and high-mindedness; she had not presented herself on the landing to play her appointed rôle in a moral universe of this outsider's, this foreigner's construction. And how familiar this gradual transference of power and glory, this imposed suggestion that all problems of real importance lay always elsewhere – always within Dinah's sphere of vision, just beyond her own.

'Perfectly maddening,' agreed Dinah. 'Such a sell for me. We'd had quite a pleasant hour, the three of us. I invited him to come to Brighton with us. It would have been a tough day for me, considered as a jolly outing – I've never known anyone relax with such intensity. But worth it to see him doing the Pier and playing darts in the pubs with Rob. Ah well ... I must ring him up, I suppose, and tell him it's off for the present ... No, I won't!' she exclaimed, springing to her feet. 'How *can* I? And anyway he'll know by now. By now he's on the watch again. Ugh! I'll keep out of the whole mess. After all this, let me get you a drink.'

Without awaiting yes or no, she went swiftly out of the room and presently returned from the direction of the kitchen carrying a bottle and two tumblers. 'What do you like in yours?' she said, without a glance at Madeleine. 'I haven't much in the way of dilutions. And the more dainty cocktail glasses seem to have got broken.' Then as Madeleine shook her head and made as if to rise: 'No? Why not? Do you mind if I do?' She filled one tumbler half-way up with gin, swallowed half of that, and sat down with the glass in her hand. 'It's Rob's, this bottle,' she said. 'But he won't mind.'

'I must go,' said Madeleine. She got up.

'Must you really?' She looked aside for a moment, her eyes flicking as if blindly round the room. She drained the glass and wiped her lips on the back of her hand.

'Unless,' said Madeleine, 'you'd like me to stay.' Avoiding Dinah's, her eyes went hunting for a focusing point and came to rest on a spot on the wall, on the drawing of Rickie.

'No, I don't think so, thank you.'

'Will you – why don't you come back with me? Come home. It would be quite all right, I'm alone. I'd like it so much. Please do. I don't like ...'

Dinah's eyes widened, came to dwell on her, a blank enormous look.

'I think I'd rather not,' she said after a moment. 'Thanks all the same. I'll be all right. I shall have a good sleep. Selby left me some more dope. That's one blessing about being in the hands of a foreign medical man. He's very free with it. I don't make a habit of it, you know, but I like to know it's available.'

'Yes,' agreed Madeleine nervously. 'I've got something I take too – quite mild and harmless. At least I did when I was sleeping badly ...'

Suddenly, simultaneously, their ears began to strain. Someone started to come up the stairs: a free step, bounding, echoing. Then it was cut off. On the floor below, a door slammed.

'Besides, he might come back any moment,' said Dinah, rapidly, in an unreal voice.

But Madeleine now was silent, biting back what rose, insistent, unformulated, to her lips. *He won't come back: don't think it, get out of this: don't let him ...* Words to that effect. And when presently the theme's last variation, final resolution, broke out of Dinah, causing her to say:

'But he knows, I suppose, there's nothing to come back to. I'm nothing. It's not him I want here. He's known it all along ...' – it was still impossible to answer.

'Well, good-bye then,' continued Dinah without getting up, without a smile. 'Thank you for your kindness.'

'There's – isn't there anything I can do?'

'Well, actually *yes*,' said Dinah, in the voice of one struck by a bright idea. 'Could I touch you for a smacker? I'm stony broke, for the moment.'

Eagerly, apologetically Madeleine dived into her handbag and laid on the table beside the gin bottle the contents of her wallet; five pounds.

'All that? Sure you can spare it?' said Dinah, squinting at the flame of the match with which she was lighting another cigarette. 'Much obliged.'

Making shame-faced for the door, Madeleine stopped. Something important had been forgotten. She strove to remember what it was; remembered.

'I – there's one thing. I shall never tell – *anyone* – anything about this. Not even that I ever did this – came to see you. I don't want him – I very much don't want it to be known. So far as I'm concerned it never will be. I swear it. I told you it was my own idea: it was. But I might be asked ... Though I don't think I will be. If you should ever be asked, would you – will you do the same?'

Curt, final, Dinah's answering nod dismissed her.

And so far as she was concerned, the door that let her out, that shut in Dinah on that evening, had never been reopened. In her inward eye Dinah remained closeted, waiting for two, or for one, or for no one, with a sketch of Rickie to look at, and Rob's bottle in her hand, and some pound notes of Madeleine's that she would have picked up later and spent on drink perhaps, or perhaps used frugally as pocket money; or perhaps torn up and pulled the plug on. That was the last encounter until they had met across the death-bed in the Nursing Home, with Dinah in the flesh. She, Madeleine, had hurried down into the freedom of the streets and re-entered that sufficiently going concern, her home, leaving Dinah sealed off in her high-up, empty room. Even under sore temptation, she lay reminding herself, under the onslaught of Dinah's last monstrous, so nearly victorious offensive, she had kept their pact unbroken; even at that pre-ultimate moment when she could have pushed Rickie like a *voyeur* to the keyhole, forced him to discern the ambiguous goings-on, the com-promising positions: Dinah in the alcove, abandoned in a smother of red roses, tangled with a young man cold and shining; and an old one, hot, in a voluptuous dressing-gown.

What had held her back? Loyalty to Dinah? Rickie? – to the fine codes and manners of an irremediable lady? Fear of Rickie? – Dinah? – of their contempt and mockery? – of playing straight into their hands, playing up Dinah's mysterious duplicity, Rickie's mysterious jealousy; his surrender, part appetite, part self-pity, to the innocent criminal, the drifting waif in her? Intuitive certainty that it was too late, that he had already slipped from her grasp, flowed out of the house, was being carried on or under a full flood tide towards that room awaiting him, even while the shell of him stood upright before her?

Yes, all that had been enough, more than enough, to hold her back. It was only years later, in rooms with Jocelyn, that she guessed or suspected the possibility of another motive – the card up her sleeve she had always shut her eyes to guessing that she held: motive of profoundest self-protection, planted in still undirected impulse, rooted in a quite unacknowledged premonition: one day she too would find that traitor she was looking for, would require a concealed place in which to lay out with him what Rickie had given her to spend. Buying Dinah's future silence with her own. Premonition ... or willed event-to-be?

And how had that ended, if it had ended, that affair of Dinah's? What had Rickie known? What had become of Rob? What would become of herself and Jocelyn? Where was he at this moment? She had only to lift the receiver by her bed to reach him in London where he was spending the week-end. He was not going away, he had told her so. She could call him out of sleep – not yet, perhaps in two hours' time. She imagined the number ringing, saw his crested head turn on the pillow, blinking, frowning, as if incredulous, his hand going out reluctant for the receiver. She heard his characteristic 'Hello?' – cautious, appealing, musical. 'It's me,' she would say, as usual. His voice would break into a smile, expand to welcome her. Perhaps round about eight o'clock ... or nine ... she would give herself this pleasure. Perhaps not? ... Several times during the last year when he had declared his resolution to stay locked in his flat and get some work done, his plans had changed unexpectedly at the last moment: conscience pricking him, he had gone down on the spur of the moment (he had explained later) to stay with his boring married sister or his maniac father. Then the number rang, rang, rang, hollow, rasping her eardrum till the operator's voice said briskly: 'No reply.' Horrible. More than once it had been worse in a sense than no reply. He had sounded – not pleased but the reverse: put out; had said: 'I thought you weren't going to telephone till this evening.' Exasperated. 'Yes, of course I *want* to talk to you, but I thought that's what we arranged. You arranged it yourself.' As if caught off his guard, claws out, a snarl before he could stop himself. She had been astounded, wounded, frightened most of all. After a period, long or short, of torture by silence, he had rung up penitent and cajoling with a plausible explanation: trouble in the office, one review scrapped by his editor, another promised not delivered in time for press, he had had to write both the damned things himself and rush them to the printers and then stay up nearly all night squaring the outraged inebriated contributors, both his friends.

'Darling, don't sound so dignified and majestic. Everybody's been telling me they've got their dignity to consider. If you're going to say it too I cannot bear it.'

'Well, you were so nasty. You sounded as if you were accusing me of laying traps for you.'

'Never, *never*. You're the only person I can trust not ever to lay traps for me.'

'I don't think that statement altogether bears examination.'

By the time she had said that, terror of course had vanished, suspicion had become a mere titillating hazard in the delicious game of reconciliation. He had closed the conversation on the note she most approved – it so reinforced her pride in him, her confidence in her good influence over him; the firm, ambitious note about his job. He was determined not to fall down on it; to justify to her as well as to himself his decision to give up schoolmastering and earn his living on the staff of an intellectual publisher and editor: this as a step towards his true aim, his single one, he said: 'To write a good book.' 'What kind of a good book?' He shook his head, smiled through a mask: 'You'll see one day perhaps . . .'

More than once during that first tranced period of watching him move, so much at home, so much a stranger in her house, drawing near and nearer, yet seeming still remote, untouchable, she had been traversed by a flash of recognition. Of whom, if not of that young man of Dinah's, seen only once, so long absent from her conscious mind, had he reminded her? The clues lay in the apparent openness, simplicity and trustfulness of the initial self-presentation; in the noiseless animal lightness and suppleness of movement; in the ... something unsubstantial, romantic, out of time or out of the contemporary, that endowed them both with what could be acknowledged as, or mistaken for, authority.

Yes. But no, no: the resemblance was superficial and only a hint at that. Jocelyn stood in sunlight; he was penetrated with warmth in all his fluid fertile essences. The other stood the other side of light. As she had seen him once, once only, she saw him now: moving in his orbit like a planet fed by thin air, infrequent dews, nourishing only grey forms of life – lichens, seaweeds. What shone from him as he stood in Dinah's doorway to receive her, as he passed through the room, returned, then vanished from it was a kind of reflection, deceptive, intermittent.

Lying in the shroud of this November morning she stared at his risen image as clear to her as if she had received, suppressed it only yesterday. He stood in his pale, silent, moonlike coldness, obscuring her potent child of light. Then they changed places, and Rob stood a tall shadow behind the other's shoulder. She saw his eyes, more than opaque, extinct. Jocelyn's were mobile, brimming and darting, not fixed on her. Then these eyes, both pairs, faded; and as she turned over, drowsy now, the eyes of Rickie opened on her, suspended in darkness against no background. They were the eyes of his youth, of the time of their first meeting, so clear, large, lustrously blue that, as she had remarked to a confidential girl-friend in her bedroom after a dance one night, his face seemed to have a window on to a patch of blue sky inserted in it.

The eyes became abstract, incandescent flares; at the peak of their intensity went out. With a memory flitting across her – surely irrelevant, uncalled for? – of their honeymoon – midday, southern French coast, heat of baked rocks enveloping their beautifully coupled, water-freshened, sun-strengthened limbs as they lay after swimming relaxed – his face bent to hers, suddenly wild, dumb, brilliant against the whole Mediterranean sea and sky.

'Rickie, what is it? Why do you look at me like that?'

No answer.

Moment of despair and ecstasy? ... Trick of transfiguration, of bewilderment from the enormous, pure and savage light?

With this transparent memory opening and closing on her, she fell into a morning sleep.

Midnight

EMERGING from Knightsbridge tube station and exploring in the direction of Harrods, Rickie hit finally upon the street he was almost sure that he was looking for: a brief by-street of miniature late-Georgian houses, half boarded up and shuttered, but still intact from end to end, and agreeable by reason of the compact small-scale yet generous simplicity of its perspective. A slightly soiled bedraggled free-and-easiness had come to overlay – it was Spring, 1944 – what must have been a pre-war character of modest domestic elegance. Children were playing hopscotch in the middle of the road; one or two prams were parked upon the pavement; several raffish dogs converged with prurient competitiveness and studied *méfiance* upon a dustbin; two middle-aged housewives, their heads tied up in kerchiefs, called to one another across the street from upper windows; another, young, trim and pretty, leaned out as he passed to water some hyacinths in a window-box. Her pose, lyrical, devoted, offered to all and no one the charming smile she gave as he caught her eye; presenting him suddenly with an image of romantic decoration; with the forgotten taste of an unthreatened vernal intimacy.

For a moment, in a spirit of almost abstract contemplation, he saw himself anonymously, one of a young couple starting married life on a small income, in a delightful little house. No, he could not put actual names or shapes to the pair whom he envisaged. Without much curiosity he pondered, as he went slowly down examining front doors, whether it could be a symptom of premature senility, this day-dreaming habit that was growing on him – if indeed it could be called daydreaming, this recurrent state of – what? – of sleep-walking, this phantom-like observation, fluid, undirected, without personal desire attached to it. Directly he knocked off work it was apt to happen:

he became like one waiting in an ante-room, not with particular anticipation and not with apprehension: the state, more, of one to whom waiting has become a habit, a way of life disassociated from its original *raison d'être*; so that expectation of ... whatever it was ... summons to present his case, or to hear judgement passed on it, had in course of time evaporated, leaving him with a tenuous internal freedom ... Not turning backwards to recapture his own past, but fading out at will, slipping his identity; intently, idly playing with all possibilities, selecting one substitute-identity, then another, to fill out – or scale down – or put a frame round the amorphous semi-transparent mass of low-powered energy that seemed himself. For instance, just now he had been a young man, not recognizably his youthful self, simply a youth in love going eagerly home in the evening to the loved one ... as it might be Colin if he survived the war; as it might have been Anthony; or one of those scarcely known friends of his who had written letters of condolence; or any young sailor, solider, airman. Any piece of humanity could invade him like a cloud and like a cloud pass through and out of him. Any women could move him. 'Anything in skirts.' Dangerous condition to be in: regression to adolescent sexuality, prelude perhaps to becoming a dirty old man? ... But so far the element of the chase seemed mercifully absent. If he wanted in a sense to go to bed with all of them, equally he wanted to go to bed with none. He simply found himself endeavouring to *learn* them; speculating, as it were incorporating their femininity and then in a disinterested way relinquishing its manifestations ... If this was the result of sexual frustration, it was an unexpected one. Sometimes he wondered if he would be any use any more to any woman. Why not find out? No time; or too tired; or could it be too lazy? Nobody he could think of went to bed alone these days, or not for long. He could not say that he had remained chaste latterly from choice or out of principle. Every Government department including his own seemed stuffed with oncoming far from ill-favoured girls; he had taken several out to dinner, gone back to bed with one called Rachel: divorced, dark, hungry, clever, Jewish, rather beautiful; had had to retreat quite soon from an adventure for which he had only appetite not heart.

At the time – two years ago it must be now – when she had started to make it clear to him that she envisaged something tremendous, permanent, his basic emotion – underlying some affection, some gratitude, remorse, dismay – had been astonishment. How could she have imagined ...? What could have so misled her? It was his need for love, she said, the way he asked for it. He was appalled. Of all the men she had ever known, she said, he was the most capable of a real relationship with a woman. If, as she guessed, he had been badly hurt she could assure him he was not permanently damaged. Let him only surrender, be healed, not be afraid. He couldn't help feeling frightfully annoyed, he was not afraid – merely not prepared to harbour so much more than he had space or welcome for. Another thing, she declared he was such a homeless person, so without a shell ... Oh, she was a jolly understanding girl. The net result had been to make him long suddenly for one, for the one who from first to last had beckoned and dismissed him, bound him and set him free so magically, so non-committally that any other woman's touch seemed leaden, or rasping, or insipid ... As for his being homeless, if that meant anything at all, it meant only that he was like most other people nowadays; that he partook of the destiny of thousands all round him all over Europe. Perhaps it was this that lay at the root of this loss or intermittence of personal identity, this perpetual sense of ... of breaking through boundaries into a vast uncharted waiting twilight. Certainly this sudden attack of – well, curiosity, that had overtaken him a few hours earlier and had driven him out on his present search – certainly this was the sort of thing that happened to the homeless, to the homesick. Must look up Georgie, find out how she was getting on, what news she had of Jack. There was something he wanted to tell or hear from Georgie ... not quite sure what or why, but it had suddenly got itself hitched on, like a makeshift rudder, to this whole state of paradox, this *passive urgency* ... (he turned the phrase over on his tongue) this flux, this drift.

He wondered if something – curtains, some object in the window – would mark her house for him with a suggestion of her personality. Coming to a standstill half-way down the right-hand pavement he took a survey: a tall straight slight figure in naval uniform lifting his head warily; a young man's eyes, alert and quizzical; yet veiled; a sunken face, lined, young, not without noble essence; at once spirited and quenched: a failed Olympian look. From the door of the house opposite, where a pram stood, a woman ran out, whisked a shawled bundle from its repository, and hurried in again. Her figure, silent, purposeful, suddenly gave focus and animation to the street's perspective. He glanced back and saw that the hop-skipping children, the busybody dogs had vanished, as if by arrangement; or as if ... But no, that was impossible. For weeks and weeks London had had no Warnings. They could not surely have sounded within these last few minutes; the intermittent benumbing of his senses could not have reached that pass. All the same the mad imprudence or imperturbability of Londoners! – these children leaping with infinite tomorrows, that woman putting her baby out to sleep, that other growing flowers ... in view of what he knew to be about to be unleashed from the other side of the Channel. *When?* ... He found himself staring at the perambulator which a few moments ago had seemed a normal part of the paraphernalia of human living. Now with one twist of an inner lens he saw it crushed, twisted, empty with a difference ...

'What have you lost?' a low penetrating voice remarked from an unexpected quarter.

He swung round, looked down to see Georgie, none other, halfway up a flight of area steps, staring up at him from ground level through iron railings. Below her an arched recess led to what appeared to be a basement entrance.

'Nothing,' he said with a broad grin, flushing. 'At least I've found it. You. You asked me that once before. Why do you?'

'When did I?' she said, advancing up the steps. 'It isn't an opening gambit one should use twice. I am mortified.' She emerged on to the pavement beside him, her large eyes fixed unwaveringly on his face. She was dressed in a candy-striped shirt and dark red linen slacks. 'When did I?'

He shook his head, stooped to kiss her cheek, saying: 'A sight for sore eyes.' Then: 'Perhaps I dreamt it. Never mind.'

'Well ...' she said vaguely. Looking away, she drew an audible quick breath. 'Always I get this feeling when you appear that you are wondering what you are doing, where you are. Or rather, where you could possibly have left part of you.'

'Now now!' he said, a light half anxious, half provocative in his eyes, 'don't start on me. I'm horribly selfconscious. Like all Englishmen – as you know. Please say you're glad to see me.'

'I am glad.' She raised her eyes to his again. 'How glad I am. I thought you'd never come.'

'Oh, darling Georgie ...' He took her hand up, kissed it, dropped it. 'I know I've left it late. It was because ... All these last few months I've been so diabolically hard pressed.'

She nodded, confronting his rueful coaxingness with a guarded smile.

'But suddenly, today,' he went on, 'things began to look more like a patch of clear weather towards nightfall in my department, and precisely as I lifted my cup of tea I had a vision of you, looking almost as nice as you do – not quite. So I left the office helter-skelter and came questing for you through these enigmatic by-ways. Instinct my only guide, darling – who was it said what a great matter instinct is? It brought me to your very door with practically no deviation.'

'You hadn't my address?' Her voice made a statement of the query.

'I lost it, darling. How could I have?' He noted her averted cheek. 'You wrote it down for me, I know, last time we dined. But where? My memory – some days honestly, I have to wrestle to remember my own name. My wallet seems stuffed with little pieces of paper bearing cryptic signs, but the clues don't stand up to scientific analysis. It isn't,' he added with a faint unease at her continued appearance of reserve, 'under your name in the book, is it?'

Her lip twitched. 'No. It's under Jack's aunt's name. Maybe I didn't tell you that. She's a refugee in Ireland and she offered me the house rent free. She was scared her china might get stolen if she left it empty. But I can still be contacted at the Ministry – American Division. I'm still there.' She flicked him a glance of almost open mockery.

After a slight pause he said in a sociable way: 'I like your street. Attractive bijou residences.' He scanned the façades with an appearance of intentness. 'Funny how our meetings seem to develop a repetitive design. This is the second time I've seen you rise from basement level. Remember?'

'I do.'

'1940 that would have been, I suppose.'

She nodded. 'The time I spent the night in the coal-hole. Nobody came to look for me because the house was supposed to be empty. When the corner house came down I thought it was mine, on top of me ... It seemed – well, there aren't any words really for total obliteration alone in a black underground trap. I'd have been glad

of a rat for company. But the resurrection is the only part I remember.'
She put her arm through his. 'I remember it totally every day of my
life. Coming up at dawn, as soon as I saw I could get out, not daring
to see what I expected – and finding you on my doorstep. Knowing
you had come to look for me. Being wrapped in your overcoat. Taken
away, fed, warmed. The most beautiful morning of my life.'

'I haven't forgotten either,' he said, quickly pressing her arm against
his side.

'Well, won't you come in?' she said, leading the way into the house.
'What luck you came just when you did. I was just starting out to
visit some girl-friends down the road. They have a high-class
gramophone and some records I enjoy. But I would much rather talk
to you. Jack's fine – he's somewhere in the Apennines, I had a letter
yesterday. How is Madeleine? – and that honey girl of yours? And
the boy?'

Following her into the living-room, he gave her a somewhat perfunctory account: Clarissa had enjoyed her first term at a new boarding
school, Colin had had a sharp illness in the summer, virulent
pneumonia, just after passing out from Sandhurst. His last Medical
had not been altogether satisfactory – strained heart, though very
slight. He, Rickie, could not help hoping that when he had his next
board they would invalid him out. Madeleine was very well, she'd
been having a bit of a holiday in Cornwall or somewhere with a friend
– needed it, slaving in the garden as she did.

'You haven't seen her lately?' His eye followed her as she mixed
him a drink, moving about with light economical movements that
reminded him – always had – of Dinah.

'No.'

'Why don't you run down for a week-end? She'd love it.'

She made no reply but set her lips; and presently he went on with
a sense of compulsive blundering; 'You and she hit it off all right,
don't you?'

'Oh, we hit it off fine.' Her voice seemed to give out the same
sort of clink as the cube of ice in the cocktail glass she now handed
to him. 'Yes, I like your wife a lot.' She sat down opposite to him,
crossing her knees. One small foot in a crimson velvet mule, poised
in mid air, held his attention: aesthetically pleasing, oddly inviting.
'Does she complain of solitude? Do you fret about her?'

'Oh no,' he said hastily. 'But I hardly ever manage to get down. Apart from the local rustics she doesn't seem to see anybody . . . much. At least in term time.'

'I guess all our horizons have narrowed socially.' She paused. 'Madeleine never liked a lot of company . . . Well, I suppose you know that.'

'Do I?' He assumed a puzzled expression. 'I should have said – before the war – she couldn't get on without a crowd of people, morning, noon and night.'

'And how she disliked them!'

'I wouldn't have said that.' His voice was stubborn.

'Well that's a simplification, maybe. Scared of them. Straining to keep them at arm's length. No wonder, in the circumstances.'

He rubbed his eyes, yawned slightly, sending her a cramped apologetic smile. 'But that's a big subject,' she added, still in the same clarified, edgy voice. 'I wouldn't worry about her too much. I guess she has all the company she wants. When I last saw her she certainly gave me that impression. Completely engrossed. But that's some time ago now. Things may have changed.'

'Oh, I don't think so.'

He looked about him, as if vainly searching for escape. The room they sat in, in stiff armchairs, was a double drawing-room, extending the whole width of the house with a window at either end; all faded chintz, brocade, fringed velvet; and thick with maiden aunts' water-colours framed in guilt, and with miniatures, photographs and samplers, with glass-fronted cabinets containing a job lot of Dresden figurines and Oriental plates, bowls, teacups; with spindle-legged small tables displaying, also under glass, a miscellany of trinkets, silver snuff-boxes, objects in ivory, amber, mother of pearl and other forms of semi-demi-precious curio. He got up and started to prowl up and down, idly absorbed, it seemed, in a meticulous examination of the walls and shelves.

'Doesn't it get you down,' he said presently, 'living with all this junk?'

'Dusting it gets me down. Jack's aunt's sole condition was that I should attend personally to the dust. I can't be said to live with it. I guess I'm too tired in the evenings to think of the room as anything but functional – four walls for privacy.'

'You're tired now?' he said in a voice of concern. 'Was it monstrous of me to drop in like this without warning? You ought to have told me to go away.'

'That would have been kind of infantile,' she said in a pleasant voice, 'considering what long hours I've spent hoping you would come. No, I'm not tired. You go on looking around.'

He glanced at her with a curious, attentive expression, as if hooded in surmise; as if he had received some expected alert or confirmatory message which, even as he took it in, he lacked the equipment to acknowledge. She said still pleasantly:

'But why do you act always as if nothing people say – have said – to one another needed to be remembered? Need have any meaning, continuity?'

'Do I? I didn't know I did.'

'If you don't know it, that's the worst of all.'

His eyes narrowed. 'Well, if I do,' he said, not pleasantly, 'it must be because that's the way I feel about the things people say to one another. They're not meant to be remembered – or else not fit to be. Or it's best, you know, to start off again as if they were forgotten.'

'Is that a warning? Or just a cynical speech?'

'I hadn't thought of giving it a label. It seems like the truth, but perhaps it isn't. You would know.' He looked over her head, pushing out his lower lip, ironic, hostile.

'Well, not polite, let's say.'

'I'm sorry, Georgie. My faculties are dreadfully blunted.'

'It is I who should apologize. Blurting out lopsided reminders.'

With an urgent but almost imperceptible shake of the head, he turned and walked off a few paces, came to a halt and with his back to her presently remarked:

'It's not even functional. It's parasitic. A whole life history, but it all seems dead. Like a shed cocoon.' He turned round and looked at her, saying with a stiff smile: 'You look so incongruous in it.'

'Exiles look out of place wherever they are.'

Surprised by the words, he brought his eyes to focus on her, and saw suddenly as if he had touched, separated, and held it up before him, a core of isolation in her, a shape coldly illumined, contained, defined, like a dark crystal with a grain of incandescence in its heart. Whatever it was – moment of intuition, recognition, unconscious interpenetration, it left him at once shaken and mysteriously eased;

as if a clue still held – a long overlaid or forgotten clue. Let it go, he told himself. Let it bury itself again. Once or twice as a child, he had seen into people in this way; not since.

'But I never had a background,' she said, as if picking up his train of thought. 'Maybe that's why physical surroundings don't make much impression on me – or me on them. I guess I'm underdeveloped visually – maybe humanly. If all you've done in youth is to check out from countless apartments and hotels you don't get much training in aesthetics. You had a different start. I imagine you integrated into your background like a figure in a conversation piece.'

'Do you indeed? It's an interesting theory,' he said, coming to sit down again, 'like all your theories, darling. It's not for me to question it, but that word integrated ...' He shook his head. 'No ... Have you read *Alice* – Lewis Carroll? That's more how it was. My so-called background seemed to me an extremely dubious affair: I never could get to grips with it. If I began to appear, as you might say, it disappeared; and vice versa. Nothing was ever *all* there. Don't ask me why. My Mamma frequently told me no woman had ever gone through what she went through in giving birth to me – perhaps that accounts for it. Now shall I tell you my first memory? – then you tell me yours. It was snooping around the attics at home, looking into the maids' rooms. Our old cook's. The sewing-maid's. Everything struck me profoundly, – it was so sacred and mysterious, and so vulnerable. With such a stuffy, personal smell; so – uninherited and without taste, and so crammed with mementoes. So – *organic*. I used to creep from one room to another and stare and sniff and touch the ornaments and the photographs. I can't describe the churned-up feeling ... rooms like that belonged to *safe* people, people without misgivings. I always had misgivings. Particularly in the drawing-room with my Mamma, and in her lovely, pale, shining bedroom.'

She uncrossed her knees, put her feet up on a tiny tapestry-covered fender stool, tilted her head back slowly. The thick creamy plastically modelled lids sank down. Her head, compact, almost austere, had the same trick, he thought, as Dinah's of turning itself into the Portrait of a Woman: an uncontemporary head, with those full-globed eyes, rounded full neck, high breasts, small sloping rounded shoulders. Nobody had ever called her beautiful. Why then did he want to go on looking at her for ever?

'Go on,' she said. 'Now I see it, at last, from the beginning. I've tried so often. I only saw external things, the same as Jack had: ponies, guns, fishing rods, cricket bats ... And a kind of a retinue to give you individual attention from birth. I never saw *you watching them.* Now you have given me some images for it. Before, I could never visualize the start of it.'

'Of what?'

'Oh ... you separating yourself and ...' She added: 'Well, the thing we mentioned earlier: wondering where you were.'

'Oh, that.' He sounded bored, or else impatient. 'Oh, I see,' he suddenly exclaimed, 'you think I'm still in the attic! What a preposterous idea. But you may be right ... I must say, the connexion never struck me, but it's odd, since the war I do find myself remembering these trifles, from infinite ages back; though in fact, this particular gem had altogether escaped me till I came to mention it. I suppose that's highly significant, you'd say. *Don't* pin me down to it, I beg. It makes me seem such a clown, and I should be sorry for myself. I'm always so sorry for clowns.'

'I'm not sorry for you. It would mean I saw you at a disadvantage in comparison with myself. And that would be ridiculous.' She paused. 'Compassion is a large word, but that more expresses it. I do feel compassion for that little boy. Some of the things you tell me seem so – uncorrupted. Like poetry in a way. Maybe you should have been a poet.'

'Rubbish,' he said harshly. 'Poets write poetry.' He got to his feet, stretching himself with an unconvincing air of langour. 'Oh, it was all right later,' he went on vaguely, the look of faint irony or self-contempt reappearing on his lips. 'I had a wonderful time – at least, after I got into my teens. No complaints. Friends, fun ... I was thoroughly spoilt. My father being killed affected everything of course. It was utter disaster for my mother – for me too, I suppose. But I don't remember missing him.'

He wandered away again towards the farther window and stood looking out.

'What do you do in an air raid?' he asked presently.

'I remain in my bed. There is a sort of basement, full of trunks and crates and things in newspaper and camphor, and iron bedsteads. I did try going down at the beginning of those fire-raids, but I didn't care for it. Rickie, is it true there is something distinctly unpleasant on the way?'

'Might well be. I wouldn't actually know.'

'Jack's aunt is superstitious about her ornaments. She said she had the feeling this room must be left just as if the war was not. Otherwise it would attract the bombs.'

'You'd be a fool,' he said, returning to stand over her on the hearthrug, 'to stay among all this glass and china nonsense if anything heavy started dropping. I sincerely hope you won't.'

'Then I won't.' Seeing him glance at his wrist-watch, she added quickly: 'I'll go and fix some supper for us. You will stay, won't you?'

'Georgie, I can't to-night. I wish I could.'

After a pause she said: 'Well, that's too bad. This has been a short visit.'

'I'm sorry. I've got a tiresome appointment.'

'Can't you cut it?'

'I wish I could.' He added with reluctance: 'It's a doctor, actually.'

'Are you sick?' Her eyes searched his face in their myopic way, at once remote and intense.

'No. At least I don't expect to be told so. Though sometimes I wonder a bit ...'

'What, Rickie?'

'Oh, nothing much. Whether that accounts for me, I meant. Whether I'm reduced to – a sort of wheel turning, automatically. Till it stops turning. I don't want to be taken unawares. Or perhaps I do.' He flushed, looking suddenly ten years younger; enabling her to discern by contrast his former greyish pallor. 'No, it's just that I have to be a thought prudent about my damned boring guts. I nearly died of them once – that was before your time. I'm supposed to go and be overhauled every few months or so and I've kept postponing it. He's fitting me in after hours as a special favour. Nice chap – very busy man – can't very well skip it.'

'No,' she said heavily. 'I suppose you can't. And judging by the way you look you shouldn't.'

'Don't tell me I look fragile. I assure you I go on as well as most – better than some. My poor dear boss has had a breakdown, that's why I've been so loaded. But my stamina is exceptional.'

She got up, saying with a hard-wrung smile: 'Well, try to come back before next Spring.'

Their last meeting had been in May the year before. Walking in Kensington Gardens one Saturday at lunch time, she had run into him. They had gone down to Kew on top of a bus.

Without looking at her he picked her hand up, dropped it.

'I remember all about that day. Don't think I don't.' He hung his head.

By one of those azalea bushes, its every fabulously laden branch in shimmering soft explosion of carved and honey-breathing coral, he had pulled her into his arms and kissed her. Going back to London in the evening, alone on the upper deck, they had sat hand in hand, laughing at everything they said, saw, heard.

'It was the happiest day I've had since the war,' he said. 'Since – oh, God knows how long!'

'You wanted it left like that?'

He looked at her dubiously, nervous. She said:

'Without a sequel.'

He said in the tone of one attempting a scrupulous self-examination: 'I suppose I did.' He opened his mouth as if about to explain himself; but no words came.

'Is that how you feel about happy days? That they are – well, sufficient in themselves? – should not be followed up? Or need not be?'

'I suppose I do.' He glanced at her again, the bright, measuring glance of the antagonist.

'Not even out of a sense of obligation to the one with whom the happiness was made and shared?'

'I don't think in terms of obligation about the people – the very few people – whose company I enjoy.' He spoke quickly, with more assurance, as if she had given him the opportunity to score a point.

'Oh, ordinary social obligations, no. I guess the word is gratitude. The thing that gives affection continuity – or makes you want to try for it, anyway ... want to try to carry on its promises.'

'I was grateful,' he muttered. 'I don't think we talk the same language.'

'We did once. That day we did.'

'Yes. At least I thought so.'

'We don't any more?'

He remained silent. Hands thrust in the pockets of her slacks, heels braced in the shaggy wool hearthrug, she tipped slowly back until her shoulders touched the mantelshelf; and in this position said with harsh flippancy:

'Ah well, it's just one of those things – one of those differences that always trip one up. Now I come to think it over, that is the way of course that a man feels about a casual date ... Girls have more personal curiosity, so generally speaking they are more interested in the follow-up. Also, more likely to be suckers.'

Unable as she was to look at him, she felt that something unexpected had taken place: a change of temperature, a softening warmth. When finally she glanced up it was to see him watching her with a grin – tenderly mischievous, genuinely amused. He said:

'You are a silly girl. I knew another absurd girl once who liked to generalize, particularly about men and women: differences between relationship of, physical, emotional, intellectual – every imaginable heading, sub-heading, etcetera etcetera. I was fascinated.'

'I wasn't trying to fascinate you.'

'Ah, fascination is a peculiar thing. It's not always what the books tell you to look out for that gets under your skin.'

She turned round, propping her elbows between a pair of Dresden shepherdesses in daintily provocative, toe-pointing postures.

'Well,' she said, her voice sinking to a strained, almost guttural note, 'if that one went out of your life, maybe it was because she got – because one gets – to the end, in the end, with a person who cannot be prevented, in the end, from preferring the beautiful memories.'

'Oh, you think that was the reason?'

His face underwent a sudden violent contraction; then as suddenly relaxed. As if relinquishing once and for all the effort to maintain the artificial dam in him, for the first time he looked openly at her, surrendering an area to be explored. She thought: 'At last'; and penetrating this conviction, felt the time lag in him, his demand upon her to wait, wait, in case he should yet choose to require her to let him remain in his stopped earth.

'Darling,' she said softly, 'it's no use. Knock it all down and begin again.'

She heard her own words drawn out of her on a plane of meaning beyond her conscious control; and on the same plane he answered:

'It's too late.'

'Don't be scared, Rickie. Why are you so scared?'

He said with a smile:

'I'm not. Why should I be?' But his tone reminded her to keep her place, make no assumption. And firmly he added: 'I really must go.'

'If you must you must.'

'Georgie, good-bye.' He put his hands on her shoulders, stooped to kiss her cheek; then his fingers tightened, he shook her. 'Yes, I am scared of you,' he said.

She put her arms lightly round his waist; but he threw his head back saying:

'I don't know how to behave, you told me so. I'm telling you if it is so, it's much too late to learn. I never did know what to do about women.'

'Oh, they're hell, we know.' Her long fingers wandered over his chest, brushing off invisible specks, twisting a button on his jacket, straightening his tie with a touch as light and intimate as tender mockery. 'What is a simple Englishman to do? His Mom has learned him to respect them. His Pop has advised him to take a cold sponge if he has trouble with his sex glands. It all adds up, doesn't it, to *keep them at a distance*. They never, never can be up to any good. When a crisis threatens, fly, fly, *fly*.'

He uttered a brief laugh. 'What rubbish. You don't understand anything. And I don't care to be put into one of your boring pigeon-holes and labelled a simple Englishman.' Then with a slight change of tone: 'Not to mention other impertinences.'

She dropped her hand and moved away from him, saying after a silence: 'Forgive me. I stick needles into you because ... to see if the anaesthetic is total. Because I cannot bear it that you have come again and looked at me and said good-bye for now, Georgie, thanks for a pleasant time. Now I suppose you will put me out of mind again for – how long?'

'I don't put you out of mind.'

'Don't quibble.'

'It's the truth.'

'But we are never to be together?'

'No,' he said very low.

'I can think of reasons, but I want to know your reasons.'

He said with the stiff severity of a youth: 'I'm sorry to be tiresome, but you are Jack's wife.'

He looked sadly at her bent head with large blue eyes that repudiated, admitted and deplored his hint of moral criticism.

'You think I forget it,' she said presently.

'No, no,' he hastened to say. 'At least, no – but you seem – I don't know ... you make it difficult.'

'Difficult to remember?'

'Yes. For me, I mean,' he muttered.

'Oddly enough,' she said, lifting her head to smile at him, 'the first time of meeting you was the first time, for me, of having to remember that I was Jack's wife. Can you recall that dinner party?'

'I can.'

'The first time,' she said, 'of looking at one another and saying good-bye. Not that you took that in – or not for more than a moment. You were all in pieces. But I was happy, whole – or so I thought. You were a terrible shock for me: like having a bad accident at the start of a hopeful journey. Just my darned luck, I thought.'

'That was a hellish evening.' A spasm of distaste twitched his forehead. Then he added in a naïve way, as if recalling a simple moment of astonishment: 'There was a moment at dinner when I suddenly found myself wishing I could go to bed with you. I do remember that. But I thought that was just one more sign I was going off my head. I wasn't drunk.'

She turned round again as if to examine the decorous Lilliputian Arcadia disposed upon the mantelshelf; and speaking into it said presently:

'When I first married I was seventeen. My husband was a boy from my home town – we were a small-town boy and girl in Georgia. He turned out to be an alcoholic. In the end he shot himself. It sounds too glib and fictional, doesn't it? – the story's turning itself out at mass-production level. Afterwards I went to New York and starved for a while before I started to get on my feet. By the time I met Jack I was a girl on her own who had made good. I was running a radio serial feature and editing a Personal Problems page on a women's magazine – answers to intimate female queries – you know, the up-to-date psychological angle. I was also having another tough time in my private life: the man whose mistress I had been for five glorious years had just walked out on me. Well, what he had done was to find Salvation: he had turned R.C. and re-married the wife he had divorced. And the result was that all my jerry-built super-structure of being an independent career-woman with a successful love life on the side began to crack. I wanted to throw my hand in – resign: anything for security, for a reliable protector. And Jack seemed sent by the Lord for just that purpose. The good Lord was as sorry for me as I was for myself, so he sent me Jack. I never have understood why Jack fell for me, but he truly did. Instinct told me to grab him, I was on to a good thing. I grabbed him. And then, you know ...' She stopped, brooded, continued with no alteration of her flat, narrative tone: 'Something new began to happen to me. The cause of it was Jack's sheer goodness. For the first time in my life I got a notion to try cutting out the thing in myself that was my enemy – the hard core of being always on the make ... also in the know, because I was so smart – a real smart girl always a jump ahead. And then so honest in my dealings: whatever they were, their honesty never could be called in question. From my vantage point of drawing dividends on Jack's investments – that's really what it amounted to, though of course it was all wrapped up in fancy wrappings – from being a profiteer I began, as I said ...' She broke off again, frowning, then faintly smiled: 'Did you ever read *The Woodlanders*? Do you remember the last page – Marty alone in the churchyard, speaking to her lover in his grave: "*You was a good man and did good things*"? When I read it just a few years back I thought that could be written on Jack's tombstone. I had come to see how real he was – his kindness real, his loyalty, his sense of honour. Looked at one way, he is quite a tough old battle-axe; but he has what most people don't have – he has a developed heart. He doesn't need to watch it or take thought to educate it, as I do: which means that mine is naturally an inferior organ. *His* works like a kind of intelligence through all his actions. Well, you know all this. You are one of his oldest friends.'

He nodded; said after a pause: 'Exactly.' He gave her averted cheek and lowered eyelids the same look as formerly, – watchful, measuring her with pupils shrunk to pin-points. 'Since you know all the reasons, and express them so admirably besides, why have you got to try and drag them out of me?'

'They are not the last words,' she said. 'Not to my mind.'

'Well, they are to mine. I'm not prepared to prove to our satisfaction – yours and mine – that if we did him an injury he would be magnanimous. Or is he not to find out? Or if he does, is he to be lied to? Or am I to say to him: "It's only too true, old chap. I knew you would forgive us."'

'He wouldn't,' she said quickly. 'He'd not forgive anyone a dirty trick. I've managed not to put him to the test, but I'm sure of it. He's got an edge inside him that cuts through mess. His first wife was a tricky little bitch, if you remember. When he discovered it he cleared her out. No, I'd never play common tricks on Jack.'

'Very well, then,' he said, curt. 'There's nothing I need add.'

She went on musingly: 'He's not worldly enough to be a shrewd picker; it's too bad, considering he's a born husband. Almost any woman he truly concentrated on would be apt to forget within six months that she had ever had a maiden name. But he picked me. Even after I began to feel committed, I still had to go on remembering to make *acts* of surrendering my bachelor life. I haven't a generous nature ... And then not belonging to the Club ...'

'What Club?'

'Oh,' she cried, suddenly bitter and impatient, 'the Club of all of you!'

'What *do* you mean? Were we unwelcoming? Surely we couldn't have been. We all took to you like – like hot cakes.'

'Oh, you were all very kind. I can't say you were high-hat. None of you made me feel you were deliberately withholding any initiation rites. And I'm not unteachable: I learned to be a respectable Honorary Member. But what used to rile me' – again her voice swelled indignantly – 'was the *assumption*, the unquestioning assumption, the Best Club attitude of mind, the lack of curiosity about ... I may as well say it, about *me*, what I was, where I came from ...' She checked herself. 'I'm not including Jack, of course: any moment Jack might have made – might make – a dignified decision to resign. And you were never included. The moment I saw you I felt naturally more at home with you than anyone. Because there was something about you that suggested ...'

'What?' he asked stiffly.

'That something was going on in you that might end in your being
– well, *requested* to resign.'

'Was that your well-known perspicacity? Or were you briefed? I
suppose so.'

'No. At least, not till later. But I wasn't referring to that. That's
too particular for what I mean. I mean something intrinsic, general
– the same as in me.'

He shrugged his shoulders. Enough, he thought, of this web-
spinning round and round the nature of his nature: why must she
so persist? Since it had been agreed that there was nothing to be added,
why did he feel that she still held a skein and was coming closer and
closer, deviously winding? Yet he saw her looking up at him with
an uncertain smile; a vulnerable creature, sad, young ... as he had
now and then caught Dinah looking at him in those far-off days when,
confronting her in one of their blind alleys, he had found her weapon-
less, against the wall.

'Were you lonely?' He felt irrationally remorseful, as if realizing
too late a responsibility he should have shouldered.

'Yes. Sometimes. But that was inevitable, in the circumstances.
People like me never manage to get planted. Wherever one goes, even
if one settles down, even if one is protected, one is always aware of
something one is deprived of – one's sense of the past perhaps, one's
own instinctive one. The instinct of other people for it can be understood, but not incorporated. Children would have helped, but I didn't
have any. Other people's children did *not* help. As far as Jack's relations
are concerned, I have gone on being the foreign woman, divorced
– and barren.'

'You shouldn't worry about in-laws,' he protested with anxiety.
'They're a problem everybody has. Not that I speak from experience.
Mine were angelic, I adored them.'

'Are they dead?'

'Oh no,' he hastened to say. 'No indeed. At least *he* is, not she
– Madeleine's mother. I can't think why I used the past tense – except
that I've seen her so rarely – oh, for years now, worse luck. I love
her as much as ever and I think she ... But you see, it got awkward.
She being Dinah's mother too.'

The silence seemed to hum between them. Georgie said finally:

'That's the one name I have never heard you speak before.'

'Well, it's out at last.' A flush ran over his face. 'Oh yes, it was murder.'

'Poor Rickie.'

'Not at all.'

'It doesn't trouble you any more?'

'Oh – yes and no. No, never. Yes, always, for ever. But ...' Again he shrugged his shoulders; adding in a light hard voice: 'I'm simply inadequate. Perhaps as a result. Or perhaps – more probably – as you suggest, my inadequacy was the prime cause. I've often felt it was.'

'Everybody is inadequate.'

'Some more than others. And some who are don't care to admit it. So these crimes get themselves committed.'

His colour had faded, leaving him so ashen that she exclaimed:

'Rickie, what about that doctor? You should go.'

'Yes, I should.' He looked at his wrist-watch. 'I shall be exactly one hour and a half late.'

'Shall I call him?'

'No, don't bother. Georgie, good-bye.' This time he drew her into his arms, clasped her close and kissed her lips. 'Little one, precious,' he said, 'forgive me. You mustn't think I don't remember *some* things – just a few. I always shall.'

'Would one of them be ...' Heavily she sighed, her face hidden on his shoulder.

'Be what?' He drew her closer, with a sort of desperation that gave her the impression of being asked to help him in his resolution of silence. She went on, however:

'That day in 1940, you sent me to the country, and I wouldn't promise to stay there. Do you remember why I wouldn't?'

'Yes.'

Drawing apart from him she said: 'It does seem only like a string of words, the way things have gone. But it also is a grain of comfort that words don't always quite disappear. Well, take them away with you again. I said I wouldn't promise, because a promise made to you I would always have to keep.'

'God bless you, Georgie. Then will you, won't you promise ...' She looked at him, expectant; but with a sharp intake of breath he shook his head.

'Will you come back?'

'Yes, I will,' he said in a distraught way. 'At least, if I can. I'll try.'

'I am not to ask when?'

'It won't be so long this time. It shan't be.'

But now everything, these sighs, his staring look, his tone of distraction seemed to her suddenly hollow and theatrical. She saw him gone already, tearing down the street. She covered her face with her hands and her voice came through them thin and elegiac.

'Ah, it's no use. We are back at the beginning. That day at Kew was out of time, I suppose. We knew we were lovers then, didn't we? But we never will be lovers. And I don't want anything else with you. I never did – you know that, don't you? At Kew there was no need to say it. I thought the only reason why we didn't go home together that night after that day was that we were war-time casualties of love, we had no place to go. You living at your club, and I ... Perhaps you don't remember, do you? – walking half over London in the blackout after supper, taking me back to that God-awful flat I was sharing then with Jack's romping great clown of a niece in the Ministry of Food. We knew it must end at my front door with her sitting up for me, you bet, in her Jaeger dressing-gown the other side of it; but that only made it more credible, more true to life – to the human condition. At least, I said that, you just nodded; and then you said, was the human condition always frustration then? And I said yes, but could be like *The Three Sisters* or that story *The Dead* – the kind that starts echoes afterwards, backwards and forwards for ever wherever you strike it – one echo picking up another till the whole thing *sounds out* like a fulfilment ... I said I would move soon into a house, and you said good, please do. I know you went abroad soon after; you called me to tell me so. I said you would have my address when you got back. I wrote it to you but you didn't answer. As time went on it occurred to me you might have decided to run out on me. Believe it or not, I was incredulous. I called you twice at your office, but you were out; I left my name but you didn't call me back. I thought: well that's the pay-off. But when I came up the steps this evening and saw you standing there, I thought at last you had come back, at last. It was all so blindingly simple again – to myself, I mean. But things don't happen like that, we know. As well they don't, you'll say. You don't need to remark what a lot of grief and pain has been saved all round: if you do I shall never forgive you. Don't come back. I don't want to give you news of my husband or hear how your wife is. When I listen to us shooting that line I want to say: "Mind your own treacheries, and I'll mind mine." How dare you offer them to me so blandly, trying to force me to agree they are acceptable? You trust me unwarrantably, Rickie: I was not at your public school. Now listen – you can listen, what I am telling you is posthumous. I have always been in love with you. I don't want an affair with you. I want to live with you. Now go.'

She listened to the sound of the front door closing after him, swerved sharply to prevent herself from seeing him go past the window, ran upstairs and fell upon the bed. She lay there prone, her eyes upon the ceiling, her arms along her thighs, legs straight, feet crossed; withdrawn into her own stripped outline and making herself an effigy, formally pure, anonymous, inviolably exposed among the tasteless crowding intimacies of the life of another woman: life of an old sterile woman, she thought bitterly, who has jettisoned these fragments of her human history and run away to save her fruitless skin.

She said aloud, with pride: 'At least I did not save my pride.'

The night came down, nothing flowed in to fill her emptiness, she dozed; started awake with the howl of the sirens in her ears. She waited for the guns but nothing followed. An immense silence swung her off the bed and on to her feet while she still lay flat, without a movement, and in darkness; and in intent expectancy. Presently she heard what she was waiting for: someone's rapid footsteps, louder, louder on the pavement, stopping at her door. Someone rang the bell, a long imperious peal. She was downstairs ahead of her own conscious impetus, and opened the door to Rickie.

Under the narrow downward shaft of light from the shrouded electric bulb in the ceiling they confronted one another. She saw the sweat on his forehead: this and something *fauve* in the aura emanating from him made her think of a fugitive, a hunted animal. But there was no panic in his voice and no appeal when he said after an immeasurable moment:

'I had to come back.'

It was a statement, definite, unemphatic. The slant of the light obscured his eyes, so that she had the impression of being scrutinized by two scooped-out sockets under the brow's wide faintly illumined ledge.

'Wonderful,' she breathed. 'Not expected.'

He shook his head, then nodded, with a kind of indrawn sigh. The house began to vibrate – tremor of falling bombs? – or distant gun-fire? . . . He took her by the shoulder, and swung her round, pushing her firmly backwards with him.

'Come along down at once,' he ordered her. 'It may well be about to be very noisy. Where's your basement? Lead the way.'

She went before him down a short twisting flight of stairs to the room from which earlier in the evening she had emerged by way of the area to greet him. Groping, holding him by the hand, saying, 'Mind your head, it's a low ceiling,' she drew him to the far inner corner and switched on a brass table-lamp fitted with a faded green silk shade and set on a brown tin trunk beside a camp-bed piled with old rugs, and topped with a couple of cushions in holland covers.

'Dismal, as you see,' she said. 'Enormous locked receptacles for skeletons and camphor. Look at that parrot cage. And those volumes of God knows what I cannot even lift. It should all be obliterated; but not with me underneath it, please the Lord.'

She sat down on the bed and watched him pace to and fro examining his surroundings in his customary padding noiseless way. He put a hand up and knocked on the ceiling with his knuckles; frowned; stepped over to the area door that stood ajar, pushed it wide open, stooped to peer out, drew back again.

'You act like a sanitary inspector. Leave that door open, you *must*. It's my escape hatch.'

He brushed some flakes of plaster off his jacket and came and sat down beside her on the bed.

'What do we do now?' she said.

Without a word he put an arm round her, drawing her to lean against him till her forehead rested against his cheek. Presently with his free hand he took a handkerchief from his breast pocket and wiped his face. She felt him tremble.

'You are shivering,' she said. 'This vault . . . Why do we stay here? Please let's go upstairs.'

'No,' he said, 'not yet, we're better off here, honestly. And anyway . . .'

She heard what he had left unspoken: the necessity he was under to take no more thought or action. He had reached her by a hair's breadth.

'Lie down,' she said.

Obediently his body fell back, till his head rested on a cushion; still holding her, he stretched himself out along the rug. The wire springs sagged, grinding under their weight as he drew her down beside him.

He fell asleep at once and she lay with her ear against his very slow heartbeat, listening to that and to his loud shallow breathing. With infinite precaution she managed to loosen his tie, undid his collar, pulled it from beneath the back of his neck. After about fifteen minutes he woke up with a little groan, part apologetic protest, part relief.

'Darling, have I been asleep? Sorry. Manners.' He raised his head a few inches to look at her, touched her cheek with his lips, said: 'Beautiful,' and lay down again.

'Are you happy?' she said.

'Yes.' He sighed. 'If you are.'

'Yes.'

'Did you take my collar off? Thank you. Clever girl. What a couch to lie down on with my love.'

'You chose it. Would you rather move?'

'Sh! No.' He shook her shoulder lightly. 'If you don't mind. Poor Georgie. Horrid rough blankets for you. Pretend we're on the battle-field.'

'We are.'

They turned towards one another, exchanging words of endearment against one another's lips. But before long he broke the trance in which they were beginning to lapse together, turned away from her again and lay on his back, staring sombrely at the ceiling.

'What is to be done?' he said.

She felt, or heard, his heart beginning to race as if in nervous anxiety, like an inexperienced boy, and put her hand on it, letting a moment or two go by before making a sound of soothing query.

'I want,' he said, his voice hard, toneless, 'to make love to you more than anything in the world. But you won't be able to believe it. Because also I want not to. So what is to be done?'

She laughed softly to reassure him and to cover her mixed feelings.

'How can I answer questions that don't make sense? If you want me to say I do believe it, I will; and that I understand why not, I will. There! It's said, it's meant. Forget it. Only stay with me. Everything is all right.'

'You're sure?' he said gratefully, at once relaxed, responsive. 'You won't – you'll let it be? You won't explain me to me?'

She shook her head. It was her turn to sigh, but too inaudibly for him to hear.

'When I opened the door and saw you,' she said, 'that moment, there was nothing left for me to want. Was coming back an impulse? Or is that part of what I'm not to ask?'

'I don't know.' He rubbed his nose vaguely with one hand, pushed his fingers through and through his hair, till it stood up in a crest. All his gestures and inflexions had suddenly become young, spontaneous, confiding. 'Oh, the moment I'd gone, I wanted to come back. I suppose I knew I would really, but ...'

'The doctor, you saw him? What did he say?'

'No, I didn't see him. He must have left, there wasn't any answer.'

'Oh dear ...'

'It doesn't matter. Though I do feel rather bad on his account. I went back to my flat in case he'd telephoned a message, but he hadn't.'

'You've got a flat?'

'Oh, just a beastly thing in a warren off Russell Square. I share it with another chap who comes and goes, like me.'

'You come and go.'

'Well, I'm sometimes away, and sometimes on night duty.' He yawned. 'Thank God, not to-night.'

'Thank God I'm not fire-watching either.'

'Do you wear a tin hat? I couldn't bear it.'

'Did you have some supper?'

'No, I wasn't hungry. I had a sort of gnawing, so I drank a glass of milk. My intake of milk these last seven years or so would float a battleship.'

'It hasn't made you fat. I wish I could look after you. I'd cook for you – so well, too. Won't you come and stay with me?'

His arm tightened its clasp around her shoulder, slackened. She thought she heard him utter another rapid: 'Sh!' After a moment she said:

'So after that, what did you do?'

'I went out again. I walked ... I was trying to decide – I couldn't. I simply started walking across London in your direction, hoping for a sign. I was just about to turn into your street or pass it without turning when the Warning went. So I did turn, double quick.'

'That was the sign?' It was half a question.

He said in a helpless way: 'I couldn't bear to think of you alone. But after I had rung the bell I was terrified. With no light showing, one never knows ... You might have gone out. Or guessed it was me and been too cross to let me in. Did you guess?'

'Yes. I knew. I was lying down, and the Warning woke me; and then I began to expect you. I was certain you would come – but I still cannot believe it. I thought men never came back of their own accord. I thought they went for good. Not that I was thinking in those terms – they had no relevance.'

'Why hadn't they?'

'Because I had entirely relinquished you.'

'That's what I thought,' he said at once, in simple agreement.

'You might have waited for the rest of your life. I would never have called you back.'

'Ah, the rest of my life ...'

She raised her head to discover his expression. His lips, whose sensuous distinctive modelling had long been stamped, like an obsession, upon her tactile memory, looked peaceful and severe. He gazed at the ceiling with transparent eyes that seemed to her unfathomable.

'Procrastination comes natural to me,' he said, as if puzzled, or impressed. 'So this sort of current running so strong, all of a sudden, the other way ...'

'Do you think it's ominous?'

'I don't know. I can't help wondering.'

'You mean to-night? Here? Both of us?' Her arms tightened round him and an icy sweat broke out on her and trickled over her stomach, down her back. Next moment the uproar of guns burst over them, enveloped them to roll them round and round, as she thought, against the inner side of a roaring giant funnel, a Wall of Death on which they were to circle, pinned, till in a thunder of suffocation, pulped obliteration, any moment ...

But: 'No,' he was saying, patting her shoulder, his voice level above the fading reverberating snarl as if he had barely noticed it. 'No. Don't be afraid, darling. We're not going to be killed.'

At once the trap became a private fantasy, ignoble. She said, slightly abashed:

'I'm not generally so scared. I've been in it alone and with strangers and with friends and acquaintances – and never much doubted I would survive. It ought to seem like a pushover now we're together, but it doesn't. I've never felt responsible for lives before: yours, mine because of you. They are too precious to be lost.'

He turned his head on the pillow to look at her and smile; yet, at the elliptical angle from which she watched him, the structure of his face seemed to express more of austerity than tenderness, his almost closed eyelids less of union than of separation, distance. Her fear started again; different, aching, like a pang of labour.

'I had a very silent uncle,' he said presently. 'A queer old chap, a bachelor. He used to come for long visits and I don't remember that he ever spoke. Till one day he arrived unexpectedly at tea time, and his tongue was loosened. And instead of being cramped and sour, he was a dear amiable old buffer with a chuckle. He never stopped, it was a perfect torrent ... Mamma was alarmed; she thought he was drunk. And then she thought he must be sickening for something. He must have been. He died a few days later.'

She swallowed, waited; her voice shrank as she asked:

'What is it you are feeling?'

'I don't know.' Then flippantly: 'Couldn't rightly say, and that's a fact. Don't know no more than the dead.' He put his free hand up, spread out his fingers and examined them. He had a strong, finely turned hand that never looked less than conspicuously clean.

She cried: 'But this always had to be!'

'What did?'

'This – us. I told you. You knew it too. You told me, you said you had to come back.'

'Yes. I suppose so. Yes.'

She told herself that the fight was not over after all; that she was losing ground.

'Only it's strange still,' she said. 'It is for me, too. We can't be expected to get accustomed to it yet.'

He made a patent effort, saying: 'It's more . . .' then checked himself. 'Tell me, if you can.'

'It isn't exactly strange. It all seems – sort of inevitable. But so peculiar. More than anything else, a feeling amounting to conviction that – that I can't afford to wait.'

'Is it – does it seem to be – connected with me – with us, this feeling?'

'Could it be?' he asked apologetically; adding: 'Poor Georgie. You see what an unsatisfactory lover I should have been.'

Now she was seized with such petrifying apprehension that her heart missed a beat. Regretful, helpless, he was offering her himself in the past indicative; he was asking her to accept him in that tense.

'This trance,' he said, 'I've been in such a horrible long time . . .'

'And now you feel it's broken . . .'

'Well, something like that.'

The stone in her chest contracted, bled out a heavy drop. There was nothing to share, but she must follow his experience; shadow him while he moved about in worlds not realized.

'I love you,' she said; an uninflected affirmation, disregarded, whether heard or no.

'It's like bracing up for the high dive. Were you ever simply unable to go? Getting to the edge – but you can't: you find suddenly you're nothing but a hollow cylinder stood upright, you've left your impetus behind you. You can feel yourself still attached to it, but separated from it, which is such a humiliating feeling that you can't look back. You teeter on the edge, and rock the board a bit to test the spring, and lean out a fraction pretending to mark the exact spot where you mean to hit the water: all this by way of preliminary for the great dramatic moment, the dive of your life, of all time . . . But you're paralysed: head first or a jump feet first equally inconceivable. Not even the nasty expectation of a belly flop: simply, the water has become so huge, so deep and dark, so infinitely far away . . . and you have become so – weightless, an object without gravity . . . Nobody, *nothing* is what's down there where you were just about to launch yourself. You've realized it in the nick of time. No sensible chap would risk even bouncing the bloody springboard. So you stand dead still, with your hands on your hips: a balanced chap in a calm attitude . . . entirely impotent.'

Another volley of gunfire opened out beyond his cut-off voice: this time more distant, less dangerous, more ominous.

'But now you've gone?'

Faint, dizzy, downward, she shot his endless arc with him; yet stayed rooted at the point of his departure, seeing him wheel and vanish.

'I didn't *go*. I mean, there wasn't a moment of going but it seemed to happen.' He paused, corrected the statement, as if intent on accuracy. 'It seems *to have happened*. If that makes sense. I suppose not.' The snort he gave, part helpless, part self-mocking, brought him once more just within her orbit. 'Can you imagine it at all?'

'Of course I can.'

He said rather crossly: 'Where am I then?'

'Inside yourself.'

'Oh, am I?' He considered. 'Well, I never! ... It seems to me more like – I don't know ... Being in space. Too much of it.'

'It's that too. Don't worry. It's real.'

'How do you mean, real? You could call madness real. But I don't *feel* mad. Madmen never do, do they?'

'You're not mad.'

'How do you know?' he said defiantly. 'I was mad once – or on the verge of it. I got back by the skin of my teeth.'

'When was that?'

'Oddly enough, that night when we first met.'

She nodded; and he said sharply: 'Why do you nod? I suppose it's no surprise to you – you're such a clever girl. Or was it fairly obvious?'

'No. But I couldn't help – recognizing you, the moment I met you. I fell in love with you, if you prefer that term.'

He pulled one arm from beneath her shoulder, crossed it with the other behind his head and lay silent, looking backwards into what, as she lay beside him, was only communicated darkness.

But he was seeing clearly: himself and party – late party, the latest place, place of lugubrious eroticism, sexily spot-lit, shaded, choking with fatigue and expensively procured hangovers and cigarette stubs, with vacuous puppets shuffling to the compulsive whipped-up rhythms of impotence. Suddenly in the thick of all these ambiguities, *graffiti*, innuendoes, he saw Sex; and he was terrified, though he concealed it. But She recognized him; and picking him out from the whole gaping roomful made him sing Sex with her in the old cavern of her mouth. Everybody sniggered. So after that there was nothing for it but to flog himself round and around the dance floor. He was half shouldering, half dragging a lead sarcophagus: he was inside, crammed in, preserving himself. No collision could jar his shrinking flesh through that dull thickness; no filthy sight, sound, stench offend him through so much opacity and weight. All the same he gasped, he ached, he burst with groans. He must set it down, must be set down; he must be disconnected. He became disconnected. He was now an automaton, a man-machine, enabled to record but not to correlate, let alone feel, a variety of sensory impressions. For instance, two curiosities: Madeleine stretched a peahen neck and pecked at his dry heart. The wrenched-off head of Dinah swirled away, a *papier mâché* mask washed down by never-to-be-wept torrential tears. Avoiding trapdoors, trick mirrors, dummies – particularly a jigging Negro drummer with a conniving leer – pretty obscene that one, even for a show like this – he stalked out into the crooked streets all shadowing his shadow, or running ahead of it to lose it.

'No,' he said loudly in Georgie's ear, 'that couldn't have gone on. I'd have had to end it. It was touch and go.'

'What did you do?'

He laughed to himself. 'I don't suppose you noticed when I left the party ...'

'I did notice.'

'I went to look for someone.'

'Dinah.'

'Yes, Dinah.' He dropped the name out simply, in absent-minded corroboration. 'But I didn't find her. I mean she wasn't where I – I'd got it into my head she still might be.'

She said after a pause: 'Well, that makes one appreciable difference.'

'What do you mean?'

'You didn't find her that time. You did find *me*, this time.'

'Oh, I see ... Oh, but the whole thing was different. That was all a nightmare. I was only tracking down the cause, the core of it because I bloody well had to: that's what you do in a nightmare. In fact I was relieved in a way when I found she'd gone. The sheer emptiness gave me something to hold on to. I mean I saw everything was so to speak in order, just as I'd thought when I left her earlier the same evening – until this explosion, brainstorm, started up.'

'What did you do then?'

'Oh, then . . .' He sighed rather helplessly, like a questioned child. 'I went home and apologized to my wife for behaving like a cad. She was very nice about it – extraordinarily nice. I got into bed with her in the end. The result of *that* was Clarissa.'

'You must have been tickled to death.'

'We were rather. Though a thought disconcerted.'

He sounded sardonically amused. She scrutinized the picture so trustingly presented: confession, reconciliation, gratification in its somehow comic outcome: a ruefully intimate, caught-out, philo-progenitive couple. Later perhaps, when the two-way time traffic in possessiveness had begun, it might be that such satiric outlines would grow human, all too human, such innocence be called in question. Better to find out now what she had often asked herself.

'Do you still go to bed together?'

'Oh no, never. In fact,' he added with detachment, 'after that occasion by tacit consent we turned it in. It was never a star turn – my fault, I expect. We were too young when we married. Poor Madeleine.'

'Has she had lovers?'

'One – I think only one. She's had one for – oh, some years. At least, I believe it still goes on. She never mentioned it to you?'

'She did tell me someone had been a support – no names – that time I went down after Anthony was killed. I didn't ask questions. She's kind of reserved by nature, isn't she? Or else she has never trusted me. That was the time she asked me to see you as often as I could.'

'Did she indeed?' He raised his eyebrows, mildly surprised.

'She was worried about you being lonely.'

He remained silent; and presently she said:

'You don't mind about this lover?'

'No. I'm glad she's got someone to keep her cheerful. *I* can't do anything.' He sounded rather fretful. 'I don't know the chap – it's a different world – he might not be quite my cup of tea. Not that that is essential in one's wife's lover. The accent, I gather, is on culture – lots of slim vols in the house now; and classical gramophone records. Very nice, of course, no harm in it at all. Clarissa thoroughly approves:

it seems it was due to his coaching that she was top last term in Musical Appreciation. So she told me. She flourishes his name about with almost tedious lack of inhibition: I dare say that's normal. Colin used to mention him a good deal too – he doesn't any more. That's normal too, I dare say. He was Colin's contribution in the first place, you see – he was keen on Bach fugues, like Colin. Poor boy.' Still the note of irritation predominated. 'Oh, I don't want to poke my nose in – let alone inspect the chap personally. I only hope he won't let her down, that's all. Don't know why he should ...' He jerked his hands apart from beneath his head and started picking at paint blisters on the wall beside him. 'I feel it's none of my business,' he finally declared, 'and yet I feel responsible. You may think it a conventional point of view, but I'd feel happier if he seemed to want to marry her ... if they'd *sounded* me, at least, about a divorce. Of course they may have excellent reasons for not doing so. Principles. I doubt it somehow.'

'You mean you would like to have the chance of obliging her to kick him out?'

'Well ... yes ... or of ...' He uttered a faint snort of laughter. 'Or of letting her go to him. Yes, I suppose so. One or the other. My guess is, he's a chap on the make. Quite a lot younger; humble background, scholarships all along. No harm in that. And bags of charm. But these ruthless, sharp-witted orphan types – do you know what I mean? – have you come across them? ... Orphan is the word, they're a damned sight too frequent nowadays, forgive the pun. They're a flourishing cross-section of the community, and they're on the up and up – there'll be a lot more presently. I doubt if my objections are altogether snobbish, though no doubt you'll say so. It's not that they behave any worse than our sort – my sort – on the whole: it's just that they don't behave at all. Behaviour has ceased to be a concept. I've got a hunch they simply don't know what it feels like to feel *disgraced* – personal, moral, disgrace – dishonour if you like. You could say it was innocence, lack of humbug – end of the code of the Decent Fellow and high time too. Seems to *me* more like something left out, subtracted ... like a dimension missing almost ... She wouldn't know what to look out for, Madeleine wouldn't. She had an old-fashioned bringing-up and she's still awfully like a girl. She wouldn't know what to expect.'

'You mean she's so naïve? She wouldn't expect to be walked out on?'

'Well ... does any woman?'

'I always would.' Her voice was firm and loud.

He was silent, then said curtly:

'Oh, I dare say they have rows.'

'I don't mean,' she hastily corrected herself, 'that I'd spend my time courting nemesis. But I never have expected permanence: maybe it's a question of conditioning in childhood. I never had what you and Madeleine had. It makes it all the harder to learn how to drop your past without getting poorer and thinner with every breakaway you choose – or have – to make. Perhaps I never have learnt. Perhaps that's why I love you. I think you would never get a withered heart. And I guess anybody who lived with you would be helped not to shrivel up.' Above her head, unseen but felt by her, his mouth became contemptuous. 'And whether Madeleine knows it or not, she *does* know it. She would never leave you.'

He turned his head as if listening more intently.

'And apart,' she continued, 'from that basic fact my guess would be that it may have crossed her mind there's no for ever and ever with this guy. Which, without being over-cynical, would be an added reason for preferring to have her cake and eat it. I guess she kind of hopes that one day she'll stop being crazy about him and sweep him painlessly off her doorstep.'

'Oh, she'd never sack him,' he said decisively. 'She's very faithful. Very loyal. Anything she undertook she'd stick to.'

This statement too she scrutinized: important item in the collection.

'I don't quite know how to put it,' he went on. 'She's really awfully nice. Very just and – well, wholesome. Generous. Anyway she couldn't be ungenerous to someone who trusted her: not in the last ditch she couldn't. I've reason to know that. She's a disciplined character – they all are, that family. Her mother's a wonderful woman. Her father was incredibly nice too. She's done well by the children: I didn't make it too easy for her at one time; and what with that and the war ... What I'm trying to say is, she's not got much self-confidence, but she has got values. She won't expect to be let down *in the way she will be*.' Then as if to retract from his own dogmatism he added a vague: 'Though she's fairly realistic ...'

'Is he neurotic?' asked Georgie after a pause.

'Oh, Christ, I expect so. I dare say it's a word he makes good use of.'

'I wasn't using it loosely.'

'How then? What does it mean?'

'Not a term of excuse, or of approbation. Something quite specific. Never mind. Say what *you* mean by "let down in the way she will be".'

'I mean,' he said, his voice loud again, 'it will be: "Yes, I did love you yesterday, I don't today." Or more likely: "Yes, I did want to go to bed with you two nights ago, that's why I did. Last night I wanted to go to bed with someone else, so I did. What's the objection?" First she'll think he must have been tight. She knows about drink, that's part of what she can accept. He got roaring tight, as chaps do, and played the fool, it was quite excusable because of course he's sorry. But he'll tell her he wasn't tight at all – at least no more than usual. He had a very enjoyable time, so why should he be sorry? ... She won't understand *that*. She'll go crashing on, trying to make sense of it, building up a pattern for him, pushing motives and codes into him, when there simply are none, none at all. It was so, it isn't so. It isn't so, it was so. What is equals what was equals nought.'

The spate of his words abruptly ceased, and she lay listening to his breathing. Presently she said:

'Is this a simple case of prophecy?'

'I don't know,' he said. He stretched himself, to lie afterwards not so much quiet as inert, and with a suggestion of stiffness, like a body pinned down, resisting pressure. 'I don't know why I'm saying any of the things I've said to-night; or why they seem like the truth.'

The lips of dying men ... The words flashed out of hiding. Oh, after a long détour he was coming again towards her with something hidden in his hand. *'Guess what I've got for you!'* This time he was going to present it to her, she would have to take it because it was his gift to her, the offering of a lifetime. Almost under her breath she spoke his name.

'Must it be called prophetic?' She discerned in his rather tentative tone a wish or an attempt to reassure them both. 'Oh, can't you see I'm talking really about myself? It's something I understand. I've got it in me – this something, which is nothing, in the centre. You don't understand do you? – you're a woman. So much the better for you. I'm simply telling you for the tenth time I'm no good to you. Sometimes I think a new thing is happening: men aren't any good to women any more. But why can't you stop it happening? Sh!' He shook her sharply. 'All right, laugh.'

'I wasn't laughing.'

'Well, don't cry then. Are you crying?'

'No.'

'What then?'

'There's nothing new in what you're saying. It's only too familiar. *Get thee to a nunnery* ... That's all you're saying.'

'Oh, that's the last thing!'

'Yes. Sooner or later it's what men always say to women. So it must be what they want.'

'We certainly want to keep women in their proper place. That's a well-known aim of ours.'

'Yes, you do. But it's not so well known as it should be – you see to that. I'm not altogether blaming you – you start at a disadvantage. It *is* kind of unmanly being carried around the way you are all those nine months. And then having no choice but to submit to all those female processes – being born, fed and all the rest. It must be a big humiliation – confusing too. No wonder you're scared you may be women in disguise.'

'Perhaps we are.' His voice had become cheerful. 'It's the kind of loose talk, you know, that goes on in clubs.'

'You don't have to tell me. That's just the reason wives always urge their husbands to go to clubs – you must have noticed. They love to think of them being able to relax and let their hair down and compare notes. The only thing that gets us irritated is the silly look on your faces when you come out again. The fatuous self-important smirks.'

He twisted round and propped his head on one elbow to look down at her. When she raised her eyes she saw that he was smiling broadly. He said:

'Does Jack think you're funny?'

'Sometimes.'

'He's quite right.'

'He thinks all women are funny. He's a great tease.'

'Ah! there's not enough of that – hence all these bills we can't meet

– trunk calls, drink bills, sleeping tablets ... these shocking little objects chaps find in their pockets next morning – tiny sopping handkerchiefs, I mean.'

'I promise not to add to your store of those.'

'Oh, couldn't you possibly? I've so few – it makes me feel inferior I know a chap who keeps a special drawer for them, all different initials. What's so touching, he says, is the different scents still lingering in them even after they've been to the laundry and had the tears and lipstick taken out ... No, my trouble is I'm always the one to cry: it's embarrassing for both parties. Promise not to make me cry.' Between phrases, he was showering light kisses on her face. 'That's the only thing I'd ever mind about,' he said. 'Someone else teasing you. The laughing together. One can't leave someone who ... I don't mean laughing *at* ... God, the time we've wasted to-night! Darling, you are so silly. You think I don't want to make love to you, don't you? How am I to stop you talking? If I did all the things that keep on occurring to me, I might go too far, and then where would we be? But we're not going to die together in one another's arms – so don't flatter yourself, see? We're not going to die together.'

Later – how long later? – he raised his head from her bare shoulder and listened attentively to the silence.

'What time is it?' she whispered. 'Is it still the middle of an air-raid? Could we have missed the All Clear?'

'I wouldn't put it past us. But I doubt it.'

'What kind of a raid can it be? Does it seem to you it's a new kind?'

He sat up beside her, than swung his legs down and started to pick his clothes up off the floor. She watched him pulling on shirt, socks, trousers, adoring the lazy peaceful grace of all his movements. When he was dressed he looked down at her with a smile that calmly embraced all of her known unknown body, bent to kiss her, saying: 'Don't be cold, my darling,' covered her gently with her wrap. Gazing at him, she was hit suddenly by a great wave of giddiness; a blinding conviction. The eyes shining on her with such unearthly brilliance stripped her body of its identity; not Georgie lay exposed to that look of tender coldness – not she, but another ... Dinah ... Madeleine ... or any woman.

'Stay where you are,' she heard him say. He padded across the room to the area door, stooped and disappeared through it. Next moment another stupendous crash of anti-aircraft gunfire split open the marrow of the world. She stretched herself out, pinioned beneath its mounting gigantic tension; dissolved into the uttermost spasms of its release; lay limply with closed eyes. It had come about as he had told her; they would not die together. He was gone, hurled into limbo; and she alive, alone.

Feeling an imponderable weight above her, she opened her eyes to see him bending over her, then lowering himself to sit on the edge of the mattress. She found a thread of voice to say:

'Did you arrange that?' He raised an inquiring eyebrow, and she added: 'I thought you had been blown up.'

'Don't be so silly. There's nothing dropping. The searchlights are carving up the sky like mad, but whatever they caught, if they did catch anything, they've lost it, or I didn't see it.'

'Blown up,' she persisted, 'or else gone to *her* . . .'

'To whom, for Christ's sake?' He took her by the chin and turned her face round to meet his.

'You know.' He looked at her dumbfounded. '*Her*. Your love.'

'You must be mad,' he said, his easy affectionate manner suddenly cut off.

'Well, maybe it's infectious.' Tears started to roll down her cheeks from under her closed eyelids and she felt him watching them with a bewildered frown. 'This dimension you have been mentioning – maybe I'm in it too. I see no cause to scold me. If you're not crazy, I'm not. If you are, I am.'

'What is it?' he said presently, with paternal patience. 'Tell me what's the matter.'

'Only that . . . since we made love, I don't know who I am.'

Two or three dry sobs shook her frame and he uttered a rather perfunctory, soothing 'Sh!' Then after a pause:

'Darling, wasn't it all right for you? What did I do wrong?'

'Nothing wrong – nothing you can do anything about. Only – I thought we had found one another at last. But afterwards – just now – when you were standing over me, looking down at me . . . No blame, no reproach . . . but what happened?'

'What did happen?' His voice was blankly stubborn.

233

After a long silence she said:

'Nothing.'

'Darling, you're being dreadfully difficult,' he said, with mixed gentleness and impatience. 'Didn't you see me go out just then? I'm so sorry if I gave you a turn.'

'Yes, that was it,' she said after another pause. 'Being unexpectedly alone all of a sudden.' She sat up. 'All I remember is ... you were looking down at me so beautifully, and it crossed my mind to wonder, as one does – if anybody else – who else – how many others had made your face shine so.' He interrupted her with another, this time violent 'Sh!' and she continued: 'Yes, I know. One doesn't say these things. But they're not meant as questions, I'm just telling you what happened. Whom were you looking at? That's not a question either. But who is it we look at, speak to, if we only knew? Whom are we trying to find? Well, it's just that – I thought I did know suddenly. But I can't explain. Rickie ...' She put her arms up and drew his face down against hers. 'No. My love. Anonymous ... You've tied your tie in a revolting knot.' She reshaped and straightened it. 'Long ago I knew a girl who was not a virgin when she married. Her husband knew she had had a lover – she didn't deceive him. It had been a big experience. One night on her honeymoon when she was almost, not quite, asleep, she said this lover's name by mistake instead of his. She could have bitten off her tongue a second after, but it was too late, the damage was done: this boy she had married was most deeply shocked and hurt. As he saw it, he was married to an adulteress: this lover had invaded their marriage bed. She knew it was not so: she really loved her husband, she didn't miss the other guy one jot. But after that lapse she could never reassure him or trust herself to go to sleep. The result of their joint efforts was the first guy, who had been duly laid below and – not forgotten, that was self-evident, but totally sterilized and incapacitated – this guy got kind of raised. It was terrible: there got to be a third person in the bed. She tried everything – all sorts of interesting experiments, and jokes, and twin beds, and psychiatry, but it was no use: nothing worked for long. The marriage was destroyed. The husband started drinking and in the end, as I told you before, he shot himself. He was a self-pitying type – emotionally adolescent, so I guess if it hadn't been one thing it would have been another; but at the time she bitterly reproached herself. Now she knows it was a thing that might happen to anyone. But equally she knows that if it happened to her – was done to her, I mean – she would be terribly piqued.'

'It won't be done to you.' His voice was light but hostile. 'Speaking from my somewhat limited experience, I doubt if it is one of the things men do. In spite of their being, as we know, *capable de tout* ...' He turned a disagreeable look and smile on her adding: 'I wonder what you're getting at in this somewhat oblique fashion.'

'I don't know,' she said, struggling. 'Can I be jealous? I think I must be.'

'Jealous? Who on earth of?'

'Dinah, I suppose. Yes, Dinah. I always have been.'

After a dead silence he said quietly: 'I told you I never think about her.'

'"Never and always" is what you said.'

'Oh well ... perhaps that's my ham-handed way of describing my quite outstanding ineffectuality as a *feeler*. I came to a dead end once, you see, and there I've stayed ever since. Propping up the wall at the end of the dead end.'

'But you are not there now,' she cried. 'Not any longer, Rickie: you've said so. Don't unsay it because it wouldn't be true and I wouldn't believe it.'

He shrugged his shoulders lightly as if to say: 'Just as you please.'

'Though maybe I deserve it,' she went on. 'The last thing I meant was to try and pull a fast one, but I guess that's what I'm doing – the way you are talking to me makes me know it. Listen. The truth can't be more dangerous now than hiding it. This is what happened. We were looking at each other, at the whole of one another ... and all of a sudden I saw you, thought I saw you – not with me. Free – in a different way from what I'd expected, from the kind of freedom I had been sharing with you. I saw you with – with the last trick up your sleeve. And playing it. Behind your loving face your look was so – triumphant. This is what seemed to come out of it to me: "Now I can say good-bye to her at last".'

He only looked at her, but with curiosity now, the patient look wiped out.

'To *her*,' she repeated. 'Yes, to me perhaps – but I thought – to the other. Or were we interchangeable? She and I. All of them. The

Loved One: good-bye to the entire experience, the whole wonderful appalling, impossible idea.'

After a moment or two he slightly shook his head. He looked very much at his ease, sitting bowed forward with his knees apart and his hands loosely locked between them. The ear she could see, well-turned, flat against his skull, struck her as functional, a simple instrument made for impartial listening. Her words would be recorded, not interpreted.

'What comes next?' she said, addressing no one in particular. 'The love of God?'

'Oh, does that mean something to you?' he said with polite interest. 'No, but it might.'

'Yes. I suppose one can't be certain ... I mean, that one might not suddenly get the hang of it. Another faculty one has simply not noticed was dormant even. Or like beginning to understand music, or a problem in higher mathematics. But that takes concentration, doesn't it? Damned hard work, and something to drive you on. A longing ... But can you even conceive of becoming convinced one has been let into the secret? – if there is a secret. One would have to go mad; or else one would have to be absolutely simple.'

She said under her breath: '*Go love without the help of anything on earth.*'

'What's that?' He bent his recording ear towards her, and she repeated into it the words, adding: 'Something Blake wrote. A poet called Blake'; to which he replied with a nod: 'I've heard of him.' Presently he said: 'Clarissa's absolutely simple. She believes in God; she finds no difficulty.'

'Do you think about her a lot?'

'A fair amount.'

'Worry about her?'

'Oh, I worry about everybody I'm responsible for. Bad habit.' He reflected. 'Yes, I do worry about her.'

'I bet she worries about you too.'

'Why should she?'

'Well ... that's the effect you'd be likely to have on an impression-able young girl.' Her voice was dry. 'The handsomest man in the world and the sweetest – and then something so kind of sad about him ... She would set herself an aim in life: to be your ideal woman. I guess she already has. I guess you have ruined her life.'

'Shut up! You're the beastliest woman I've ever come across.'

'Don't you dream now and then of going down the vale of years, a resigned distinguished figure of a widower, hand in hand with her?'

'Certainly I do.' His faint grin, directed at the floor, was appreciative. 'Oh, the whole works. Already I detest her lovers. They'll make her unhappy and – the thought upsets me. We won't go into *that* if you don't mind. The imagination boggles. At least mine does, I'm sure yours preserves its equanimity ... Quite right. She'll do better without my guiding hand. Poor little ...' He stopped abruptly. 'Oh, she'll be all right, she's as sound as a – sound apple. Cox's Orange. She'll be a hostess in a transglobal airline, tending tired business men on the long hop.'

'You're nothing if not consistent.'

He cocked an eyebrow.

'If there's one type more than another that could give a tired business man cleansing subduing thoughts, it would be those ministering, well-groomed, airborne girls. One hears that they do marry. But I never have believed it. They seem so immaculate and plucky. So at ease with their bright restful personalities.'

She saw the planes of his profile begin to alter in amusement; but next moment they fell once more into their fine-drawn lines and hollows.

'I wish ...' He stopped. 'I hope you'll see her some time.'

'I might get on better with your son.'

'Colin ...' he considered. 'Nice chap. Reliable, intelligent. Madeleine thinks he's on the dull side, but I think he'll add up one day to more than she imagines. Hope so. He's the only male of this generation either side.'

'Dinah has no children?'

'No. She married a chap who was killed in the Spanish Civil War. She got caught up in all that anti-fascist class war business – struggle of the worker, all that. I only heard about it, of course. Never set eyes on him.'

'I'd like to have set eyes on people like him. And her. I'd love to know her, to have known her: people like her.'

'Would you?' He turned to look at her, thoughtful, then turned away again to say with an inflexion that caused her an uncontrollable

237

pang: 'Oh, but she was never like *people* ... However much she may have changed, I can't believe she's growing older like everybody else and going about her business. And then her business ... Well, you know, darling, I don't much hold with party politics for any sex, but when it comes to women, my lower nature gets the upper hand. They're so bloody cocksure and tigerish – not that I know any. I just don't like their hats. If Dinah now – if Dinah were to call me a fascist hyena or even a bourgeois lackey, I should be irritated. I wouldn't know how to talk to her. I might say rude things – appalling things about the British Empire and tradition and Christianity and who betrayed who and the barricades and God knows what, I can hear myself. We might come to blows, it wouldn't be the first time ... Or I'd detect that well-known look of disappointed expectation.'

He was talking to himself, she thought, or muttering in his sleep: a monologue broken with an occasional faint sigh, fading out with the brief headshake of one presenting a somewhat regrettable statement of expenditure.

'I'm a notable disappointer,' he resumed. 'Championship standard. People were always expecting – I don't know what of me. I can't remember a time when I wasn't secretly convinced I wouldn't come up to scratch. That was something I never got the hang of: I'd obviously deceived them into believing there was more to me than there was. It was the last impression I wanted to give – or intended to. And yet at the same time I suppose I must have wanted ... felt called upon. Well, I suppose I was trying to prove it to my own satisfaction one way or the other. *How?* By taking action. Doing the best or the worst I was capable of, and seeing if I fell down on it. Committing the ultimate ... "*He's ruined his life.*" That simple positive statement started ringing in my ears from an early age. Why? God knows. I was born with every advantage, as they all pointed out. I had such good examples set ... and in my turn I was to produce my quota. And I honestly did want to have a bash at it, what's more. I did care about – well, *goodness*: trying to be good. If I may say so in a whisper, I still do. But I think I must have been born with some congenital defect of vision: anyway, even in the nursery I couldn't see life steady: there always seemed something coming up to fog the issues. For instance, the persons I was taught to look up to and respect, virtuous persons, often struck me as untruthful and unkind. I won't mention any names, but I felt absolutely ashamed sometimes of virtuous persons – and sickened by highminded ones. Also I felt a strong distaste for saying my prayers, particularly at my mother's knee. It shocked me that God, of all people, had to be begged and implored not to lead me into temptation. God knew everything, so he must know I always fell when tempted. It must be that he set temptations in my path for the pleasure of witnessing my falls. He looked forward to punishing me – for my good, because he loved me. It appeared he loved me too much to grant me any mercy, unless I could get Jesus to put in a good word for me: and though I knew poor Jesus meant well, I couldn't feel much confidence in him as an intermediary, considering the failure he'd had himself – not managing to persuade God to get him out of being crucified ... No, but seriously, Georgie, the love of God's no joke. You mentioned it just now.'

'I wasn't joking.'

'No, I dare say not. It's no joking matter. Not a fit subject, to my mind, for children's ears at all. You hope your kitten won't die and it does: that's bad enough. You *pray* for its life and it dies: that's devilish ... Can you see Christ as a pleasant chap to put a pipe on with and thrash things out? A chap who's interested in insurance schemes and bonuses and benefit performances? Christ never said anything cosy or agreeable, to the best of my recollection – supposing he did say what's on record – moot point, of course. But *supposing* he did – and it does seem to bear a personal stamp, it's hard to imagine it having been invented – either he was raving mad, or he was what he said he was and the whole thing hangs together – the *whole* thing, mind you: pretty formidable and drastic. As for me, the scales won't tip, they never have. All or nothing, in the balance: I prefer it so. Don't imagine I'm smug about it, though. I hope I'll die before I start forgetting to feel uncomfortable ... Darling, are you listening? I *have* said all this before – in my cups, in my salad days, you know – but everybody else was always talking more and louder and faster, I never got a fair chance. Now I say to hell with everybody else. I'm sorry to harp on my dead uncle but I cannot help being reminded of him. Most modest of performers, never offered even an elementary parlour trick to justify his existence, suddenly one morning doesn't give a fig, takes on all comers, no holds barred ... He said some pretty raw things,

I can tell you. Do you know what I thought at the time? Young as I was, I thought: "The reason my uncle is being so embarrassing is because he knows he's God." Is that what you're thinking about me?'

'No.'

He bent his ear towards her with the air of one prepared to grant the semblance of a deferential hearing.

'She doesn't think so,' he resumed, addressing the carpet. 'Not that he cares, one way or the other ... When it was broken to me that my uncle had passed on, I remember thinking: "Well, that's all right, there's nothing to deplore." As he saw it, my uncle had overcome every impediment to the full apotheosis. What is there left to live for, once you have become God? But personally I shan't go so far as that. In fact, one interesting fact comes to light –' he slightly turned to send the fraction of a quizzical spark in her direction, 'I've made no fresh discoveries about the nature of the universe. What you're learning now I could have told you twenty-five years ago or more, my poor, dumb, unenlightened girl. In my end is my beginning. Who said that? Another secret I will impart to you – that poet Blake you quoted from just now – I've more than heard of him. Dinah used to read aloud to me – she read very nicely, or so I thought ... According to Clarissa, What's-his-name reads aloud divinely too: well let that pass ... There was one thing, a love poem I suppose it was, but a very peculiar one. I can't remember any of it except two lines, and they've always stuck in my head.'

'Say them.'

He repeated, without expression:

> 'And throughout all Eternity
> I forgive you, you forgive me.'

'Ah yes,' she said. 'He asks her to agree to give up love. *Root up the infernal grove*, is how he puts it.'

'Was that it? I believe you're right, that was the gist of it. Cryptic sort of thing. Dinah always claimed she understood it and saw absolutely eye to eye with him – with the sentiments expressed. Forgiveness. That was her great theme. We had a pact to forgive one another everything, always, beforehand, if you see what I mean: the idea was hers. So that whatever might go wrong ... Well, her theory was, if we stuck to that, nothing ever could go wrong. So after all was over, I . . . well, it was a morbid notion. We'd parted in a ghoulish sort of way – I fell down dead in her bathroom and was removed to hospital in the nick of time – in more senses than one. What with months of skilled medical attention and unrelaxing domestic vigilance I was granted an opportunity given to few of *coming to my senses*. All the same, I couldn't get rid of this obsession . . . We hadn't said good-bye, you see. I was taken into custody only a few hours after we'd finally joined forces for the big record-smashing break-out. For quite a while I went on uneasily imagining her standing waiting for me at the prison gates. Then I got a hint from her mother that she'd gone abroad. *Gone abroad!* . . . Oh, the waves, suns, mountains, islands, jungles – even jungles! – that used to pass whirling before my eyes in glorious technicolor, while I lay sipping junket and being knitted at and trying to force space to yield up one glimpse, just one, of the real figure in the actual landscape . . . The landscape was always enormous, exotic, sinister, and the figure was sinister too – like a faint print of an old photograph, never quite plausible or life-like – disguised-looking; and always alone. Ironic really, considering the facts of the situation disclosed at a later date. I don't resent the deceit practised on me, I couldn't have faced the facts. As it was, I was enabled to preserve some sort of sickly exalted illusion . . . that at least I had managed to set her free; at least she wouldn't taste me tasting of milk and soda or touch flesh with a raw hole hidden in it when she touched me. I tried to tell myself I welcomed the humiliation of being the one on a couch in a decline while she went off big-game shooting. And among other obsessions I went on having this one – about commemorating my loss in some particularly striking way; something no one else in her life would ever think up, whoever she replaced me with, whoever she would torment in the absolutely horrifying, howling black future . . .'

'What was your idea?'

'My idea was a practical one – that is, technical. To have a bracelet designed, and those words engraved inside it, to run round and round in a circle – eternity, you know – and in my own handwriting to underline the message. I actually got as far as hunting through the whole of the works of Blake to verify them and copying them out on to a piece of paper and putting them in my wallet, to take along to a jeweller as soon as I was allowed out without a keeper. But I never got round to it. The thought of hearing them read back to me by one of those dignitaries behind the counter – that defeated me. I used to break out in a cold sweat imagining the conversation. "Interesting sentiment if I may say so, sir. Quite an original note struck." "Oh it's just one of those tags, you know, that stick in your head. Forget who wrote it. Some poet or other." "So I would have assumed, sir, from the tendency to rhyme. I would have fancied possibly Miss Ella Wheeler Wilcox." "Oh, really? I expect you're right. Anyway, I sort of wanted it done for a kind of anniversary." "Quite so, sir, very appropriate. Something any lady would appreciate were she to take it in – well, more in the playful spirit, as would, of course, be the intention. I would have ventured to suggest a more formal type of lettering – but I appreciate that the inscription in your own personal hand – very individual hand, sir – would add a more intimate note, highly acceptable no doubt."' A suppressed chuckle shook his shoulders. 'So I procrastinated. I sometimes wish I hadn't. I cut such a graceless figure so much of the time, I'd have liked to manage to let her know somehow that ...'

'What?'

'That's just it – what?' After a pause he said slowly, searching for accuracy:

'That whatever stretch one cared to give those words – and I don't see any limit really – she could never be outside their scope. Whatever they do mean, she's the meaning of them, as far as I'm concerned. Always was. Always will be. That though it all turned out so badly, the meaning didn't go. It changed almost out of recognition, but it didn't turn sour, or get cobwebby. I'd like to tell her the real reason she didn't get a bracelet was that it got clearer and clearer there was no way, no way at all, of putting my – limitless gratitude into any sort of form that wouldn't mean, for me – a diminishment of my feelings that caused me too much pain, disgust, to contemplate.'

'You must tell her.'

'Ah, but where is she?' He raised his head, his nostrils dilating faintly with an effect of irony; or of sniffing for a trial through space and darkness. Again she was made aware of what he concealed so warily within him: the feline electric animal with quivering senses glimpsed like a dark twin sleeping by the flicker on his hearth; or ranging, lightly leashed, always within recall in the tingling night.

'Yes,' she said. 'Where is she? Do you know?'

'Oh, not far off. Somewhere in London. Has been from the beginning, working in some particularly grim form of Civil Defence – I'm not sure what. I've never run into her even in the street. Her mother sent me her address – unsolicited – I'm not quite sure why – in case of an accident probably, poor old dear. It would be like her to think all enemies should be reconciled at a time like this. She's a great believer in families drawing closer. She thinks remorse the worst form of human suffering. I'm certain she's still convinced she helped save me from a lifetime of it once ... Yet, you know, I also suspect sometimes *she*'s the one, still, who goes on being gnawed at. She weighed in to stop a crime, but she feels guilty. Hence these infinitely discreet impartings that have gone on ever since. The hints she drops are always designed to make me feel that Dinah's very much *alive* – or so I fancy. And I get the impression she's saying: "Go on, prove I was right, live too." I've often wished I could take away her remorse at the spectacle of me. I know she loves me. I'd like to leave her a legacy. That would buck her up.'

'A legacy?'

'Well actually, to Dinah.' He shook his head brusquely at the sharp breath she drew. 'Oh, nothing concrete. Nothing in print to be read out after the funeral. There's obviously no way to do it, and it's of extremely little consequence, except perhaps to myself, but I'd like to make my point. But supposing I'm mad? Supposing it's a case – as I dare say it is – of recording one's gratitude to the person one has most damaged, most betrayed? – who remembers you, if at all, with scorn and bitterness?'

'It would not be a case of that.'

'How do you know? You don't know what the look on her face was like, the last time I saw her. I'd given her nothing, not a groat. If she'd put her hand out ... but that's like saying if she'd had wings, or I'd had ... Sheer stark impossibility, at the time. Keys on the table. I picked them up and pocketed them. She did return my cuff-links: she dropped them in my hand, without touching me even with the tip of one finger. The cuff-links simply vanished – dematerialized, as I've noticed things of that type do – small personal objects with any sort of magic attached to them – at a time like that. Queer to think that piece of paper with the poetry on it was in my wallet.

243

"Eternity", "Forgiveness" ... Big words, written with blood, tears, sweat, hidden against my heart. Totally inoperative. Not one vibration coming out of them.' Smiling secretively, he felt over his breast pocket; then slipped his hand inside his coat, drew out his wallet.

'I think it's still there.'

Unfastening the stud of an inner flap, he pulled from one of the compartments a sheaf of rather crumpled papers – snapshots, several letters, torn-off flaps of envelopes with addresses scribbled on them – sorted them through with a faint frown. 'All sorts of junk,' he murmured. His frown deepening, he pushed them back, peered into another compartment, drew out a piece of notepaper, grubby, grey, folded in two, opened it, rapidly doubled it up again. The paper stared at her from between the thumb and first finger of the hand hanging loosely flexed between his knees. In the other hand he held the wallet, which he closed, then opened hesitantly again as if uncertain of what action to take next.

'Fairly incriminating document,' he said. 'Unmistakably my own handwriting. Well, there we are ... I wasn't even sure if I still had it. But I remember now debating – shall I, shan't I burn it? – at the time of the big burning – letters, you know, photographs; and not being able to bear it. Thinking with scarcely any hope, that it was my last grain of hope: there was no knowing, *one* day it might germinate. One ought always to bear in mind, in times of destruction, that it's wise to give the last word of all the benefit of the doubt. Save it, just in case it's got it in it to acquire virtue somehow again, some day. You never can tell. It's the great thing to impress on people when they're in trouble. It does seem odd to think I've carried it on my person without giving it a thought for years and years. This wallet was a twenty-first birthday present – from I've forgotten who. Stood up well, hasn't it? Best pigskin.' He looked down at his hand. 'It could go now. Where's your waste paper basket?'

In one unbroken movement she swiftly leaned forward, took the folded paper from between his fingers and slipped it into the pocket of her dressing-gown. This he observed absent-mindedly; made as if to put away his wallet; then with a faint start reopened it.

'Yes ... Here's an odd thing.' He rummaged through the contents, pulled out a sheet of flimsy, cheap-looking notepaper. 'From a chap called Edwards.' He peered at the few lines of pencilled script; an uneducated, backward-sloping hand. 'Almost too faint to decipher. Over a year I've carried this about, according to the date.'

'What is it?'

'Polite note I once had from someone, thanking me for a pleasant evening. I kept it because – well, because I can't bear destroying letters from my boy-friends.' He pursed up his lips and whistled a few faint bars of a popular cabaret song.

'Does it tie up with anything you're saying?'

'Oh yes. Yes, it might be said to. Here's where the story acquires a touch of drama. Can she bear any more? She can? Yes, easily. Well now, let's see ... One week-end I got away unexpectedly and went down to the cottage. Madeleine wasn't there. I knew she'd gone away – I rather wanted to be alone, so I didn't let her know I was turning up. On the Sunday afternoon, I went for a long walk along the river. Coming back, I saw a chap, a sailor – able seaman – standing in the road looking at the church tower, which is a rather nice one. I passed the time of day with him, and he asked me one or two questions about the place – date and so on: he seemed to take an intelligent interest in architecture, which I thought surprising. In fact I felt surprised altogether: he had a striking face: in fact I never saw a better-looking chap; and his voice was unexpected somehow ... and the whole thing seemed to ring a very, very faint bell. Presently I asked him where I'd seen him before. He gave me a queer look, then shook his head. Then he hesitated and said his name was Edwards: but that meant nothing to me. Then he said he'd served in a certain ship about six months before: was he right in thinking I'd been aboard and if so would my name be – what it is? He never forgot a face – sometimes wished he could, he said with a bit of a not very cheerful laugh. He had a frozen sort of face – when he laughed it didn't brighten up. I said I was rather the same ... I thought perhaps I might have spotted him sort of subconsciously. But all the time I knew that wasn't it, and I knew that he did too. It was as if spurts of electricity were running between us ... And he went on standing stock still beside me, not a muscle twitching. I asked him if his home was in the neighbourhood and he said no, he'd lived in London before the war but the whole street where he'd hung out had bought it in the blitz: he'd been along to look for his old lodgings but there was nothing left, only rubble. He'd had some very nice furniture of his own, a smashing suite, he said, it had upset him losing it. What with one thing and another he wouldn't be sorry when his leave was up. He'd come down this way on foot, and thumbing lifts, to look up a lady he'd once made the acquaintance of, to explain something he'd done that might have left her with the wrong impression. I heard myself saying if he had nothing better to do would he care to come in for a drink? My wife was away for a few days, I told him, and I was on my own. He accepted very promptly and we strolled up the road and into my house. There wasn't much in the way of spirits in the cupboard, but – with a little help from me – what there was he put down in no time. I never saw such a thirst. He loosened up bit by bit, and started talking. I thought he was one of the shrewdest, most observant chaps I'd ever come across. A born story-teller – a natural, with this poker face he had, and a quiet voice – slightly nasal, flat, rather mournful. God, he made me laugh! He had opinions of his own too – about politics, and the war, and the way things would go afterwards. I don't say he was a deep thinker, but he was no fool. He'd acquired his point of view the hard way, and nothing would shake it. Sour, tough, cynical – formidable in a way. As cold as ... It crossed my mind ...' He stopped. 'It crossed my mind there might be murder in him – something abnormal anyway. But the point is I never felt more drawn to anybody in my life. I'm not a pansy – did you realize? – never felt even a touch of queerness since I left school – well, Oxford to be strictly truthful – but my sensations about him were very peculiar.'

'What about his for you?'

'I don't know.' His voice was rueful. 'I didn't pursue the matter. I've always regretted it. Don't laugh.'

'I'm not laughing.'

'Dinah would have laughed. She'd have been fascinated; and it is rather fascinating if you'll kindly listen quietly and not interrupt. We'd been drinking and talking for about an hour when he said suddenly: "It's funny it's turned out like this. I was positive in my own mind you'd be away or I wouldn't have intruded. It was your wife I was wanting to see really." He let this drop in the most casual way as if it was a perfectly natural remark to make ... I'm not sure to this day whether he was putting on an act or not. But I don't think he was. As he saw it, the whole thing had gone swimmingly. He'd entered my house at my cordial invitation, and our relations were entirely satisfactory, on a basis of mutual confidence and drinking. Anyway, I know *I* felt: "This must be accepted in the spirit in which ... and so on." So I said rather feebly: "I didn't know you were a friend of my wife." "More of an acquaintance," he said. "It's some years back now that I had the pleasure. She might recall the occasion or she might not. It was Dinah introduced us."'

He held his head up as if requesting her to refrain from comment; then presently:

'Story's too long,' he muttered. 'Cut it short ... He explained he was referring to an occasion when my wife had gone to call on Dinah. He opened the door to her when the bell rang. My wife now, she was his idea of a really beautiful woman: the way she carried herself and her taste in dress and all: smashing. And her gracious manner, I remember that expression. He'd never forgotten her. He hadn't stayed long with them – slipped out and left them chatting. The fact is, he'd gone on a blind that evening and not come back at all. He came round to find himself I think it was at Brighton. Took a fancy to the south coast and stayed down there all summer: fell in with a chap with a smashing yacht, got taken on a cruise all down the French coast. Fact is he was browned off with London just then, didn't care if he never saw the place again or anybody in it – except for just one friend he had, a foreign chap. That stuck in my mind because when he spoke of this exception his face did alter, for the first time. It gave a sort of spasm; and I was interested to detect what appeared to be a sign of strong feeling ... However, that comes later ... Then he said: "You may be like me, you may not, when it comes to living with a woman, but there's times I have to cut and run." I agreed I'd had the same temptation once or twice. "They suck your marrow," was the way he put it. Then a certain amount more in the same vein, not highly original, but a bit unnerving because it was so – so scientific. One's heard chaps in their cups cursing women, but it's usually *one* they're bashing at – one unfaithful wife or mother; and generally dripping with self-pity or self-reproach or disgust or some other form of twisted love. This wasn't. He didn't want me to sympathize, or corroborate, or contradict, or help restore his confidence in women – he was just passing on the results of his clinical investigations. Plague–carriers – that's how he saw the fair sex: either that or diseased – infected. He struck me as a pretty serious case himself, I must say: in fact he seemed to me to have the look of an Incurable ... that kind of unnaturally separated, fastidiously sterile sort of aura. Weak stomach. You saw him pushing his plate away, or throwing up what he couldn't swallow – which was the human race in general, women in particular. With one or two exceptions – morbid cravings: my wife for one! What could she have represented? Some kind of fare that had never come his way, I suppose, the one thing he could have fancied – wholesome, really tempting. The other he mentioned – that one friend he'd had, his special diet, was also unobtainable: he was dead. The one person, perhaps, who could have persuaded him not to become a chronic case. As it was, there was nothing left but to pass the time dissecting other people's antics. And *yet* there was such sadness in him – the sadness of a creature in the Zoo – irremediably displaced ... Yes, I know I'm a romantic: but why shouldn't there be these creatures to be met with, classified as human beings but ... well, living at a different level? As if they hadn't quite made it – the human status – or else side-tracked it – or risen above it, maybe? Anyway, when you come across one you feel disquieted: partly you feel the creature's dangerous ... partly that he's at your mercy. There's something you ought to do for him – but what? Some place you ought to send him back to, or send him on to, where he'd be at home – but where? Social problem – biological deviation – anything you fancy. *He* only wanted to be let be to be a misfit. But oh, I did feel so disquieted, I did feel so at home with him! – more and more so because of habits of speech he had that seemed familiar. I can't describe them – turns of phrase I'd heard her – Dinah – use that time I took her to the sea-side, the last time we were together. And something she said then that I wasn't aware I'd remembered suddenly surfaced and exploded in my face. We were discussing love – our expendability, you know; whether, if we parted, we could ever love again: one of those honest conversations chaps wish girls wouldn't start. I said I supposed – knowing myself – I'd go back to Madeleine and make do with her. She didn't like that – and to tell you the truth nor did I – for different reasons. Suddenly she said there was one person she could, would go to, if I left her. She wanted to tell me all about him, but I didn't want to hear. She volunteered that it was nobody I knew, and nobody I need be jealous of. I wasn't. Women don't understand how discreditably unjealous men can be. Yet what she said did obviously stick: because here he was, the missing link, all those years after, and I was on to it – not like a knife exactly, but well before he handed it to me. He handed it without any fuss: and the only shock I had was a social one: I mean his absence of class-consciousness *vis-à-vis* myself – and Dinah. "You walked out on her too, didn't you?" he said. He didn't blame me: of all the shockers he'd ever come across she took the bun, in his opinion. The trickiest bitch that ever set herself to eat a man alive. She'd properly shagged him out. I did get a pang then, a nasty one, in my competitive instinct, but only for a moment: because he went on to explain with great indignation the total technical impasse he'd been in every time he found himself in bed with her. So I realized he was using the expression in a ... shall I say spiritual sense. I understood his feelings, but that had never been my trouble.'

'Did you tell him so?'

'Well, I didn't stress it. It didn't seem quite fair – the chap was upset.' He shot an equivocal glance in her direction. 'No, and I didn't compare notes either. Men don't, you know: they're not like women.'

'So I've heard. This impasse though – he felt it was her fault?'

'Oh yes, entirely.'

'He explained that to you?'

'Not in so many words. He had his reserves: in fact in some ways he seemed to me rather delicately spoken: or oblique where I wouldn't have been ... and contrariwise. For instance, I couldn't have said one thing he said ...' He paused. 'He said: "Of course I knew it was you she was after all the time, though she pretended not. She'd cry in her sleep. That used to rile me." I couldn't have said that ... I didn't at all like hearing it.'

'It made you miserable.'

'Horribly. But pity wasn't a word in his vocabulary. He thought women who cried in their sleep were a bloody nuisance. All the same, she did make him miserable. What he couldn't say – couldn't find words for – was this feeling she gave him that she took the virtue out of him. *He* thought, or decided to think, she was – well, no good at her stuff: and he was fairly explicit about his tastes and types. But I saw what the trouble was – the thing that caused this sexual humiliation it nearly choked him to remember. But I couldn't tell him because

I was afraid of him, see? Because he was lower class. It would have taken – oh, years to reassure him ... No, I never could have – any more than Dinah could have; we were both his enemies. I bet nobody could have been more *careful* than poor Dinah to treat him as an equal; but I bet too, not a day passed that she didn't show him she took her superiority for granted. Quite unconsciously, of course, on her side, quite subjectively on his. How could he pity her? And how could I tell him to put his shirt on pity for his enemies? It takes a lot of experience to conceive of *that* as a gamble with any point to it; and he was browned off with experience. What he was really saying was that the whole thing wasn't *natural*. In fact, he was shocked by her. She had ought, as he saw it, to have stuck to her own sort and left the likes of him alone. He didn't give a fig for her disinterestedness, her social conscience: or rather he didn't credit the possibility of their existence. Most of the upper-drawer rag-bag stuff he'd sampled – he'd pretty well got their measure: they were to be preyed on. But what was *she* up to? A real killer in disguise she must be – a real female Dracula. I even think he half suspected she might be after hiring him to blackmail me or stick a knife in Madeleine. Pathetic, isn't it? In a manner of speaking we were akin, you see. Both orphans of the storm. That word *bourgeois* ... we'd both been tipped the wink it was a term of abuse, but, secretly, as rude words go we didn't mind it. Our orbits had touched – though all unknown to me. We had come out together in Society – and a fine pair of twittering debs we were, I must say, scared stiff of cutting a dash – or of not cutting one. He said he'd seen me once or twice with Dinah – I hadn't noticed him. He must have been one of the Ace glamour boys; but I incurably only noticed the girls – or rather just the one girl. The point is we neither of us took kindly to the goings-on. We were out to better ourselves, but we were both too respectable. We agreed we had that old-fashioned feeling about sisters – we wouldn't have cared to take along our sisters, let alone see them enjoying themselves in that company. "I bet your wife didn't fancy those kind of capers," he said. Right he was – poor Madeleine. But Dinah did fancy them – she seemed perfectly at home; and this upset us both for rather different reasons. As regards *amount* of jealousy, inferiority complex, there couldn't have been much to choose; but it worked in opposite ways. He didn't want to touch her, he wanted

to send her back to what she was busy cutting herself off from –
to where good girls, ladies, didn't get seduced by common chaps, and
the lower orders knew the form and kept their distance. I wanted
to possess her: the more she gave me the slip the more I wanted her.
In fact we were all hard at it deceiving ourselves and cheating one
another. Dinah too – Dinah most of all. God, she was terrible – what
a girl! She would *not* accept we were no use to her. She claimed if
only we tried we could be truly strong; but we wanted to be truly
weak. That was a disappointment and a puzzle, but she tried to take
it. Poor sweet, she was so humble – so set on learning – *learning* to
be wiser, truer than anybody else; and oh dear, oh dear! – stronger
into the bargain. We saw her bracing up to be strong for two; and
it was beastly of us, we were not grateful. We didn't say all that to
one another, I'm just making you a present of it for your casebook,
darling. Neither could we have been said to come together in the spirit
of two mourners clasping hands at last in yearning and remorse over
the one romantic grave – though I know you'd be happy to think
of us in such an ignominious pose. We didn't so much as mention
love. It's not a word he would have sanctioned, and I should have
hated to embarrass him. Pity, isn't it? Poor Dinah! Aren't men brutes?
Not even able to admit we'd both loved the same woman ...'

'The same two women ...'

He burst out laughing. 'What a farce!' He shook his head, sank
into silence.

'How much did you say?'

'Nothing, simply nothing. I decided it was the most gentlemanly
way to protect everybody's honour.'

'But he was no gentleman.'

'No. He was a cad. Also a bit of a prude. But he did love her just
a little bit. There's practically no doubt in my mind that he was trying
to tell me so. So what came out should have made me want to kick
him.'

'You didn't want to?'

'No, I didn't. Wasn't too advantageously placed for that ... No
... I did rather want to once though: when he said he'd thought
it so very friendly of Madeleine to come and visit her sister under
the circs. The presumption of the twirp! How did he know what she'd
come for?'

251

'What had she come for?'

'*God* knows . . . There was never any knowing what went on between those sisters.' His voice had become loud, querulous.

'You really don't know?'

'Oh, *I* was never told. Neither of them ever mentioned it to me. Oh, I suppose I did get hints . . . Oh well, that's neither here nor there.'

'I do see why you wanted to kick him.'

He said in a normal voice:

'I wanted to kick the lot of them. Very unfair on my part, most uncalled for. I'm sure it never occurred to him that he was treading on my toes. He was really talking about himself, which he did for two hours without drawing breath, saying he too had had a lovely sister who'd stood by him, taking the rap from his drunken old sod of a father, but she'd died young. He envied Dinah . . . All the same I felt, quite unjustifiably, they'd all combined to make a fool of me behind my back.'

'What makes you think he was trying to say he loved her?'

'Oh . . . I expect that's nonsense. I expect it was just booziness, and being lonely . . . I think it was chiefly the way he laughed about her, a *real* sound it was, a good long chuckle. And the way he said suddenly: "Poor old Dine, she was a silly girl." Girl, not cow or bitch, sounded strange on his lips, like a compliment, – or a tribute rather. "Always a sucker. Give away her last sixpence without a thought for herself." He himself owed her one pound, he said. It had been on his mind a long time – that's one reason why he'd been so anxious to see Madeleine: he wanted Dinah's address, to give it back. Why this one pound should prey on his conscience I don't know. I bet he'd set her back considerably more than that. It must have stood for something in his mind: perhaps Madeleine had happened to be present at that particular transaction.'

'Did you give him her address?'

He fingered the sheet of paper in his hand.

'No,' he said after a pause. 'I didn't. That's rather on my conscience. I told him I wasn't sure myself, I knew she'd moved, I'd send it later if he'd leave me his address; but he forgot to in the haze of the occasion. He wrote and gave me one a few days after' – he held the paper up, still folded – 'and thanked me for the only pleasant evening of his leave, he said. He was off to sea again, but he'd look for a word from me on his return. He didn't return. He was killed in the Battle of Narvik – blown up with the rest of his gun crew, bombed from the air. I saw the whole report. I thought then I ought to write and tell Dinah the whole thing – but I somehow didn't ... I feel bad whenever I think about him. I couldn't help being so relieved when I knew he was dead: I dreaded his coming back into my life – turning up again at the cottage for instance, and giving the whole show away to Madeleine. He was quite unaware of all the taboos attached to the situation – or impervious to them anyway. He'd have been the hell of a nuisance. On the other hand, I wanted awfully to do the poor chap a favour – such a simple one too – just send him an address he wanted. I couldn't have let him down; but the thought of him sort of passing back to her through me appalled me. Almost like using my secret knowledge of her whereabouts to – to conjure with. Black magic ... What wouldn't I let loose? I told myself it was my duty to protect her from him. But I didn't believe it. I knew I had it in my power to give her back something she'd value. Should I? Shouldn't I? Hopeless predicament as usual. But he let me out – I was always let out somehow ... I was curious to know who would have been informed as next-of-kin, so I checked up. The name was a foreign one: Selbig, that friend of his he told me about – the name that caused his face to twitch when he pronounced it. He must have written it in when he joined up, before he discovered there was no more Selbig. He said he'd knocked around the world for several years before the war – South Seas, America, all over the place – but he got back somehow in the September and enlisted in the navy straight away. And then what with being pushed about and one thing and another, he hadn't found out for months that his friend had taken poison a few days before war was declared. Despair, perhaps ... That's me talking, not Edwards. Poor chap. I do hate to think of no one missing him when he went. So did he hate to think of it, I know he did. That's why he wanted to find Dinah, and why ... That sentence in his letter about looking for a word from me, that went on haunting me.'

He got up, stretching his arms above his head, then with a sharp gasp bent forward, doubled up; sat down again.

'Rickie, what is it?'

'Sh! – Nothing. Bit of a stitch. I get it sometimes.' He reached for her hand, held on to it tightly for a minute or two, then took a deep breath and sat up straight again. 'Gone now ... I've sometimes wished I'd come across that Selbig. He was a doctor, perhaps a quack, anyway a perfect wizard, according to Edwards – nervous complaints his speciality. My ulcers come from bad nerves, in case you didn't know. According again to Edwards he performed miracle cures. He had this Dostoyevsky-sounding tenement – lodging-house – clinic – I don't know what, down Stepney way, where he treated people free. I rather think he wasn't allowed to practise officially in this country. It struck me much later that it was through him that Dinah managed to get enough phenobarbitone to do herself in one time she tried to. Keep that under your hat along with everything else, but even more so.'

'I'll be discreet. When was it?'

'Umm ... round about the time we went to Wales. I was sent for suddenly ... I had to take her away, try to get her on her feet again. She – she'd been played the devil with, left alone in London. I was no use to her, I'd ... And then she took this blighter in and looked after him, and a rare rewarding job that turned out to be. What staggers me still is the cold-bloodedness – walking off as if he'd just dropped in for a bit of a sit-down in a station waiting room. Not once, but twice ...'

'Did she talk about Selbig to you?'

'Never mentioned him. She wouldn't let on to a soul where she got the stuff. Not that I pressed her ... I suppose he was – well, part of her secret life with Edwards. Otherwise she would certainly have described the set-up. She loved curiosities, and loved describing them. And this must definitely have been one of the minor fun-fairs of our late blasted civilization. I still can't picture her in it.'

'Do you have to?'

'It's not imperative, but I do sometimes: merely, I mean, because that's where she was. It was there that she retired with Edwards after I was carried off to hospital – I don't know how long after ... but there she was in purdah, while I lay spooning up my sops and seeing her skip over oceans and dance over lands ... Yet I don't know ... It strikes me now, this minute, I may not have been so far out? Granted that you believe, and I do, in the possibility of telepathy, and that

254

she was still – well, tied up with me, as I was with her, and trying, as I knew she would – ferociously – to root me out of her and tear me up ... there must have been some moments – in her sleep perhaps – when she'd have been – oh, meeting tidal waves and lions and wandering through ruins and falling over precipices ...'

'How long did that go on, her life in Stepney?'

'That I don't know ... Well, in a sense it's gone on ever since. She never came back as you might say, to the West End. Very odd story, isn't it? I've never understood what precipitated that leap to Stepney.'

'Craving for the absolute,' said Georgie reflectively. 'Could it have been? Part of the pattern of her fanaticism. It does seem as if' – he looked at her suspiciously, but she went on: 'as if she couldn't break the pattern, couldn't let it go. Always trying to get back to where she started. I don't see her as that free independent breast-forward marcher you describe. I see her *driven*; trapping herself over and over again because she hadn't found out her own enemy – the one inside herself ...'

He looked glum, obstinate, and she added: 'If that seems unacceptable, presumptuous, forget it. I know I'm inclined to type casting, as Jack calls it – it irks him too. But I can't help identifying myself with her, a bit: suspecting our shadows might be the same shape ...'

'Oh, I don't mind. You do rather remind me of her – in one or two ways. I suppose everybody's more or less the same ... with variations.'

Frowning at the carpet, he did not notice her expression, which was melancholy.

'She was extremely domesticated,' he said presently, in a constricted way. 'More so than Madeleine: more like her mother. She wanted to settle down – she always wanted to. I know how it must sound to you, but she really did revel in – well, making a home for me. Whatever you may have heard about her reputation, she was a *settling* person.'

She said untruthfully: 'I know nothing of her reputation.'

'Oh, don't you? She was considered promiscuous and unscrupulous. But you can take it from me, however reckless, misguided, ridiculous she sometimes was, she never was corrupted, never could be. No doubt a more ingratiating figure would have got away with more. She was very uncompromising – ruthless perhaps. It was her innocence.' He jerked his head up, said with a look of exultation: 'She burned in the flame.'

He did not observe the shudder that her body gave, or catch what darted at him from her eyes. All the same, when he spoke next, his tone, though stiff, was tentative.

'I suppose she went to Stepney to make a home for Edwards. She always had a feeling ...' He stopped. A look of surprise suddenly broke up the aggressively triumphant mask he had been wearing. 'Well, it might have been,' he exclaimed in a natural voice, appreciatively amused. 'I see what might have made her ... This curiosity she had – great curiosity about animals. Non-human creatures. Respect for them, you might say. Pity. Rather what I felt myself about him ... Wish to let him be himself on his own level. Make him feel *at* home, that's more like it – acclimatize him to his environment or artificial habitat. Her naturalist's – no, her *keeper's* instinct. She was always inclined to treat people as if they needed *handling* ... as if she were saying: "My poor fellow, you require a more humane approach than people realize. You may not even realize it yourself." It was apt to irritate sophisticated people. And Edwards would have suspected a trick in it: it was too respectful, too careful, for the likes of him.' His faint smile broadened to a grin, self-mocking yet not ungratified. 'It suited me all right.' Glancing at her in expectation of response and getting none, he sobered quickly; said after a pause: 'I'm afraid it was what always caught her out. If you put it into people's heads they may be dangerous, they're apt to be so.' Then, with a diffident inflection: 'Is that what you meant by being one's own enemy?'

'Let's not talk about me, or what I meant.' She turned her face away.

An unaccountable nip in the air dismayed him. He said regretfully: 'I'm sorry. It's all very boring. You shouldn't have let me go on.' He took her hand.

After some moments of silence she said: 'I like you to go on.'

He shook his head. Presently their fingers yielded to one another with a reconciling pressure. He shifted his position to take her hand more comfortably into his lap and began to stroke it in an abstracted, gentle way.

'What are you thinking about?' she said, knowing the question this time a safe one; seeing beforehand the way he smiled and started, like someone rousing from a pleasant dream.

'Oh, wool-gathering,' he said apologetically. 'Matter of fact I was thinking about the country. My old home.'

'Do you often think about it?'

'Quite a lot.'

'Miss it?'

'Oh always ... I generally try not to think about it much because it's rather painful. I mean I've never got over regretting that I sold it. At the time it seemed the only thing to do – my economic crisis was acute. And Madeleine didn't fancy living there, quite understandably. However, spilt milk and all that ...'

'Tell me about it.'

'I'll show you some pictures of it.' He made as if to pull his wallet out again; then withdrew his hand and replaced it over hers. 'Not now. Some other time ... No, I was only thinking how extraordinarily lucky I was. Since the war particularly, the whole thing has often come back to me – come over me so strong and sharp it's quite uncanny. Not as a craving exactly ... more as if it was in me, as if I was still there ... Perhaps one never does leave really ... I can really smell the smell of the woods in winter, where I used to spend blissful days alone with Marshall, our angelic keeper. And the smells: Frost. Ferns and brambles – all those heavenly smells. And the smell of fishing – and of lake water. I used to go fishing with Charlie; he was the chauffeur's youngest, a year or two older than me – my father's godson. I used to have high tea afterwards with his Mum and Dad. I always wished I didn't have to go home: cottages were cosier and I preferred Charlie's Mum to mine as a mother-figure, and the taste of Mazawattee tea to ours. Charlie made up for not having a brother; I always deplored my status of only son. I adored him – I think he liked me too. Once when we were sitting on the bank of the lake he suddenly put his arm round my shoulders. My heart beat like a sledgehammer, I can't vouch for his. Anyway there we sat, quite dumb. I couldn't take my eyes off his hand. For some reason I was thinking about it just now ... It must have been about November. Clear green sky, beginning to get dark. Presently we heard a sound above us, coming out of the east ... oh, if you've ever heard it! – but it's indescribable. Rushing, creaking, unearthly ... Geese flying over. It was the first time I'd ever heard it. We counted them. Charlie said: "Greylag". He knew a lot about birds, far more than me. Can you imagine what it was like? – waiting, bursting with expectation – then that sound? It was the Annunciation. I mean that's how it took me. Charlie had simply had the luck to see the geese, I should imagine, and in my company, which made it even more jollier. That's all that happened. We started to walk home – five miles to go, and I began to feel horrible – horribly low. He whistled and I bit his head off. I could hardly wait to get away from him – be alone – be sick – be nothing. I don't know if he noticed. But he wouldn't have held it against me: he wasn't one to crawl away bleeding if a chum told him to shut his beastly row. He was a nice chap, awfully good-looking too. Talking about poor Edwards made me think of him – I don't know why, they weren't a bit alike ... except that Edwards had the same kind of hands – broad, rough, open-air hands, blunt fingers. I noticed them that night, and they reminded me ... Not that *he* put his arm round my shoulders. In the end we were both nodding in our chairs. In fact he was snoring heavily. Yes, it was a rum start, that evening.'

'Did he stay on?'

'Yes, he stayed the night. I shoved him into my dressing-room and removed his shoes and stretched him on the bed. It's where I sleep as a rule, but Madeleine being away I slipped into the nuptial couch. I looked in on him pretty early next morning with a cup of tea, but he'd flitted: he must have slipped off at crack of dawn – leaving no trace beyond some creases in the bedspread. Oh no, I'd forgotten ...' He gave a chuckle. 'He did leave a trace. I never spotted it, but Madeleine did in no time. *Wrote* to me about it.' Again he chuckled. 'How could I be so careless, since when had I taken to smoking in bed? Well, I hadn't; that's never been one of my vices. It seems a burning cigarette had been placed on the rather good Regency pedestal beside my bed – ruined it. I had to take the rap – couldn't give him away. So he managed to leave her a memento: jolly funny I think, don't you? I saw why she had to get on to me without delay; some other poor innocent chap might have come to stay and got the blame. See?'

'Yes, I see.'

'She'd always have held it against him, I'm afraid. He'd have been upset to know he'd done himself no good with her that time either.

Rough justice, isn't it? – seeing he'd come to eradicate a former bad impression – social impression, quite trivial, still weighing on his conscience. Whereas any bad impression he might have left on Dinah ...' His smile fading, he shook his head. 'But it's not for me to judge him. It's scarcely a parallel, but I also wronged one of those girls rather more than the other. At least, I think so.' He sighed. 'But I don't exactly feel guilty about her ... and I always do about my wife. Odd, isn't it? There must be something guilt-erasing about Dinah. Edwards seemed to think so.'

'I call that a pretty high compliment.'

'So do I. *He* didn't.' He got up suddenly, and stood with his shoulders hunched. 'Oh no, of all the shits! His conscience didn't trouble him a jot: because it was all her fault, if you please, that it ended as it did.'

'Oh, you did discover how it ended?'

'Yes, I did.' His shoulders went higher: he paced up and down in front of her, burst out impatiently, reluctantly: 'It didn't last long the second time – not much longer than the first, I gathered. He couldn't stick it, he said; he wasn't cut out for that sort of life. It was her idea, not his, this setting up in Stepney. All he meant was to breeze in on her in a friendly sort of way when he got back to London in the autumn: that was after his cruising holiday – if you remember, he'd walked out on her earlier in the summer – on her and Madeleine. He'd left some shirts in the flat, and he needed them, he said. She was ever so pleased to see him ... Yes, I can imagine she would be – she always was: she never had any bones to pick, no matter what ... She made herself such pleasant company it came over him again he wouldn't mind having her – see what came of it this time. But bless me if she didn't say no to that! Quite a change. Reason: she'd shut up her bedroom. A friend that had been staying there a few weeks back had been taken very queer there in the night one night, the ambulance had come for him ...' He paused to glance at Georgie. 'That would be you know who. I suppose he knew too: but he kept a poker face and so did I ... Since when she hadn't fancied that room to sleep in any more. She'd taken to dossing down on two chairs in the sitting-room, and he could see for himself there wasn't room for two. Small low chairs she had with high sort of padded backs to them, hard – not his style (I remembered them too). He saw how she felt about that bedroom: he wouldn't have fancied sleeping in it himself knowing an ambulance case had been there. Then it seems she got low in her spirits and told him to get out and leave her be: he'd never known her like that – quite sarcastic. But he hadn't hardly got to the other end of the street when he heard steps coming after him in a hurry, and it was her. "I'm coming with you," she said, just like that. You could have knocked him down. She seemed all worked up, like as if she'd seen a ghost. So he didn't argue, he took her along back: not meaning for more than just the night. But he was stuck with her. Once she was there she wouldn't budge: went up the other end once for a few clothes and came straight back. What's more, after that she never stirred from his room except of an evening when she'd slip out sometimes to do a bit of shopping to cook him an evening meal – very tasty too, he'd give her that. He'd be out all day, of course, but when he came in of an evening there she'd be, sitting smoking cigarettes and listening to any old programme on the radio, and well, just taking big breaths as if she was short of air. Carrying on more like something moping in a gilded cage than a Christian. Though she'd always brighten up when they got talking – the evenings weren't so bad: specially when his friend who owned the house – the doctor – dropped in late and got her to read aloud. Poetry mostly – bits of Shakespeare, Milton – his friend enjoyed it, and the fact was she did speak it nice. Then she and his friend would get talking, more after the philosophical style, or politics: they'd talk their heads off, he didn't complain of that, but it couldn't go on like it, could it? (I saw his point). Funny thing, in spite of her clinging on so, in another way she didn't seem to take all that much notice of him; and whichever way you looked at it, it wasn't like her. In the old days she was always after him to start leading what she called a constructive life – (can't I hear her!) – even to getting a job somewhere in the country and setting up with him in a caravan she was going to buy, or some other such daft notion – but now she didn't seem to trouble much what he did with himself. She'd stare through him with her great eyes like as if she was simple. Money was getting short too – not that he was having to keep her (no, you bet he wasn't) but she'd always been the independent sort ... That's true enough. She'd never let me ... except for the rent of the flat which I insisted ... She had a bit from her father; and she did odd jobs of writing

260

when I knew her – fashion notes or sketches or cooking hints or something, she never let on exactly what. But she had quite a flair as a journalist. She was the most frugal, saving, discreet little creature I ever knew. I suppose he took it for granted he only had to stretch his paw out ... However, not my business ... only when he mentioned money matters I felt upset. It was exactly what I'd suspected the last time I saw her ...'

'She told you she'd been borrowing?'

'No, not that.' He started pacing again, the glum look heavy on his face. 'She wouldn't let on. When I raised the subject she sort of set her lips and thanked me with great formality – said she was managing perfectly well. But Edwards told me she took to borrowing from Selbig. That was so incredibly unlike her – nothing could have brought it home to me more disagreeably that ...' He stopped.

'She'd folded up?'

'Mm. Given up hope. Demoralized. I felt quite sick.'

She rolled over on to her side and lay with one elbow propping her cheek, in a meditative attitude.

'And in the end?' she said.

'Oh, in the end his nerves got bad. Somehow he didn't fancy telling her to clear out, but she got him down so he started walking in his sleep – or talking, I forget which. They'd certainly left him with a sense of grievance, those broken nights of his. But the very end of it was he got browned off again. Cut the painter. Did a bunk. She'd bought it, hadn't she? ... Bought it, paid for it, wrapped it up and taken it home.'

'Did he leave her there?'

'He left her fast asleep. Very sensible I think, don't you? She might have made a scene.'

'Leaving her with Dr Selbig,' she said reflectively.

'Yes. He was there I suppose. History doesn't relate.' He sat down again listlessly, scratched his head. 'As you know when he finally came back there was no room, no Dinah and no Selbig ... The only thing that goes on bothering me is ...' He brooded.

'Is what?'

'Whether that might have been what she came to tell me, that last time. Whether it had already bust and she needed help and I – failed to make it possible for her to say so. She looked ... I think there was something on her mind – more even than could be accounted for by the obvious awkwardness of the occasion. I left her in a taxi to be taken to wherever she told the driver. She wouldn't tell *me* ... merely said she was expected back, there was someone waiting for her.'

An infinite boredom seemed to be invading him.

'Maybe there was,' said Georgie, still propped on one elbow. 'I should think probably.'

'Ah well ...' He yawned. 'It's not a fruitful subject for conjecture. If she was in straits there was Dr Selbig, as you say. Perhaps he looked after her. I hope so.'

'The missing link,' said Georgie.

He looked at her vaguely, puzzled; and she went on slowly: 'The one person she could go to after you left her. No one you need be jealous of. I guess that wasn't Mr Robert Edwards she had in mind.'

Not light, but a look of nullity, collapse, smoothed his face suddenly. He said without apparent curiosity: 'Oh, I see.'

'Don't be mad at me,' she pleaded.

'She's putting up another candidate,' he remarked, ignoring her, addressing himself or no one. 'Selbig the missing link, not Edwards ... Well, she may be right. I hadn't thought of it. Or had I? No. But she's a clever girl ... It wouldn't be singular, would it, if such a clever girl was right?'

She lay down again flat on her back.

'I haven't been lying here,' she said after a silence, 'with my subtle smile, seeing it all quite clear from the beginning; casting my line and seeing you swallow the bait. It's just that I'm ... Oh, can't you see? I have to feel the pull, I'm hooked as well as you. Tied up in all the lines. Oh, I pray I never meet her! I'd be too tempted to wind her in.'

His mouth opened; but as if something in her voice had suggested second thoughts, or an attempt at making contact, he said quite kindly: 'There'd be no need.'

'My needs are not yours, alas for me. Never mind all that.'

He hesitated, looking at her now.

'You think she had this foreign chap in tow?' His tone conveyed open-mindedness. 'Got him up her sleeve perhaps, all the time?'

'Perhaps. But you know what a stickler I am for my own hunches.

Total sceptic about other people's. Or maybe it can just be put down to wish-fulfilment. It would seem more on the side of life, if you understand – kind of counter-deafeatest more ... Well, let's say more natural. Whether it turned out an asset or not I wouldn't know, but I guess she had something more positive than Edwards in the bag when she went to Stepney.'

It was her turn to address herself to no one in particular. She put her arms behind her head and lay with her eyelids almost closed; as he had seen Dinah lie a hundred times.

'I place myself in her shoes,' she presently continued. 'Re-united with you on that shore ... situation fraught with happiness, intensest happiness ... All the same, not a situation to give her total confidence. She was a girl in a precarious position. She had had it proved to her – not once but twice – that she was one of that class of girl that is rejectable: acceptable until getting on for zero hour, but then rejectable. She was to have it proved to her a third and a fourth time; but twice is enough to make any girl suspect she may have to scratch for good from the mixed doubles. Or put it another way ... That going together to the seaside the way you did, that was not – life-like – was it?'

'I suppose it was pretty crazy,' he said, conceding the point dejectedly but fully. 'Like everything we did. Considered as a piece of folly it was certainly a high spot.'

He stopped abruptly, startled by what had suddenly appeared to him: the figure of a girl in a bright blue cotton frock, bare-legged, honey-brown, streaming with wind and sunlight, turning to hold up a bunch of wild flowers: tiny split-second image seen through a stereoscopic lens. 'Quite mad. Mad, bad ... And considered as ...' But once again he stopped, hearing the words just uttered circling her vanished image as they left his lips. *Sad ... mad ... bad ... sweet* ... An entrail-piercing cry, like seagulls.

'Yes, I know,' said Georgie, putting her hands up and pressing her eyeballs hard with her finger-tips. 'Like our Kew Gardens, if you will forgive the analogy. Not for human nature's daily food. She knew it, you knew it, both of you: you were compelled to say so: though you would have preferred more delicacy. If you lost, you were still – not unacceptable, to someone, as a partner. But she had nothing, no one: not Edwards – he's not in the match at all – or not playing on any court anywhere she knows of. He'd disappeared. Not Edwards: not her sister ... If this girl is to survive, – and she will survive, she's a determined girl, she hasn't lost her passion for adventure – she must go on, further and further, to get – oh, anywhere near home again.'

'You're very cryptic,' he said wearily. 'I can't say I follow.'

'Well, let me see ... In that conversation you spoke to me of having, that kind – deep questioning – men wish women would refrain from, you were admitting to one another, weren't you, your secret knowledge that you – hadn't reached, together, the – the point of no return? In case of need – and the need was a sad certainty – you would go out separately, by different emergency exits. You had yours in reserve. And she had hers. It's only my hunch, as I told you, backed with a little circumstantial evidence, that Selbig was her point of no return. Something, someone, final to fall back on. Not a substitute lover. Maybe a kind of father figure? I'm only suggesting it. We realize that's what he was to Edwards. Protector, admired comforter, one true friend. Maybe it's purely subjective and irrelevant, but I keep on investing his personality with mystic symbols: The everlasting Arms, The Hound of Heaven ... Waiting. Shadowing them – in and out of the picture, in and out of the room – Dinah as well as Edwards. If that makes him even more of a mystery, even more unreal than before as a person, it seems to *me* to make his rôle – this rôle I am assigning him – more possible, more plausible. The *one* person left for her to go to. His crazy set-up the place where one thing anyway was certain: she'd get off the merry-go-round for good.'

She opened her eyes and sat up, then swung her legs down to the floor and sat on the edge of the bed to search under it for her bedroom slippers. Fallen beside one of them lay a piece of folded paper; the letter from Rob Edwards. Let drop absent-mindedly by Rickie? Forgotten about? ... She screened it carefully with one bare foot; heard him remark, from a long way off, over his shoulder:

'Be done with love, you mean.' His voice was hard and flat.

'Oh, that would be too sweeping: though I guess at the time she may have felt that that would be salvation. I just mean one kind of love: passion ... Romantic love, perhaps. We do know, don't we, that though she never came back, in the end she was all right – she made a happy marriage?'

Thrusting her foot beneath the bed, she touched the dropped paper with the tip of her big toe, pushed it a fraction further in. Then easing her heels into the crimson mules, she got up, crossed the room and went to stand on the threshold of the open door, taking breaths of fresh air into her lungs. After a moment he came and joined her. They stepped out and stood together in the narrow well of brick and stone, in the loaded silence of blacked-out London at four o'clock in the morning.

'What are we waiting for?' she murmured. 'Something is going on.' With her mind's eye, she discerned his profile above her, lifted, sniffing the dark. 'I wish the skies would fall. I wish we could see Christ's blood stream in the firmament.'

He put his arm round her waist and held her close against him. She thought she heard him say faintly: 'Hush!'

'Wait for the All Clear,' she said. 'It hasn't sounded, has it? Surely we can't have been cut off even from that?'

'Well, I don't know what's happening ...' She could feel him busy with matter-of-fact surmises, calculations.

'What is it? Robots? Are you informed about the nature of the secret weapon? Are your lips sealed? Shall we be saved?'

'Hush,' he said again, gently patting her hip. 'Don't worry. I expect we shall soon know a lot more.'

'Honestly, is it going to be a little more than we can bear?'

'No, no, that's one thing certain. Whatever it is, we shall get over it – find the answer to it, I mean. There may be a nasty patch before we do: it's bound to take time. But nobody has any doubts. Do you honestly not see that?'

'Yes. Yes, surely. It's only the suspense. Not knowing precisely what to stiffen up our sinews for.'

'We shall be told,' he said, mild, reassuring. He lifted his head to scan the sky. 'It almost looks as though ...'

'As though what?'

'I was going to say, if anything has started, not much of it seems to be getting through. But I may be dead wrong.'

He reflected carefully on what, by pure chance, he had seen go over, extraordinarily low, at the exact moment when he had emerged into the area two, three, how many? – hours before. An aircraft with a tail of fire, like a streaking comet. An aircraft engine with a thrumming and buzzing note – a clockwork sound. He had been keeping half an ear strained ever since for its return, but he had not heard it again. He considered whether to mention it to Georgie now; decided not to. Time enough. If she had not said all those hours ago when he came back: 'I thought you'd gone to Dinah' – fantastic nonsense! – he would have described it to her.

The thought of the work facing him in the Admiralty was beginning to weigh heavily on his mind: a particularly tough day ahead, and he was in no shape for it. He had begun some time ago to long to be back at his desk; had, regrettably, been unable to give his whole attention to the important subject they had been discussing. He must leave her now.

Contrite, he took her invisible face in his two hands, tilted it up to cover it with loving kisses.

'I must go,' he said, not liking the sound of the words as soon as they were uttered.

Something more was obviously expected – more adequate, more personal, more ... What on earth? Quite beyond him. But he wished very much not to leave her with too disappointing an impression of him. He tried.

'So you think that's what happened. She went to Stepney to find Selbig ... Oh well, he's dead now. We shall never know.' It sounded in rather poor taste, almost jaunty. He tried again. 'Perhaps he had the answer. She was always after it: but I never knew what the question was, let alone the answer ... Yes, she was all right in the end. She married this nice chap – from all accounts – in Stepney. Don't know how that came about. Nor did Edwards, of course. She didn't marry Selbig, did she? Whatever that proves ... or doesn't ...'

He could only hope that the ground had now been more or less completely covered, because he couldn't, really *could not* go on. There was nothing left in him except for this compulsion, so fatal, so familiar to say that he must go: nervous compulsion of the departing traveller wishing to show a creditable last-moment spirit, but already in transit, busy seeing himself out. His expectations, such as they were, lay all ahead of him: but here she stood, silently holding out to him the load (rather heavy for her, take it, hurry) – the question there was never time to answer.

'It's getting light,' he said. 'What time is it, I wonder? My watch stopped hours ago. Precious, go back to bed, and get some sleep. I can see your face, it's a ghost. And oh, you're shivering! What a selfish brute I am.' He drew her to him, wrapped his arms round her and kissed her lips hard, long, once. 'My darling, thank you for everything. I must go.'

'I must see you to the top,' she said, following him as he went up the steps. They stood on the pavement in the greying street where nothing stirred.

'Thank heavens I can see you now,' she said, able to smile. 'This is my third resurrection.' But he was inattentive. She could just discern him in silhouette looking up, down the street and at the sky.

'Not a cat or a dog ...' she said. 'Dogs will be in the shelter still, I guess. There are several regulars who bustle along the moment the Warning goes and don't stick their noses out again till the All-clear. I wish there weren't so many children in this street. But I suppose if anything is going to start they'll be evacuated again.'

'I hope to God they will. And double quick,' he muttered. 'I must say I wish you weren't in London. If I were to telephone and suggest your leaving if you could, what would you say?'

'I'd say I couldn't and I wouldn't. If I were to telephone and ask you to come back and see me soon, what would you say?'

'Of course I'll come,' he said, in a hurry again. 'I shall be absolutely up to my eyes for the next few days, but I promise I'll telephone. I'll come as soon as I can.'

The singing began in his ears. Giddy. A bit sick too. He must get going, start at once. He looked down at her and her face seemed to have gone far away, to be a paper mask. His lips opened to speak; but he was dumb; seeing hollow eye sockets, nostrils, mouth, stare back as she receded ...

One more effort.

He waved his hand and turned away: a brusque farewell, an almost graceless self-dismissal; too pushed for time to smile; heading too urgently away to linger, even a second, for her answer. She would have blown him a kiss ... Her hand dropped down. She watched his shadow-outline fade into the tenebrous nullity of the void street: listened to his footsteps. Slow. Curiously faint. Not the loud-ringing, driven-sounding stride she had heard approaching hours ago. He did not once look back; and she too withdrew, went below again, locking and bolting the door between herself and this continuation of suspended time.

She went at once to stoop, feel about under the bed and retrieve the evidence. Unfolding it, bringing it close to her short-sighted eyes, she saw less than a dozen lines of mauve pencilled script, blurred, cramped, ornate, impossible to decipher apart from the known signature: R. Edwards. On the other side something had been scribbled in ink. This also she scrutinized, seeing it to be a capital D and an address, in Rickie's harum scarum scrawl. She hesitated. Her spectacles were upstairs in the bedroom. She tore the paper into minute pieces and threw them into the grate. The other piece of paper, the one upon which Rickie had, with less than customary illegibility, copied out a line of poetry, remained in the pocket of her dressing-gown. Later she transferred it to her notecase.

So that three days later when his life was spent, when after a long vigil Madeleine had seen the end, had had his personal effects silently, respectfully returned to her, and with Colin's arm supporting her, left him alone, and dead, no clue remained. It was some time before she was able to summon enough courage to go through the papers in his wallet; but the only secrets brought to light were a ticket for shoe repairs, a roughly jotted list of investments and securities, some childhood snapshots of the boys — one including herself; a recent laughing one of Clarissa; two of his old home; also one he had never shown her of his mother as a pretty little girl with a fringe and a mane of fair hair, wearing a black yoked pinafore tied in at the waist and holding a kitten up to her cheek; also a letter: the good letter Jack Worthington had written after Anthony was killed.

Touchingly trivial odds and ends to leave behind. All above-board, simple and clear as his blue English eye. Yet she had watched a stranger die. Body and limbs inert, anonymous, concealed beyond recovery under the neatly tucked hospital sheet and blanket; wax face, discoloured with a two-days' growth of beard; anybody's dying face, relentlessly exposing its indifference. Only his hair, its shining brown just touched with grey, but thick still, youthfully energetic, made him seem Rickie asleep on his pillow. Some time in the small hours of the night, the nurse having taken his pulse and raised the lamp to look at him, murmured a change, she thought, she must fetch Sister ... hurried out. Madeleine was left alone with him.

Last chance, last minute opportunity, chance of a life-time to resist ... restore ... Fight for him, fight ... Call back. But stooping over him to speak his name, she found herself prevented. His lips and lids were a closed frontier, behind which he had been irrevocably taken over, claimed by eternities of change and dispossession. She dared not touch him. She raised herself to stand passively beside him, hearing swift feet advancing in the corridor. Then on an impulse of compunction – he must not think she feared him – she put her hand out and touched his unaltered hair.

His lids flew open. She looked into twin globes of crystal, shining without comment, without recognition; one moment lighting the finished portrait; then extinguished.

The Early Hours

SWITCHING off the engine at the top of the lane – a long-established petrol-saving device – Madeleine let the car run down the slope towards her house, steering it to come to the expected standstill in the bay of grass beneath her garden wall, just under the shelter of the holly tree. She sat on a moment watching its moulded thicknesses, floodlit by her headlamps, spread like some glazed monumental Gothic canopy above her, darkly glittering, incised, fire-bead-encrusted. Then switched off, took the ignition key, got out, locked the doors. All the motions, all the precautions gone through just as usual.

She stood still in the vaporous mild moony dusk, hatless, hugging her fur coat to her stomach, forcing herself to breathe in and out ... Thank God for the light behind the curtains in the lower windows, for the narrow comfort of being expected back. Dinah, instead of no one, waiting in the house: Dinah, of all people ... Incredible. On the long drive from London, shivering, crawling through fog-patches, the thought of Dinah waiting had been the one point of rest. The urgent longing to reach this point ahead of her – she saw it featureless but precise, blocked in like a mark on a battle-map meaning Ambulance, First Aid behind the lines – had focused her shocked mind and body and pulled her, magnetized, back home again.

Unimaginable turn of the wheel; stranger-than-fiction fact. Yesterday, only yesterday, Dinah, that fifteen years banished phantom, had re-materialized; solid enough after one night of domicile to detect the sudden atmosphere of crisis, to say: 'What's wrong?' to receive the answer: 'Nothing,' with an air of unperturbed acceptance of the necessary interval: before it came, the breaking-point, the painful confidence, accepted, discussed, deliberated on, judged finally in the style of the old schoolroom days, the salad days of suitors –

pressed-flower, dropped-handkerchief, sealed-note, keepsake-and-token suitors: aerial, stinging, wild-fire, harmless swarm, transparent ephemeridae ... Not these clay effigies, these stagnant eyes and hands, this congealed, oh, not even animal indifference ... .

Thus it had come about that morning after breakfast that Dinah from behind the Sunday papers had remarked, with no preliminaries:

'Shall we take a turn or would you rather not?'

'I don't know. I don't mind which.'

'Did you sleep?'

'Fairly well only. Did you?'

'Like a log ... ditto Gwilym. Till you came in, in fact. Or did I come to a few moments before? I half thought I heard the telephone.'

'You might have. I'd promised to ring up someone at nine o'clock and I couldn't get on. It's that half-witted girl at the Exchange, she drives me raving mad. "*The lines are all engaged: you'll be rung later.*"' Vicious adenoidal imitation. 'When she feels disposed, in fact, that means.'

'Maddening. Were you too late?'

'No, but the line to London was so bad it was hopeless. I couldn't ... Nothing made sense. Was I talking very incoherently?'

'If you were, I didn't hear you. I only heard the bell.' Then presently, laying down the newspaper: 'Would you like to talk, or don't you want to?'

So with reluctance and relief the outline had been revealed, then sketchily filled in; and a couple of hours later, having agreed suspense intolerable, nothing to be lost, possibly much gained by immediate interview with Jocelyn, Madeleine had dressed for London, Dinah had brought the car round, checked the oil and water, slipped a brandy flask into the dashboard pocket, said: 'You look a knock-out. Expect you when I see you. I'll have something cooked. Good luck'; and stood to watch her start.

Keeping to the grass to make no noise, she reached her gate and opened it. Almost at once the dog started to bark; one pair of curtains parted, an outlined form appeared: Dinah, alerted by the iron gate's creak and click.

I hope I don't outlive her. What provision have I made against an empty house? ... Old age meant, among other things, fewer and fewer people coming to one's door. One would end by being pleased to see the caller

271

with the collecting box, the Whist Drive ticket seller; one would be wishing to detain the postman and the milkman for a chat. *What if no man, no real man, ever comes back into my house?* One should take more trouble to invest in women friends. Two or three pleasant neighbours yes, but occupied with families, chores, local interests, envisaged only as parents of young people in the holidays. No one to drop in for a good gossip on a lonely evening: I never wanted that enough to take trouble about it. Shyness? – self-sufficiency? – distaste for mental picture of Women without Men, cosily resigned, exchanging recipes, knitting patterns, confidences . . . ? More and more rarely girl-friends of youth turned up to stay: Clara gone to live in Ireland, Sylvia become a drunk – boring, distressing; Georgie Worthington . . . As she went up the paved path and saw the front door open to reveal Dinah, stock still, in slacks and jersey, waiting on the threshold, Georgie, dead and so long out of mind, startled her with a stab of memory. Killed in the black-out one night – only a few months after Rickie's death – not even in an air-raid: knocked down by a car of all futile ways of being a war casualty. And why walking over Putney Bridge alone at 2 a.m.? Nobody ever discovered . . . But she had always been odd, uncommunicative, cat-like: for instance, that going all the way to Norfolk to see where Rickie was buried . . . that letter to Clarissa:

I want to tell you I saw your father quite a short while before he died. We talked for a long time not about the War but about really important things – people, human relationships, personal feelings, which he understood about better than most people. He was very happy himself, and he gave me an idea of what love and happiness should be: that made me happy. Since you were a big part of this idea he had . . .

That was how the letter began, or near enough – extraordinary letter, wonderful really; perhaps Clarissa's greatest comfort; shown to me with tears, in struggling silence, locked up by itself in a mother-of-pearl box Rickie had once given her . . . I wanted to write to Georgie about it, thank her for the thought; but I never did, not wanting to seem intrusive, or suggest that I thought myself included in what was intended only for Clarissa . . . What had she gone on to say? – something about Rickie's home, his childhood . . . the things he remembered . . . something about wild geese, about inheritances, losing and not losing them: Rickie had done that, she said. Then a quotation, a line of poetry: '*Heart of this heartless world* ...' That could be said, she wrote, of a few rare men and women: it was true of Rickie, Clarissa must remember that, it was the reason why he gave people this idea of love ... (less true of others – experts, dealers, professionals, black marketeers, who also were able to give people ideas of love) ... Georgie always made me feel inferior, same knack as Dinah of conveying there was something which I didn't know or was unfit to hear ... or was that just my guilt? Perhaps she was in love with Rickie: I sometimes wondered ... But no, an ideal marriage, poor old Jack, completely broken, married however less than a year later, such a relief to all, very nice girl, father of twins already, fatuously proud ...

She called 'Hullo!' and Dinah came slowly out a step or two to meet her. The dog sprang at her with rapture; then immediately sped in the direction of a clump of viburnum, emitting in his hurry an urgent, whirring and growling sound like a shaken rattle.

'Hedgehog trouble,' said Dinah. 'I found him prodding it under that bush at tea-time. He thinks it's still there but it isn't. I put it in your shopping basket and carried it up to the edge of that near wood and decanted it. He's had another spiffing day, but he's hideously demoralized.' With scarcely a pause she continued: 'There was a call for you about a quarter of an hour ago. From London.'

Through the iris-coloured lucent gauze made by the fog-filtered, windless air and the three-quarter moon her face came swinging towards Madeleine like a balloon on a string. She said in a medium's voice:

'Oh, was there? Who was it?'

'I don't know but I think it was him – Jocelyn. He didn't say, I didn't ask him. I said I was expecting you but you weren't back yet from London, should I give you any message.'

'What did he say?'

'He said no thank you, no message, and rang off.'

'You might have ...' She took a lunging step forward as if to push past Dinah into the house; then stopped. 'Well, I suppose you couldn't – you weren't to know. What time is it? Does your watch say eleven? I'd better ...' In the act of taking another step, but this time slowly, almost languidly, she checked it. 'No. There's no hurry. I don't know whether to – I'll wait a bit, I must see. What do you make of it?'

273

'Of what? His telephoning? I can't make anything of it, can I, at the moment?'

'I didn't expect it, I must say.'

He had moved, he had been the one after all to take the first step through silence and separation. This proof that he felt *something* strongly enough to ring her up – the mere report of it enabled her to move and breathe again. Like one pinned down under beam in fallen house, suddenly released ... Briefly, self-deprecatingly, she laughed. 'It would seem on the face of it to show concern.'

'On the face of it, yes,' said Dinah unemphatically.

'How did his voice sound?'

'Well ... I don't know his voice. It's got charm, hasn't it? It doesn't sound quite English for some reason.'

'He can't pronounce his r's – he makes them French. Yes, that was Jocelyn all right.'

Yes, his voice had charm: would at once assume it to speak to an unknown woman at the other end of the line. She felt a spasm of sickness; then of shame at her schoolgirl questions.

Dinah strode away a few paces, grabbed Gwilym, snapped a lead to his collar and returned.

'I've made some onion soup; and an omelette would be the work of a moment,' she said.

'Darling I couldn't, thank you all the same. I don't feel as if I could swallow. Perhaps the soup a little later. I adore it.'

'It's the real McCoy. I had a pudding-basinful with toast in it for supper.'

'I hope you gave yourself a drink.'

'You bet.' Flanking the door, the Italian tubs exhaled an ashen gleam. Dinah sat down upon the edge of one; and at once, flexing his rear with military precision, Gwilym perched his hind quarters on the alert beside her. She observed him with attention, defining his pose and outline as heraldic; then turned her face up to the sky. 'Unearthly,' she murmured. 'Is November often like this?'

'Often. Though I'm always apt to forget it.'

'I had quite forgotten. Isn't this the month for shooting stars?'

A winter-flowering stellar essence misted earth, air and sky. The tilted moon rode tangled in a long angelic drift of blossoming unearthly cloud-dapple. A faint rhythmical noise, a kind of reedy croaking came from the region of the crown of the big chestnut tree beside the gate.

'What can that be?' said Dinah.

'I'm not sure. It starts up every night. I think it must be young owls talking. Or snoring perhaps.'

Dinah laughed softly in her throat, a sound of satisfaction.

'I saw the big one again, going over the river this afternoon. One way and another I've had a blissful day. I found a very classy paint-box in the attic, and a drawing block, and I did a sketch. Some time or other I want to have a bash at making a proper picture of it. Perhaps you'd let me come back some other week-end?'

'Please. Promise to. Any time.'

'Though I should make a ghastly mess in oils. There was a nice concert on the Third this evening – Fauré and Debussy. You must be tired. The water's hot, I stoked the boiler. Do you want to go straight to bed?'

'No,' said Madeleine slowly, after some hesitation. She glanced through the door that stood ajar. On the drive down, everything that her walls enclosed had been exposed to her. Room after room and over and over again in two-faced images: one welcoming, familiar, to be hurried to for shelter, comfort; the other cynical, estranged, condemned, giving out a suspect breath. In every room some object contained some aspect of him, some jack-in-the-box about to spring. And now, since hearing of his telephone call, swaying as she was in the first pluck of some untested current, her dry craving to push forward, know the worst, had left her. To remain in suspension was enough; to rest a moment on this bare unencroaching verge, among these interlucent spaces, in this thin world of ghosts, outlines, abstract densities.

As if to image her mind's nebulous collapse, the moon's face blurred, webbed over by a drift of spreading vapour. Forms stood extinguished – non-created specimens in some grey pre-natal chamber of creation. The dog uttered an experimental bark.

'Sh! Pipe down,' said Dinah. 'There's nothing anywhere. Must write and tell Master about horrible heroic exploits.'

'Here,' said Madeleine, 'wrap this round you.' She threw the soft plaid rug she was carrying over Dinah's shoulders, and then sat down on the rim of the other tub. 'Is his master a great friend of yours?'

'Yes, he is. He was Jo's best friend, actually. They were together at Guadarrama when he was hit.'

Guadarrama. Spanish name, of course – but it evoked an echo. There was another ... Guernica. Elegiac syllables; lament and outrage in the very sound of them ... Apocalyptic brutal vision, on canvas, by Picasso: fury of teeth, horns, blood, steel, entrails, men and monsters; agony of women. Name meaning catastrophic moment in other people's history, like Messina, or Pompeii ... or Hiroshima.

The name is Tobruk for me: for Dinah Guadarrama.

'Their section of the front was cut off,' continued Dinah. 'He carried Jo, somehow or other, all one night; eight miles, and Jo a deadweight – paralysed. His back was broken. It was a miracle they ever got back to the Battalion at all. But it was too late for Jo: for Danny too, I suppose. He never really recovered. He was sent home a few weeks after with a collapsed lung. I nursed him and he got much better. But this war finished him. He volunteered in the Fire Service and had a hellish time in the first East End blitzes; and he developed t.b. He can't live more than two months now.' She stood up, opened the rug, wrapped herself in it and sat down again, folded like a Red Indian in his blanket.

'You'll miss him terribly ...'

'I shall,' said Dinah in a light brusque voice. 'One way and another he's the last real link with Jo – and he's been a wonderful friend to me. However, it's much worse for his mother. She's getting old and she's alone. Luckily I've got more money now, I can look after her better.'

Silence. The dog moved uneasily, but with Dinah's hand rhythmically stroking his head, refrained from further vocal effort, even when, presently, a distinct commotion arose from the direction of the paddock: horses brushing and stamping over grass; an equine snort; a muffled whinny.

'That's that ghastly Gertie,' said Madeleine with indignation. 'Clarissa *would* beg the farmer to put her in with Jasper for company, but it couldn't have turned out worse. She works on his emotions in and out of season: she's a neurotic frustrated shrew. Whenever I go near him she comes tearing up and bares her teeth at me. I complained to the farmer but all he said was if she offers to bite just hold your hand out to her, she's only having a game with you ... I ask you!'

'Is Jasper the bay?' asked Dinah, sounding amused. 'He's handsome.'

'Yes, he's a good pony. He was Rickie's present to Clarissa the last Christmas before he died. He scoured five counties to find just what he wanted for her.'

'Does she ride a lot?'

'Yes, she loves it. Thank God, though, her ardour for the Pony Club is wearing off: two years ago it was positively religious. But now she's got a decadent local boy-friend who's down on all forms of competitive professionalism, I quote her very words. They take long cultural rides together and visit old churches and rub brasses and photograph effigies and fonts ... Couldn't you stay over to-morrow and have a ride? He ought to be exercised.'

'Wish I could, but I can't. Anyway I'd fall off, I haven't ridden for years.'

'Clarissa urges me to mount, she feels it would do me good – but I can't start again, I've lost my nerve entirely. Jocelyn occasionally ... when he comes – came – for the week-end ... But he wasn't ... He's not ...' Her throat constricted. Past, present, future twisted for a moment, gripping her like locked snakes. 'Clarissa's got a natural gift,' she went on stumblingly, 'the only one of the family, like Rickie. He was wonderful on a horse – if you remember ...'

'I don't, as a matter of fact. I don't remember ever seeing him on horseback. I'm sure I never rode with him. Not once.'

'Oh, didn't you? We used to – when we were engaged. Not much after we got married. But then living in London ... and I was never really mad about it – not like you. You were, weren't you? You were much better than me, I was always too nervous ... It was a pity he ...'

She stopped, afraid of her own voice and what she heard it saying. But silence was more frightening: something, *something* must quickly be declared. 'Sometimes I think it was all a mistake,' she heard herself declare. Without looking, she saw Dinah's face turn towards her, stay arrested, a pale spheroid in its shawl of rug. She went on: 'I mean, not staying in the country. I think we ought to have gone on in Norfolk and made our life there. This – this that's happened to me, which I never expected – I mean preferring the country, would have happened sooner, that's all. And with Rickie and the children to ...' She choked. 'To make more point ... It would have been a damn sight better for everyone, that's putting it mildly. How could I know? Why didn't I know? It was Mother who was so sure I was hopelessly unfitted ... She

277

saw me shining ... Well, I didn't shine. Still, it's stupid to blame her. She only had a dream of my having the sort of brilliant social life she would have liked to have herself. Rickie was to shine too – in politics perhaps, the Diplomatic being out. Poor Rickie, he didn't want to be a star. I don't think anybody – any kind of woman – wife – could have managed to push him on in the world. He had an innate resistance to furthering his own interests. Anything with a whiff in it of asking a favour or getting influence exerted on his behalf made him absolutely neurotic with anxiety. That's why he couldn't bear the Uncles. They thought the world of him in the end; to hear him talk about them he might have been a guilty thing surprised.'

A faint snort perhaps of laughter came from Dinah; and she continued:

'Yes, I know, but it wasn't that: it was simply his horror of career-making. All the same you know, I believe if he'd lived he'd have – done something. In spite of me ... and you ... we can say that now, can't we? ... and everything that went wrong. I don't quite know how; but if you think he was done for when he died you're wrong.' Her voice sharpening, she added after a pause: 'You did think so, didn't you? I know Mother did.'

'Why should you suspect me of such impertinence?' said Dinah pleasantly, but on her dignity. 'If you got that impression from Mother, you must have misunderstood us both.'

'Oh, she may not have said so.'

'She neither said nor thought so. He was a person she very much admired – as well as loved.'

'Yes, yes, she did love him,' agreed Madeleine, contrite, but as if deprecating her own contrition. 'She adored him. And she did feel – what did she feel? ... anguish about him, I know she did. And I could never tell her, I can't think why I never could tell her ...'

'What?' The word thrust with a sharp point of bitterness; of warning. When Madeleine next spoke, it was more carefully, more simply.

'I wanted to tell her, but I wasn't sure enough. Besides, she always made me shy. She thought I neglected him, but I don't really think I did. It isn't – terribly – on my conscience. He didn't want *me*: he wanted me to look after the children and keep away; which is what I did. The thing is, he didn't want anybody any more. But not out of –

apathy. He was one of those people who takes a long time to find himself; but that's what he was doing – emerging somehow. I felt it for quite a long time. It wasn't just that he was doing a very responsible job superbly – though I dare say that was part of it. No, it was more a feeling he gave me that he was beginning to be – at home with – well with himself. As if he'd made up his own mind about something or other – about what he thought was important.'

'I thought he would,' said Dinah under her breath.

'What's that? What did you say?'

The speak-up-I-can't-hear-you insistence in the tone of voice resurrected the youthful Madeleine comically, pathetically in Dinah's ear: schoolgirl echo of the person still urgently, crossly seeking to be confirmed, or contradicted, in her point of view.

'Nothing. I was thinking ... what you said about him reminded me of how he behaved the last time I ever saw him.'

'Oh really? How did he behave?'

'It's hard to describe – though nothing could have been simpler – more elementary – on the face of it ... As if he was sure of himself; of what he was doing; though what he was – outwardly – what he was doing was – simply nothing. So far as I was concerned, he wasn't in the room: he was an empty shell. But at the same time I was conscious that something – inside him – that I'd never suspected – was somehow releasing a lot of weight. If that makes sense to you ...'

'Oh, perfect sense!' said Madeleine bitterly.

'But it wasn't like resistance,' corrected Dinah, as if the tacit parallel had been explicit. 'There was no need for that. He hadn't got to extricate himself – it was all over. He did impress me,' she suddenly added, as if talking to herself.

'When was it?'

'Oh, ages ago, of course,' said Dinah absent-mindedly. 'I can't pin it down exactly to a date. It was after I'd gone to live in Stepney. I asked him to meet me at the flat I had: it was in his name, I don't know if you knew, and I was clearing out of it. It was a brief encounter.' Her voice became sardonic. 'He had to make it snappy, I remember – you were dining out.'

'Oh yes ...' She stopped short; but Dinah was still preoccupied and failed to notice the corroboration.

'Actually,' she said, 'it's only occurred to me this minute, but what he seemed to have was – space round him. It made him look sort of disguised – a disguised personality. Like someone prepared to go over the frontier, travelling incognito. With feelers out in space in case he's stopped. But he won't be.' Madeleine could guess her expression as she added: 'I know I'd been hoping very much he'd look smaller than I remembered. But he didn't. Quite the opposite.'

'Yes,' said Madeleine after a long pause. 'I think I know what you mean. I noticed it when I saw him after he was dead. With a space round him; filled out; but blank. Perhaps all dead people look like that.'

'He had something in him that didn't need human beings,' went on Dinah, busy pursuing her investigation. 'Although he was so gentle. An explorer personality – don't you think? That extra abstract dimension. He might have been one? . . . I would never have been surprised to hear he'd gone off somewhere in the end.'

But: 'He looked so majestic,' was all that Madeleine said; and Dinah found nothing to reply. They sat motionless, straining their eyes into space, as if from the prow of a ship at sea they were scanning the dark waters for targets; rocks and shallows; or for something that had seemed to float, glimmer unexpectedly across their line of vision; might rise, signal again. Garland of foam? . . . Wraith fatally beckoning above the foundered wreck? . . . Or a man drowning, his arm flung up in what might be a last farewell, or dumb imploring cry, or exhortation; or final gesture of acceptance of a man surrendering life.

'When Papa died,' said Madeleine, breaking a long silence, 'Mother wrote to me. I couldn't come, Clarissa was just born. She told me she had covered him with her wedding veil. I remember what she said: "He looks so majestic." '

'Yes,' said Dinah, 'he did. I saw him.'

'Do you suppose it was a sudden inspiration? Or did she keep it folded away all those years for that? Is that what brides did with their wedding veils once upon a time? . . . I wish I'd had the sort of life that would have made me able to do a thing like that. It would mean an *achievement* – something carried through: like what I was saying might have happened if Rickie had stayed put in Norfolk and made me help him. Really, it should be drummed into one in youth, the importance of living so as to be able to face one's memories when one's old.'

'You oughtn't to blame yourself about the place,' said Dinah. 'From the way he used to talk about it to me, he didn't miss it.'

'Oh, he did talk about it to you? He never did to me – at least I can't remember it. Why can't I remember ever talking about it afterwards? Did we have a sort of pact, really, not to mention it? And was that the reason – one of the reasons – why we had less and less to say? How did he talk about it to you?'

'With great detachment,' said Dinah cautiously.

'How do you mean? Politically? Did he discuss it as a piece of social history?'

'No.'

'I thought perhaps he might have, to you. He might have seen himself as a social or historical anomaly or something. You were violently anti all that weren't you? Landed gentry, ruling class, inheriting property – what you call Debrettery?'

'Not *violently*,' said Dinah with an effect of determined equanimity. 'You make me sound like a Hyde Park tub-thumper. However, perhaps he did talk about it to me in the way he thought I'd expect him to talk. He may have felt I wouldn't understand – or anyway be sympathetic.'

'Well, you wouldn't have been would you?'

'All I meant was,' said Dinah, still resolute, 'he never gave me the impression that he looked back on the decision as a great mistake. A major crisis.'

'Well, it was one,' said Madeleine vehemently after a moment of reflection. 'It must have been. It couldn't have been simple for him. As if places, homes, responsibilities could be shelved like old cricket bats, sold like one's out-grown bicycle . . . ! No, it was all a muddle. As a matter of fact I never, never would have minded being poor, whatever you may think. It was he who minded at the time: he couldn't bear the thought of living in a small way, not keeping up a style. He had such lavish conceptions; and he'd flung money about at Oxford; and then when he came of age he found all the estate affairs had been mismanaged – to put it politely and draw a veil, as everyone did, of course. Between them, his mother and that Colonel Something, that trustee of his she was in love with – his dearest father's dearest oldest friend – had simply played fast and loose; more out of idiocy on her part anyway than crookery. But imagine letting that bird-witted feather-pate have any control! Oh, what an awful woman! I couldn't stand the thought of her moving bravely out to live near by and plant her poisoned honey darts in everything I did. I loathed her everlasting widow act and her sweet thin smiles and all the insidious mother-and-son humbug with Rickie. Oh, how she got him down! – specially over his father's anniversaries that he was always well-nigh breaking her heart by forgetting to go to church on. "Our Beloved" – that's how she always referred to his poor father. She was like a sour pickle with a coating of marshmallow ... And even apart from her, I felt I couldn't cope: I saw myself falling down on the responsibilities – I always saw myself falling down on everything. I suppose we both needed more support than we could give each other: or both secretly too unsure of ourselves ... You were never unsure, were you?'

'Of course I was.'

'Do you think you could have made a go of it if you'd been married to him instead of me?'

'No. I couldn't have made a go of being married to him, or to anybody else in those days. Besides – oh well ...' She gave a sniff, then laughed. 'It's an unreal question.'

'Is it? I wouldn't have said so, considering.'

'Oh, don't you *see*? ... It was bound to be you, not me – well, anyway, bound not to be me – he fell in love with, wanted to marry, when he did. He would never have thought of me then. In fact, he didn't think of me – he told me so more than once. What happened happened because ...' She paused. 'I suppose a number of things contributed to it.'

'For instance?'

'Propinquity. Hysteria. Escapism. Sense of failure. Impulse of self-destruction. Me. You, Rickie ...' She sniffed again; then sighed. 'Can't think of any more.'

In the darkness Madeleine could be seen to rub her eyes and forehead.

'I suppose,' continued Dinah, 'my jealousy of you had gone on growing. I couldn't compete in your world. And you made it so plain I wasn't really acceptable. I don't mean you particularly – all of you.'

'Oh, nonsense! Anyway, *you* were the one; you despised my friends. At least you behaved as if you did.'

'Yes, I did.' Her voice was brisk. 'They didn't like me. I tried so hard too! They simply couldn't stomach me. Plain, highbrow and intense ...'

'You weren't plain. You can't have been. You were always very attractive. Much more attractive than me really – anyway, to men.'

'That's nonsense. Simply more business-like. More determined not to fail. I was bound to feel more competitive, with a handicap like you know who.' By the tone of her voice, Madeleine discerned her broad characteristic smile.

'My handicap seemed big enough, God knows. I don't know why, it always was so.'

'Everybody starts by feeling unfairly handicapped.'

'I was always afraid to look ... I don't know what at. At myself I suppose. Or sex – particularly sex. But seeing I was considered so very pretty, I blindly hoped I might get by. Or rather it was a double thing: I *assumed* I would; but all the time I was convinced I wouldn't. If you really want to know, the whole damn thing was one long horrible dream: stuck up, I was, on the platform of something like the Albert Hall with my big aria to sing and no voice at all, and no inkling of how it ought to go. I bet you never felt like that.'

'No,' said Dinah after a pause. The smile stroked her voice again. 'I couldn't afford assumptions. I knew I'd got to work hard to pass the exam at all. I took a good look at sex at an early age. And the more I looked the more extraordinary it seemed. Fascinating, I thought.'

'You weren't afraid – ashamed of it?'

'Not in the least, at first. Simply curious.'

'How very – very – odd.'

Another silence fell. They gazed at the sky, watching the moon's shoulder begin at last to push off shreds and fringes till, disentangled, the whole unfleeced globe slid clear, on to illimitable floors of polished sapphire. As if the world had lightened audibly as well as visibly, their ears caught now, from nearly a mile away, the weir's drowsy, pulsating, ethereally singing breath; and miles away, the diminishing rumble of the last night train from London as it ran over the railway bridge to draw into the station.

'Not at first,' said Madeleine, slowly. 'Do you mean, afterwards, you were?'

'Yes. More and more.'

Silence again.

'Well, it is terrifying,' said Madeleine in an expiring voice.

Against her high fur collar her face, turned upward, seemed to lie with an unanchored look, like a floating *plaque* of lustre with moon-like open lips, distraught yet dreaming, painted on its surface.

'You must be dead beat,' said Dinah softly, having looked at her.

'Yes. No. I don't understand. You mean after you started actually going to bed with people you started being afraid?'

'Oh no. I liked it very much. At least, on the whole I did. I actually' – she gave the word a lightly teasing stress – 'ceased to be a virgin rather prematurely for a girl with such a good home and careful bringing up. They say a woman never forgets her first experience. I can't say I ever give mine a thought.'

'Was it – did you ...' began Madeleine delicately; then plunging: 'Charles, I suppose? Charles Mackintosh ...'

'Oh, the barrister, my fiancé!' She chuckled briefly. 'What became of him? I'd forgotten his existence. Horrid man.'

'I thought he was rather nice.'

'You were quite wrong – we both were. I'd also assumed he would be, he had such a gentlemanly appearance – so clean-cut and magisterial. And such an eligible bachelor – one had to agree with him on that important point. But nice he was *not*, in bed or out; particularly after he'd decided to honour me with his hand in marriage and I confessed my past to him in all good faith and innocence. He said I was no better than a tart. I said I didn't want to be better than a tart, men seemed to like them. It was a term of opprobrium, I said, I'd never understood. Priggish! ... I was a prig.'

'You didn't strike me in that light.'

'Yes, sexy and priggish – disgusting mixture ... But Mr Mackintosh was really very nasty ... vicious.' She sniffed.

'But he wasn't the first,' persisted Madeleine on a point of order.

'No, no,' said Dinah, keeping up her tone of airy readiness and reticence combined. 'Not by a long chalk.'

'Who was it?'

'Oh, nobody you knew. When I was sent to that dear family in Paris to be polished – if you remember. A married man I met. Sort of *ami de la maison*.'

'Did you fall in love with him?'

'Not in the least. It was entirely his idea, my defloration. But he was very considerate and charming. And a thorough expert of course, which made a difference.'

'You enjoyed it?'

'Yes.' She reflected. 'Yes, I did. I was grateful to him. I learnt a lot of French, too.'

'And there were others after that,' said Madeleine after a pause; eliminating, she hoped, any suggestion of a prying attitude by putting the question in the form of a firm statement.

'Oh, one or two. Several. I forget really.'

'Experimenting . . .'

'I dare say that was it.'

'More like a man . . .'

'I suppose so.'

'How very extraordinary. All that going on and I never knew.'

'It wasn't so sensational or abnormal as all that. Besides, we never did swop that sort of confidence. You may have had lovers too, for all I know.'

'Well, I didn't. Neither before nor after marriage . . . What *would* Mother have said? – about you, I mean, if she'd known.'

'I can't imagine . . . I think it was on my nineteenth birthday she did bring up the matter of the facts of life.'

'What did she say? She never even mentioned them to me, not even on my wedding eve.'

'She only said she had the impression that they were in the nature of an open book to me.'

This time the silence that fell between them was penetrated sharply with a third ambiguous presence; emptied slowly, unelucidated.

'Did Rickie know?' said Madeleine. Her head, which had been bent, returned to its former sky-gazing pose. Dinah did not reply at once; then said with a different sort of reserve:

'He knew I was in trouble.'

'In trouble?'

'Over Charles. Oh, not in the popular sense. Miserable. In a muddle. About going to bed with Charles.'

'You confided in Rickie?'

'Not exactly. He . . .' Uncharacteristically she hesitated, stopped.

'He guessed, I suppose. He would obviously have been madly jealous. I realized he was afterwards, looking back. He was already madly in love with you, I suppose.'

'No, he wasn't in love with me.'

'Well, madly attracted to you.' Before the intentness of her stare the globe in the sky divided; twin moons swam in and out of one another. 'And I suppose knew you – weren't inhibited like me. I wonder, if you hadn't already . . . If he hadn't known – which he did know. I suppose – that you weren't . . .'

'Quite likely not,' said Dinah with reserve.

'And had you started to be afraid?' She focused carefully; the twin discs slid together like a pair of folding lenses.

'Yes. Then. It was then that fear began.'

'I see. Because of the very peculiar circumstances. Well, I don't wonder . . . I wasn't getting at you. What's the point now? I didn't mean to bring that up.'

'Nor did I. It wasn't the circumstances. I was afraid because I fell in love.'

'With Rickie.'

'Yes.'

'That's like a man too,' said Madeleine presently. 'Men are always afraid of love.'

'I was afraid for years. Fear governed everything I did. That was the root cause of the appalling way I behaved – though not, of course, an excuse or a justification.'

'But you got over it? I can tell you have. When did you? How?'

'I did get over it. But not for a long time. Not till I'd been . . . broken open and pounded to pieces.'

'As I am being now?' asked Madeleine of herself with terror, with one flare of hope that arched and vanished.

'Jo saved me,' said Dinah. 'Loving him – daring to love him. Being loved by him.'

'I'm glad.' Tears came suddenly, streamed down her exposed face. 'Luckily for me, people don't always get what they deserve.'

'I'm not sure. It's not so simple as it seems. I expect you did deserve it somehow. You were always strong. I expect you saved yourself.' Speaking up into the sky she added faintly: 'How do you manage now?'

'Without Jo, you mean? Oh, I go on. I've got accustomed to it. It's a different sort of life, of course, not to be compared . . . But it's not so bad. I enjoy some of it very much; and the rest is tolerable – interesting.'

'Have you got anybody . . .'

'A lover? No. Nor want. It's all over, it won't happen any more. I like company and I've got a few friends. I don't miss having an emotional life.'

'It must be peaceful.'

The words, an extinguished heart-wrung cry, brought Dinah's eyes to rest on her again; to watch her fumble in her handbag, extract a small handkerchief and dab her cheeks. Presently she said weeping:

'Well, I shall not be saved.'

'Madeleine, you will be. You are saved. It may not make sense to you just now, but I know it is so.'

'There's a lot that doesn't make sense.' She blew her nose. 'I didn't think I needed to be broken open. I've never been put together. And now ... oh well ... Sorry to be so idiotic.'

'God blast him,' said Dinah, spitting the words.

'Yes, it was horrible. He was awful. However, there it is and I don't seem to be able to start talking about it.'

'No hurry. Let's go in. I don't know about you, but I shall be crippled tomorrow with rheumatism.'

She unwound herself and rose to her feet. Dully following her energetic movements as she folded the rug and stooped to place a kiss on Gwilym's head, Madeleine got up also and followed her into the house. Momentarily released from tension, grateful for Dinah's outburst, she trailed obediently after her into the kitchen, standing by with sagging shoulders while her sister busily put on the kettle, opened the Aga stove, riddled it, heaved up a load of coke, stoked it and closed it. What was left of her consciousness, a small dry kernel, observed these housewifely activities in a spirit of critical appreciation. Dinah was as efficient as herself, possibly even quicker, neater. A vague immense surprise at the undramatic intimacy, the naturalness of this domestic scene persisted in the background. Instead of nothing, she had been granted this breathing space, the quiet interior, sparsely furnished, without ornament or colour or perspective; but decent, ventilated: a place where some semblance of normal existence, or realistic action, could still plausibly continue.

> The trivial round, the common task
> Should furnish all we need to ask ...

One might yet find a niche in the community, serve others, put one's talents to wider use.

Refined educated lady of good appearance (early forties) cheerful disposition artistic tastes widow (one child, girl, school holidays), thoroughly domesticated, country lover, fond animals, experienced cook gardener washerwoman, able drive car, undertake all household duties, rough (coals, boots, wood-chopping, scrubbing, etc.) not objected to ...

A perfect woman nobly planned.

Emotionally frustrated unadaptable class-conscious matron victim circumstances upbringing personal tragedies, exploited rejected (grounds age, moral intellectual maladjustment) by lover renovating sexual requirements, unwilling accept suggestions re courage pride eventual resignation, unable contemplate living (a) alone (b) for others i.e. family friends community spiritual values or any other form abhorrent vacuum, seeks instantaneous return status quo, failing which immediate euthanasia ...

Dinah lifted the lid of a saucepan, peered, stirred with a wooden spoon, poured part of its contents into a soup bowl set to warm nearby.

'Try it,' she said, 'it'll slip down easily. Do you good.'

Madeleine accepted it with a show of alacrity, saying: 'Thank you, how wonderful. It smells *delicious*.'

Dinah spooned up the remainder from the pan, sipping it slowly, her expression critical, engrossed. Presently she asked:

'What about a sleeping pill? Have you got something?'

'I have, but I won't. I think I shall sleep. Besides he might ring up again ... or perhaps I ought to put a call through, just to find out. You did say, didn't you, he said no message?'

'No message.' Dinah looked into the saucepan, tilting it slowly.

'But I expect it was only he felt it might be as well to check up.' Her lip twisted. 'In case of an accident. I might have staged a smash on the way back. He may be a little anxious.'

'I wouldn't bother too much to relieve his mind,' said Dinah, carrying the saucepan to the sink and running the hot tap into it full blast.

'It would be awkward for him.' With spurious satisfaction she pictured the panic-stricken face, the stammer, the whole confident personality stripped of glamour, abject in collapse; his projects blasted ... 'On the other hand he may be hoping for it. Something to feed his guilt. That's what he lives on.'

'You must do exactly as you feel like,' said Dinah, now occupied in scouring out the pan. 'I can't advise. What happened when you got there? Was he in?'

'Yes. Alone, thank God. Eating cheese and biscuits.' She laughed weakly. 'I let myself in – I've got a latchkey. I expected – I don't know what. However, there he was, looking exactly the same, munching away and reading the Collected Poems of W. B. Yeats.'

'You startled him, presumably?'

'Yes. He went stiff all over, quite perceptibly. His eyes came out on stalks. He didn't get up. I almost thought – I still think – he looked terrified for a moment. Perhaps he thought I'd come with a gun. He said: "Hello!"' She laughed again. 'Then he quickly pulled himself together and said: "I told you I couldn't see you any more" – angrily: no, sulkily more, scowling at me. I said "I know you did, but I had to come . . ." After that he was quite pleasant in a way. Asked me if I'd had lunch. Said I was looking very smart.'

'Did he explain the situation?' asked Dinah, after waiting for a moment.

'Oh yes. He was quite collected. Said he'd intended to spend the afternoon writing me a letter. That's one blessing – I shan't have to open *that* and read it . . . Oh, it's just as I – as we supposed. He's found somebody else. It's happened before, as I told you, several times: once I found out, once I suspected and he lied to me, once I never had an inkling – and he told me afterwards. But I stopped minding when he was unfaithful – at least minding *horribly*; perhaps partly because he never for a moment stopped wanting *me*; partly because I thought in the end he might learn to be faithful – choose it, if I left him free. It seemed a sort of compulsive thing – having to make someone fall for him, or having to fall for someone, some ghastly girl who was after him. But only occasionally. And it never lasted any time. He was never serious about anybody else. He always said he knew he'd be bound to come back . . . However he says this time it's different. He won't come back.' Pronouncing the words, she totally rejected them. It came to her again, not in a flash but in a kind of dark electric storm that stabbed her nerve ends, that he had telephoned, of course, to say it was all untrue, he must come back. This must be fought. She brought out breathlessly: 'He said this time his feelings may well be permanent.'

'What a pedantic boring thing to say.'

'It's the way he's inclined to talk when he's being cornered about his feelings. He puts on a clipped donnish sort of voice ... Still,' she said, stubbornly turning the screw, 'he wasn't like that today. He wasn't superior or huffy or dramatic ... or apologetic either. Just unapproachable.' She shuddered. 'He wanted to give me a friendly good-bye kiss but I couldn't – I was afraid if I touched him I'd find he was made of concrete.' A recollection struck her and she uttered the same weak laugh. 'He kept on looking in the glass so I knew it was Jocelyn. It's one of his habits. As if he was watching himself and wondering who he was.'

Dinah exclaimed abruptly: 'Rob did that.' Adding, 'Someone I used to know. Very disquieting habit.'

'That young man – the one I met? Wasn't his name Rob? That time I came to your flat ... ?'

'Oh yes. Funny, I'd forgotten.'

'I've never forgotten. I often used to wonder ... what happened to him?'

'He's dead,' said Dinah. She took the steaming kettle and filled first Madeleine's hot-water bottle, then her own. 'He joined the Navy – killed in the Battle of Narvik. I only heard afterwards, by chance.'

'It's funny you should say that about looking in the glass. Something about Jocelyn always reminded me of him – I can't think why, they weren't a bit alike. You may think it mad considering I only saw him once for a few minutes ... but you talked about him afterwards ...'

Dinah added briefly: 'It might be there was a likeness.' One eyebrow lifted. She screwed in the caps of the bottles and shook out a few spilt drops. 'This girl – does he propose to marry her?'

'He says so.' Madeleine looked bewildered. 'It's crazy. He hardly knows her. He only met her a few weeks ago.'

'Do you know anything about her?'

'Only what he told me today. She works in some publisher's office. She's twenty-seven.'

'What's her name?'

Painfully she pronounced it. At once the obscure amorphous image advanced itself, became consolidated.

Dinah's eyebrows shot up again. 'How odd,' she said in a casual voice. 'I've met her.'

Another step – no, a leap forward, terrible, the spring in the dark in the jungle

'You *haven't*, have you? How incredible.' *Don't tell me, don't describe.* 'What is she like?'

'Oh, I scarcely know her. I came across her a few years ago. She came in on a campaign about some Spanish political prisoners I was helping to organize.'

'I see. How very interesting. He told me she was – very serious, progressive ... public-spirited.'

'Oh well ...' She made an equivocal grimace. 'Interested, certainly, in publicity. I can't say she struck me as a girl to go to town on. I rather think I didn't take to her.' She frowned, as if aiming at disinterested accuracy. 'Enthusiastic. Not amusing or amused. Enlightened more than intelligent ... and making heavy weather of it. Ambitious – yes. *Frank* ... Steel-true wanton, I rather thought. Well-developed figure, trinkets, head scarves, cheek-bones, on the grubby side. *New Statesman* girl. Not *nasty*.'

'She sounds *appalling*!'

'N–no.' Dinah shrugged. 'Just not our sort.'

'He told me she wanted so much to meet us ...'

'Ah, self-abnegation! – yes, that fits. She'd serve her Man. Total Acceptance – conflicts, impotence, neurotic drinking bouts – all the works.' Her lip curled. She added bitterly: 'Oh, she's a piece of cake for a modern hero.'

'Do you know what he said? He said he saw no reason why we shouldn't go on seeing one another – *from time to time*.'

'How very common.' She advanced briskly, nursing her hot-water bottles, handed one to Madeleine. 'What did you say to that?'

'Nothing.' She shook her head; went on feebly, shaking it; then said as if concluding: 'Well, if that's what he thinks, if that's how they've fixed it between them, if that's the sort of person he wants – prefers ...'

But it would not do. She heard her own voice, female, vindictive, counterpointing the spinsterish asperity of Dinah's, stridently vocalizing love's degradation and betrayal. She said, despairing: 'I don't understand.'

'Don't try. It doesn't really help.'

'But I must! How can I possibly get through it otherwise?'

Taking the almost untouched soup bowl from the table, Dinah poured its contents into a large enamel dish, blew on it, tasted its temperature with one finger and set it down before the dog.

Watching him drink it splashily, she said: 'I only meant don't try to analyse it now. It's too soon. One can't see the wood for the trees at first, and one goes stumbling about ... Still, one has to do that, of course Whatever I say now you'll think I'm wrong. And I may be.'

'He said he still loved me.'

'I expect he means it.'

'Then how can he ... ? We were so happy – not always, but most of the time, as he agrees. Do I understand *nothing*? He says I don't. Does it always wear out? Are men bound to get sick of making love to the same woman, even if it's – if it seems to her – very successful? Is that all there is to it?'

Glancing at the childishly quivering face, Dinah said with pity and kindness:

'It's not all there is to it by any means; but it does seem almost insoluble. I can't help thinking it's particularly difficult to be a woman just at present. One feels so transitional and fluctuating ... So I suppose do men. I believe we *are* all in flux – that the difference between our grandmothers and us is far deeper than we realize – much more fundamental than the obvious social economic one. Our so-called emancipation may be a symptom, not a cause. Sometimes I think it's more than the development of a new attitude towards sex: that a new gender may be evolving – psychically new – a sort of hybrid. Or else it's just beginning to be uncovered how much woman there is in man and vice versa.' She pondered. 'Perhaps when we understand more, unearth more of what goes on in the unconscious, we shall manage to behave better to one another. It's ourselves we're trying to destroy when we're destructive: at least I think that explains the people who never can sustain a human relationship. It's not good and evil struggling in them: it's the suppressed unaccepted unacceptable man or woman in them they have to cast out ... can't come to terms with.'

'Did that friend of yours, that psychologist, teach you that?'

'That's why when each time the destruction is accomplished, they seem to us so calm. It's a kind of death.'

'That doctor – he was one, wasn't he?' insisted Madeleine. 'I remember him too, that day. I met him on the stairs.'

'Oh yes, so you did,' said Dinah vaguely.

'I can't remember his name. You talked about him afterwards – about his theories.'

'Did I? . . . Oh, we used to have discussions. He didn't *teach* me.'

'I thought he looked as if he might be mad, a little. Do you still see him?'

'No. He died years ago.'

'Everybody's dead or mad. Everybody's going mad. Cracking up. Going out of control. Perhaps everybody *will* go mad and that's how the world will end.'

Nursing their hot-water bottles, they stood facing one another across the kitchen table. The powerful lamp in the ceiling poured light down on to their hair, the pale, the dark brown, both sprinkled with grey but abundant, burnished, soft still; and on to their down-bent faces, both faintly lined and sunken, firm in bone structure; one tense with pain, the other with concentration.

'Murder in the air,' said Madeleine in a twanging thread of voice. 'It did seem like that. It *was* like that – the aura of it, the smell . . . Such a calm face. Fixed. It may have been himself he was destroying, but it felt to me like me. Not that he was violent in any way – quite the contrary . . . He went out before me and left me there – he said she was expecting him. And before he went he looked at himself in the glass above the fireplace. Murderers are vain, aren't they? Narcissistic. Have you ever come across one?'

'Yes.'

'Rob?'

'Rob did try to strangle me once.'

'You mean really? – physically?' Madeleine's head lifted sharply; her eyes lost their film of beaten apathy.

'Oh yes. Not in cold blood – or hot blood either. In his sleep. At least I think so – half asleep – I've never been quite sure.' A smile, amused, sardonic, stretched her mouth. 'I was asleep, anyway, having an appalling dream that I was bursting: and then I woke up to find his fingers were round my throat, I was having the breath choked out of me. What a grip! – he had very powerful hands. I remember thinking what a horrible corpse I was going to make – swollen, black in the face. I couldn't even get a squawk out, but I struggled and clawed. And then just when I thought I was done for he suddenly pulled his hands off.'

She heard again the harsh gasp, felt the leap he made away from her side, out of the bed; watched him, by first dawn light, dress quickly, noiselessly, open the dressing-table drawer, find her notecase, take the whole wad of notes out and pocket them. He looked about him. He looked into the dressing-table mirror, smoothed his hair, pocketed the comb, picked up the watch. He looked at his hands. He went out of the room, not once looking at the bed.

'Were you terrified?'

'Not really. I think my main feeling was: "This is it." I suppose I'd been expecting it . . . Oh, he wasn't a real killer. Lots of respectable couples have these nerve storms, I'm sure.' She returned to the sink and gave a smart turn to the handle of a dripping tap. 'Some women do get drawn into the aura, though. They get to be murderees. You can smell it in them. I know what you mean. I was pretty rank myself once. There's nothing like that about you, don't worry. You're as fresh as a field of clover. But you need to get some sleep.' Summoning the somnolent Gwilym, now toasting his stomach before the stove, she went to the door and stood with her finger on the switch till Madeleine joined her. 'I love your kitchen,' she said, putting it in darkness. 'I love all this house.'

Going ahead upstairs, she opened Madeleine's bedroom door, ushering her within. The electric fire was on, the big bed turned down.

'Shall I run you a bath?' she said. 'I had mine after tea.'

'No. I'll have one, but I'm not quite ready. I'm probably going to telephone. Thank you for everything. Good night. I'm glad you're here.'

It was nearly an hour later when, reading in bed, her ears on the alert, Dinah saw her door open. Madeleine, in a blue dressing-gown tied with a rose-coloured sash, stood on the threshold.

'Come in.' Dinah sat up briskly. 'Sit down.' She moved her feet and Madeleine came to sit down on the end of the bed.

'I thought I'd tell you,' she said. 'I've rung him up.'

'Oh, you did. You got him?'

'Yes. He was asleep but . . . It was all right, he was quite on the spot. Not drunk.'

'It *was* him who telephoned?'

'Yes, it was. *He.*' A smile touched the corner of her lip.

'Had he got anything special to say?'

'He'd been worrying.'

'Just as you thought.'

'Yes. No, not really. Anxious about *me*, he said. Not quite so . . . Not what I said. Better, I suppose, in a way. And worse, I suppose. I mean, it *is* over.' Her huge eyes, fixed on the wall, consumed her face. 'But he wasn't like stone any more. He was like himself. We were able to talk to one another.' A long unconscious sigh lifted her breast. 'He wanted to tell me that he'd been to see her and it's all fixed up. They're going to be married as soon as possible. He wanted to tell me that he would always love me. That I could be sure – whether it helped at all or whether it didn't – that he was thinking about me all the time. It will *not* help, needless to say, it'll be one of the tortures: it is already. I thought I'd just tell you now, then we needn't mention it again.'

'You'll be glad he said it one day. Sooner than you think perhaps.'

'That's what he said. He knows too much, it's awful. I do see it should be better to feel I never did him any harm.'

'It will be better.'

'You do see he isn't worthless – infantile ... Do you? Despising doesn't help. I'd rather you didn't.'

'I don't.'

'Though it's only a temporary relief. He thanked me for coming: he said it was the most wonderful of all the things I'd ever done him. He said he was very unhappy.'

'I do hope so.'

'But he thought he was going to be very happy.'

'Well ...' said Dinah. Her voice was non-committal. After a pause she added: 'I suppose he begged you to be happy too.'

'Yes. I told him he always seemed to prefer me when I was unhappy.' She laughed, a dry vestigial sound. 'That's true. He was perfect to me when Anthony was killed. And when Rickie ...' Her breath caught. 'Deplorable, but true. He said he'd never been any use to me. I told him it was no good talking like that, he needn't falsify ... I shan't. Though of course it would be agreeable to feel I was lucky to get rid of him. Lucky to lose my happiness!' Her mouth quivered, pale, swollen, ugly without lipstick. 'And how can he possibly be happy,' she wailingly protested, 'with this ghastly girl? Do you think he will be?'

'I don't give a damn whether he is or not. And you won't either in the end. I only care about you getting to the end – to where you'll find his reactions are a matter of complete indifference to you. He'll have been painlessly expelled – after a lot of bloody pain and struggle, which seems entirely wasteful. Perhaps it isn't. Anyway, it can't be avoided.'

'Clinical prognosis.' Madeleine got up and stood with her back turned, wiping her eyes. After a long pause she said more calmly: 'He asked me to forgive him, but I couldn't answer that.'

'It's really the best we can do,' said Dinah. 'Out of pure self-interest.'

A tune, an echo, started sounding in her head. *And throughout all Eternity . . .*

Presently Madeleine turned round, her face composed.

'What are you reading?' she said. She picked up the new library novel from the bedside table, put it down again. 'I haven't read it yet. Do you still read without glasses? I wish I could.' She pushed aside the enamel cigarette box and bent down, examining the surface of the table with a frown. 'Did you ever come here?' she suddenly inquired.

'Did I ever come here?' Dinah was amazed.

'Yes. In the war.'

'What on earth do you mean? Of course I didn't.'

'All right, I believe you. Sorry!' Her look and smile were almost normal, almost deprecatingly mischievous. 'I haven't suddenly gone out of my mind. Do you see this mark? – you almost can't, the man took a lot of trouble – a local man, he's frightfully good. You'd never think so, but it was an absolutely monstrous cigarette burn. I found it after I'd been away one week-end during the war. Rickie was alone here. I thought *he*'d done it – though I never knew him to smoke in bed. When I asked him he was rather funny – first he said no, of course he hadn't, then almost at once corrected himself and said he supposed he had. He sounded a bit guilty – as if I'd caught him out. It was only afterwards it suddenly occurred to me – thinking about his manner – you might have been here. Come down for the night – to get out of London, or something.'

'No, I did *not*,' said Dinah indignantly. 'Can you imagine me? And I've never burnt any article of furniture with an unstubbed cigarette in all my life. I'm not so fussy as you, but it's a habit I can't endure. Rob used to do it – he ruined a writing-table I had once.'

'Ah well, a mystery,' sighed Madeleine vaguely. 'I didn't really think it could be you . . . Well, good night.' But she lingered by the door.

'I wish there was *something* not acutely painful I could think about,' she said. 'Thinking about Clarissa is truly terrible, I don't know why.'

'What about Colin?'

'Ah, Colin, yes, bless him. Poor old boy.'

'He's not painful, is he?'

'Not in the least. He's a comfort – should be, at least. Terribly nice, good, kind. Much fonder of me than I deserve. I haven't been beastly to him, but I always feel I haven't done much about him. I've never really got to know him. He writes such good letters too – sends me parcels. He's an angelic character. I wish he wasn't so far away. He's always asking me to go out.'

'Why don't you?'

'I might – next year perhaps, with Clarissa.'

'Why don't you go now?'

'I can't go till Clarissa leaves school.'

'Why not? You can afford it, can't you? Go by yourself – I bet that would suit Colin. Clarissa can go later. I'll look after her in the holidays, if you like. I've got room for her in London – she might enjoy it; and I could come down at week-ends. Go on. Think about it.'

'Yes, I will.' She brooded, then said less heavily: 'I will think about it.'

'I don't say travel is a solution: one takes oneself along. But it does do something. You *have* to take a step – and then another, and another. And new places and new faces, without associations; and all the practical things ... Everything does help. Getting plenty of sun and food helps enormously, I promise you. Good God, if I had a nice grown-up son waiting for me in South Africa, you wouldn't see my heels for dust.'

Leaning against the door jamb, Madeleine thought about Colin – tried to. Quiet, tall, slender young man with a quizzical expression, a nice voice – not charming but very likeable. Sensitive accomplished player; not a star personality, but absolutely reliable in minor rôles.

Dinah's hand went out to the drawer of the bedside table. Opening it with an appearance of particular caution, she took out a small white cardboard box with an elastic band round it.

'And while I think of it,' she said, 'I'll give you this. I was going to leave it on your dressing-table. I couldn't quite see myself handing it over gracefully. I've had it such a long time.' She sat up straight in bed, holding it out.

'What is it?'

Madeleine took the box, opened it.

'Cuff-links,' said Dinah, her face blank.

'Rickie's ... Aren't they?'

'Yes. I don't know if he ever missed them.'

'Yes. He thought they were lost. How very extraordinary.' She took them out and laid them out in her palm, examining them. Circles of green jade, a Maltese cross in tiny diamonds set in the faintly concave surfaces. 'I remember when he lost them.'

'He left them in the flat. I found them after he'd gone, the last time I saw him. I meant to send them back, but I never did. I mislaid them again as a matter of fact.' *In the pocket of my coat, thin black coat I was wearing, in my clenched hand in my pocket, crushed ...*

'What's on the box? Some initials.' Screwing her eyes up, Madeleine frowned at the lid. 'I can't read them, they're so tiny. E.S., is it?'

'Yes. That man you were asking about – his initials. I told you. I lost them again. I'd no idea I'd left them with him.' *I dragged my hand out, forced it to open: they were stuck to my palm, the edges biting into it – agony. I flung them over his descending shoulder, anywhere, let them go, anywhere, I didn't hear them drop ... I never looked for them.* 'I left a few things with him one time when I was homeless for a bit. Clothes, books. But I lost sight of him. He died, I told you. As a matter of fact he committed suicide just before the war. He must have felt unable to bear his life any longer. I had the obsession once that I was the loneliest person in the whole world; but he cured me of that. He really was lonely – irremediably alone. In the way outcasts are – pariah dogs. I didn't understand why until he told me: he once gave a woman poison – the woman he loved, or who loved him, he said: it was a pact. They were Jews, they were being rounded up by the S.S. She died, but he didn't: he lost his nerve and didn't take the stuff. He was put in a concentration camp, but he was got out, somehow, through influence, and came to England. That was his story. I'm the only person he ever told.'

'He must have trusted you completely.'

'That wasn't the reason. I came to him to be put out – done in. I wanted to end my life, I thought he'd provide the means. He promised me once he would if I really meant it. I did mean it; but he wouldn't. He thought we could be saved: save one another.'

'Was it then that he told you?'

'Yes. He thought I was his second chance, you see. He wanted to bring it to that, try conclusions with me – bring me to that pass. But it didn't work out like that – not in the way he meant.'

'What did he mean?'

'Oh ... Me to come asking him for death and him to give me back my life instead.' Her voice was hard.

'But that sounds rather wonderful,' protested Madeleine. 'Why wasn't it?'

'Because he was so ...' She stopped, with an effect of violence.

'So what?'

'Unlovable. I thought I was past caring what was done to me, but I found I did care. I got away.'

'Perhaps he meant you to.'

'Oh no, it was in spite of him.' She shuddered, almost imperceptibly.

'How do you know? He might have meant to force you to, in spite of him. Force you to live.'

'Well, I did live.' Her face set. She opened her lips again to speak, closed them again. After a long pause she muttered: 'No, people aren't so magnanimous ...'

'I suppose not.' Madeleine stared at the links. 'Though I should have thought, after what he'd been through, there was just a chance of his being capable of anything.'

'He was.' For a moment her face opened, vulnerable, with a look of inner doubt, distress and wonder; then closed, secretive.

'How did these come back to you?' asked Madeleine, still staring into her hand.

'In a package through the post, addressed in his handwriting – no message. I got them the day he was found dead in bed.'

'You'd no idea he'd got them – kept them?'

'None.'

'You must have had a shock.'

'Yes.'

'I should have felt horribly upset. He must have been thinking of you. He must have been asking you to remember him.'

'Yes.' Dinah lay down in bed, flat on her pillow, looking at the ceiling with blank eyes.

'Why do you say unlovable? Didn't you love him then? I should

299

have. But we always, automatically, love the dead. Don't you find that?'

'Yes.'

'It seems a waste.' She touched the little buttons curiously. 'Are you sure you want to part with them?'

'I think Colin ought to have them. He'd wear them, wouldn't he?'

'Oh, yes, I'm sure he would. He'll be pleased. Aren't they pretty? I believe they belonged to Rickie's father. All right – I'll give them to Colin when I see him. Tell him they got mislaid, they've just turned up. Would that be best?'

'That would be much the best.'

She closed her fingers over them, letting them slide into the hollow of her palm, feeling them nudge lightly, settle there; anonymous abstraction: questionable solid; cold, almost weightless weight.